LIGHT

LACEY LEHOTZKY

Copyright 2024 by The Lehotzky Group LLC

First paperback edition January 2024

ISBN 979-8-9883620-3-6 (paperback)

ISBN 979-8-9883620-2-9 (e-book)

Book cover and formatting by Beholden Book Covers

Edited by Kaitlin Ugolik Phillips

Published by The Lehotzky Group LLC

www.laceylehotzky.com

PRONUNCIATION GUIDE

Agrenak - AG-ren-ak
Aress - AH-ress
Béke - BE-k
Blire - B-lire
Cazius - KAZ-ius
Drazen - Dray-zen
Domi - do-mi
Endre - EN-dre
Északi - EE-sah-kee
Este - esh-te
Félvér - fell-ver
Izidora - iz-i-dawr-uh
Kazimir - kaz-imir
Kaztar - kaz-tar
Kirigin - ki-ri-gin
Kriztof - KRIS-tof
Liliana - lil-i-ana
Radence - RAY-dense
Ruslan - Rus-lan
Ryza - RYE-zah

Telivér - tell-i-ver
Vaenor - VAE-nor
Vadim - vaa-deem
Valynor - VAL-noor
Vasvain - vas-vain
Vaszoly - vaas-o-ly
Vlisa - vlis-a
Viktor - vik-tor
Zalan - ZA-lan
Zekari - zek-AR-i
Zheka - zeh-kah
Zuriel - ZUR-iel

CONTENT WARNING

Light is suitable for audiences of 18+. It contains scenes that sensitive readers might find disturbing. Your mental health matters, and you should make the choice with which you feel most comfortable.

This is by no means an exhaustive list of trigger warnings, and you can check the author's website for the most up to date list.

Trigger warnings: Torture, kidnapping, mentions of rape and sexual assault, nightmares, flashbacks, panic attacks, suicidal ideation, graphic violence, death, and mentions of physical, verbal, mental, emotional, and child abuse. The explicit sexual content in this book contains anal play, light impact play, light blood play, breath play, and more.

Északi
Iron Realm
Day Realm

Night Realm
Crystal Realm

A CHOICE OF LIGHT AND DARK
PLAYLIST

Hunting Season - Ice Nine Kills
Watch The World Burn - Falling in Reverse
There's Fear In Letting Go - I Prevail
Werewolf - Motionless in White
Masterpiece - Motionless in White
No Masters - Bad Wolves
I Will Not Bow - Breaking Benjamin
Fallen Angel - Three Days Grace
Infinite - Silverstein, Aaron Gillespie
Riot - Three Days Grace
TRIALS - STARSET
Don't Stay - Linkin Park
Face Everything And Rise - Papa Roach
Say You'll Haunt Me - Stone Sour
Last to Know - Three Days Grace
Without You - Breaking Benjamin
Pain - Three Days Grace
Whispers in the Dark - Skillet
Take Me Back To Eden - Sleep Token
Whatever It Takes - Stephen Stanley

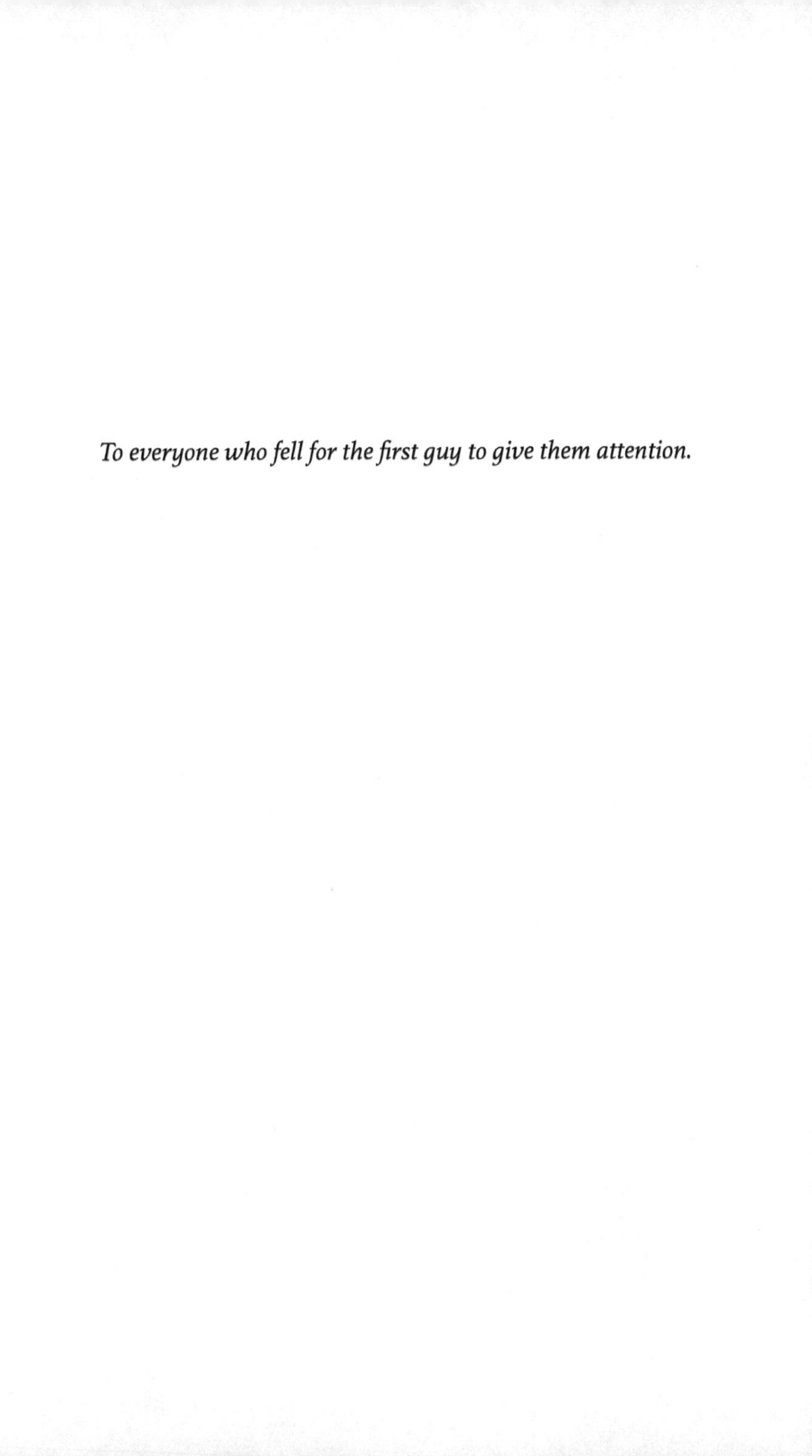

To everyone who fell for the first guy to give them attention.

***

PROLOGUE

Wickedness exuded from the two kings. The clink of crystal glasses filled the air as they toasted their plan, and the roaring fire before them crackled with sinister energy, as if the Fates themselves stood in the large hearth, witnessing as they sealed their deal.

The king of the Night Realm threw back his drink, hissing as the burn trailed down his throat. "Now, as for my role in our new world, Azim."

The king of the Iron Realm leaned forward, resting his elbow on the polished wood table between them. "What did you have in mind?"

"I grow weary of ruling. So many complaints, so many bullshit meetings and papers to sign. I want a handsome pension and a country home with enough rooms to house my harem," he stated. "But first, I want my daughter to be broken, like I broke her whore of a mother. With any of Liessa's blood in her, we run the risk of our plans going awry if she is not brought to heel."

King Azim's eyes glittered at his counterpart's proposition. "How do you propose we do that, Zalan?"

King Zalan's smile was oily. "We keep her away from the

world, so when she emerges into it, she will listen to everything we have to say. When I found Liessa, she'd already had too much worldly experience. Better to mold her exactly the way we want her to be than to risk interference from the thousands of Fae who would be clambering to get to her."

The king of the Iron Realm sat back in his chair, running a finger along his clean-shaven jaw. "I think we can manage that. I have a location that would be perfect."

Opposite him, the king of the Night Realm held up a hand. "I want full control over her care. Whatever I say should happen to her or with her will be law."

"With Rares's input," King Azim interjected. "After all, it was with his help that all of this came to pass. He knows what needs to be done."

The Night Realm king waved his hand dismissively. "Fine, fine."

"So, do we have a deal?" King Azim proffered his hand to King Zalan.

"We do," he replied, clasping his hand against the other king's. "We'll keep each other's secrets from the other realms until our weapons are ready to deploy. Until then, let's drink and fuck."

King Azim rang a bell, and when the door opened a moment later, females dressed in scraps of fabric sauntered into the room, gathering around the kings. The king of the Night Realm leaned back in his chair, allowing three to fawn over him with a look of cruel pleasure spreading across his face. "They certainly are pretty," King Zalan commented to King Azim before pulling one onto his lap and groping her.

"Have as many of them as you want. My gift to you," King Azim replied, rising from his chair and heading toward the door.

"Don't you want to join the fun?" King Zalan asked, words

muffled by the placement of his face against the breasts of one of the females.

The king of the Iron Realm declined, his body buzzing with excitement and the desire to work on other things while his new partner wasted his life away. That was the difference between them, in his opinion. King Zalan was a greedy bastard driven by sloth and lust, while he was a true king, driven by a thirst for power. It was for that reason he deserved to rule all of Északi, and he had just placed the final piece into the puzzle.

Soon, King Azim thought, as he traversed the halls of his home.

I

THE REVELATION

1

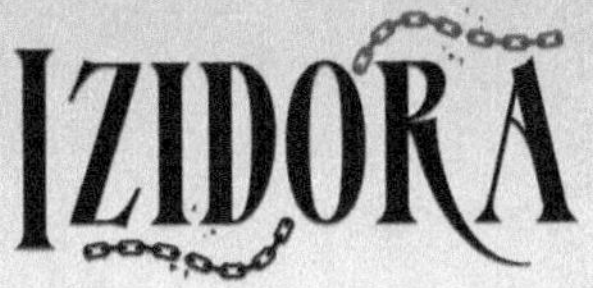

Darkness surrounded me. My head pounded as if someone chiseled away at my forehead, tap, tap, tapping until I was sure my skull would split on the next strike. I groaned, the sound vibrating within the fuzziness that coated my mouth, which was drier than a field during a drought. As I lifted my arm to rub the ache from my temples, a too familiar sound struck my ears – the clanging of chains. Panic clawed up my throat, robbing me of breath and jerking me out of my stupor as my memories came flooding back.

Did I dream up Kazimir, Liliana, and the Nighthounds to save myself from my miserable existence in the cave? Was any of it real?

Not a hint of light trickled through the oppressive darkness, and I was unable to ground myself in time or space. My hands groped the area around me, searching for the rough rocks I knew better than my own face.

I found none.

Instead, smooth wood pressed into my shaking fingers, and my left hand brushed against something soft and furry. I pushed myself to my hands and knees, but when I tried to crawl forward, I pitched to the side, my legs trapped together with tight fabric.

The dress! The feast! Kriztof! And Kazimir, something was wrong with him...

A sob wracked my chest as my final moment with him flashed before my eyes. I had reached for him, the world fading into black around me as I struggled against the hands that grasped my limbs. His deep emerald eyes were broken as he lay on the polished floor of the ballroom at Este Castle, unable to move, unable to protect me. My love, my mate, shattered and agonized by my pain as I was dragged away.

Ruslan.

The male's wicked smirk flashed through my mind – the one he wore when he had revealed the truth of my kidnapping to all those present at the feast celebrating my return to the Night Realm. My father and his father – they were the ones responsible for all the pain I'd endured the first twenty-one years of my life. King Zalan sold me off before I was born, then contributed his soldiers to guard me in a cave high in the Agrenak Mountains, far away from anyone who might dare save me. He must have thought he was so clever with his ruse, leading the Nighthounds on a chase around the continent searching for his beloved daughter.

Ruslan thought I belonged to him, and that he would take me as his bride when I came of age – which happened at the same time that Kazimir had rescued me. Ruslan was pissed and ready to claim his prize, all so that he could have me for some power-grab the Iron and Night Realms had planned for Északi. When I fought back, he had ordered his soldiers to drug me, to subdue me, to chain me, all so he could control me. Typical male.

My head throbbed anew with the burning rage building in my chest, the embers that remained from my drugged stupor spreading into a wildfire. That inferno wrenched a scream from deep within my body, a high-pitched shriek to accompany the harsh metal clanking as I flailed my arms in a manic burst of energy, ripping at the iron that bound me as if I could simply break free of my chains. I screamed and screamed and screamed, my hands glowing white of their own accord as fury exploded from the depths of my soul.

How could this be happening again?

Footsteps raced closer, and I stilled, waiting to see where the first crack of light would appear. My survival instincts broke through the surface of my rage, and I banished my magic before anyone saw its free reign around the iron that should have snuffed it out like a candle. I sat back on my heels, crouched and ready to launch myself like a wildcat at anyone who dared lay their hands on me. Wood creaked off to my right, then the ground dipped beneath me as though something heavy joined me on the floor of my prison, just out of reach. The faint click of a lock jerked my gaze forward, straight into Ruslan's darkly handsome face. Even in the dim light, his arrogance was blinding.

"Sleep well, Princess?" he smirked.

I bared my teeth, a threatening snarl tearing from my peeled-back lips. "You fucking bastard."

"That indeed I am," he grinned devilishly. "But enough about me, how are you?"

"How am I? Are you fucking serious? You just kidnapped me, ripped me from my mate, killed my friends, and disrupted my whole life! How the fuck do you think I am?" My voice rose with each venomous statement flung in his direction.

"Sounds like you are hungry and thirsty. I bet you didn't eat much in that dress." His gray eyes perused my crouched form with the leisure of a male in total control. My teeth ached from how hard I clenched them. "Here, I'll be back when you're feeling better." He tossed a canteen in my direction, the metal clattering to a halt at my knees, followed by the soft thud of a hunk of bread.

My jaw dropped as I stared incredulously at the male backing away from the entrance. Before his face disappeared completely, he accosted me with that fucking smile again. "By the way, that male isn't your mate. I am."

The door slammed shut, lock clicking into place before he trapped me in a thick blanket of utter darkness that felt more like an executioner's hood. My shock rooted me in place as I tried to process what the fuck had just happened.

He thought he was my mate? He was absolutely insane.

I wrinkled my nose at the bread and water in front of me, the offering more likely to drug me than make me feel better. Risking a hint of light, I cast a spark into the air, directing it around where I was confined to discern my surroundings – and look for potential weapons I was trapped in a low wooden box, just high enough for me to sit on my knees with my hair brushing the top. The beautiful headdress that accompanied my outfit was nowhere to be found. In one corner, a pillow and pile of furs sat crumpled together, while the opposite corner held a bucket. I was free to move about save for the iron clasped around my wrists and ankles. There were no other clothes to be found, no other items save for the canteen and bread Ruslan had chucked at me.

The door of my box opened outward, which meant I had nothing to hide behind should he return. This box was within something else, something that dipped when Ruslan put his weight on it, but didn't move in any other direction, as far as I could tell. If I could break the lock outside this door, I might find keys or even a weapon to aid my escape.

But I would accomplish nothing in this skin-tight dress. Grasping either side of an existing tear in the glittering gold skirt, I yanked, trying to rip the fabric apart to create more room for my legs. It didn't budge, my arms not quite strong enough to accomplish the task. A few fruitless pulls later, I relented with a groan. My head pounded vigorously, and I could barely grip the fabric between my trembling fingers. Water and food would banish my weakness, but what Ruslan had left me was equally likely to render me unconscious yet again, delaying any chance of escape. Making a break as soon as possible was better than allowing Ruslan to put extensive distance between us and Vaenor.

I needed to get back to Kazimir, to Liliana, to my friends... if Ruslan had left any of them alive. Though he seemed to only want me, his soldiers had created enough chaos to distract the crowd while isolating Kazimir and myself. Even if I asked, I doubted that I would trust his answer. I had to see with my own eyes.

Heavy footfalls gently shook the wood beneath me, and I banished that tiny spark of hope to avoid revealing my unchained magic. I snatched the metal canteen from the floor in front of me, gripping it tightly in my hand, preparing to strike with it should the need arise. It wasn't much, but I would take what I could get.

Two soldiers cracked the door to my wooden prison, and without hesitation I hurled the canteen at the closest one, causing him to flinch back into his companion. I leapt over them, rolling over my shoulder to take the impact of the landing, then popped into a crouch. Taking quick stock of my surroundings, I discovered two doors flung wide and scrambled toward them, seeing my freedom within reach. My racing feet were hindered when one of the soldiers caught the chains between my ankles and yanked them out from under me. I hit the wood of the outer container with a thud, all the air whooshing from my lungs, but I managed to snap the male's grip with a harsh kick to the face. On hands and knees, I darted forward, leaping for the earth not far beneath my feet and landing lightly before running as fast as I could with my limited range of motion. The iron clanked and clamored, and I gritted my teeth against the sound that was sure to give me away. I glanced over my bare shoulder for my pursuers, then ran straight into a wall of stone.

My breath fled again, but two rough hands caught me before I collapsed to the ground. Ruslan towered over me, his eyes glinting with excitement like a predator that had cornered its prey. "I did tell you that I like when they fight back," he purred, his eyes heating with black flame. "Trying to entice your mate already?"

"You are not my mate," I spat out, teeth bared. He may be a predator, but I was no prey.

He only laughed, as if my fiery spirit amused him. "You are so cute when you're angry. Like a little sprite."

I glared, willing him to catch fire and burn before my very eyes. If my magic were capable of that, that would have been a great time to see it.

"Come, let's get you some real clothes. I can't have my mate freezing out here," he tutted, wrapping his arm over my shoulders and guiding me back to the wagon that confined me like an animal. My mind worked over every detail, searing its every angle into my memory, noting that the boxes lining its insides didn't quite reach the ceiling and that I might be able to use something stowed in another compartment to aid in my escape. The two soldiers waited at its open doors, smug grins on their faces as their leader held me captive under his massive arm.

"Stop calling me that," I demanded.

"Then tell me what pet names you like, and I will oblige." His voice was smoky, raspy, and grating me in all the wrong ways.

"I am not your fucking pet, I am not your fucking anything,

and I do not want you to call me your mate!" I shrugged him off me with a scream.

His hand snatched my upper arm, spinning me to face him. His face was deceptively serene with the half moon peeking over his right shoulder. It cast light on half his face, shrouding the other in darkness – a darkness that was only accentuated when he crouched, leveling his iron gray eyes with mine. "I know this is a lot for you right now, so I am going to excuse your behavior. But you will see what I mean soon enough." He snapped his fingers at the soldiers, who appeared by his side with a pile of clothing.

"I am going to remove your chains so you can change into something more comfortable. We're going to trust each other here, okay? I know you want to run off, but I am trusting you not to. The three of us will stand here, watching you, an arm's distance away. You will not get far. If you choose to run regardless of the trust I place in you, then I will have no choice but to punish you. If you choose to be good and change without issue, I will allow you to ride alongside me today instead of in the cage. Whatever you decide, you choose what happens next. Understand?"

My eyes narrowed as I weighed my options.

Run in darkness in a skin-tight dress with my ankles and wrists chained, or run during the day with a horse beneath me?

I knew which option was better.

"I will change in front of you, and only you, and I will not run away," I sighed, feigning defeat.

His eyes darkened with the promises held in our aloneness. I schooled my face into a neutral expression as his soldiers unlocked the iron from my wrists and ankles. Rubbing my wrists, I eased some of the ache from the weight and friction on my skin. With a jerk of his head, Ruslan dismissed the soldiers, and I stood before him in the dress created for me to look like the Goddess, feeling like anything but.

His smile was feral as he assessed my soft curves. I squared my shoulders and lifted my chin, unwilling to falter under his heavy gaze. He circled me slowly, like he was memorizing every inch of my body covered in glittering gold. My spine tingled with anticipation, and my low belly heated in a traitorous way. When he went out of my view, I held my breath, waiting for his next move. The hairs on the back of my neck rose as he closed in behind me, and if I weren't already so tense, I would have stiffened.

"Looks like you might need help out of this," he purred in my ear, his hands finding the back of my dress.

My heartbeat was erratic, and I was certain he could hear its thundering pace with his keen Fae senses. Cold sweat trickled down my spine, and it took all my willpower not to flinch as his rough hands met my back.

How would he react when he saw my scars?

With one mighty pull, he accomplished what I could not and ripped the dress in two, snagging a few of my long chestnut strands that were tangled in my dress and yanking them from my scalp. I gasped, clutching the front of the dress to my chest with both hands as it nearly fell away and left me exposed to the chilly night air – and Ruslan.

"You won't be needing this dress anyway. Everything will be better where I am taking you." His hot breath floated over my ear as he whispered his promise, then he brushed past me, his arm barely caressing mine as he stooped to collect a pile of clothes.

It must be too dark for him to see the deep lacerations marring my back, the scars a physical reminder of the torture and abuse I'd suffered at the hands of his kin. They were hard to miss; perhaps he didn't care – maybe he inflicted some himself.

Yet he didn't smell familiar, and my body did not react to him the way it had reacted to the male I killed when our camp was attacked along the Northern Route to Vaenor.

With one arm, I snatched the fresh clothes from his outstretched hands, desperately trying to hold the remnants of the fabric to my chest. He waited for me to inevitably drop the dress with barely veiled amusement, his fingers splaying over his lips as he watched my struggle. I screamed internally as the shimmering fabric pooled around my feet, but kept my face bland, almost bored, and resisted the urge to cover each part of my body. Throwing the tunic over my head, I tugged at the gray fabric, grateful that my breasts were covered and the hem kissed the tops of my thighs. I yanked on the leggings while simultaneously tossing Ruslan an aloof look, and wrapped the jacket around my upper body, the thick fabric immediately soothing the rib that was irritated whenever I caught a chill. I had no shoes, but my toes were content to wriggle in the grass, the most freedom I could obtain for the moment.

Ruslan growled appreciatively, my new attire not leaving much room for imagination either. The leggings hugged me perfectly, and the jacket was crafted from flexible leather that fastened on one side, the high collar framing my neck. My long chestnut hair tumbled over one shoulder, the soft moonlight casting a shine on its tangled mess.

He closed the distance between us, and I didn't dare move, didn't dare breathe, as he sniffed me. "Much better. Now his scent no longer clings to you." He spun on his heel, yanking me along by the hand, and I stumbled behind him, my foot catching on a rock. A string of curses left my lips as he kept pulling, dragging me deeper into the wood.

We broke into a clearing where dozens upon dozens of soldiers clad in intricate metal armor gathered around small fires. The smell of roasted meat assaulted my nostrils, my empty stomach rumbling appreciatively at the idea of food. Each soldier held a tin plate piled with thick slices of bloody meat and bread, and as Ruslan stalked to the fire, I couldn't help my hungry gaze glancing over their plates. He selected a log, and the other males shuffled to adjacent ones without a word. Guiding me to the ground at his feet, he caged me in with his legs, and I had no choice but to settle there like a dog at the feet of its master.

"Bring me food," he ordered to no one in particular. A male appeared with a plate in hand, and Ruslan handed it to me.

"Eat," he commanded. His tone brokered no room for argument, but I spun the food around at eye level, searching for signs of tampering or drugs anyway. He scoffed, yanking the plate from my hands. "I'm not trying to drug you again. See?"

He took a bite of the hunk of meat, chewed and swallowed, then handed it back to me. I eyed him warily, waiting a moment before taking a tiny bite off the opposite side. When nothing happened to him, I tore into the bloody meat, juices dripping down my chin and onto the plate, only to be sopped up by the fluffy roll before it disappeared into my mouth. With each bite, my headache abated and my shaky hands stabilized. He sipped from a dented canteen, then passed it along to me. I gulped the cool water greedily, my desert-dry mouth relieved at last.

The smallest hint of sun graced the sky, the pitch black of night fading into the deep blue of early morning. "Let's move," Ruslan ordered. The grim-faced soldiers packed up in minutes, stuffing everything into the carriage, which was nestled in the trees near a packed-dirt road that was visible in the quickly rising light. He kept me at his feet until the last male mounted his horse, leaving only a thick black steed with white feathered hooves at the front of the traveling party. Ruslan grasped my arm and dragged me toward the stallion that pawed at the ground, shaking the ground beneath my feet as his hooves struck the earth.

"Where is my mount?" I demanded.

"I said you could ride alongside me. That means with me, on my horse," he grinned, his deception well played.

I scoffed, then approached the beast, who calmed his restless stomping as I neared. Ruslan reached for me as if he would throw me on his mount's back, but I shot him a sharp look. "I've got this," I snapped, stepping away from him.

Though I could almost walk beneath the trunk-like legs of the horse, I managed to grasp the saddle and haul myself atop the black beast with graceful ease. With my chin lifted high and gaze glued forward, I did not deign to give Ruslan attention as he pulled himself into the leather saddle behind me. His warmth immediately enveloped me, followed by an intoxicating combination of cedarwood and vanilla. Muscled arms snaked around my waist, trapping me against the hard planes of his torso. I arched away from him as much as possible, though it was futile, and he snapped his mount's reins, leading the group away from Vaenor, away from my friends, and away from my mate.

2

KAZIMIR

I was numb. As I walked around the massive ballroom in Este Castle, Fae wailed, both from physical pain and grief. The sound was distant, like I passed a symphony playing in a far-off venue. Glassy eyes gazed up at the ceiling that imitated the night sky, their owners never to see the real one again. Healers ran through the obstacle course of bodies, living and dead, scattered throughout the room, saving those they could, granting peace to those they could not. Occasionally, another shard of crystal lost its battle with gravity and shattered against the floor, knocked loose by my earlier roar, which had left my throat bloody and raw.

Endre barreled into me, grasping my shoulder, shouting in my ear. But I did not hear him, could not process the words that flew from his mouth. I shrugged him off, continuing my harrowed march. My best friend in the entire world, and I could not stand his sympathy, for I had completely and utterly failed.

Izidora... I swore I would protect her, keep her safe, never let her be chained again; yet I watched as they drugged and dragged her from me, unable to lift a finger to reach her. I could not protect her.

My father... with his dying breath, he'd told me what I knew deep inside but didn't believe was true. Izidora was my mate. If only I had listened to him... I would be able to contact her, mind to mind. I could have saved her. Mate magic was strong enough to break barriers, cut poisons, and more, with a beacon that always guided mates home to one another. If I'd listened, I could have tracked her, saved her from the Iron Fae's clutches.

I rode Fek, my dependable mount, through every forest surrounding Vaenor last night, and I screamed for Izidora over and over, ignoring the sharp pain in my throat until my voice was utterly gone. But I found no trace of her – not even a hint of her sweet, rosy scent. It was as if she had disappeared into thin air.

Now a strong hand lay across my face. I blinked, registering that Viktor stood in front of me, covered in blood, his eyes frenzied and fearful. He slapped me again. My reverie began to fade. He raised his hand for a third strike, and I let him hit me, needing to feel the pain, taking the punishment for my failure as a mate.

"That's enough!" Endre roared, catching Viktor's hand before he could land a fourth stinging strike to my sweat- and tear-stained face.

"He needed to pull his head out of his ass!" Viktor snapped back. "We've got to do some serious damage control, and we need him coherent. He's the head of House Vaszoly now."

"He just lost his father and his mate, you asshat! Give him a minute," Endre fumed.

"We don't have a minute! Valintin is in the council room right now making his claim for the throne. None of our houses are there to stop him, and if we don't get there soon it's going to be too late," Viktor barked.

"Let's go." My voice was raspy, hollow, and barely there – just like me. Walking between my two best friends, I stepped in too many ruby puddles until we broke into the hall outside the ballroom, where the dead lay side by side beneath white shrouds. My two closest friends continued their argument with silent glares around my head as we left a bloody trail in our wake, all the way to the council room.

Over my dead body would High Lord Valintin install himself as King of the Night Realm.

Izidora was out there somewhere, and she still had the strongest claim to the throne. I threw open the double doors to the council room with a bang. With that aggressive action, my head cleared enough to stalk to my father's seat near the head of the table, eyes like daggers as they stabbed into Tomaz Valintin. His son Alekzi shadowed the wall behind him like a pathetic puppy begging for a scrap of attention. Neither sported a drop of blood on their unruffled formal attire.

Endre and Viktor took their fathers' seats, both Tibor and Erik having been badly injured during the chaos as they defended their realm, unlike the two sniveling pieces of shit that sat across from me. High Lord Kaztar Rass limped into the room moments later sporting a blood-soaked bandage around his thigh. Viktor shot to his feet and helped the young High Lord hobble to his seat at the table. Kaztar dipped his head to me, his jade eyes hard and cutting to the High Lord seated across from me.

Tomaz Valintin stood, casting an accusatory glare at Endre and Viktor. "Where are your fathers? We cannot take a vote without them."

Viktor shot to his feet with an affronted snarl, knocking the heavy high-backed chair to the ground. "Our fathers are both with healers who are tending to their wounds received from defending their realm and kin. Unlike you two, they fought like heroes. They have named us delegates with freedom to hear and decide on any argument until the time that they shall be healed enough to return to these seats."

High Lord Valintin paled under Viktor's ferocious stare. His thin lips popped open to retort, but I interrupted him. "So, tell me Tomaz, what is it that we are voting on? You see, Houses Adimik, Zadik, Rass, and Vaszoly were not present for the debate. We'll need a rundown of the proposal before we can proceed." My knuckles braced against the polished red wood of the table as I towered over it, my jaw clenched around the words I really wanted to whip into the spineless male before me. My father taught me to be a damn good politician, and I refused to allow Valintin to win this battle of words by succumbing to my raging emotions.

He cleared his throat, glancing to High Lord Vaklav Luzak down the table. "We were just discussing succession plans, now that King Zalan is dead. He never named a successor, making it plain he wasn't planning on doing so for some time just before the Iron Fae stormed in. Given that Izidora returned and wasn't immediately named heir apparent, I think this council should decide what's best for the Night Realm."

"Princess Izidora was kidnapped, again, only hours ago, by those Iron Fae soldiers who breached our walls and killed King Zalan – whose body still remains in that room – and yet you are most concerned with who will next wear the crown?" I questioned.

"Well, I... I mean we... we can't lead forces against another realm without proper leadership, and besides, we don't really have any evidence that she is who she claimed to be–" I stopped him mid sentence with a growl so low and threatening that even Viktor and Endre blanched.

"Am I to believe that there are others in this room who question Princess Izidora's identity? To speak those words is, in fact, treason. And while King Zalan may no longer preside over this council, his laws still exist. So tell me, does anyone else share Tomaz's opinion?" My regard landed heavily over the other High Lords gathered around the table.

High Lord Jaku Volak averted his eyes, and only High Lord Vaklav Luzak held my gaze, contempt lining every wrinkle on his aging face. "I share this opinion," he spat.

"So we have two traitors among us? My dear brother Kazimir, it seems we cannot take their votes into consideration," Viktor purred. "According to the Law of Árulás, any noble house that commits treason is automatically stripped of its voting rights, with or without trial." Viktor righted his chair and settled into it with a relaxed posture. These were the moments he lived for, twisting words and weaving tales to line up his chess pieces in just the right way to corner his opponents.

"We aren't traitors!" Vaklav shouted, banging his fists on the table like a child, his face flushed and filled with fury.

"Oh? So then you do believe that Princess Izidora is the daughter of Queen Liessa and King Zalan, and she has a claim to the throne?" Viktor questioned, leaning forward with a dark brow raised toward his black hair, which was somehow just as neat as it had been before the feast last night.

"Yes, of course–" Tomaz started.

"So then, if she has claim to the throne, why are we discussing who else to crown when we, as her loyal council members, should be planning to rescue our monarch?" Viktor interrupted.

I smirked as Viktor laid his cards on his carefully crafted table of words. The two could try to backtrack, but they would lose face with the other members, who assessed them closely, their faces neutral as they analyzed their potential alliances.

Neither Vaklav or Tomaz spoke, both silently fuming at the trap they had so easily fallen into. "It sounds to me like we should vote on a war council instead," Kaztar Rass ventured.

"I quite agree, Kaztar. And since my mate is the one whose life is in grave danger, I volunteer to lead the effort." I laid my cards onto the table as well, daring anyone to challenge me.

A hush fell over the room as the information sunk in.

"Your mate? Are you certain?" Kaztar raised his brow in question.

"Yes. We have not yet accepted the bond, given the circumstances. But I have no doubt." My voice was laced with conviction, and I held his gaze until he nodded.

"Viktor and I watched from the very beginning. It was Kazimir who led us on our mission to rescue her, and Kazimir who held her attention from the moment we found her. I think we all knew before he did," Endre explained.

"I have yet to hear the full story of what happened to Princess Izidora. Can you please explain from the beginning? I am certain I am not the only one who feels left in the dark about the whole ordeal," High Lord Jaku asked.

Sucking in a deep breath and flattening my palms against the cool wood, I launched into the tale of our discovery and subsequent rescue of Izidora, followed by our race to Zirok and journey here. I explained what I knew of Izidora's abuse at the hands of the Iron Fae – and Night Fae, if Ruslan was to be believed – leaving out more personal details regarding the repeated torture and her unashamed killing of one of her abusers. Those were not my stories to share. I rounded off my tale by repeating what we had learned only yesterday about King Zalan's involvement – a secret marriage contract between King Azim and King Zalan, the murder of Queen Liessa, and Izidora's kidnapping.

Every male in the room was stunned into silence. Kaztar blinked repeatedly while he processed my words, fist covering his hard-pressed mouth. If I had to guess, his mind was on his wife, Domi, and what he would do had she been taken from him with the same brutal force with which Izidora had been taken from me.

"All hail, Queen Izidora Valynor," High Lord Jaku uttered.

"Long live Queen Izidora," Endre, Viktor, Kaztar, and I chanted in unison.

The room held its breath as every eye trained on Tomaz Valintin and Vaklav Luzak. They glanced at each other, knowing they were outnumbered. "All hail..." they muttered, looking away and crossing their arms, pouting like children who'd had their favorite toy snatched from them.

"I second your appointment as head of the war council, Kazimir," Kaztar pronounced loudly, shooting a deadly glare at Valintin and Luzak.

"I would like my second to be High Lord Viktor Adimik," I announced. My friend bowed his head to me in acceptance.

Kaztar volunteered next, and then, of course, Endre.

Jaku stood, garnering the attention of all those around the table. "May I request that the traditional war council be expanded so that my house may join?"

Without missing a beat, Viktor instructed, "All those in favor, say 'aye.'" There were four ayes and two nays. "The vote passes. Welcome, Jaku, we will be grateful for your expertise."

The five of us had drawn a line in the sand with Luzak and Valintin. I smiled at the latter with enough venom that he shrank into his seat. "I think we'll begin our first session now. Leave," I barked. They both scampered from the room like dogs with their tails between their legs.

My chest loosened with the certainty that Izidora's claim was safe, and instead I could focus on saving her again. I could not penetrate the Iron Realm alone, and we would need allies. This step was a necessary evil, but no matter what, I was going to get her back – even if I had to fall into darkness to do so. That darkness called to me, beckoning me to my dimly lit room at Zirok, where Izidora's bright, aquamarine eyes pierced me as I moved inside her. My groin heated as I recalled the face she made when I buried myself completely in her, her pink pout spreading into an O while a whisper of breath passed her lips.

Viktor cleared his throat, bringing me back to the present moment. I settled in my seat at last, and Viktor spread a map across the massive council table in front of us, pinning the corners with weights before spreading figurines across the scaled map of Északi.

It was time to take down the Iron Realm.

3

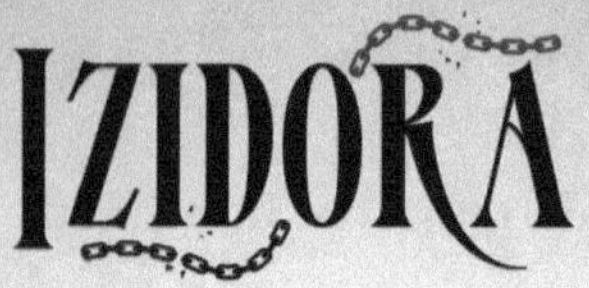

IZIDORA

The Agrenak Mountains peeked over the horizon, shadowed by the golden light of the setting sun. My brow furrowed as confusion swept through me.

How long had I been unconscious?

It should have taken weeks of riding to see the jagged, snow-tipped peaks this close. As if he could sense the direction of my thoughts, Ruslan whispered in my ear, "Aren't the mountains beautiful? They are my favorite place on the continent. I could sit on a cliff's edge for hours gazing over the vast landscape. Maybe I will show you my favorite spot."

I cringed both at his closeness and the thought of spending any time with him, but my curiosity got the better of me. "Shouldn't we still be weeks away from seeing them?"

His rumbling laugh raised the hairs on my arms. "You don't miss anything, do you, my sprite?"

I rolled my eyes at the nickname, not deigning to respond. The only sound around us was the clip of the horses' hooves against the hard-packed road. When it became obvious he had no intention of speaking, I snapped, "Are you going to tell me or not?"

Ruslan's only reply was a sharp whistle and quick jerk on the reins, halting our progress to the mountains. "Make camp," he ordered, and heavy boots thudded against the ground, metal armor clanged, and hushed conversation fell across the soldiers behind us.

Instead of allowing us to dismount, Ruslan yanked on the reins, carving a wide arc around the clearing where his soldiers busied themselves pitching tents and building fires. His pace was lazy, slow, and leisurely, while my mind screamed for something, anything to happen. Yet I remained silent, waiting for his next move.

"What do you know of the other continents?" he inquired.

Was my brain broken, or did his responses to normal questions make zero sense?

I answered anyway. "Only that there are other continents. I can see trading ships coming and going from the windows in my room at Este Castle."

"There are four continents, plus many outlying islands, each with its own people who have different magical abilities. Déli is filled with Shifters, whose magic allows them to take the shape of different animals. There are powerful Mages who harness magic using spells and potions on the continent Nugati. Keleti is filled with Angels and Demons who are nearly immortal, some living for thousands of years."

My curiosity begged me to ask questions about the other continents, but I silenced my inner voice, instead firing back with a sliver of information I already possessed. "And the Iron Fae traffic females from these other continents, selling them for slaves in Északi."

Ruslan stiffened at my back, sending my already tense shoulders even higher as his anger rolled off of him in waves that knocked me off balance. "They are not slaves," he gritted out, his knuckles white around the black leather reins. "Nor do we sell them."

That struck a nerve.

In one swift movement, he leaped off his horse, spinning to face me while he gripped his stallion's bridle. His smoky gray eyes flashed as he stared at me, struggling to regain a semblance of control of our conversation. I studied him in turn, taking in the dark lashes fanning against his pale skin as he blinked through an array of emotions. His dark hair was close cropped on the sides but longer and slicked back atop his head. Sharp cheekbones contrasted with a strong jaw dusted in stubble.

His horse was massive, yet he held his own against the beast, legs thick as tree trunks holding his broad shoulders straight. Metal armor fit snugly over his body, leaving no doubt that he could break your spine across his knee and not even blink. The smallest hint of a tattoo peeked through his armor near the nape of his neck, the rest covered by the leather collar of his under-shirt. Another tattoo peeked between his sleeves and wrists as he clenched and unclenched his fists, attempting to rein in his wild emotions.

His inner turmoil mirrored my own, and if I weren't trying to survive this kidnapping and return to my mate, I might have sympathized with the male. That wall behind which I hid my intense emotions was too cracked to repair, and I needed every bit of control over them to make it out of his clutches alive. There was no room for mistakes or pity. My only focus was me. Reaching inside, I stoked the white flames that had become my comfort in moments of turmoil, relieved when they flared to life alongside the spear of crystal, both ready to fuel my magic should I need to fight and flee.

Ruslan circled his neck, once, twice, three times, before releasing a breath, seeming to relax once again. "Will you please dismount and walk with me?" he asked, his voice strained as if it pained him to play nice.

"Do I get to walk on my own, or will you chain me like a slave?" I retorted, looking down my nose at him.

His eyes flashed with violent black flames again, and his teeth clacked with how hard he snapped them shut. Through those gritted teeth he seethed, "You may walk beside me, without chains."

Keeping him in view, I slipped off his mount's broad back, landing lightly on my toes. I braced myself against the horse's furry hide, wanting something to ground me as I faced off with the male who towered over me. The familiar musky scent and the rippling muscle beneath my fingers was enough for the moment. Tossing me the reins, Ruslan allowed me to lead his horse as we traipsed through the dead grass toward the camp.

"So, the continents? Were you going anywhere with that story?" I prodded, wanting to shift the dangerous air that lay between us.

"The Iron Realm is the smallest in Északi. My father has long searched for ways to expand his power and bring wealth to Iron Fae. The other continents are how he has accomplished that. We bring rare metals, jewels, and people to the Iron Realm, creating beautiful new items like none have seen before. Like me," he explained.

He thought he was rare and beautiful?

He was like every asshole who had abused me for the twenty-one years he had me chained in a cave.

"My father is King Azim of the Iron Realm, but my mother was the result of careful selection in a breeding program designed to create Fae with superior power. You see, the other realms think that blood purity is the way to build and maintain magic power, but they are wrong. Their prejudices have made them weak, and I intend to show them the error of their ways.

The Félvér – what we call those with mixed blood – will rule this continent, with me as the king of all realms."

Breeding program? As in, they forced those they brought from the other continents to fuck and produce offspring?

My brows pinched together, but I forced myself to refocus as he continued.

"Rares – King Azim's director of the breeding program – selected my grandfather, a Mage, to breed with my grand-mother, who was half Demon, half Dragon Shifter. And then my mother was born, with a mix of all races except Angel and Fae. My father bred with her, and then I came into the world." He stopped so suddenly that his mount nearly crushed me beneath his hooves in my attempt to slow him. With his back to the camp, Ruslan leveled a look at me that sent chills skittering down my spine. "I have magical abilities far beyond what any Fae on this continent can manage, and I can partially shift into a Dragon. But the best part is that I can bend space with a simple spell. So, my sprite, you were only out for a night. But I moved us three fourths of the way out of the Night Realm in that time."

Holy fuck.

My breath caught in my chest as panic clawed its way up my throat, threatening to suffocate me as the weight of his words crashed over me.

Ruslan was bred to have abilities beyond what most imag-ined possible.

In a short time, he could move massive distances.

How was I supposed to escape if he could follow me like he was leaping from one stone to another along a river?

I was trapped with no escape yet again – not on this conti-nent, and not on any other. I was powerless in the face of an enemy who carried the prowess of every race behind him.

How was I supposed to overcome this, especially alone?

My white flame dimmed in my chest, doused by the tidal

wave of despair that rose from my trauma, and tears burned in my eyes as that helpless feeling pulled me beneath the surface. Faster and faster my breaths came, pricks of black dotting my vision as panic exploded from my core. Bile rose in my throat, and I gagged on my breath before dropping the reins and bolting to the nearest tree. Bracing myself on it, I heaved the contents of my stomach onto the array of pine needles coating the forest floor, though not much came up. Ruslan made no move to follow, and for that I was relieved. The tree slightly obscured him, and I used the opportunity to regain control of my breath, using the flow of air in and out of my nostrils to ease the sharp pain that gripped my chest.

I was a survivor. I was strong. I was powerful. I was an insidious bloom, and he would not see my thorns until it was too late.

I repeated the phrases over and over until the threat of further gagging subsided. Wiping my mouth with the back of my hand, I returned to where Ruslan and the horse waited patiently.

"Are you alright?" he murmured.

I hoped the hate in my eyes was evident as I stared him down. "No, I am not. I have panic attacks when I get over-whelmed, or startled, or fear for my life. Why? Because you fucking people abused me from the time I could talk. I spent my entire life chained in a cave. I had no contact with anyone besides males who would beat me, tear me down psychologi-cally, or rape me, and a group of females who pretended like everything was perfectly normal when they showed up once a month, despite the fact that more often than not I was covered in bruises or blood or both!

"And now, I have to sit here and listen to you tell me how fucking amazing you are. That you are my mate and we're going to conquer the continent with your father. That all of that abuse was meant to break me so that you could mold me into a weapon for your own desires. But guess what, I am not broken! I am here, I am angry, and I am tired of males acting like they are so superior. You are no better than my father – who I killed, by the way – or the other High Lords of his court. Why would I be alright when I am with you?"

Ruslan only blinked as I finished my verbal assault, my chest heaving with unreleased anger. I had so much more to say, and I was ready to unleash another torrent when he fell to his knees before me, grasped my hands, and brought them to his face. I flinched, ripping my hands away, but he reached for my waist instead and pulled me into him. Pushing against his shoulders, I struggled in his hold, turning this way and that, but as he buried his face into my jacket his grip was as unbreakable as the irons that had chained me for so long.

"I had no idea that you suffered so much... they were never meant to hurt you, or touch you," his words were muffled by the fabric of my clothing. "They were meant to show you the way – our way, so you would be compliant when the time came."

I shoved at his head again, wanting no part in this insincere apology. He only gripped me tighter, his shoulders shuddering with wracked breath.

Was he seriously faking tears?

"Save your breath, I know you don't mean a single word of what you're saying," I spat. "The only education I received was how to numb out of my existence as your kin made me bleed."

His black hair shifted as he tilted his head up, his slate eyes shining with a desperation that made me cringe. "Izidora, I will spend my whole life making this up to you, helping you heal these wounds you carry. I should have checked on you, rather than leaving you in the hands of others. Our fathers were the ones who arranged for your care, and they would not allow my involvement until you came of age. On your twenty-first birthday, I was on my way to surprise you and to whisk you away to the palace I built for us, where I planned to shower you with treasure and love. But when I arrived, all the guards were freshly dead, and you were nowhere to be found. I waited for that day for so long, and to find you were not there almost destroyed me. I went out of my mind trying to find you, fearing the worst. Please, Izidora, see that I mean this," he begged, his hands fisting in the fabric of my jacket as he clutched me to him.

He used my name for the first time.

All I could do was blink as I absorbed his explanation, sincerity and despair weaving among his words. My father was a sick bastard who admitted to allowing the abuse to happen, even contributing guards from the Night Realm while he sent Kazimir and the Nighthounds racing around the continent looking for me. For that, I killed my father without regret, and King Azim was next on my list. The two self-important males could rot in hell together.

Ruslan must have sensed my wavering resolve, because he relaxed his hands, resting them on the backs of my thighs instead of nearly tearing my jacket and tunic from my torso. The tension in the air between us was palpable as he waited for me to speak, to acknowledge his words. Escape was high on my priority list, but I had to be smart about it. I knew, more than anything, how *not* to escape after so many attempts in the cave. I also knew how to manipulate and pretend to be who someone wanted me to be. I didn't believe a word he'd said, but heaving a sigh, I backed out of his embrace, holding my hand out to him as my keepers in the cave had taught me. "My Prince, I see that you mean your words. Let's start over. Hi, I'm Princess Izidora."

He grasped my outstretched hand like it was a lifeline and he was drowning. His rakish smile flashed his white teeth and jolted my low belly. "Pleased to meet you, Princess. Can I get you something to drink?"

"Some water would be lovely. Thank you, Your Highness," I said, giving him a tight smile.

I was so fucking tired of doing what I had to do to survive.

He pushed to his feet, his hand never leaving mine as he led me and his horse to the camp. I cringed internally, but his shift in mood - however sudden and strange - was welcome, and if I could maintain it, maybe he would let his guard down long enough for me to flee.

"I'll be right back," he promised, dropping me in front of the fire, returning only a moment later with a canteen and a blanket. He wrapped the thick fur around my shoulders like he was wrapping the most precious of gemstones, gently tucking in each corner until I was fully enveloped in warmth. His tenderness was antithetical to his earlier aggression, and I was developing whiplash from his abrupt shifts in mood.

In another act of kindness, he sipped from the metal canteen, then handed it to me to drink. The water was cold and refreshing, washing away the taste of bile in my mouth. Satisfied that I was comfortable, he seated himself behind me, caging me in with his legs to keep the blanket firmly in place when I accepted a plate piled with food from one of the soldiers. Hunger overtook caution as I tore into the roasted meat and vegetables, my belly demanding sustenance. Funny how I went years without a proper meal every day, but a few months with good food completely reversed my body's tolerance for starvation.

The lack of camaraderie was apparent around the crackling fires, which highlighted grim faces and unmoving lips. Few dared sit near Ruslan and me, and despite my hatred of the current situation, I was desperate for a joke from Kriztof or a trick from the twins, Zekari and Kirigin. Endre's quiet companionship held none of the tension that lay between Ruslan and me. I'd even settle for Vadim's licentious tales or Viktor's brilliant mind.

My eyes burned, and I bit down on my lip to suppress the sob that wanted to break free. I missed the Nighthounds, my friends, and the wood smoke scent surrounding me sent a stab to my heart as it reminded me of our time together.

Don't think about it, don't think about it.

I repeated the phrase over and over while I stared, unseeing, at the food in my hands. But it was no use, not as the scene at that damned feast played out over and over behind my eyes.

Kriztof leaping to his feet, hurling a dagger at King Zalan, only to be pinned by the king's guards, the executioner's blade poised to strike. Vadim tackling the would-be executioner. Liliana's scream as her brother launched himself from their table. The Knights jumping to action, Zekari and Kirigin leading the charge against those who sought to kill their brother-in-arms. Viktor and Endre preparing to die so Kazimir and I could escape the chaos as Ruslan's soldiers flooded the ballroom.

A lone tear mapped my cheek, dripping onto my plate as I ducked my head and chewed my food, hiding the grief that surged from my soul. Food turned to ash in my mouth at the thought of my friends lying dead in Este Castle, and it took all my willpower to choke down the last few bites, needing all the sustenance I could manage to get me through whatever came next.

When my plate was clean, Ruslan lifted it from my hands, then spun me to face him. Even squatting on a fallen log, I had to tilt my chin up to look upon his face. "Do you want to know how I know you are my mate?"

I narrowed my eyes at him in response.

"The Goddess's Prophecy."

My breath caught, mouth popping open involuntarily. "You know the prophecy?"

"I have every word imprinted on my heart, because it promises me a mate – someone who will love me no matter what. I'm assuming you haven't heard it recited?" His stubble-dusted lips turned up at the corners in a knowing smirk.

Clenching my teeth, I gritted out, "I have not."

"How badly do you want to know what it entails?" His words were no more than a whisper, and yet they struck with the force of a well-placed blow. Because I did want to know, more than anything; I wanted to know what the Goddess had laid out for me, and if I would have more choices stripped from me.

"I'd like to know what else I will be made to do against my will," I hissed. His eyes darkened for only a moment before they sparkled with amusement.

"And what would you do to receive this information?"

I wanted to scream, to claw his fuck-me eyes out. He must have sensed the direction of my thoughts, because he offered up a list of options. "You could sleep in my tent with me, or you could kiss me."

His options did not quell the firestorm building in my chest. "Only sleep? Nothing more?"

"Not unless you want to do more." His slate-gray eyes heated as they searched mine, waiting for an answer.

"Fine," I gritted out, fisting the blanket around me until I ripped a few tufts of fur from the pelt. "I will sleep in your tent, but there will be space between us."

His smirk told me that I had lost this battle, but I planned on winning the war. "Then we have a deal, my sprite. I'll tell you the prophecy."

Clearing his throat, he recited my fate.

"The ones that are part of all will be born under a full moon
Her white light will fill the land
But her mates darkness will rise

Kings will fall
Rivers will run with blood
There is a choice
Follow the light
Descend into the dark
The harrowing pass decides it all"

Every word was seared into my memory, my only chance of recalling them later when I had time and space. Even if Ruslan wrote it down, I would not be able to read it. Cazius had only managed to teach me the letters, and there was no way I could string them together into words.

The second line snagged my attention with the mention of white light. That must have been the part that Endre remembered all those weeks ago when he saw my magic for the first time.

But the first part... *the ones that are part of all?* I was only Night Fae, so how would that involve me?

My face must have slipped from anger to confusion, because Ruslan offered, "King Zalan isn't your real father."

All semblance of self-awareness and control disappeared as my jaw slackened. "How do you know that?"

"Because your mother was mated to an Angel who lived in the Iron Realm. He was there under the guidance of Rares. When King Zalan and Queen Liessa arrived for Béke, he was roaming the streets of Radence and saw her. After trailing them to the citadel, he sought out Rares to explain. Mates are different with Angels and Demons – they know immediately when they've found their mate. Rares involved my father, who then revealed his plans to King Zalan. He couldn't wait to breed his wife to the Angel after seeing the powerful Félvér Rares created for King Azim. What better way than to start with his wife, whose child he could claim as his own?

"King Zalan was insanely jealous, though, and he insisted on watching every second they were together. But since Liessa was mated to the Angel, their draw was beyond anything they could resist. He caught them several times together without him present. If she weren't already pregnant with you, he would have killed her. As it stands, that's what he did after you were born.

"And because we had intimate knowledge of the prophecy, we knew that you too would be born under a full moon, based on the time of your conception. So my father proposed a marriage alliance to strengthen our houses and conquer the continent. Though your mother was Night Fae, she had a hint of Crystal and Day blood in her from generations back. So together, we are part of every race on this planet."

Ruslan's face spun and my eyelids fluttered as I tried to process all this information. Everything I thought I knew about the world, about myself, was completely upended in the span of a day. I no longer knew which way was up or down, only that I was spinning out of control, on a collision course with the Fates and the Goddess who deemed my life to be the center of this choice of light and dark.

I needed to lie down.

Whether Ruslan sensed my wavering consciousness or my thoughts were said aloud, he swooped me into his arms, my head lolling back as he carried me to a lavish tent steps away from the roaring fire. Ducking inside, he placed me gently on a fur-lined pallet in the center of the space. My teeth chattered uncontrollably, and Ruslan piled additional blankets on top of me, tucking them up under my chin. When my body stopped shaking, he fetched more water, supporting my head as he brought the lip of the canteen to my lips.

"Drink," he pleaded, voice cracking over the word. I obliged, too overwhelmed to argue. After a few quick sips, I turned my head away, and he gently released me to the floor. When I closed my eyes to the world around me, my stomach churned with the dizzying motion that hadn't left my head.

I prayed for a deep sleep where I could forget about Night and Iron, Angels and Demons, and a Dragon that was getting way too close for comfort. The Goddess must have heard my plea, because not a breath later, I was unconscious in a massive tent that still did not have enough space for all the questions that buzzed like an angered beehive in my head.

4

KAZIMIR

By the time I finally exited the council room, all bodies of the dead lined the hallway outside the ballroom. Too many Night Fae, young and old, lined the wall – and not enough Iron Fae. Viktor and Endre trailed a few steps behind me as I searched the bodies for our fallen friends and family. I spotted Tibor, Endre's father, and Erik, Viktor's father, sitting near the body of my father, both heavily bandaged but alive. Erik's good arm lifted in a wave, beckoning us toward them.

"How did it go, son?" Erik asked Viktor.

"Valintin and Luzak are on the outs. The rest of the houses aligned with us. I backed them into a corner they couldn't escape from, and now they have all accepted Izidora as queen," he smirked.

"Really?" Tibor looked stunned.

"Really. And High Lord Jaku asked that the traditional war council be expanded to allow him to join," Endre added.

As the fathers and sons conversed, the heaviness in my heart became unbearable. My father's lifeless body was covered in a white shroud with the black sigil of House Vaszoly splayed across it. The crescent moon, surrounded by a smattering of stars, frowned at me, mirroring my own expression. Stepping around Tibor and Erik, I crouched at his covered feet, bowing my head and allowing the chilling loss to spread through my limbs. My father, my mentor, the last bit of my family... gone. Never again would I hear his voice, take his council, or fly through the skies with him.

We'd worked so hard, for nothing.

King Zalan had known, for the past twenty-one years, exactly where his daughter was. Of all the fucked up games he played around the court, this was by far the worst.

If Izidora hadn't killed him, I would have. His body lay only a few paces away, and I nearly shot to his corpse and stabbed him again, if only to relieve a whisper of this rage heating my chest like a white-hot fire.

Silence fell behind my back as my friends joined me in my grief.

"Your father was a good man. He will be greatly missed." Tibor clasped my shoulder, lending me what little strength he held in his injured body.

I ran a hand over my face, exhaustion seeping into my bones. I hadn't slept, hadn't eaten, and I desperately needed a break from the desolation that crowded out every other feeling in my heart.

But I hadn't seen the other bodies yet.

"The rest are a little further down." Tibor motioned to where the bodies of our friends lay.

Pushing to my feet under the heaviness of what felt like a thousand hands pressing me down, I trudged with Endre and Viktor to three bodies covered in white sheets stamped with black swords. Sorrow swelled from deep within my chest, robbing me of breath as we stopped in front of them. A choked sob wracked Endre's chest, and I pulled him into me, his breath rasping as Viktor knelt to reveal the faces of our fallen friends.

Kriztof, Zekari, and Kirigin's bloodied and lifeless bodies lay side by side on the cold marble floor. Viktor inhaled sharply, hands trembling as he tried to rein in his agony, while my eyes burned and Endre fell to his knees. His dark, unkempt hair fell into his face, concealing his pained expression that no doubt mirrored my own. Viktor closed his eyes, fingers pinching the bridge of his nose as he straightened.

I allowed the salty wetness to wash away the blood that stained my face, for Kriztof's last act was to stand up for Izidora and me with an attempted assassination of King Zalan. He deserved my tears and more. Kriztof lay with an unfurrowed brow, a soft smile playing across his bloodless lips, joining his father in death, both executed for speaking the truth.

Zekari and Kirigin were far too young to die. They had been with the Nighthounds the shortest amount of time, but I would never forget the laughs we shared, the jokes they played, or how they risked their lives time and time again for what was right. We found their bodies among those of over a dozen of Iron Fae who lay dead or dying. The twins fought fiercely to the end, despite the deep gouges marking their young skin, evidence of the iron-tipped whips that had rained down on them.

The bruised faces of the twins brought me to my knees beside Endre, and a moment later another pair of leather boots appeared through my blurred vision. Vadim's head was bowed, his thick locks messily tied up in a bun, though many pieces fell across his face. He placed a hand on Viktor's shoulder, as he tried to remain strong for the rest of us, but the barest shake of his chest betrayed his true feelings.

Half our group, gone in one night.

None of us had been prepared for chaos to erupt. Vadim never went anywhere without his daggers, but the rest of us were barely armed, either with decorative weapons or our magic. There was no armor at the feast, with all Fae dressed in their finest clothes, meant to impress and not defend. The Iron Fae bastard struck when he knew we were most vulnerable.

I planned to tear Ruslan to pieces with my bare hands, slowly carve the flesh from his bones, then flay him alive to rip out his still beating heart. Maybe then he would understand the pain I suffered when he ripped Izidora away from me.

Pure, unbridled fury dried the wetness that covered my cheeks and sent heat creeping up my spine until it surrounded my neck. I swallowed my grief like a bitter potion, then pushed to my feet. It was my time to lead the Nighthounds, and these males would follow me to the ends of the continent. The three looked to me expectantly as we hung on the precipice of the words they knew would spill from my lips, my first official order.

"Let's go get my mate," I commanded.

Providing my friends with a new goal was exactly what we needed to take back control amidst the chaos in the Night Realm. Endre pushed to his feet, then one by one, a vengeful, bloodthirsty grin spread across the face of each male.

"Let's fucking go," Vadim growled. "When can we leave?"

"As soon as possible," I said. "The funeral is in a few days, but after that, we have no obligations." I'd lobbied for King Zalan's royal funerary rites to be stripped from him, given the revelations after Ruslan's arrival at the feast, but I had been overruled at the council. We'd hold a mass funeral, honoring everyone who'd lost their lives defending their realm. As we spoke, servants were preparing the pyres in the grand courtyard in front of Este Castle, open for any Night Fae to attend. I expected most of Vaenor to turn out, especially since word of the attack two nights before spread like the plague into the city in a matter of hours.

I needed food, a bath, and sleep, in that order. I found myself walking to the Royal Wing, toward Izidora's room, without thinking. The call of her rosy scent was relentless even as the distance grew between us. I wanted her beside me, to share in the crushing grief of losing my father and brothers.

More than that, I was worried about her; Ruslan did not seem like the type of male who cared about the wellbeing of females. A muscle feathered in my jaw at the thought of his hands on her. I had to get to her, and soon.

I had to save her again, because she was mine.

A servant scrambled by us as we reached the Royal Wing. I stopped him with a shout. "Please have food sent to Princess Izidora's apartments."

He nodded, then scurried off. The four of us entered Izidora's sitting room, each sinking onto a couch by the hearth as we waited for a proper meal. The silence stretched between us until servants appeared, laden with trays of food that they placed on tables surrounding us. A familiar female followed, carrying two bottles of alcohol in each hand.

"Pardon me, my lords, but I have some information that might be useful." She curtsied as best she could with her hands full.

I remembered her from the feast two nights prior. "Tamara, is that right?"

"Yes, my lord," she dipped her head. Tamara had spoken to Izidora about her mother at the feast.

"Please, take a seat." I motioned for her to pick an open spot.

She placed the bottles beside Endre, then opted to perch on the edge of a chair somewhat in the middle of us before glancing around the room, taking in the food and opulence that spread throughout. A sandwich caught my eye, and I reached for it, taking a small bite as I waited for whatever information she had to impart.

Remembering herself, she cleared her throat. "Queen Liessa

helped me find employment at the castle, right after she arrived here. I was one of her first maids, and we became friends after I earned her trust. She was an incredible queen, so kind and generous. But she suffered living here. There were very few people she trusted, and I was lucky enough to count myself among them. I traveled with her every year during Béke. About twenty-three years ago, we attended one held at the Iron Realm." She paused, tears welling in her eyes as she recounted her tale.

Viktor, Endre, and Vadim sat straighter, leaning in to catch every word Tamara uttered.

"A male - one of the most beautiful males I had ever seen - followed her relentlessly around the citadel. He came to her rooms every day, sometimes twice a day, during the month we were there. I asked her why we hadn't left in our fourth week, and she revealed to me that the male was her mate. He was an Angel, from another continent. She broke down, and I had never seen her so distraught. She described what King Azim and King Zalan were making them do..." Tamara's eyes glistened with tears, falling across her round cheeks like a dripping faucet. She shook her head to clear them, sniffling, and I handed her a handkerchief. She accepted it, drying her eyes with dainty dabs.

"They were forcing them to breed, so that King Zalan could have a half Night Fae, half Angel heir. King Azim promised that their union would produce an offspring so powerful that they could conquer Északi together. Queen Liessa was merely a vessel. She never loved him, and she was broken by his treatment of her. She asked me to help her and the Angel escape so they could be together. Of course, I agreed, knowing how awful King Zalan was. She gave me every jewel on her body to pay for assistance. I hired a boat that would spirit them away to the Crystal Realm, where she had distant cousins who could hide them both. But as they left under the cover of darkness, King Zalan spied them, chased them down, and then beat her in front of the whole citadel before they'd even made it out of the gate. The Angel had tried to shield her from the onslaught, but King Azim had his guards pin him to the ground. The only thing that stopped him from killing her right there was that she revealed she was pregnant. So King Zalan ripped the Angel's wings from his back to punish her. We left two days later to return to the Night Realm.

"She swore me to secrecy, and I knew both our lives and the babe's were in danger if anyone knew what really happened. So I said nothing. She found me another position in the castle, to protect me further. But I still checked in on her as often as I could without it raising suspicion." She hiccuped and looked at the ceiling, a new wave of wetness spilling across her cheeks. I had to lean in to catch her next words, so broken and filled with an anguish that was familiar and raw. "I discovered her body after she had given birth. Her neck was purple and broken, and I knew King Zalan was the one who killed her, though I had no proof and never voiced my suspicions aloud. I felt as if my own sister had died."

Tamara dabbed her eyes and blew her nose. "She didn't deserve the life that the Goddess handed her."

The room was deathly still and filled with the sound of silence as she waited for us to respond.

Endre brought his hands together in front of his lips and reclined back against his chair while Vadim rubbed his own hands together, still leaned forward on his elbows.

Viktor broke the silence. "Did she tell you anything else? Or did you ever hear of Ruslan prior to the night of the feast?"

Tamara shook her head. "No, most of what she told me was pieced together from overheard conversations between King Azim and King Zalan. But I did hear from the Angel that he was trapped in the Iron Realm, along with many others from other continents, by a powerful Mage who wanted to create a race more superior than any that walked the planet."

Vadim let out a low whistle. "So that's why they're always trafficking..."

A blush spread across Tamara's round cheeks, and she ducked her head to avoid our gazes. Her hands wrung round and round before she opened her mouth to speak once more. "I only want the princess returned safely. I was so glad to meet her at the feast."

Patting her knee, I reassured her, "We will retrieve *Queen* Izidora, who would love to speak with you, of that I am certain."

She beamed as my words sank in, then hopped to her feet, dipping into a low curtsey. "Thank you, my lords. May you stay safe on the road."

Once the door clicked shut behind her, Vadim opined, "What the fuck."

"I'll second that," Endre replied, snatching a bottle of wine and tipping it back.

But this explained so much – why her magic was white and why her wings did in fact look like an Angel's.

"Give me that." I swiped the bottle from Endre, taking a long drink myself. "So we're not telling anyone what we just learned, yeah?"

"Absolutely fucking not," Viktor said, reaching around Endre for another bottle of wine. "It would provide Valintin and Luzak with everything they need to claim the throne for themselves."

Vadim nodded at Viktor's words.

"They'd still need to win a majority vote to place one of their greedy asses on the Night Throne," Endre reminded him. "Right now, it's five against two. But I agree with Viktor, it's too risky. We should keep it between us."

After another pull from the bottle, I wiped my mouth with

the back of my hand, catching a stray drop of red before handing it back to Endre. "Good. Glad we are all in agreement."

After draining half the bottle of wine with only half a sandwich on my stomach, my shoulders dropped and my chest loosened as the alcohol took effect. Finally, some of the numbness I craved was setting in, and I could forget for a moment about the deaths of my father and friends, and my missing mate.

Viktor chugged from his bottle before passing it to Vadim. "Remember when we got shitfaced after Béke when we were twenty-one and decided it would be a good idea to go for a midnight swim?"

"Yes, because my dick and balls were too frozen to make sweet love to that female I was fucking at the time," Vadim shuddered.

"You seriously can't remember her name?" Endre laughed.

"I'm not good with names," Vadim waved him off.

I snorted. "That's because you'd slip up if you remembered them."

"Baby is a universal name, one that has saved me too many times to count," Vadim raised the bottle in toast and then drained the last of it.

Viktor yanked the cork out of a bottle of hard amber liquid, then hissed after he took a pull from the glass lip. "Kriztof had just joined our group that year. We told him in order to stay he had to jump off that insanely high cliff without the assistance of wings or magic. That crazy bastard did it, too. I felt bad afterward because I would never jump off myself."

He handed the clear bottle to me, and I gulped the smoky liquid, welcoming the burn down my throat and into my stomach. "He hated King Zalan more than any of us, especially after his father's death. Kriztof died trying to protect Izidora and me from being torn apart. He is a hero."

I passed the liquor to Endre, who poured a shot into a glass, then tossed it in the fire. "To Kriztof," he said solemnly, raising the bottle then pouring an unhealthy measure into the glass for himself.

Vadim fetched the bottle from his hands when the amber liquid reached the rim of the glass. "Zekari and Kirigin didn't come from a noble house, but their promise as fighters shone brighter than many sons of both High and Low Houses. It was an honor to fight alongside them, both last night and in many skirmishes before that." He toasted them with the bottle, then drained a large enough portion for the three of them.

It was Viktor's turn to snatch, and he poured two fingers into another glass, then threw it over the embers. "To Zekari and Kirigin."

He filled the glass for himself, then another for me, placing the bottle in the middle of us as we sat in silence, lost in the memories of our fallen friends. After I finished my second nearly full glass, the alcohol said, "Who is up for a swim? I need to bathe anyway."

"Let's do it," Endre said as he jumped to his feet, then caught himself on the arm of the chair before he swayed to the side. Or was it me who swayed? I jogged to the wall of windows, opening one to a slap in the face by the salty sea air. My bloody clothes were tossed away, and I called my wings to me as I stood naked in front of my friends, all in various stages of undress. The window was wide enough to leap through and take flight, so I backed up a few paces then charged through it, my wings catching a draft and sending me soaring over the angry waves that crashed against the jagged rocks below. Endre leaped out the window behind me, followed by Viktor and Vadim, and we whooped as we glided toward the surging sea.

"What are you idiots doing!?" A female screamed from the window, and I flew in a loop to find a red faced Liliana standing in the frame.

I swallowed down the alcohol that threatened to come up with a laugh, then banished my wings and plunged into the icy water. My brothers mimicked me, all of us gloriously drunk and sharing a light moment together before the reality of the impending war sank its claws into our lives.

5

RUSLAN

zidora would come around. Not a single doubt plagued my mind as I watched her sleep.

Was staring at my mate as she slept creepy? Probably, but I didn't give a fuck.

I'd waited twenty-one years for the day when I could lay eyes on her. When I saw Izidora in that ballroom, in that gold dress, Angel wings on full display, and a halo around her head, I knew. She knocked the breath straight from my lungs, and if I hadn't been on a mission to save her from those Night Fae who thought they knew better than me, I would have fallen to my knees and crawled that thread pulling me straight to her.

I should have killed that motherfucker Izidora clung to like a liferaft. His scent still lingered, and I knew they'd been intimate. My fists clenched so hard at the thought of him inside her that I drew blood into my palms. But that wasn't the worst of what had happened to her.

She'd been raped by her guards, my father's soldiers, and probably some of King Zalan's, too.

My blood boiled as I swore to avenge her, sodomizing every last one with my sword until they begged me to end their lives, and only then would I wrap my hands around their throats and watch with glee as the life dimmed in their eyes.

No one hurt my mate and lived.

Izidora shifted in her sleep, brows creasing, and I was instantly alert to her every breath and movement, my violent thoughts vanishing like a cloud in the wind. I had to take care of her, to show her that I wasn't going to hurt her, and to convince her to conquer the continent with me. It was what we were meant to do, prophesied to do, together.

Fuck my father's plans. I had my own.

As a soft sigh escaped her, I nearly died with the need to join her under the blankets, wrap my arms around her, bury my face in her chestnut hair and suffocate on her rosy scent. But she'd fallen apart over the truth that had been kept from her, and I couldn't risk pushing any more until she had time to adjust to her new life.

And she would adjust, because if what she'd been through hadn't broken her, nothing would. This little spitfire was everything I wanted, needed, and I knew without a shadow of doubt that the Goddess made her for me. She had blown up my whole world the moment I laid eyes on her.

"Ruslan," hissed Drazen, my lieutenant and closest friend, through the canvas tent. He was half Dragon, half Iron Fae, and technically we were related through our Dragon kin. With one last glance at Izidora, I exited my tent to find him waiting, arms crossed over his chest.

"What?" I snapped, annoyed that on my first real night with my mate, he had torn me away.

"Why did you dump all that information on her? I thought we agreed to wait until we were safely in the Iron Realm to reveal our secrets," he chided.

"There's no way they'll catch us before we get there. Besides, if I see them coming, I'll just move us away," I shrugged, not caring whether he liked my response. I answered to no one but my father, and even that was becoming rare. King Azim knew I could take him down with a single thought.

"Your cockiness is going to get us all killed," he snarled.

I rose to my full height, baring my teeth as I growled, "I am your alpha, and I make the calls here. I don't need you to question my judgment."

"Don't pull rank on me to get me to shut up. I am calling you out on your bullshit. You can't think clearly when it comes to her," he seethed, gesturing to the tent where Izidora lay sleeping.

"Of course not! This is the first day I've had with my mate, who I have waited twenty-one years to see. And I find out that she was abused while my father's soldiers held her captive. What the fuck do you think I should be doing? Because what I think I should be doing is killing every last male who had a rotation in that cave," I growled.

"You really had no idea that was happening?" he snorted like he didn't believe me.

I had him by the throat, feet dangling in the air a half second later. "And you did?" My voice was like daggers, and I was ready to snap his neck, kin or not.

"No," he coughed, his face turning purple as I crushed his windpipe. Releasing my grip, I dropped him roughly, and he fell to his hands and knees, gasping for breath.

Crouching so I was level with him, I purred, "Are you sure about that?" The gleam in my eyes was a warning to be truthful with his next response.

"I swear. I figured you were such a fucking control freak that you'd gotten a daily report on her all these years," he grunted.

He had a point. I had been tempted to demand to know every detail on more than one occasion, but that was a point on which my father relentlessly stood his ground. He claimed it was so I could "heroically" save her when she came of age. But I think he owed King Zalan a debt for not speaking of his program and looking the other way when the other realms got involved, trying to stop the "trafficking," as they so termed it. I'm sure King Zalan was the one who permitted the abuse, simply as a way to maintain control over her even from afar. I was an Angel compared to King Zalan when it came to controlling others. But with him out of the way, thanks to my ferocious mate, nothing could hold me back from making Izidora mine.

She already believed her "father" to be a narcissist capable of such atrocities, so who was to say I couldn't be her knight in iron armor? There was little light in me, but my darkness had already brought enough females to my bed to satisfy an army. I would lure her with honeyed words and trap her with me. She already had enough of it in her; it was only a matter of bringing it to the surface and showing her how alike we were. Already I had witnessed her kill in cold blood, and she would do it again and again before I was through with her. Maybe I'd even bring her along, let her toy with the males who'd abused her before I finished them off, showing my mate just what I would do for her. The nightmare I painted in my head of us killing together and fucking like wild animals afterward had me hard in seconds.

I held my hand out to Drazen and he grasped it, pulling himself to his feet. "When we return to the Iron Realm, I want you to find every last motherfucker that had a guard shift in Vasvain, and I want you to take them there. Chain them up like they did to her. Their deaths are mine."

Drazen didn't even blink at my violent words. "Consider it done."

My vehemence relented, and I sighed. "Would it make you feel better if I moved us to the Iron Realm tomorrow?"

"Yes, I would feel better, but you'll burn yourself out. I know your magic isn't fully recharged from moving everyone to

Vaenor and then rushing the survivors away. Let's ride harder instead." He clasped my arm, reassuring me that no hard feelings lingered between us.

"Wake me before dawn," I instructed before dismissing him.

Lifting the tent flap with the barest amount of force so as not to wake Izidora, I ducked into the space. Her bright blue eyes cut through the dim light, though she quickly closed them, feigning sleep. I tuned in to my heightened senses and listened to her erratic heartbeat and shallow breath. Her fear covered the awful stench of that male she thought was her mate. Turning my back to her, I stripped my armor away piece by piece.

Her eyes raked my backside as I undressed, and I slowed my pace to allow her to drink in the view. It was a nice one, after all. Tattoos lined every inch of my muscled torso, the stories of my races mixing with one another to form artwork more beautiful than you'd see on any royal residence's walls. Gradually, I made my way to a chair where I could remove my heavy boots, ducking my head so Izidora could continue her perusal of my form. Her gaze landed on the ridges of my chest, the dips and valleys of my abs that trailed into the pants I unbuckled.

Her scent changed from fearful to aroused with a hint of anger. I smirked, knowing that she liked my body and likely hated herself for it right now. Dragon senses were fucking incredible. As were my wings, talons, and horns, and in time, she'd see those too, ratcheting up her arousal to a dizzying height.

My groin heated under Izidora's stare, and as I stood to remove my pants, her eyes snapped shut, pretending to be asleep once more. By the time I was ready to crawl into the pallet, she'd evened her breaths, but her heart still pounded as wildly as she had pounded the walls of her cage early this morning.

As promised, I kept my distance, pulling up a blanket to

cover my naked lower half, then turned my back to her. I itched to yank her to me, to press my erection into her back, but I had the self-control of a god. She would willingly crawl on her hands and knees to me, begging to be fucked, and soon if I had to judge by her scent. But Drazen was right, and I need to sleep to recharge my magic. So I closed my eyes, ignoring the hardness that threatened to become a kickstand, and forced myself to sink into a restorative slumber.

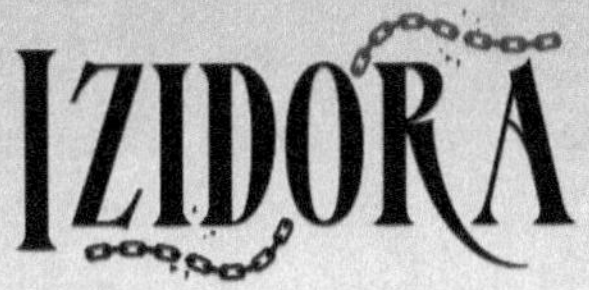

6

*H*oly fuck. *There was no way I was sleeping anymore.*

Earlier, I had been drained to the point of collapse, and even the threat of unfamiliar males was unable to prop me up. But with Ruslan at the other end of this too-small pallet, my heart and mind raced out of control. I didn't trust him not to touch me, especially since he claimed he was my mate. Liliana had said the attraction between mates was undeniable, and as much as I hated him, my body clearly did not, if I had to judge by the dampness between my thighs.

Goddess help me, even his muscles had muscles, and he shamelessly flaunted his body before settling down beside me. He was taller than Kazimir, but where Kazimir's size was threatening but not terrifying, Ruslan's was aggressive and alarming, like I'd always need to be on my toes to avoid unleashing the beast within. I had to keep up my training, if only to give myself a fighting chance should he ever want to take from me what I was unwilling to give.

His soft snores broke through my racing thoughts, and I wondered if escape was possible.

It was late.

I was unchained.

He was asleep.

There might only be a few soldiers on patrol.

If I could only sneak to a horse undetected, I could be far away before anyone could wake him. But then I remembered he could move through space like it was nothing, and my dreams of flying through the night on horseback back to Vaenor ended before they even began.

There had to be a way to evade him, and I needed time to figure out what that was. Resigning myself to staying for the moment, I decided to feel him out for any weaknesses and learn as much as I could about the breeding program to prepare for the impending battle. Because, without a doubt, Kazimir would fight his way back to me, and I needed to help him win.

But staying didn't mean I had to stay in this bed.

Noiselessly slipping from between the furs, I crept to the tent's entrance, then shimmied through the flap, preventing too much light from spilling across Ruslan's face. The night air was cold against my face and bare feet, but I would soon be too sweaty to care. As I presumed, only a few soldiers sat awake around the fire. Their eyes snapped to me, none of them a familiar shade of green, and I was glad my plan was to train and not to escape, because I would not have made it two steps.

"Which direction has enough space for me to exercise?" I whispered.

The male closest to me looked at me as if I had three heads. "Exercise?"

"Yes, you know, like squats and push-ups?" I explained.

"I know what exercise is, I'm not an idiot. But why?" He assessed me with his deep blue eyes.

"Because I like it? Do I need a reason?" I shot back, crossing my arms over my chest.

He huffed a laugh. "Guess not. I'll escort you. My name is

Drazen." He led me between a few tents until we were in a small clearing. Propping himself against a tree, he picked at his nails, paying me no mind as I eyed him warily. Crossing to the middle, I put as much distance between us as possible without pushing his boundaries. A breeze lifted wayward strands of my hair, and I was loath to shed the warm jacket as I shivered, but I unfastened it, tossing it to the side so I was dressed only in the tight pants and gray tunic Ruslan had given me. I boxed an imaginary opponent to warm up, moving in a square pattern as my blood heated and chased the chill away with it.

Sweat dampened my long, loose hair, darkening the chestnut shade into a rich auburn. My bare feet crunched dried leaves that dusted the forest floor, creating a harmony with my heaving breath until I brushed against some fallen limbs and paused my movement to gather a few sticks of different shapes and sizes. Selecting two of similar size, I danced with them in my hands, slashing imaginary opponents and imbuing my rage into each successive strike. Anxiety and anger melted away as if my pouring sweat stripped them out of my pores, my body flowing easier, lighter, the more I worked.

I sealed my tentative inner peace with a stretching flow that involved intense breathwork, collapsing against the cold, hard ground and staring through the scraggly canopy overhead, finding a sky filled with twinkling stars much too bright for my dark situation.

Drazen scrutinized my sweat-soaked body when I rose from the ground, brushing at a few leaves stuck in my hair and against my back. He tossed me a canteen, and I drank down the water, my throat parched and stinging against the chilly air as my breathing returned to normal. "You drop your left elbow a little too much when you throw hooks, but other than that your form is spot on. Who trained you?" he asked.

"A friend," I snapped. There was no way I planned on

sharing information about the people who loved and supported me in the Night Realm, especially with this unknown male.

"Chill, Izidora, I'm not trying to interrogate you for information. Just trying to make small talk."

I raised a brow, saying nothing, and studied his face for any sign of deception. Drazen seemed like an honest male, his demeanor a combination of laid-back and take-no-shit. His dark hair was long but slicked back into a bun at the top of his head, showing off his dark complexion, though his eyes were the color of the deep ocean outside my window at Este Castle. His frame was bulky, like every Iron Fae I had seen up until this point, but there was something about him that reminded me of Ruslan.

Drazen was not to be trusted.

He jerked his head toward the flickering fire. "I'm freezing my ass off, and since you are finished exercising, I want to warm up. Let's go." He waited for me to pass him before following behind me.

"Someone is bossy," I muttered under my breath, stalking away from his commanding tone.

"I am the lieutenant of this regiment, so yeah, I am the boss here," he responded.

My cheeks flushed at his words, and I whipped my head around to see a thick brow quirked. "How did you hear what I said?"

"I'm Félvér. Half Dragon, half Iron Fae. Dragon senses are even better than Fae. They are, after all, the apex predators." He waved me on, and I spun on my heel with a huff.

"Like Ruslan," I said flatly, remembering our earlier conversation where I learned I was part Angel.

"Not quite. Ruslan is the most powerful Félvér to ever exist. I heard the conversation you two had earlier. Everything he said was true, and there is much more to him than you realize."

My limbs tingled with more fatigue than they had moments

before as my anxious thoughts came roaring back with yet another volley of unexpected news.

As if escaping wasn't going to be hard enough, they had even more acute senses than Fae?

Was there any chance of saving myself?

Or would I have to rely on others once again to save me?

I ground my teeth as magic stirred beneath my skin. The white flame burned hotter under perceived threat, and that spear of crystal flared with light as I fueled the fire, my magic ready for my use at a moment's notice.

My spirit would not die under the weight of despair.

I would figure a way out of this because I was an insidious bloom, and I knew how to play pretty while waiting for them to be cut by my thorns.

The light of the fire licked the shadows surrounding the camp, and I strategically selected a seat where I had my back to no male. The night was dark and deep with barely a whisper of wind rustling the bare branches above us. Yet sleep did not call to me, for my body once again coursed with adrenaline, surrounded by males with unknown intentions who had been instructed to guard me.

It was an all too familiar situation, and one I hoped I'd never experience again.

The brilliantly red and orange flames lulled me into a meditative state, their color blending with the woody smoke that filled my nostrils. The sharp pops of a crackling log punctuated the otherwise silent air around us, but all I heard was the snapping of whips that filled the ballroom and my cave the times when I was held down and beaten for my insolence. Shuddering, I refocused my mind on the prophecy and its vague words.

Her white light will fill the land.

All I knew was darkness until very recently, so how was it possible to fill the land with light? Every day was a battle of wills in my head: the side of me that wanted to rage and destroy anything and everything that hurt me, and the other that wanted to thrive instead of survive. The magic that filled my chest may be white and pure, but my soul was anything but; I had killed and would not hesitate to kill again if my life depended on it.

There is a choice
Follow the light
Descend into the dark

Was this about my inner struggle? Or something larger than myself?

My lips flattened, and I clenched my fist around the words that slipped through my fingers like sand.

Kings will fall

One king had already fallen – my father, at my own hands. Though, he wasn't my father after all, but a narcissistic, mad king who preferred to rule through fear and took pleasure from lording control over others. Ruslan did not mention whether my real father, the Angel, still lived, but I presumed he'd died, given what I knew about King Zalan and King Azim. The power-hungry males got what they wanted, and he had likely outlived his usefulness.

My newfound heritage explained my white, seraphic wings. Half of my blood was Angel, while the other half was a mix of Night, Day, and Crystal Fae. It closed so many of the questions left open in my mind, and finally, I understood why my magic was different from my friends'. And if Ruslan's claim that half breeds – Félvér, as Drazen had called himself and Ruslan – were more powerful than regular Fae, was true, then...

My breath soared on the wings of hope as realization settled over me like a warm blanket.

I was fucking powerful.

Ruslan wanted to use me as a weapon, so I would allow him to make me into one. When the time to deploy his weapon arrived, I would turn on him, bringing him to his knees, utterly destroyed under my wrath. And when I landed the killing blow, I would have slayed the last of the demons that haunted me.

I would be free.

7

KAZIMIR

Liliana was pissed. A promise of death lingered in her light green eyes as she stood, arms crossed, before Viktor, Vadim, Endre, and myself. The four of us were soaking wet, wrapped in wool blankets, seated in front of the roaring marble hearth in Izidora's room. The cold water was refreshing, but we remained roaring drunk, trying to sober up under the ferocity of Vadim's sister's glare.

"What the fuck is wrong with you? You are drunk! You could have died. Then what would we do? Izidora would be gone forever, and as if losing Kriztof, Zekari, and Kirigin wasn't bad enough, I would have lost all of you too! And while you four were drinking your sorrows away, I was following High Lords Valintin and Luzak. Kamilia still plans on marrying you next week, Kazimir! King Zalan announced it before he died, which means the engagement still stands unless another monarch chooses to break it. So you all need to dry the fuck up, because we have shit to do," she seethed.

That sobered me up. I ran a hand over my face, remembering what happened moments before Ruslan disrupted the feast. High Lord Luzak's disgusting daughter became my fiance.

She had been after me for years, but even being racked and stretched wouldn't make me touch her. "Is it too late to kill her? She could have died in the ballroom?"

Viktor and Vadim sniggered, and Liliana looked at me as if she would throttle me instead of Kamilia.

"Yes, it is too late, and if you asshats had hurried back when I called for you the first time, we might have been able to interrupt the meeting. But now, they are gaining support for their cause through the Lower Houses. There are more than twice as many Lower Houses than Higher Houses, and you know how power hungry they are. If Valtinin and Luzak promise them seats, they might win enough support to overthrow the current council," she warned.

Viktor smiled proudly at her. "I am still drunk, so there is no way I would ever say this to you sober. You are a better strategist than I was at your age."

Her eyes rolled, then she leaned forward, dropping her tone so low it scraped against the floor. "And I'll be twice as good by the time I am old like you."

Endre snorted and Vadim whistled as her words hit Viktor like a whip.

Viktor glared at them, then announced, "I am going to puke up all this alcohol, then we need to plan our counterstrike." He strode to the bathroom and made good on his word as retching reached our ears moments later. When he returned, he grabbed a plate full of sandwiches to soak up the rest of the alcohol. Unwilling to purge my stomach, I stuffed my mouth full of food from his plate. Endre and Vadim did the same.

"Liliana, what do you think our next move should be?" I asked, if only to temper the storm building in the small space.

She tapped her fingers against her arms as she considered. "Izidora is your mate, or will be once you accept the bond. She has a lot of popular support among the common Fae, who currently are unaware of your *engagement*," her nose crinkled as she spoke the word, "but are preoccupied with the death of King Zalan. I'd assume not many other details have been shared widely. Make a public statement announcing the war council, and that you are working tirelessly to retrieve your mate, their queen. Wrap up all the big shit in one speech, but leave out the bit about the engagement. If Valintin and Luzak manage to sway the Lower Houses, popular support will not be in their favor, especially once the common Fae know who sits on the war council."

Vadim spoke around a mouthful of food. "Let's gather our allies and inform them what the traitors are up to."

Viktor remained quiet, but his expression told me that he was plotting. Finally, he spoke. "First, let's gather them, but Liliana, can you get your friends to snoop on their parents and find out where their loyalties lie? We might have common support, but the Noble Houses still rule. If most of them choose the traitors, they have enough force to shutter any rebellion. Second, we need eyes on Luzak and Kamilla at all times. Vadim, can you trail them? Run interference if you feel it necessary for our goals. As a backup option, someone needs to pull the records for delaying a marriage without the direction of a monarch – the librarians are a good place to start. We need time to send a message to King Airre and Queen Immonen. They will be sympathetic to our cause and likely will end the engagement.

"Now that I think about it... they will likely ally with us against the Iron Realm, especially since Kazimir and Izidora are mates. Once we've got this mess sorted out, we should make our way to Vlisa with our army. We have to pass through both Crystal and Day Realms to reach the Iron Realm. I would rather not get caught up in Zherza Pass where the Iron Realm would surely slaughter us."

"Béke is also in the Iron Realm this year, and the time is fast approaching," Endre reminded us.

Viktor slapped his forehead. "Fuck, yes, this is exactly what we need. The monarchs are already preparing to leave anyway, why not show up with an army too?" His white teeth flashed as an impish grin rounded out his plan.

"I'd like to get going so I don't have to marry against my will," I announced, rising to my feet. My clothes were soaked from yanking them on after our swim and still stained with blood from the feast, but at least my skin was clean.

Liliana took a judgemental perusal of my attire. "Uh huh, but first you need some dry clothes. Appearance is everything."

Viktor barked out his orders: "Let's take the passage to our rooms, then grab whomever we can find and herd them to the council room. Liliana, head to the library and ask for help with delaying the marriage. Then go spy on the Lower Houses and meet us in the council room once you have intel. Vadim, track down Luzak and his daughter." Viktor swayed slightly as he dropped his wool blanket and teetered in the direction of the secret passage we'd discovered only days before in Izidora's room.

"Fine," Liliana huffed, uncrossing her arms and stomping along behind him.

"I'll be right behind you," I called as Viktor opened the door and my friends started down the path that led to the High House Wing. Once they were out of sight, I scoured Izidora's closet, sniffing every piece of clothing scattered across the floor until I found a sweat-dried tunic that smelled as if it had been dipped in my mate. I selected the tunic and a few torn scraps of lace – entirely my fault – and bundled them together. Holding them away from my saltwater-filled clothes, I traversed the tunnel until I arrived at the entrance to the High House Wing, the door cracked a hair, my friends having left it open for me.

Looking left and right, I slipped through then sealed the door before darting into my apartment to avoid curious eyes.

Lifting Izidora's clothes to my nose for one last sniff, I stowed them in an empty drawer, promising myself to return to them later. Then, I hurriedly showered and changed into fresh clothes. Clarity returned to my head as the alcohol finally wore off, though my faculties hadn't entirely returned. I bumped into a side table, knocking something off during my hurried exit from the room. On instinct, I caught the object just before it hit the ground.

My father's journal.

Shaking hands lifted the leatherbound journal and I sucked in a few steadying breaths, both to calm the nausea rising from my belly and to lock down the grief that surged as the smooth cover pressed into my chest. I desperately wanted to crack the spine and soak in my father's words, but there were too many situations warring for my attention, and assuaging my grief was falling further and further on my priority list. Gently tucking it into the couch where it would remain unseen, I promised myself to look through the journal later. His words would always be there to provide me comfort, but I urgently needed to stop some scheming lords from ruining my life.

I found Kaztar wandering the hall as the door to my apartment swung shut with a groan behind me. "Hey, we have a situation. I'm convening a meeting as we speak. Do you know where Jaku is?"

He furrowed his brows over his darkening jade eyes. "Is it Valintin and Luzak?"

Pinching my brow to stave off the oncoming headache, I nodded. "They're working with the Lower Houses to ensure my engagement stands."

"Fucking Fates," he swore, then shook his head. "I'll find him. I'm assuming you don't want Valintin and Luzak there?"

"Just the war council. We have much to discuss."

He nodded, running a hand over his close-cropped dark hair, letting it linger on the back of his neck. Blowing out a breath, he said, "See you in a few, Kazimir." He spun on his heel and strode in the direction of the stairs to ascend to the second level of apartments.

Endre and Viktor emerged a minute later, followed by their grim-faced fathers. We fell in step as we marched through the marbled halls of Este Castle, passing servants bolting in every direction and markedly removing themselves from our path. The heavy wood doors of the council room clicked shut behind us as we settled in our seats, waiting for Kaztar and Jaku. Endre and Viktor shadowed the walls behind their fathers, welcomed as participants even though they did not have seats at the table.

Jaku nodded to me as he took a seat across from me. His heir, Havel, leaned against the wall behind him, followed by Kaztar, who leaned forward, elbows braced on the polished wood as they waited to hear why I'd called them together.

"It has been brought to my attention that High Lord Luzak intends to uphold my engagement to his daughter, despite the widely shared knowledge that Izidora is my mate. We discussed this earlier, so I won't get into it again. Our laws state that it must go through without the intervention of a monarch, which we currently lack. Again, not going to rehash that."

Especially because Izidora technically was not the daughter of King Zalan.

"We have yet to honor our dead, whose bodies still remain with us. So, I request your support in delaying the engagement in light of recent events and with a looming war on our hands. I propose that, during the funeral, we reveal to the common Fae what truly occurred at the feast, save for a few minor details – like the engagement. We should also emphasize our unity on this council and highlight our plans to rescue Queen Izidora. Any questions?"

Jaku was the first to speak. "I support you fully, High Lord Vaszoly. I do not see the engagement as valid, and I believe King Zalan acted maliciously in proposing it."

I dipped my head respectfully in his direction. I didn't need Tibor and Erik to voice their support to know they were with us, too. So, I looked at Kaztar, who almost certainly agreed with us, but I needed his confirmation regardless.

"What engagement?" he smiled wickedly.

My answering grin mirrored his. "Shall we draft a speech for the funeral?"

"I'd be happy to write it," Tibor offered. Endre's father was a great writer, and I'd happily read anything he drafted for me.

"While you are working on the speech, we have another matter to discuss," Erik added. "My son reminded me of the upcoming Béke, hosted by the Iron Realm. We will need to make haste to reach Radence if we are going to stop along the way in Vlisa and Zheka to ask for the Crystal and Day Realms' support in our war against the Iron Realm."

Jaku challenged, "But are we actually planning on attending a feast meant to celebrate peace when we know they captured our monarch, and we are planning on waging war? Surely they know the consequences of their actions."

"The other realms do not yet know, though, and that's our advantage," Viktor chimed in. "I doubt King Azim will reveal his actions by sending them a letter. He's much more likely to flaunt it in everyone's faces when we arrive. If we can convince King Airre of the Crystal Realm and Queen Viktoria of the Day Realm to ally with us, we could leave our armies waiting in the Day Realm and arrive as usual to the Iron Realm for the feast. If we recover Queen Izidora prior to attacking, it would put us at a strategic advantage. Her magic is very powerful."

The High Lords around the room nodded as they thought through Viktor's plan. His logic was sound, and no one could find much objection.

A knock sounded at the door, and Havel strode to open it. Liliana peeked her head in, mouth set in a tense frown. "May I please speak with High Lord Vaszoly?" she asked.

At least she could be polite when it mattered .

"Of course." I nodded to the councilors, then slipped out of the room to speak with Liliana.

"Do you have their support?" she whispered.

"Yes. What's wrong? Where is Vadim?"

She glanced around us, and seeing no one, leaned in closer. "I spoke with Mari and Viara, and their parents can't stand House Luzak. But Luzan and Ivan told them that their father is allying with the traitors. All the male heirs are being sequestered with their fathers, Vadim included. Mari and Viara only saw them in passing as their fathers went to the Blue Room. That's where they are all meeting. I snuck into the passages behind the room to see what I could hear. It's not good, Kazimir. Valintin and Luzak have swayed a lot of them to their side. My father argued against it, but he was quickly overruled."

"So, that's like three against eleven?" I calculated.

"Pretty much. I spoke with the librarians as well, they are looking into options for you."

"Thank you, Liliana. I need to get back in there. Lie low and don't let anyone catch you spying, please. Vadim will kill me if anything happens to you," I pleaded.

"I'm going to Izidora's rooms. I'll meet you there later," she promised, then turned on her heel and walked briskly in the direction of the Royal Wing.

I re-entered the council room as Jaku and Erik were discussing who should speak at the funeral. "... Honestly, Jaku,

Kazimir has the most to lose in this situation. We need passion, and he can show that."

"But how will we prevent anyone else from speaking? If we get hijacked, this is all for nothing and our hands are tied," Jaku argued.

They debated back and forth while I gazed out the window. Night had fallen, which meant that we didn't have much time to plan. We all needed rest, having been up for the better part of two days. A heaviness encased my body, calling me to my bed, and I decided to act. "We need to get to the priestesses before anyone else. They will control the show, so to speak, and we need them on our side. King Zalan's pyre will be lit first, and then the pyre for my father, since he is the next-highest rank. If we can convince them to allow me to light both, it will give me time to speak. Who wants to contact them?"

"I will," Kaztar said. "You look like shit, Kazimir. Go get some rest."

I smirked at Kaztar, grateful that he was stepping up. "I suggest we convene the war council early in the morning. See you all at first light." Bracing my hands on the table, I pushed to my feet, my bones weary as I trudged from the room and toward the Royal Wing. Endre and Viktor weren't far behind, their heavy footsteps the only sound tracking me at the late hour. We wouldn't be sleeping apart, especially since in the coming days our brothers would turn to ash, and then they would only exist in our memories.

We found Liliana curled up in Izidora's massive bed, her breaths slow, even, and deep. Endre's peridot eyes lingered on her sleeping form, and I knew my best friend well enough to know he wanted to lie with her and comfort her. She was grieving like the rest of us, especially since she and Izidora had been instant friends. Her brother found us lounging in the sitting room, his face grim as he flopped down beside Endre.

"Tell me you have a plan, because otherwise we are fucked," Vadim stated.

"We're going to hijack the funeral," I offered.

"Fucking Fates, Valintin is planning on doing the same," Vadim groaned.

I ran my hand over my face and blew out a breath. "I need sleep. We'll figure it out as we go along."

"Where's Liliana?" he asked.

Viktor jerked his head in the direction of the bedroom. "Passed out in there."

"That bed is big enough for all of us. She can move over," he yawned, rubbing his eyes. Vadim walked into the room first, then strode to the bed and pulled her to the edge of the mattress.

"Hey, what the fuck!" she exclaimed, waking and slapping him before she realized who was moving her.

Viktor, Endre, and I roared with laughter. Viktor ribbed, "At least you know she's ready to attack at any moment, Vadim."

"I trained her too well." Vadim rubbed the small red handprint stinging his cheek. "Scoot over so we have room."

"Ugh, but I am not sleeping next to you, that is weird," she huffed.

"Fine. Anyone who touches my sister loses their hand," Vadim threatened.

Snorting, I stretched out across the foot of the bed where I could lie on my back, my limbs begging for rest and reprieve almost as loudly as my soul. Liliana scooted to the edge of the soft mattress, Endre positioning himself beside her. Vadim squeezed between Endre and Viktor, shooting a sidelong glare at Endre and then Liliana.

The velvet canopy above me reminded me of our game of hide and seek, Izidora nimbly scaling, and then hiding above the bed. A stone settled in my gut at the memory of her unguarded laugh that took so long to coax from her perfect pink lips. Waves crashed against the rocky cliffs beyond the windows, the rhythmic sound lulling me into a hazy sleep, where my friends were all alive and we raced around these stupidly large rooms, carefree and happy.

———

THE MORNING of the funeral came with a tidal wave of grief. The few hours of sleep I had managed to get over the past few days were not enough to temper the storm of sadness that enveloped me as I rose for the day. My body protested with every small movement as I dragged myself from the massive bed that still smelled faintly of roses, despite my brothers and Liliana sleeping in it with me the past few nights. With heavy limbs and an even heavier heart, I bid goodbye to my friends and hurried to change into my sharpest attire for the funeral, painting a picture for the onlookers I needed to sway to my side. I needed to appear to those in attendance like a strong, level-headed yet impassioned male who would stop at nothing to return his mate to her throne. King Zalan had proclaimed Izidora to be his daughter, and though he had not named her heir apparent, those words had been enough to sway the crowd that already adored her.

The sun crested the horizon, sending streaks of gold across the polished wood table in the council room where Kaztar and Jaku sat, dressed as formally as they had been at the feast, and waited for the rest of the High Lords to arrive. Tibor and Erik, followed by their sons, arrived moments after me.

As soon as they'd settled into their high-backed chairs, I opened the meeting. "Lord Arzeni's son, Vadim, reported that High Lord Valintin is also planning on disrupting the funeral for his own gain. Kaztar, please tell me you got to the priestesses first."

Kaztar's smug grin was all I needed in response. "They were most pleased to receive a visit from the oldest house in the Night Realm. And Domi may have promised them a foal from our upcoming season."

I released a shaky laugh, my chest lightening with his news. "Thank the Goddess. What's the plan?"

"The High Priestess will begin the rites, and once it is time to light the pyres, she will hand you the torch. You will have an opportunity to speak as you light them. She has instructed the other priestesses to chant during your speech. She also recognizes that the Goddess has blessed Queen Izidora and you with her love, and she will recite a blessing for both of you at the end of the ceremony," Kaztar informed us.

"Tibor, did you finish the speech?" Erik inquired.

"It's right here. I kept it short so that you could memorize it in the next few hours, Kazimir," Tibor said, handing me a piece of paper with his elegant script. I read through it once, smiling to myself as his words flowed passionately from one subject to the next.

"Thank you, Tibor, this is perfect."

"You have always been like a second son to Katalin and myself, and we only want you to be happy. I am honored to serve alongside you now, and I know your father would be so proud of how you've stepped into your role." Tibor placed his hand over mine, giving it a light squeeze, the fatherly gesture causing my throat to thicken with emotion.

All I could do was nod around the tightness, unable to speak as sadness swelled in my chest. I would release my father from this earth, never again to ride through the Night Realm by his side, never again to knock on the door to his study at Zirok House, our family home, and never again enjoy a meal with him beside the crackling fire or around the table with the other Nighthounds. Zekari, Kirigin, and Kriztof, too, would never experience those simple moments again.

"Let's eat together before the funeral," Jaku suggested, sensing my rising wave of melancholy.

My breath shook as I sucked down much needed air, saving myself from drowning in the never-agains. "I'm ready when you are."

Trudging among the other High Lords toward the dining hall, Endre and Viktor bumped my shoulder in an effort to pull me out of the haze that clouded my mind. Rubbing my eyes with my fingers, I banished the last of the whispers, perking up as we stood in line for the buffet of pastries, eggs, bacon, and cheese. My stomach rumbled as I seated myself beside my two closest friends, the three of us working together to memorize the speech that Endre's father had written, making notes here and there to add my own inflection. I continued to bury myself in it long after I had it completely memorized, trying to squash my grief into a box much too small to contain such an over-whelming emotion.

Too soon, my friends told me it was time for the funeral to begin. The large, cobbled courtyard in front of Este Castle was lined with tall wood pyres, the stacked logs wrapped together with twine. White shrouds covered the bodies and the pyres holding King Zalan and my father were decorated with winter flowers and other offerings laid by the priestesses. The crowd of Night Fae stood on the other side of the raised platform, where rows and rows of chairs waited for the Noble Houses. The High Priestess stood in a pure white gown behind an altar, gazing down on those below her and beyond the pyres. Her midnight black hair was plaited into a single braid that fell down to her waist, highlighting the black lines painted across her face. She locked eyes with me, her gaze piercing and assessing as if she could see into the depths of my soul, and judged what she saw.

Settling into my seat, I glanced around, locating Valintin and Luzak, who were seated at the far end of the row, away from the High Priestess. I smirked, deciding I needed to thank Domi personally for her gift, even though it wasn't meant for me. My vantage point on the platform provided unparalleled access to the faces in the crowd beyond the pyres, and my brows leaped at just how far the crowd stretched beyond the gates. Every street was filled with males, females, and children hoping to glimpse the rites, but closer to me, the wealthy merchants had fashioned themselves a seating area near the pyre that would burn their brethren.

We would release many souls to the Goddess; all had someone to grieve. The realization that I was not alone in this opened my chest a fraction, relieving some of the crushing pressure that made it hard to breathe. Though I did not want to attend more of these rituals, war would inevitably bring death, and countless more Fae would face the pain that now speared into me. But those who fought on the battlefield would die in glory on their own terms, instead of being slaughtered at the whims of a madman.

The High Priestess began chanting, as the other priestesses with black-painted faces and creamy robes stood near the pyres, harmonizing. Their eerie song rose higher and higher into a crescendo, filling the air with unearthly vibrations. The hairs on my arms and the back of my neck rose as they wove magic into their words and danced around the pyres. Raising her pale arms above her head, the High Priestess looked past her fingertips toward the chilly blue sky, her voice directed at the heavens. A sudden gust of wind blasted the courtyard as she screamed, her white dress billowing behind her, the gale stinging my eyes. Squinting against the bitter wind, I continued to watch the hauntingly beautiful dance unfold in front of me, unable to tear my eyes from the young females' writhing forms.

The High Priestess snapped her arms to the side, and the wind died as quickly as it lived. Silence filled the still air, a heaviness settling over the crowd like an invisible fog. A chill wracked my body, and it was not only from the cold winter morning.

At the altar, the High Priestess's eyes rolled back in her head, and she began to shake. I never believed that the Goddess entered their bodies, but I wasn't about to tell her that, especially after the huge favor she had done for us. Her shakes ceased, and she turned her face to the paled crowd in front of her, opening her mouth wide to speak.

"Millennia ago, I spoke a warning of a pivotal time when world order would come under threat. It seems many have forgotten or obfuscated this prophecy, and I am most displeased. I am merely the creator of life, and I have no control over your actions. And yet I urge you to heed my warnings. The Fates are fickle, weaving many futures into the fabric of possibility. You must choose quickly and wisely, for too many are filled with horror."

Oh shit, had the Goddess heard my thoughts and appeared to us through the High Priestess?

She cocked her head at me, her neck craned in an unnatural position, pure white orbs trained on me as she opened her mouth to speak once more.

"The ones that are part of all will be born under a full moon
Her white light will fill the land
But her mates darkness will rise
Kings will fall
Rivers will run with blood
There is a choice
Follow the light

*Descend into the dark
The harrowing pass decides it all"*

The High Priestess seized, folding violently over the altar in front of her, arms splayed wide. No one breathed as her limbs stilled. Then, she picked up her head, righted herself, and strode to the waiting torch as if nothing had happened. Blinking, I watched her pull it from its holster, then walk directly to me with the flaming torch outstretched and ready for me to take. Her eyes had returned to their normal color, and there was no sign of possession left in her.

Dipping my head to her, I accepted the torch, then strode with my chest proud toward the stairs that led off the platform. Pushing aside all the anguish and despair that wanted nothing more than to drag me into their den, I reminded myself of who I needed to be to lead the Night Fae through the war, to their queen, and to the light as the prophecy indicated.

Sucking in a deep breath, I began my impassioned speech.

"Five nights ago, we were attacked by the Iron Realm."

A hushed murmur rose from the crowd, and I let it ride as I descended the wood stairs, my boots clacking with each step across the courtyard toward the pyre where King Zalan's bejeweled form lay.

"Little did we know, King Zalan had invited our attackers into his home, because he made a deadly promise regarding his daughter, Queen Izidora. Their leader, who claimed to be the bastard son of King Azim, kidnapped your queen because King Zalan promised her hand in marriage once she came of age."

A collective intake of breath swept through the audience, and I advanced past the pyre holding the servants who had died at the feast.

"The Iron Fae killed dozens of your brethren, my father

included, while they stole your monarch. Three of my closest friends lie in this pyre."

I gestured to the pyre beside me, where Kriztof, Zekari, and Kirigin's lifeless forms lay alongside three other knights. I bowed my head, honoring my friends one last time, and the priestesses surrounding me followed my example. When I straightened, I saw many others in the crowd had done the same.

"I grieve with you today, for I lost many important people to me only a few nights ago. The most important of whom was my mate, your queen, Izidora."

A wave of gasps turned into a crescendo of cheers as the crowd, both angry and excited, swelled with emotion.

"I am leading the charge to return your queen and my mate to her rightful place, here at Este Castle. We will wage war on the Iron Realm, and put them in their place once and for all!"

At last, I reached the standalone stack of wood that held King Zalan, pausing dramatically as I held the torch inches from the kindling that would set it alight.

"Who wants to fight for their queen alongside me?"

I dropped the fiery torch to the pyre, and the dried wood flared in time with the crowd's answering roar. The cries did not die down as I continued lighting the wood, sending our loved ones into the sky where they would fly forevermore. Once I climbed the stairs and reached the altar, I faced the sea of Night Fae, eager in their grief.

"We leave tomorrow for the Iron Realm. Every able-bodied male willing and ready to fight, gather in the courtyard after the rites are complete."

Dropping into a deep bow before the crowd, I blew out the tense breath I'd been holding, then handed the blazing torch back to the High Priestess. Tibor shot me a wide grin from the seat next to mine, and Endre and Viktor both clapped my shoulders from behind me as I settled into my seat. The air thrummed with exhilaration, the promise of vengeance and bloodshed calling to a primal part of us.

The haunting chant of the priestesses rose with the flames that burned hotter and hotter, arcing so high into the sky I was sure they would reach the stars. Sweat broke out across my face from the scorching temperature, and I was certain my stubble would be singed. The crowd opposite the pyres backed a few paces to escape the boiling heat that broke the chill of the otherwise cold day. But the intensity of the pyres' light was nothing compared to the depths of darkness currently filling my heart as I steeped in the hate I held toward Ruslan and the Iron Fae.

They would all die by my hands for hurting my mate.

I felt eyes on me, and when I glanced over my shoulder, a furious Tomaz Valintin glared at me as if he wished he could shove his magic down my throat and suffocate me. To his right, Vaklav Luzak's reddened face dripped sweat, and his horrid daughter Kamila perched on the edge of her seat behind him. We had succeeded in foiling their plans, and with the thousands of Fae gathered for the funeral, there was no way to challenge our statements. They should count themselves lucky that Tibor had a good heart and left their abominable actions out of that speech.

The High Priestess finished the rites with a blood sacrifice, the bleating goat's blood pouring off the sides of the altar, caught in small bowls by the young priestesses and flicked from their fingers as they danced relentlessly around the pyres. Once the ruby river that flowed from the sacrifice ceased, the High Priestess dismissed us.

The war council remained seated as the rest of the Noble houses wound their way through the massive metal doors marking the entrance to Este Castle. Valintin and Luzak shot one last death glare in our direction before ushering their sniveling children along. They were defeated, but I had no doubt they'd try their hands at another scheme, so long as a power vacuum remained in the Night Realm. We needed to get Izidora back.

By the time the crowd thinned out, hundreds of males milled about the courtyard, whispering to one another as we approached. We gave the pyres a wide berth, though my eyes lingered on the one second from the end, where the roses that lined my father's body had already become nothing more than ash. Vadim and Liliana jogged to join us after bidding their parents goodbye, and I was glad for their assistance, especially since Vadim could easily tell which males were fit to join and which were not.

"Thank you for volunteering for the war efforts," I began. "Lord Vadim Arzeni will assess your fitness and select those best suited for our mission."

The males nodded, and Vadim began shouting instructions.

Kaztar slid to my side, a sly grin splaying across his face. "That was quite the speech. It had its intended effect. Congrats on not being engaged."

I smirked in response. "Yet. I am never letting Izidora out of my sight again once we find her." I'd save her, then chain her to me so no harm would ever come to her again.

He laughed, clapping me on the shoulder. "Like any good male should do. You'll make a fine king consort, Kazimir."

As his words sank in, a hint of an idea sparked in my mind. "I think we should promote House Arzeni to take the place of House Vaszoly, should that ever come to pass." Vadim and Liliana's family deserved a higher status for everything they had done for us.

"I couldn't agree more," Kaztar grinned.

The future High Lord Arzeni assessed our potential warriors with his keen eyes. Though our Knights were prepared for battle at a moment's notice, we'd lost too many during the feast and many others were spread throughout the Night Realm. We needed more bodies, especially because a battle in the mountain passes leading to the Iron Realm would be deadly for those unaccustomed to fighting among the cliffs. Though Night Fae could fly, the Iron Fae had a strategic advantage: the ability to hide among and shift the giant boulders that perched precariously along the sheer rock faces.

In the end, Vadim only dismissed a handful of males, leaving a solid number to join our ranks. He instructed them to return to their families, say their goodbyes, pack their belongings, and return tomorrow at dawn for further instruction. The war council watched the males disappear into the streets of Vaenor before returning to the castle.

Liliana seized the opportunity to speak once we'd begun our trek through the halls. "I'm coming with you," she announced.

"No fucking away," Vadim shot back. "War is no place for a lady."

"Females fight in the Iron Realm!" she challenged.

"Yeah, because they are bigger and stronger than other Fae females," he retorted.

"Exactly. Iron Fae are bigger and stronger. So what is their weakness? They are slow. And I am small, light, and agile. I can dance around them all day. You need females like me to help you win this war," she argued.

She had a point. I had watched her and Izidora both outmaneuver Viktor, who fought similarly to Iron Fae with his brutal strikes. He could be light on his feet, but when he focused on using his strength to overpower an opponent, he was slow to move.

Vadim shook his head. "I am not letting you join us. You'll die, and mother and father will kill me for putting you in harm's way."

"I think she has a point," Viktor added. Vadim whipped his

head to Viktor, the former's eyes threatening violence if the latter uttered another word.

"I'd be your secret weapon, a female that is stealthy yet deadly. Plus, I could get to Izidora easier than any of you," Liliana pointed out.

Kaztar saved us from witnessing the siblings' brawl in the middle of Este Castle. "Domi would love to be a part of this. No one will expect it, so we have the element of surprise. Besides, we're supposed to arrive as a neutral party first, right? Liliana is already known as Izidora's ladiesmaid, so we can explain their presence easily."

Vadim had no choice but to agree. "Fucking Fates. Fine, but all the females are training daily, vigorously, with me. You will fight faster, harder, and more fearlessly than any male in our company."

"Deal!" Liliana beamed, bouncing to Vadim's side and wrapping him in a hug.

"But you have to tell mother and father this was all your idea," he warned as Liliana bounded away, off to find Goddess knows what trouble.

"Let's convene the war council after lunch. We have much preparation to do if we plan on leaving tomorrow," Kaztar said. We parted ways in the main hall, promising to meet again in a few hours.

Fatigue, both physical and mental, washed over me as all the adrenaline that had been fueling my body the last few days dried up. Sleep sounded better than food, so I said my goodbyes to my friends and jogged to Izidora's room. Her scent called to me the moment I opened the door, and my knees went weak as I lifted the blankets on her bed and scented her lingering arousal. Stripping out of my finery, I crawled between the sheets, burying my face in a pillow that held a few wayward strands of her chestnut hair.

My groin heated as I remembered her seduction, how she dragged me to the shower and sucked all of me down before bending over so I could enter her. I crushed a firm pillow against my body, imagining it was her laying in front of me. My hand found my hardness, and I pumped into it as if it were the wet core of my mate.

Mine, mine, mine.

The words repeated over and over in my mind, marking each thrust of my cock. It was her, only ever her. Trembles wracked my legs and spine as I closed in on my release, imagining her perfect pink center dripping for me as she begged me to finish inside her.

The image of her belly swelling with my child drove me over the edge, and my hot seed spilled across the bed where we'd lain together only days before. She may not have wanted children, and I might have gone along with it, but no longer. I would save her, impregnate her, and then she would be mine, in every way, just as I had imagined it for so long before rescuing her from that dark cave.

INTERLUDE

The summer sun beat down upon the three Night Fae males walking along the crowded beach. Waves crashed against the pebbled shore, dragging the stones against each other in a soothing, repetitive motion that allowed the males to think and process what they had overheard only moments before.

A trader from the Iron Realm had planted himself among a group of females bathing in the sun and sea, not so subtly flashing his wealth and wares as he glittered in the light. Two large diamonds adorned his earlobes, and gold hoops looped through the point of his ear. He had bragged to the group attracted to his shine about a recent adventure he'd taken through the Agrenak Mountains. He told them he'd seen new mining shafts popping up beneath the harrowing peaks and revealing new precious stones, like the one that adorned his pinky finger – a stone that looked like black smoke curled inside it, undulating as the stone was moved from left to right.

But it wasn't the stone that caught the Nighthounds' attention – no, it was the mention of new tunnels being carved into the mountains over the past twenty years and the new caves being discovered along the way. Throughout the years they had searched for the lost princess, the one place that had eluded them was the Agrenak Mountains. Flying among the peaks was deadly, and with the vast majority of them in the sovereign territory of the Iron Realm, searching them was nearly impossible.

To hear this Iron Fae bragging so obscenely about their successes was rare, as the Iron Fae were notoriously secretive, and if something of this magnitude was happening, there must have been more to the story. Their suspicions raised, the three continued down the beach, returning to the rocky outcropping that provided a path up the cliff and back to Vaenor.

Only once they had returned to the confines of their apartments at Este Castle did they speak. The broadest male with neatly styled hair said, "This is definitely a lead."

"Where are the twins and Kriztof and Vadim now?" the one with the messy hair asked.

"Last my father heard from them, they were near the Iron Realm border," the emerald-eyed leader replied.

"We need to tell Cazius what we've learned, then have him send word to them, telling them to ask around about these new tunnels and caves. If the Iron Realm has been having success with this endeavor for the last *twenty* years, that means they must have started digging before then. We've never been able to search more than a few places in the mountains, which means they could have hidden her there all this time without us being able to find her," the broad one concluded.

The other two nodded their heads in agreement.

And the one with the emerald green eyes knew, deep down, that this was the information they had needed to find the lost princess all along.

II

THE RIDE

8

IZIDORA

Much to my disappointment, I rode in front of Ruslan every day as we entered the Agrenak Mountains. The path narrowed with each step we took, winding between high cliffs, dipping briefly into a rocky valley, but always steadily climbing. The biting wind tore at my hair, and I grinned smugly each time my hair whipped Ruslan in the eye. The air grew colder the higher we climbed, and I wished for some furs to cover my achingly cold legs. At least I had thick wool socks covering my toes, though I'd lost feeling in them long ago. Ruslan's muscled front pressed firmly into my back, especially as our path steepened and we had to lean into the angle to assist our horse's climb. His body was hot on my back, and he wore only a light jacket despite the chill.

"How long until we pass through to the other side?" I asked through chattering teeth.

"We'll camp tonight, then we have a few days of long rides before we break through the pass that leads into the Iron Realm," he explained.

Ugh, more days of this endless chill.

I hoped my fingers wouldn't freeze off before then. A shiver wracked my body as the uncontrollable clacking of my teeth grew louder. Ruslan abruptly pulled his massive mount to a stop, the procession behind us nearly smashing together to avoid hitting us. With a lethal grace, he dismounted, holding his hand to me. "Let's get you in the wagon where it's warmer. I can't have my mate freeze before we arrive at our home."

I made a face at his suggestion, but I was too cold to argue. My legs were too numb to move, and I huffed as I allowed him to lift me from the saddle. His strong arms carried me to the wagon where I had awoken caged like an animal over a week before, and I squirmed in his arms as the idea of being locked in the dark flooded my body with fear. "On second thought, I'd rather ride."

His smoky gray eyes searched my aquamarine ones, and I schooled my expression to one of cold aloofness. He would not see my fear of being chained, stripped of control, and victimized once more. A hopeful grin spread across his face. "I can ride in the wagon with you, keep you warm? Then we won't have to be apart," he offered.

Pressing my lips into a thin line, I debated my options.

Ride in the freezing cold and possibly lose a limb, be locked in the darkness of the wagon, or allow Ruslan to ride with me?

I sighed, resigned to my fate. "That would be lovely, My Prince."

What could possibly go wrong?

He set me gently on the rocky ground, his hand wrapped around my upper arm to steady me as my numb legs wobbled. Placing his palm against the small of my back, he directed me to the wagon, and I flinched internally at the intimate touch. He dropped it when he went to open the doors, and I released the breath trapped in my chest. Sucking in a handful of icy breaths as he unlocked them, I steeled myself for whatever may happen with the two of us sharing the small space. Images of him shirtless and then naked flitted through my mind, and I quickly clamped down on those obscene thoughts.

The doors swung wide, then Ruslan lifted me into the wagon without asking. "I'll be right back," he promised, and strode off. As light illuminated the interior of the wagon, I took the opportunity to study it. My cage was merely one of many boxes that lined the sides of it, some holding piles of furs while a few overflowed with food and one contained metal jugs of water. I discovered a small metal lantern and was fumbling around for something to light it with when Ruslan returned, closing the doors behind him and bathing us in darkness.

The wagon jerked forward a moment later, and I lost my grip on the lantern. It crashed against the closed doors, only to ping off of the metal of Ruslan's armor. Dim light sputtered to existence, and Ruslan's devastating face was cast in shadow as he held the lantern and sauntered toward me. My back hit the smooth wood of the wall as I crawled away, Ruslan's predatory grin following me. Once he was within arm's reach, he glanced upward and placed the lantern on a hook hanging from the ceiling.

I was suddenly much too hot, my body in shock from the extreme temperature changes. Ruslan's gaze raked up and down my body, sending tingles flitting over my skin. "I'll get you some furs," he purred, then spun on his heel, gracefully moving through the wagon despite the jostling as it moved. Gathering an armful of furs from my former cage, he spread them over the top of the boxes that held the food and water, creating a soft pallet for me to rest on. He rolled up an extra plush one, forming a small pillow for my head. Holding one last fur above the rest, he waited for me to settle on the pile so he could cover me. The gesture was gentle and kind, and in absolute contrast to his earlier aggressive behaviors.

I was getting whiplash from his mercurial temperament.

On shaky legs, I hobbled in his direction, holding onto the walls as I went, half from fear of falling, half from fear of him. When I reached the furs, I slid slowly between them, muscles taught and ready for the moment I would have to defend myself. But that moment never came. Ruslan covered me with the last fur, a thick gray pelt that engulfed my petite frame. He tucked it around my shoulders with the care of a lover, and I did not dare breathe until there was distance between us once more.

He settled himself on a thin pelt stretched across a row of boxes across from me, legs splaying as he made himself comfortable. The movement pulled my eyes to his groin, and my cheeks flushed as I was reminded of his hardness. I averted my gaze as quickly as I could, berating myself for thinking of his beautiful dick.

"So, you like to exercise?" he asked casually, trying to make conversation.

"Yes," I replied. Then, remembering my earlier promise to start over, I added, "I find that I am much calmer afterward. It helps me cope with... everything that happened."

His jaw clenched, and I sensed his anger rising to the surface. His emotions were deep, raw, and volatile, flooding my senses and leaving no room for my own. I inhaled sharply, trying to regain control of myself and block him out of my head.

How did he have this level of influence over me?

He leaned forward, resting his elbows on his knees as he brought his face close to mine. Too close. His cedarwood and vanilla scent filled my nostrils, a dizzyingly intoxicating combination.

"I will kill every last one of them for what they did to you. Their deaths will be slow, agonizing, and by the time I am finished with them, they will beg for death," he swore, and black flames danced in his dilated pupils. A shaky breath escaped my trembling lips, and Ruslan glanced at them a little too long before meeting my eyes once more. Heat pooled deep in my belly as his murderous words and smoky orbs engulfed me in his madness. That primal, vengeful part of me that had enjoyed killing my assailant purred at his words, preening at the thought of extracting even an ounce of pain from those who had abused me. But I shook my head, trying to clear the dark thoughts from my mind. I was nothing like Ruslan, and it was only his twisted emotions bleeding into my own that caused this flood of bloodlust.

His nostrils flared, and then he leaned back, popping his knuckles one by one, the sharp cracks punctuating the silence.

Wanting to change the subject, I asked, "How old are you?"

"Forty-three," he deadpanned, checking his nails.

If he was over forty... then these experiments had been going on at least a hundred years. I nearly choked as I thought of the males and females who had been subjugated to King Azim and Rares's ideas and experiments. Nausea churned in my gut, and not only from the swaying of the wagon.

"Tell me about the palace," I whispered, needing a distraction from my rolling stomach.

He lifted his gaze, excitement glinting in his eyes at that request. I was giving him all the wrong impressions, and I was going to regret it later.

"The palace I built for you? It is carved into the side of my favorite mountain. Giant windows overlook Radence and the surrounding valley, and every night I watch the sunset over the peaks in the distance. The granite walls glitter like the stars. A natural hot spring runs through that mountain, and on the ground level I built a deep pool where it bubbles from the floor, continually filling itself with fresh water. On the next level is a kitchen and servants' quarters, then the third level has a library and formal dining room, and finally, the top level is our suite. It has the best view in the whole palace, with a spiral staircase that leads up to the roof for unobstructed views. Our bathroom has every luxury you could possibly want, two showers, another deep tub, mirrors to admire your divine figure, and a closet big enough to sleep ten fully grown Iron Fae."

It sounded incredible. Too bad the male in front of me was not the one I wanted to share such luxury with.

"The library at Este Castle was beautiful. Do you like to read?" I asked.

"I do. The library is my favorite spot besides the roof. I considered creating an entire floor for the library, but I needed somewhere to entertain guests," he shrugged, his body swaying in time with the wagon's jolts.

"But there is nowhere for them to stay?" I inquired. He had not listed any other bedrooms besides those for us and the servants.

His smile was filthy as he leaned toward me once more. "I don't want anyone to hear the sounds you'll make while you're in my bed. Those are reserved for me, and me alone."

"I won't be joining you in your bed," I gritted out, despite the hum in my belly defying my mental objections.

He only purred, "My sprite, you'll be begging for me to fuck you before the week is up."

I bared my teeth at him, but my body wrote an entirely different story. He stiffened, nostrils flaring as he scented my desire. My heart pounded furiously against my ribcage, as his face drifted closer to my traitorous body. A flush rose from my chest and decorated my face as I studied the stubble across his jaw and noticed the soft scar that graced his temple. My lashes fluttered as his nose brushed mine, and I inhaled his crisp scent. My mind screamed at me to pull away, but my body called out for him, begging for his rough hands to caress my scorching form.

A rough bump in the road sent him flying back, and our moment shattered.

I blinked rapidly, suddenly able to think without his face a breath from mine. I cleared my throat, needing to return to my earlier stage of anger with this male who dared take me against my will.

"Why did you show up during the feast? Why not wait to claim me the next day without so many people around?" I shot at him, rising on my elbow and causing part of the fur to slide off me. The cool air against my blazing skin was a welcome reprieve.

"Why haven't you used your magic yet?" he cocked his head to the side.

"Why are you so hell bent on conquering the continent?" I stoked my inner flames to fuel my bold questions.

"Why did you fuck a male who wasn't your betrothed?" he snarled, white knuckles gripping his knees.

"I didn't know about you!" I yelled.

"So, would you have fucked him if you had known about me?" His voice carried a hint of violence that I blatantly ignored.

"Yes, because I love him, and he is my mate."

Ruslan was on me in an instant, trapping me beneath him, hands holding my shoulders in place while his hips pinned mine. His lips were on my ear, and each enunciated word was punctuated with his hot breath on its sensitive outer shell.

"He. Is. Not. Your. Mate."

When he pulled back, he vibrated with barely restrained rage. I bared my teeth, my will to fight rising to the surface. I was not a victim, and I would never be again. Ruslan was too wild to notice the white magic I called into my balled fist. I shifted my left shoulder from beneath his hand, and as he slipped toward the ground, I slammed my magic-coated fist into his jaw. His body sounded like a rockslide as he hit the floor of the wagon, and without hesitation, I leaped on top of him, pinning his hands to the floor with white magic cuffs.

His fury was a kick of spice, and smoke spilled from his nostrils as he assessed his vulnerable position. My confidence wavered as the smoke thickened, and he freed himself with one easy movement, capturing my back with his hands and flipping us so he was on top once more.

"I told you once, and I will tell you again," he purred, dropping his mouth to my ear. "I like when they fight back." He ground his hips into me as if to prove his point, and I felt every inch of his length between us.

Then he stood, his erection on full display against his leather pants, and watched me with a hunter's gaze as I shrank against the opposite wall on the pile of furs.

"You feel this pull between us, just like I do."

I opened my mouth to speak, but he cut me off. "Don't deny it, my sprite. I can smell you."

My teeth clacked shut, and I forced myself to close my eyes, to ignore his presence, so that I could recenter myself.

But he wasn't having it. "I bet Kazimir told you many things that aren't true. Did he tell you how awful your father – sorry, King Zalan – was to his people?"

My eyes snapped open, then narrowed on the male, and an impish, knowing smirk played across his lips. "King Zalan was awful, and horrible to me when I arrived at Este Castle," I said.

"According to that group you traveled with, yes. And maybe him promising you to me before you were born was bad, but it happens more often than not with royal children," he shrugged.

I crossed my arms over my chest before deigning to respond. "He promised my mate to another right in front of me, knowing how we felt about each other."

"Because you were already promised to me, and he knew I was coming to collect you," Ruslan reminded me.

"He also forced my mother to marry him. And then when she found her mate, he forced them to fuck in front of him! All so he could have more power for himself," I added. In that moment, I realized my mother and I were alike, both forced into a position from which there was no escape.

How did you say no to a male that insisted on having you? No matter how hard I trained, I knew that my size and my sex were disadvantages against any male. Only my magic leveled the playing field.

"Your mother and her mate would have fucked like that regardless. The only twisted part of that situation is that he wanted to watch. He always was a kinky bastard." He covered an amused twitch of his lips with his tattooed hand.

"But I could tell people were afraid of him when I got to Este Castle. There was definitely a camp of sycophants and a camp of realists." My defense sounded weaker and weaker the more I spoke.

"You'll find that no matter what realm you're in." He dismissed my argument with a wave of his hand.

Was I wrong to think that King Zalan was an egotistical and terrorizing monarch? No, I knew that was the case, and nothing would shake that belief.

"Did Kazimir tell you that you would make a much better queen? Did he encourage you to explore options to take the throne by force?"

His words were like a punch to the gut – because Kazimir had told me I'd be a better queen, even helped me plan to take the throne.

"Did you ever stop to think that he was using you for his own gain?" Ruslan murmured, his voice dropping as what I thought I knew came crashing down around me.

"How do I know that you aren't doing the same right now?" I challenged, but there was no bite to my words.

"When have I lied to you?"

I shook my head as if the motion would clear the insane words coming from this madman's mouth. But he had been nothing but honest, brutally honest, with me from the second I woke up in this wagon. He knew the prophecy, he knew my heritage, and he could explain so many things that I had questioned since I left my cave.

I remembered the village where the shopkeeper assumed they'd rescued me, and how Cazius had covered by saying I was being trafficked and they were only sending me back to my home. If they knew about the trafficking, and if that wasn't the first time they had rescued someone, then they had to have known about Angels and Demons and Shifters and all the other races on the far-flung continents. They had mentioned how secretive the Iron Realm was, but surely they must have seen something when they visited for Béke? And they'd seen my white magic and angelic wings. They must have known.

"How will I ever know what is true if I have to rely on others to tell me about the world?" I fisted the furs, clutching them to my torso and curling up in a ball, as if making myself smaller would protect me from the overwhelming feelings surging from the depths of my heart. The organ beat wildly, robbing my lungs of air as heat and pressure flared in my head, filling my eyes with tears until I feared I would drown in a deadly combination of rage and despair. I clenched my jaw, closing my eyes to fight the tears that threatened to drop. One still trickled down my cheek, and a warm, rough hand caught it before it dripped over my nose.

"You can't read?"

Blinking through wet lashes, I found Ruslan's hand cupping my cheek, wearing an agonized expression, as if my pain hurt him just as much as it hurt me.

"No." My confession was a hoarse whisper, the saltiness that dropped from my eye holding all my shame.

"I can't stand to see you sad," he whispered as another tear slipped free, taking a little of my broken heart with it.

"I may want to conquer the continent, but I am telling you that now, not scheming to make it seem like it was your idea all along. I will always be honest with you, Izidora," he promised, using my real name to emphasize his sincerity.

I nodded, sucking in a ragged breath. My head and heart were too confused to speak any more. He retreated, lying down across from me so our prone forms mirrored each other, then tried to meet my gaze. But I closed my eyes, guarding myself against this new disorienting world where Ruslan was good and Kazimir was bad.

But Kazimir had saved me, and Ruslan had kidnapped me.

And maybe Kazimir lied and manipulated me, but I had no way of knowing if Ruslan was doing the same. I had placed implicit trust in the words of Kazimir and the Nighthounds, and I would not make the mistake of doing the same with Ruslan. My head began pounding as my brain and body warred with each other, and my mind circled and circled around thoughts of who was right, who was wrong, who was good, and who was bad.

"I need to sleep," I whispered.

"Okay," he murmured. "I know you didn't sleep last night, and sleep will make you feel better. I'll be right here the whole time."

I wasn't sure whether his words were a comfort or a curse, but I allowed the rock and sway of the wagon to lull me until I finally slipped away.

———

I woke to Ruslan sitting beside me, stroking my hair. I jumped up, backing out of range as my breath caught in my chest. "Don't touch me," I threatened, using anger to cover how startled I was. I would not fall into the clutches of panic, where my adrenaline spiked and reason fled.

"Let me guess, your precious mate asked permission every time he wanted to touch you? He probably told you that he didn't want to hurt you too, didn't he?"

He baited me, trying to see how much his earlier words had affected my resolve. He had shaken me to my very core, but I wasn't ready to admit that yet. Instead I defended Kazimir, though I was not nearly as resolute as I had been previously. "Yes, because he is an honorable male who cares about me."

"While you were fucking him, did you ever want more? Harder? Did you want him to be violent?" he smirked.

My face flushed at his insinuation, but my stomach dropped because it was true. I had baited him, bitten him, pushed back into him because I wanted more. With Kazimir moving inside me, I felt powerful, I felt free, and I felt alive. It felt like I was rewriting my story, taking back my life with each circle of my hips. But I did not want Ruslan to know that. I bit the inside of my cheek, holding back the words that threatened to spit like snake's venom from my mouth.

"I thought so. The thing about people like us is that we like it better when it hurts. It reminds us that we are alive."

"And what do you and I have in common? You know nothing about what I went through," I snapped.

"I think you'll find out that we are much more alike than you want to admit," he taunted, voice low and filled with a thickness I could not place.

I said nothing, tamping down the fear that still coursed through my veins and pounded my heart. What was with this male and his up, down, sideways, and corkscrewed thoughts?

One minute he was sweet, the next he taunted, and I rose to meet his intensity every time.

What was wrong with me?

The wagon halted, and my hands and knees smacked the ground, flares of pain stabbing through each limb as momentum caught up to me. When I lifted my head, Ruslan smirked down at me. "I like you in that position."

I pushed myself upright, hands finding hips as I shot him a look that was icy enough to kill. "Fuck. You."

"Oh, you will," he said, and he leaped off the boxes and strode to the doors of the wagon, just as Drazen flung them open from the outside.

The bitter chill flooded the wagon immediately, and a shiver started at my head and reached my toes before I pulled a fur around my shoulders.

"We're stopping for the night," Drazen announced, before disappearing beyond my line of sight.

"Come, let's get you some food." Ruslan offered me his hand. I regarded it like it was a snake, then I clutched the fur tighter around me and hopped to the ground without his assistance. Landing lightly on my feet, I strode into a massive cave dug into the side of the mountain where the soldiers were starting fires and preparing food. It was unlike the one I'd been chained in, with high ceilings and an opening wide enough for two dragons to wander through side by side.

I plopped myself down beside a random fire, Ruslan stalking behind me, his heavy footstep unmistakable even among the dozens and dozens of males hurrying about our temporary shelter. The male pouring magic flames across the tented logs glanced at me, then moved away as if I had the plague. Once the wood caught, he made himself scarce.

An influx of heat – not from the newly built fire – filled the space behind me. I masked my face in cool indifference as

Ruslan spread his legs around me, then yanked me flush to him. He wrapped his arms around me, outside of the fur, then put his lips to my ear. "You are so sexy when you're angry. I would much rather see your hostility than despair, my sprite."

I ignored him, steeling my spine and focusing intently on the flurry of activity beyond the crackling flames. But he didn't seem to mind, content to have me wrapped up in him. My mind still warred with my body, but eventually my body won, and I relaxed into him. He supported my weight fully, even moving his hands to my shoulders where he lightly massaged. I told myself it was because it was more comfortable this way, but in truth, I liked his body cocooning me in warmth, easing the tension from my muscles and that cracked rib that was extremely irritated by the bitter cold.

A hot meal made its way to my hands, and I gripped the bowl of stew, my fingers thawing as I inhaled the earthy spices that drifted up with the steam. Chunks of meat floated in the thick brown liquid, along with some potatoes and carrots. I sipped the broth, the flavors melting over my tongue and the liquid heating me from the inside out. The meat and vegetables were tender and filled my belly as I finished the hearty stew. Once I had my fill, I set the bowl next to Ruslan's already empty one and clutched the fur tightly over my shoulders.

The space behind me was cold the moment he stood, promising he would return in a moment. He spoke to Drazen, who kept his eye on me the whole time Ruslan was gone. The male returned a few minutes with his hands behind his back and a mischievous uptick on his lips. I eyed him, weighing whether he was going to kill me or if he had another trick up his sleeve.

"Come with me." He jerked his head, motioning me to follow him in the direction of his tent, which was nestled against the curved wall at the back of the cave. I sighed and stood, still clutching the fur, and followed him.

Anything to survive.

With one hand, he held back the flap, while the other remained obscured behind his back. Angling my body away from him as I strode inside, I crossed my arms and waited for him to join me. The canvas swished closed and he grinned, bringing his hand in front to reveal his package. Sitting in his outstretched hand was a leather-bound book with a worn cover. "This is one of my favorite books. I want you to have it, and I'll teach you to read with it. I know I'm not the best company, so hopefully this makes up for it."

My eyes were wide as I reached my hands out, running them over the worn leather. I took it from his grasp, flipping to the first page to view the letters scrawled there. I only recognized a few, my lessons with Cazius forgotten once we'd left for Vaenor. I murmured, "What's it about?"

"It's a book of poetry–"

Ruslan did not finish his statement before I flung the book like it had bitten me and jumped back into the canvas of the tent. Canvas that flashed in and out of my vision, exchanging with dimly lit stone walls and the feeling of iron clasped around my wrists and ankles. My knees slammed against the thin rug laid across the tent, only slightly dulling the pain of the hard stone beneath it.

Ruslan's mouth worked over words I could not hear over the ones screaming in my head, a stern feminine voice that drowned out all reason as it sank its claws into me.

The night burns brighter than the day

The day that flowers give way

I clutched the sides of my head, gripping my hair in my fingers and tugging in an attempt to rid myself of the haunting poem.

The flowers that bloom under the fullest of moons
The moon that signals the changing of tunes

"Stop!" I shrieked at the words, pressing my palms into my eyes as grainy images of my keepers slapping me, yanking back my hair, and forcing me to recite poem after poem until I spoke them with perfect poise flashed behind them. Tears spilled down my cheeks as my chest was wracked with sobs, the words echoing around and around in my head as I lost touch with the tent and the male I never wanted to see me like this.

Cold water dragged me under, and my lungs burned with the effort of holding my breath. Only a few moments of peace remained before my keepers would expect me to surface and begin our inane lessons.

The tunes that beg their listeners to dance
The dance that means it's time to rest

I gasped for air, my head spinning beneath the water.

"Izidora!" Rough hands shook me as a raspy voice screamed my name. The wide-eyed male before me had said something else, and I blinked as the cave drifted away and the tent returned to view.

With a burst of white magic, I blasted him off of me. "Don't touch me!" My entire body trembled, more than it had while I'd ridden through the icy air of the mountains, and the chill that settled over me was bone-deep. Tears continued to flow, and through blurred lashes, I watched Ruslan pick himself up and raise his hands in surrender.

"I'll stay over here," he said, though the set of his shoulders told me he wanted nothing more than to wrap me up and comfort me. Between us, the thread that I still tried to deny was there hummed with worry, and I clamped down on the connection before I gave it any more attention. I dragged a serrated breath through my lips, then another, before my tremors lessened and my chest loosened. The tension in every fiber of my being was painful, and slowly I unwound myself from the ball I had curled up in. True to his word, Ruslan remained on the opposite side of the tent, though his attention never left me.

"Want to tell me what happened?" he asked, breaking the silence. I realized then just how silent it was, not even the murmuring of his soldiers drifting through the canvas.

"No," I snapped, returning to that fiery place that had kept me safe before.

With the slowness of a predator stalking its prey, he walked to where the book of poetry had landed, picking it up and walking toward the tent flap. The entire time, I waited, tense and ready to fight as adrenaline still coursed through my veins. He lifted the flap wide enough for me to see the crackling fire only a few paces from our tent, then leveled a dark gaze at me. "I will burn every book of poetry in the Iron Realm for you, if that is what you want." He flung the leather tome into the fire, sending sparks flying from the burning logs. When his eyes returned to me, they held no hint of remorse. "You are my mate, and you and I will love each other unconditionally because that's what mates do. That book is nothing compared to the lengths I would go to for you, Izidora. I will burn the whole fucking world down for you to show my undying devotion."

My heart fluttered as the sincerity of his words settled over me. Ruslan was an intense male, and I held no doubt that he would carry out his promise to me. The tent flap closed with a whisper, and he crept toward me, crouching down so we were more level. "Let me try again. I have something you might like better."

I only nodded as he reached into his leather bag and pulled out another book encased in embossed green. "The Throne of the Earth is a fantasy. The main character must fight to the death to claim his throne. Every time I read it, I am gripped with the story. It reminds me so much of my own life, and I feel less alone." He looked away, but there was more underneath the words, a story he wasn't quite ready to reveal.

He offered it to me without meeting my gaze, remaining still as I crawled toward him. I lifted it gingerly from his outstretched hand, then scooted to my spot on the floor on the opposite side of the tent. The book smelled musty and old, and by the faded cover and smudges on the interior pages as I flipped through them, I knew it was more than a special book to Ruslan. "Thank you for sharing it with me," I replied, studying this more vulnerable side of him.

He cleared his throat, still not looking at me. "Well, I hope this helps you feel like you have some power over your life. We can work on it before we go to bed every night, then you can try to reread the pages when you can't sleep. That's what I do, at least."

"You have trouble sleeping?" I asked.

"It's the nightmares, mostly... they are so real sometimes, it's as if I am actually reliving my memories." He rubbed the back of his neck, his eyes pinching shut.

"I get them too," I confessed, glancing down at the book in my hands. Nightmares and flashbacks, like the one that had occurred only minutes before.

Maybe we did have more in common than I thought.

A finger under my chin lifted my gaze to meet his smoky one, and I nearly startled at his sudden proximity. "We'll get through them together," he promised, his voice a hoarse whisper. His face drifted closer to mine like he wanted to kiss me, but I dropped my head, breaking contact. I flipped to the first page, then said, "I think I'd like to start learning now. It's been so long, I need a review of my letters."

"Then I will show them to you again," he murmured, passing me so he could settle on the makeshift bed of furs on the floor. He pulled back the blankets and stripped out of his armor.

Pretending to be engrossed in flipping the worn pages of the book, I watched out of the corner of my eye as his tattooed body was revealed, inch by muscular inch. His bare body slipped under the covers, and I caught a glimpse of his hardening erection before he covered the lower half of his body.

"Did you really have to get naked to teach me?" I hissed.

He chuckled, the low rumble emanating from deep within his chest and stirring heat between my thighs. "I'm not lying in bed in dirty riding clothes, and I prefer to sleep this way. You don't have to sleep in the clothes you traveled in all day, either. I have something else for you to wear."

I dropped the book from my face, narrowing my eyes at him. "I'm guessing this something else is basically no fabric?"

"Correct. But it's cleaner than your current attire," he smirked.

He had a point. And I did exercise in these clothes, so wearing them to sleep was not my first choice. I sighed, "Where is it?"

"I'll retrieve it for you." He threw the covers back, revealing his nakedness. I slapped a hand over my eyes, not out of modesty but out of self-preservation.

He chuckled again when he noticed my position. A silky fabric landed on my face, but I didn't move until I heard the whispering of furs covering him again. Then I cracked an eye to ensure he was covered.

"You have to turn over. I don't want you watching me change."

His sly grin told me he would watch no matter what, but he obliged and turned his back to me. The book thudded to the ground as I hurriedly stripped out of my jacket, tunic, and pants. Without looking at it, I threw the delicate silky material over my head. I should have checked before I put it on. The hem barely brushed the tops of my thighs, and the straps were thinner than a lock of my hair. My pebbled nipples peeked through the white fabric as the cold air caught up to me. I glanced up to find Ruslan's gray orbs on me, the male, as predicted, not keeping his word. My glare was an icy dagger as I rushed under the fur blankets, pulling them up to my chin.

He rolled to his side, propping his head on his fist as he pulled the book to him and flipped to the first page. "The Throne of the Earth." He pointed to the title, but the letters looked more like a jumbled mess than the words I knew them to be. "Which letters do you recognize?"

I chewed my lip and turned to my stomach so I could see the book better. "None of them."

Without a hint of judgment he said, "Okay, we'll start with the basics. This is the letter T," he pointed to four letters mixed within the words. "Trace it with your finger. It will help you remember."

Reaching out a tentative hand, I brushed my finger over the first letter in the title, the silky parchment smooth against it. I traced the rest of the letters as he named them, then he flipped through the book until words I was familiar with appeared on the page. I couldn't help my smile when we landed on 'horse.'

He stifled a yawn, then said, "Flip through the pages until you find 'horse' a dozen more times. You can leave the lantern on as long as you need, but I need to sleep."

"Thank you," I whispered, already searching for the word of my favorite animal. Pulling the book to the pillow in front of me, I propped my chin in my hand and studied the pages.

Ruslan settled on his back, eyes drifting closed. The hushed turning of pages filled the space between us until he murmured, "I waited for you for so long... but I will wait longer if that means you are mine willingly. All I wanted my whole life was to be loved, and real love is worth waiting for."

My breath hitched as his words tapped the same wound that

scarred my heart. I wasn't sure how to respond to his statement; it was so much easier to fight him and bite my words. He had a sensitive, vulnerable side, only adding to his complexity, and the more time I spent around him, the more I could empathize with him.

"I've always wanted to be loved too." Another confession, pulled from my soul.

He said nothing, and I continued to search. When my eyes grew too heavy to ignore, I closed the book, a small smile tugging at my lips because I had found nearly twenty words in the tome. With a long breath, I banished the light in the lantern, then settled beneath the heavy furs as far away as possible from the naked male who shared this makeshift bed. The hushed voices of whoever kept watch were the only sounds in the cave that provided us shelter from the ice and snow of the Agrenak Mountains. Despite my earlier trepidation, I was warming to Ruslan. Maybe his soul was just as tortured as my own.

Whether or not he was my mate was still up for debate.

9

KAZIMIR

Este Castle buzzed with activity as I packed the last of my things, the air thrumming with anticipation. Pulling open the heavy wood drawer where I stored the scraps of fabric covered in Izidora's scent, I brought each to my nose before tucking them into a smaller bag that would accompany me on Fek's back.

I'd seen her everywhere and nowhere the past week, in my dreams and in the halls. Her bright, curious eyes followed me everywhere I went, teasing me as I ran around the castle. Her laugh haunted my waking hours in equal measure to my sleeping ones. If I could only reach out and touch her one more time before she ran away from me...

Just before closing up my leather bag, I remembered my father's journal still tucked away in the couch. Digging my hands into the plush cushions, I searched for it until my fingers brushed the worn cover. Carefully extracting it from the couch, I ran my hands along the leather spine, recalling my father's dying words.

"Go, my son. Your mate needs you..."

He knew that Izidora was my mate; he tried to tell me, in his own fatherly way, the night before he died, and his last command was for me to go after her. Behind my eyes, I could still picture his peaceful face when he read a book, his ease when he laughed around the campfire with us. My chest constricted, and I rubbed it, trying to alleviate the heaviness that rested there. "I'm going to find her, father," I promised, hoping that wherever he was, he heard me.

I tucked the notebook away among my clothes, then hefted my sword, exiting my apartment and joining the chaos that currently ran the halls of Este Castle. "Allow me to take your bag, my lord." A young male approached from my left, and I looked at him, already leaden with items headed to the war wagons.

"Thank you, but I can manage. Show me the way to the wagons, if you would," I replied.

"Certainly, my lord." He waddled forward and I slowed my pace to match his. He stumbled, dropping a pack, and without hesitation, I hefted it along with my own. His cheeks reddened. "Apologies, my lord, I can take that back."

I shook my head. "You'll be strong one day, but not if you overdo it now."

He ducked his head, then continued to wind his way through the bustling corridors until we reached the stables. There were a dozen wagons, and triple the number of people running to and from the castle carrying armloads of food, herbs, furs, weapons, and more.

The wagon in front held packs and trunks of fine make, which I assumed were for the Noble Houses. The young male beelined for that one, gently releasing his burden before hopping in to arrange everything. I handed him one bag after another, and we made quick work of balancing the load.

He bowed low once he finished, preparing to scurry off when I stopped him. "What is your name?"

"Jora, my lord," he replied.

"Jora, if you train hard while we are away, I will personally see that you are admitted into Knight training when we get back. Can you promise me that you'll take care of our people until we return?"

He smiled from ear to ear. "Of course, thank you, and I wish you a safe journey. Return our queen to us." Then he scurried off, rounding the end of the stables where horses were being saddled. He returned, leading a snorting Fek, who shook his glossy black mane and stomped his foot when he stopped in front of me. My mount was just as impatient as I was to go; after all, we'd ridden almost all night searching for her after Ruslan had snatched her.

"Thank you for fetching him, Jora," I smiled.

"He is magnificent," Jora exclaimed.

Fek tossed his head once more as if to show just how magnificent he could be. Jora handed me the reins, bowed low, then disappeared into the throng of Fae. Grabbing Fek's reins, I led my black beast to the front of our traveling party, his thick hooves clopping against the cobbled courtyard, barely audible over the clamor surrounding us. Viktor, Vadim, Endre, and Liliana were already waiting with their horses, Liliana holding Mistik's reins, and my heart swelled at the sight of Izidora's dapple gray horse.

"I hope you don't mind, but I wanted to ride Misitk. When we get Izidora back, she can ride her home," Liliana said softly, uncharacteristically sentimental.

Izidora would appreciate the thoughtfulness of her friend. "I think it is a brilliant idea."

Kaztar and Domi walked up, leading two dark bay Hunters,

undoubtedly from Domi's stock. When Liliana had informed Domi of her plan to start an all-female unit in our army, she'd volunteered without hesitation – with the condition that we stopped at House Rass's estate to check on her mares that were about to foal. Our small group would depart first, needing the extra time for our detour, then on to Vlisa, where we would meet with King Airre and Queen Immonen. The army, with their numbers slowing them down, would travel the fastest route around the Agrenak Mountains until they reached Zheka, the capital of the Day Realm. Trusted captains from the Knights would act as generals in our absence.

It should have been Kriztof leading them.

The sun reached its apex in the sky, declaring high noon, and all shadows disappeared from around us. As my friends bid their parents goodbye, I watched on with a heavy heart. The loneliness in that moment was profound, and I understood Izidora's desire to be loved unconditionally. This was what she saw and felt when we first rescued her – probably even after she warmed up to us.

Erik and Renata broke away from Viktor, then pulled me in their direction, Renata enveloping me in a motherly hug. "Stay safe out there, okay? I want all of you back, alive, and in one piece." She looked pointedly between her son and me.

Tibor, Katalin, and Endre joined our circle, tears in Katalin's eyes as she bid me farewell. "Please watch out for each other. I don't think I can bury any more of you," she sniffed.

"And please, bring your mate home so we can throw the grandest wedding to celebrate her safe return – twice over," Renata added. Then, she wrapped her arms around Katalin and herded her toward the castle, leaving Tibor and Erik behind.

The two High Lords, along with Jaku, would remain in Vaenor to rule in our absence. None of us trusted Valintin and

Luzak, which is why the heirs had been delegated for the task of waging war. Kaztar and myself were the ultimate authority, myself as general and Kaztar as my second in command.

"Take good care of our people, Tibor." We clasped arms in farewell.

"They are in safe hands. As I know my son is safe in yours." His peridot eyes mirrored Endre's, a glassiness to them as he stepped back and admired us clad in our leather armor, bound for war.

"I'll see you when we return?" I turned my attention to Erik.

"Yes, and hopefully with the Iron Realm in chains," he grinned, clasping my arm firmly before pulling me in for a hug.

Maybe I wasn't as alone as my thoughts led me to believe.

The High Lords watched us as we mounted our horses, joining Kaztar and Domi in a survey of the courtyard quickly filling with more males and horses. Digging my heels into Fek's sides, he jolted forward, trotting toward the open gate leading into Vaenor. Kaztar and Domi, then Viktor and Endre, and lastly Liliana and Vadim trailed me out the gate and onto the main thoroughfare lined with excited Fae. We hadn't had a war in centuries, and the people were eager for a victory for the Night Realm.

Flowers of all colors rained on the stone-paved street in front of us, males, females, and children cheering on all sides as we wound through Vaenor. Only a week and half before, we'd ridden this course in reverse with the same reception.

How long would it be until my boots pounded the streets of Vaenor again? And would our people have the same reaction when I returned?

The stone bridge that separated Vaenor from the rest of the Night Realm waited for us, the bubbling creek's cheery tone too pleasant for my dark thoughts. Kicking Fek into a gallop, I charged away from the city in a race that was far too familiar, and I fucking hoped it was the last time I'd ever have to make this journey. Fek's black mane whipped my face, and I chose to remain low on his neck, accepting the stings as punishment for losing her. "I'm coming, Izidora," I vowed into the wind, hoping the Goddess would carry my words to her, wherever she may be.

10

RUSLAN

My mate rode in front of me again, and I much preferred this, with her petite frame pressed against me, to the swaying of the wagon where we were forced to sit opposite each other. As we entered the pass, the wind died down, and she no longer shivered with each gust. My chest loosened as her shaking ceased, and I breathed easier knowing she was comfortable. I'd never been the type of male who cared for the comfort of his females; yet with Izidora, the ice encasing my heart melted with each passing day. Her fire was fucking brilliant, and baiting her into flashing it was my new favorite hobby. How the two power-hungry kings thought they could break her was beyond my comprehension.

No, I don't think I would have enjoyed her nearly as much as I had since I took her from Este Castle if she did not have a bite to her words, and if she didn't look at me like she wished her magic could kill me on the spot. But with each clop of my mount's heavy hooves, we drew closer to the Iron Realm, and my heart both leaped and sank.

One step closer to showing Izidora everything I had prepared for her, yet one step away from my favorite place in Északi.

The lonely mountains called to my kindred spirit, and it was the one place in the whole continent I could truly be myself. There was no pretending to be the ruthless, uncaring prince, the weapon molded from birth to bring glory to the Iron Realm. There was only me, a book, and the haunting song of the wind as it caressed the mountains.

The jagged peaks gave me peace when nothing else could – not drink, not drugs, not females, and not fighting. I often escaped to them when I was younger, finding the solitude more bearable than the tunnels beneath the Iron Realm's citadel, where so many Félvér children ran wild. That was another reason I loved the mountains – the fresh air and open space contrasted the dank and narrow tunnels dug into the ground. I'd spent too many years of my life there, too many years fighting for my place among the Félvér.

My father, King Azim, sired a dozen children of every mix, experimenting with Rares to find the best combination. My mother died giving birth to me, bleeding out after a difficult delivery. I never knew her, or much about her. My father didn't love her, and I knew he didn't love me. He saw me as a tool, and I took advantage of that, training my mind and body to withstand all types of torture.

One day, I would be king, and not only of the Iron Realm, but of all Északi. Izidora would be my queen, my mate, and we would rule from the highest peak in Északi, Vasvain, where I could gaze down on every Fae still breathing on the continent while I basked in my glory.

Those blood purists would learn that the Félvér were superior and here to rule over them.

Shaking myself from my bloodthirsty thoughts, I returned my attention to Izidora, whose nose was glued to the book I had given her. The way she'd reacted to that book of poetry...

I needed to know everything that had happened to her. It

would only serve to fuel my rage against my father, and after hearing what little she had already told me, I was ready to kill him the moment I laid eyes on him.

The prophecy stated that 'kings will fall,' and fuck if I didn't find joy in knowing that my father would be the next to die. King Zalan was lucky he was already dead, and if I had known when I burst into the ballroom that he and King Azim had conspired to abuse and break Izidora, I would have killed him too.

Izidora's attention to the book would have pleased me if I didn't know she was hunting for words to ignore my presence. Every night, I scented her fear and arousal as I lay beside her. She had yet to touch me, but she was close to cracking – and we both knew it. The passion with which we argued should lead to amazing sex when she finally gave in to what I knew she wanted. This thread humming between us only intensified with each passing day, and fuck, I never knew it would be like this. It was getting harder and harder to maintain this facade of indifference toward her in front of my soldiers. If my father and Rares saw it, they would exploit it without hesitation. I had to protect her from them as much as I could.

She still clung to the ridiculous notion that that Night Fae male was her mate. I cursed myself for not killing him when I had the chance. Then she would have no doubt, for if the Goddess allowed him to die, then they were not meant to be together. He was already after her, of that I had no doubt.

The sun's angry glare burned into my scalp, the altitude bringing us closer to the light-giving orb. Not a shadow remained as we wound our way through the most harrowing section of Zherza Pass. On one side, a sharply sloped mountain was covered in large boulders that frequently tumbled toward the ground, flattening everything in their wake, while the other side held a sheer dropoff into a raging river that meant certain death if one went over the edge.

The middle ground between the two was the safest route, and we scanned the icy ridge above us for any sign of an impending rockslide. Snow dusted the highest reaches, and it wouldn't be long before the entirety of Zherza Pass was covered in ice thick enough to prevent any unwanted visitors to the Iron Realm.

In the distance, the path began its steady slope upward. Soon, the final hill before we broke through the last of the Agrenak Mountains and all of the Iron Realm would be laid bare to see. My spine tingled in anticipation of the view and of finally sharing it with my mate. The soldiers I had taken with me to the Night Realm plodded along behind us, the steady beat of hooves on earth the only sound bouncing between the sides of the mountains.

As the incline steepened, I leaned into it, relieving the pressure on my horse to carry us upward. Izidora remained unflinchingly focused on the book, though she stiffened slightly as my body pressed hers into the neck of my stallion. I growled, deciding I'd had enough of her ignoring me, and snatched it from her hands.

She exclaimed, "Hey! I was working on my words."

"You'll have more time for that later," I scowled. "We're about to exit the mountains. Look ahead and you'll see all of the Iron Realm in a moment."

Her sigh was grumpy but held an undercurrent of excitement. I had learned over the past few days that she had a near insatiable curiosity, which I was most happy to oblige. She watched and listened to every explanation with rapt interest that made me weak at the knees. Fucking Fates, if only she knew what her undivided attention did to me.

"I don't see anything other than rocks," she pointed out.

I tried to keep the irritation from my voice when I replied, "That's because we haven't crested the hill yet. Just wait."

The rocky top of the hill came into view, and moments later a flat overlook appeared a few paces off the main path, pointing us in the direction of the capital of the Iron Realm.

"Wow," she breathed, sitting taller against me, craning her neck over the pointed ears that blocked her view. I released the reins, allowing my horse to drop his head and provide Izidora unparalleled views across the Iron Realm.

Radence was nestled in a deep valley between some of the highest peaks in Északi, all of them dusted in white year-round. It was almost as if the Iron Crown had been brought to life by the Goddess and nestled over the brow of the valley, declaring the expanse as sovereign territory. At the edges of the valley, small farms dotted the landscape, and my sharp Dragon eyes spotted cattle, goats, and sheep herded along by fluffy black and white dogs. The city was densely packed, rings of stone buildings circling one that perched atop a rocky hill in the center of the city, its black spires piercing the sky like iron swords.

"See that tall building in the center?" I asked, pointing to it.

She nodded, following the direction of my finger. "That is the seat of the Iron Realm, Ryza Citadel. It is where King Azim lives." I swung my arm to our right, where the obsidian frames around the reflective windows were barely visible. "And that is our home, Roc Palace."

Her teeth chewed her lower lip as she squinted toward the distant palace. I wanted nothing more than to take her home and into my bed so I could suck that lip between my teeth instead. The heat from that image headed straight to my groin, and I adjusted in the saddle to relieve the friction between my pants and the leather. "You'll see it as we get closer. It is meant to blend in."

"How much longer will we ride?" she asked, covering her eyes with a hand as she sought Roc in the distance.

"Why? Are you eager to see your new home?" I purred, trailing my knuckles down her ribcage and eliciting a shiver.

She swallowed as she twisted her body to face me. Fear and arousal filled my nostrils, mixing with her rosy scent, concocting a combination more intoxicating than the finest whisky in the Iron Realm. Her aquamarine eyes scanned my face through thick black lashes as she chose her next words. "I am eager to train again. I miss having swords in my hands."

I cocked my head, a wicked grin playing on my lips. "Are you planning on stabbing me in my sleep?"

Her cheeks flamed, a guilty expression flashing briefly before disappearing beneath the cool mask she loved to wear. "No."

She did not elaborate, and I did not believe her. I would provide her with a dagger once we arrived, just to see what she would do with it. Our faces were only a breath apart, and she glanced at my lips before returning her gem-like eyes to meet mine. My hand mapped a path from her ribs to the back of her neck, my fingers threading into her thick locks. Her scent was pure ecstasy as I hovered my mouth above hers. I murmured, "Have you finally accepted that we are mates?"

She was taught as a bowstring beneath me, her breaths shallow and her lashes fluttering. Her mind may not believe it yet, but her body said everything those pink lips did not.

I could wait no longer to taste her.

Crashing my lips against hers, I forced my tongue into her mouth and kissed her deeply, tasting a hint of plum as I did so. Fuck, she was incredible. My fingers tightened against her scalp, trapping her in place as I snaked my other hand around her waist, pulling her petite body flush with mine. A soft whimper escaped her lips as she relented, allowing my tongue to dance with hers. The softness of her lips and hair beneath my fingers drove me mad, and I tightened my grip on her waist. She melted into me, arching her neck to give me more access to her mouth.

With a growl, I yanked her head back, breaking our kiss before I did anything reckless. Her face was flushed, those pink lips plump and bruised from my attention, and her round eyes fluttered in time with the rise and fall of her chest. Releasing my hold on her, I picked up the reins and steered my horse in the direction of our home. Witnesses to our passionate embrace sat silently atop their mounts, and my sprite ducked her head as we passed them.

She acted sheepish, but she wanted it every bit as badly as I did. Drazen shot me a suggestive smirk, his Dragon senses as acute as my own. But he didn't have to ride half a day behind her, every breath brimming with her heady scent, like I did. There was no hiding the hardness that dug into her damning backside, but she did not move away from me as we continued our trek toward Roc Palace.

I returned The Throne of the Earth to her, providing both her and myself with a much needed distraction. "Look for the word 'tree,'" I instructed, my voice gravely and filled with unsatiated lust. Her small hands snatched it immediately, and the worn pages lifted her rosy scent to my nostrils as she flipped through the book. I fixed my eyes straight ahead, wishing my magic had recovered enough to move us the remaining distance. The only downside to being a Félvér – our magic took twice as long to replenish.

———

A GOLDEN HALO broke through the mountains in the distance, casting everything before us in honeyed hues. Reaching over my mate's shoulder, I lifted the book from her hands. "Look around you, my sprite. You were trapped too long to miss sights like these."

Her huff transformed to a gasp as the sky commenced a lightshow only for us. Jagged white-capped peaks were silhouetted against vibrant colors that bled together like melting candy, the ruby reds fading into deep amethyst streaked with a hint of coral. The first stars winked into view, while the crescent moon came to life, chasing its counterpart in an endless race through the skies.

"We can watch this together every night from the roof," I promised as the soft light brightened the wonder in her eyes.

A brilliant smile pulled at her cheeks, and a subtle nod was all I received as her eyes roved the fading sky. A tiny sliver of ice chipped from around my blackened heart as I watched her, and, fuck me, I wanted her to look at me that way.

I needed to move us home.

In my chest, a near endless well of black fire flared as I whispered the spell, casting a wide net around us and capturing each soldier within it. The trail blurred as if we moved at the speed of light, and Izidora's hands became a vice on my arms as we swayed around a bend in the path. With one last flash, we halted at the base of the mountain that held Roc Palace.

Peeling her fingers from my arm, I leaped off my horse, landing with a heavy thud on the rocky ground. As I clasped my hands around Izidora's small waist to pull her to the ground, she clamped her hands on my arm, shoving them away with a scathing look. But I ignored it, lifting her and placing her on the hard ground before me. My hands remained on her because I expected her to run at the first opportunity, and she huffed before crossing her arms over her chest and allowing me to corral her. I would not allow my mate to abandon me, not when I knew she would love me unconditionally as long as she released that other male from her heart.

A peppery spice prefaced Drazen's arrival, though his heavy footfalls were also a dead giveaway. His storming ceased when he rounded in front of me, jaw tight and arms crossed. "I'm fine," I waved him off. "Take care of the horses and soldiers. We're going up."

"You are such an idiot," he barked, but he grabbed the reins and spun on his heel, stalking to the stables and barracks that guarded the base of the mountain. Five hundred feet above us, the palace I'd built for my mate beckoned us inside, and I was eager to show her everything I wanted to provide for her.

"How are we supposed to get up there?" Izidora chewed her lip, hair tumbling down her back as she tilted her head up and up and up, following the craggy gray rocks until she spotted the black, glassy frames that betrayed the palace's presence.

"Like this." I tugged her toward an unassuming smooth section of rock, then flattened my palm against it to reveal a hidden door. It opened with a grinding groan, the heavy rock door a deterrent in itself, though it wasn't heavy enough to prevent my strong kin from entering. A wide passage lay beyond, and small sconces flickered to life as we passed them. Twenty paces in, an iron door blocked our path, and I pressed my palm into the rough stone wall beside it. The door swung open, revealing a stone slab and an upright tunnel that hollowed out the mountain. Stepping onto the slab, I pulled a trembling Izidora with me, though she balked as I tried to close the door on us. "Relax, we'll be fine. I don't like small spaces either, but it will be over before you know it."

The lip between her teeth told me she was not reassured.

I tapped into my earth magic, and the stone shifted beneath our feet before shooting up the shaft, air screaming in our ears as we rode toward our home. Izidora screamed and flattened herself against the slab, throwing her hands over her head and trapping some of the long locks that whipped wildly in the wind. A manic smile pulled at the corner of my lips; the thrill of the lift racing higher and higher never dulled for me. I slowed our ascent as we reached the second set of iron doors, halting the earth when we reached the level above them. In one fluid motion, Izidora was in my arms, and I carried her across the threshold onto the third floor that served as an entryway.

She shook like a leaf scattering in the fall wind, and she buried her face in my chest until her breaths deepened and heart returned to a steady thump against my ribcage. "Please, don't do that again."

The broken plea straining her voice was enough to soften me. Gently, I set her on her feet and smoothed her hair away from her reddened eyes. "Let me show you around our home." I took her hand in mine, and she flinched, but left her hand where I'd put it. "We'll go to the library first."

Tugging her to the left, we approached the massive oak doors that waited to reveal the wonders behind them. With a dramatic flair, I grasped the handles and threw open the doors to my sanctuary. Izidora's aquamarine eyes widened and her pout parted as she drank in row upon row of sturdy wood cases filled to bursting with books. I allowed her to wander in front of me as she touched the dark wood panels, trailed her fingers along the gilded spines, and gazed in awe at the ceiling. A battle of Angels and Demons raged above us, depicting one of the earliest and bloodiest in their history, scene after scene unfolding the deeper we delved into the library. She disappeared among the stacks when the fresco ended, so I wandered to the windows that doubled as a wall, surveying the glittering lights from a thousand fires as night fell over the Iron Realm.

I braced my arm against the window, allowing the cool pane to soothe the heat pounding in my veins, while that thread in my gut begged me to find my mate among the books and fuck her senseless until she accepted our bond. A few painful minutes later, she returned to the center of the room, nostrils widening as she inhaled the scent of leather and worn parchment, head tipped back, arms spread wide, ecstasy written on her face plain as any story between leatherbound pages.

I had started in the right spot.

Her stomach rumbled, and her wide smile turned sheepish as she righted her head. My mate was adorable, her face so expressive when she allowed it to be. I laughed, the ease with which the sound slipped out startling and surprising me. "Next stop, the kitchen."

I swooped her into my arms, leaving the library behind as we descended a grand staircase in the entryway. She swung her feet in time with my steps, and her giddiness was more intoxicating than the wine I planned on having with dinner. The aroma of savory spices wafted through the hallway as we neared the kitchen, and when we rounded a corner, the massive space opened before us. Two chefs were hard at work preparing dinner, one chopping herbs and vegetables while the other was up to his elbows in flour. I appreciated good service, and all members of my household learned to be one step ahead of my expectations.

"My Prince, welcome back," Cedomir, the premier chef, said as he picked his head up, smiling warmly at Izidora, who I had not released from my arms. "And welcome, my lady."

"Cedomir, what are you preparing for us tonight?" I inquired.

"Glazed chicken with fresh winter vegetables, and for dessert, a chocolate cake. It will be ready in half an hour. Would you like to eat in the dining room?"

"We'll take it in the suite, along with a bottle of wine," I replied. He nodded to me, then returned to chopping, the sharp blade making quick work of slicing a round yellow vegetable.

Izidora's head swiveled around the room as we continued

through it. The kitchen was a stark contrast from the rest of the palace; with its white decor, it was light and airy, whereas just beyond, the palace turned dark and gothic. Though the decor was sharp and minimal, the space was luxurious and sprawling.

Our trek to the fourth level, where our suite awaited us, was silent as she absorbed the flecked-granite walls along the central staircase. We stopped in the small corridor at the top of the stairs, the only space on this floor aside from our suite. To our left, another iron door hid the lift, and on the right, heavy black doors barred the entrance, giving us privacy and security.

Touching my palm to the door, I showed it my magical signature, another level of security in place for the Palace. Izidora would be safe here, and so long as she was with me, she could move about freely. The doors unlocked themselves and swung inward, beckoning us inside. Izidora's breath hitched when I put my lips to her ear, whispering my truth to her. "I designed everything with you in mind. Every comfort. Every luxury. All for you."

Her breath fled as we entered the first room – a living space large enough to sleep fifty. Glittering black granite walls boxed us in, and thick fur rugs rolled out across the room to trap heat in the vast space. Deep into the room, white and gray tufted couches created a sitting area in front of a bronze fireplace that reflected the light from the sconces lining the walls. To the right, a natural wood table surrounded by chairs served as a dining area. Between the fireplace and dining area, two carved doors swung wide, begging us to explore the rest of the suite.

Without releasing Izidora, I strode toward our bedroom. Her body thrummed with an intoxicating mix of fear and arousal as we approached those doors, but as we entered the space, she stopped breathing, her eyes catching on the massive chandelier that spanned the ceiling, winking and dispersing light throughout the room. Each piece of dark crystal hung from an invisible thread, the pattern creating a set of wings, one softer like her Angel's wings, one sharper, like my Demon-Dragon wings. Across from us, the massive bed sprawled across a black paneled wall, depicting a scene from history like the ceiling of the library. This one was filled with love and hope, feelings I had yet to experience, but knew Izidora would bring me.

Deeper still, the door to the bathroom waited, enticing after days of riding. I carried her there, her eyes lingering on the painting adoring the wall behind our bed. I finally allowed her to walk once we entered the bathroom. She went first to the wall-length vanity that sat opposite the windows, fingers trailing along the smooth marble as she studied it. The mirrors changed shape every few feet, one rectangle, one octagon, one square, and repeat. There were plush stools pushed under the counter to sit on, and she pulled one out, admiring it. She left it untucked as she walked to the open shower to her right, recessed into the mountain itself. I followed her there, turning some knobs on the outside as the water poured from above.

"The shower's water comes directly from the mountain's hot spring," I told her, wrapping my arms around her from behind. She tried to step forward, out of my grip, but I only splayed my fingers across her stomach, trapping her against me.

My dick was lengthening against her back, and I didn't bother to hide it. I leaned close to her ear and purred, "Let's wash up before we eat."

Her swallow was audible over the rushing water. Her nervousness was exhilarating, though the fight was not in her, really – not anymore.

I stripped off my armor, each piece of metal clattering against the floor. Then I pulled my tunic overhead, dropping it in the growing pile. But Izidora had not moved. "Is my mate feeling a little shy?" I teased, my voice husky like metal rubbed across stone. I pulled her flush, then trailed my hands along her front, reaching for the buttons that held her jacket closed. She did not move, did not breathe, as I slowly peeled the jacket from her body. The leather joined my armor on the floor after I pushed the sleeves down her shoulders, forcing her to shed a layer of the barrier she held between us.

A hitch in her breath was the sweetest sound as I teased the waistband of her tight pants, but I stepped back, leaving her frozen in place as I stripped and strode past her into the shower. The water ran in rivulets down my body, following the predefined paths of my muscled torso until finally they reached the finish line at my erection. I bared myself before her, barely containing a grin as I slicked my hair backward, flexing my corded arms in the process.

The aquamarine of her eyes was nearly overtaken by her blown-out pupils as she looked at me without hiding her lust for the first time. She moved her hands to her tunic then dropped them several times before her eyes closed and brows pinched. Her head dropped, and with a slight shake, she chewed her lip until, at last, she touched her tunic and did not drop her hands away. A war played out in those glossy orbs as she raised her head, our gazes colliding with the power of an avalanche.

"I will bite, but not right now," I purred.

Her eyes hardened, and she peeled off the tunic with a glare sharp enough to maim. "I will shower, over there, and you may look, but you cannot touch me."

I held my hands up in mock surrender. She may think she won this battle, but I was winning the war. She stripped out of her socks and pants, hopping as she struggled to get the tight ends off, then hurried into the shower at the opposite end, standing with her back half facing me, trying to hide as much of herself as she could while still keeping me in her sights. The water traced her flawless curves, lean muscles flexing as she shifted to wet her hair. Her long locks went dark as water soaked them, clinging to her back.

And then I saw them – the scars.

How had I missed them before?

Disregarding her instructions, I stalked across the shower, eliciting a wide-eyed gasp as she flattened herself against the smooth stone. Without asking for permission, I grasped her shoulders and spun her around, sweeping her soaked hair over her shoulders to examine those deeply etched lines in her back, cracking her creamy skin like bolts of lightning.

"Who. Did. This. To. You."

Each word was flung with the violence of a thunderstorm, and I barely heard her whimper over the roaring in my ears. If that motherfucker cut these into her back, he was dead. So. Fucking. Dead.

Realizing I was scaring her with my thunderous rage, I dropped my hands from her shoulders and took a half step back. I cracked my neck, then my knuckles, every instinct yanking my Dragon to the surface with one goal in mind – protect.

"I received these for daring to defy my captors," she hissed, a haunted flash of white fire entering her eyes. I'd already planned on killing them violently, and that thirst for their blood increased tenfold with her words.

What the fuck had my father and King Zalan allowed?

He'd kept me from her... so they could play their sick twisted games with my mate. This made my plan to kill him that much sweeter. His death would be fucking brutal, and he would receive no funeral, his body left in the lonely mountains to be picked apart by carrion.

"Izidora..." I croaked, falling to my knees as her fiery gaze speared my soul. "I've said it before, but I promise to spend the rest of our lives making this up to you. If I had known... I would have burned the world down to get to you. My greatest regret in life will be that I didn't come for you sooner."

Her wet hair clung to her breasts, making the heaving of her chest unmistakable. I reached for her, but she stepped back, her eyes still containing that wildfire as she looked at me. "Start by showering over there and keeping your hands to yourself," she snapped, crossing her arms.

I nodded, my neck still tight with rage, and pushed to my feet. My chest ached as each step away from her shredded that ice-covered muscle that kept me alive. I couldn't tear my eyes from her, not when I was beginning to understand the depths of depravity she'd endured.

The assault. The whips. The poetry.

I needed to know it all.

She reached for a bar of soap sitting on the inlaid shelf, and quickly worked it over her body and through her tresses, shooting a heated glare at me every so often over her shoulder. I grabbed a bar for myself, the soap turning slick as I coated myself with it. Her heady scent wafted to me on a cloud of steam, more fragrant than the soap I used to wash almost a week's worth of dirt from my body. I tried and failed to calm down, my fury mixing with lust and hardening my cock until it was painfully erect.

Her gaze locked on my shaft, swollen for her, and her body flushed from more than the hot water. Masking the bloodlust that pinched my chest with a sardonic smirk, I winked at her then exited the shower and turned the taps. Water dripped off me with every step I took toward the folded towels waiting for us to use to wipe the moisture from our bodies. She stepped out of the dissipating steam, her long chestnut hair covering her breasts. She strutted toward me and snatched both cloths from my hands – the first went around her torso, the second around her hair.

"I didn't need one anyway. I'll air dry," I told her, and that vengeful fire slipped from her eyes as they darkened. She couldn't help her reaction to me, even though she wanted to, and that knowledge loosened my chest and shoulders.

As I walked past her, she chewed her lip, and I stopped, grasped her chin, and with my thumb, pulled her lip from between her teeth. "That is for me to do to you," I growled, cock twitching as I imagined the moment I would suck her lips between my teeth. Fighting every part of me that threatened to take her to bed, I continued on to the bedroom in search of something comfortable to wear. The light pad of her bare feet followed me as I stalked all the way to the closet where fresh clothes awaited us both.

I tossed her a slinky dress and nothing else over my shoulder while I searched for a pair of loose pants for myself. The soft fabric did nothing to hide the hardness at my thighs, and I left my chest bare for her to see. When I spun around, she had yet to fully slide the dress over her head. A hint of her core caught my attention before the shift settled over her body.

The tension between us was nearly visible as we drifted toward each other, pulled by an unseen bond. I took another step in her direction, then thought better of it. Gritting my teeth, I used the sharp pain in my jaw to ground myself against my basest desires. I was so fucking close to losing control.

Nearly sprinting to the bathroom, I slammed the door behind me, my rage and desire waging war in my brain and in my body; but they had a common goal – fuck, fight, protect. Filling a basin with cold water, I dunked my face, the sting tempering my emotions, which threatened to burn the whole palace down. With knuckles turned white from the vice-like grip on either side of the basin, I stared at myself in the mirror, counting my breath until my cock no longer tented my pants and my heart beat steady and slow.

The rumble of the lift reverberated in the walls, signaling Cedomir's arrival with our food. I stalked to the living area where Izidora lay prone on a couch in front of the fireplace, head propped up by her hands, engrossed by the flickering flames. My gaze roamed over her tight ass that her thin dress could not hide, and I almost had to return to the bathroom. But Cedomir knocked at that moment, interrupting the dark flow of my thoughts, and I strode to the door to open it.

He wheeled a cart carrying plates of food and a bottle of wine to the dining table, carefully arranging our meal so that we faced each other. A handful of white candles dotted the wide space, and he laid a bouquet of fresh flowers beside Izidora's place setting. It was a nice touch, and I thanked him before dismissing him. He closed the door behind him, and I tossed some magic over my shoulder, sealing us and all sound in our suite.

Grasping the flowers, I tucked them behind my back and sauntered to Izidora's spot by the hearth. Placing myself between her and the fire, I knelt and proffered the bouquet of gold-flecked white roses. Her eyes came into focus as she noticed the gift, and the soft smile that spread on her lips made me grateful that I was already kneeling. She reached for the roses and brought them close to her face, inhaling their floral scent.

I stuck my hand out to her, hoping she would willingly take it. "Come to dinner, my sprite."

She rose from the couch but did not take my hand, and I let it drop casually, hiding the sting of her small rejection. At the dining table, I pulled out her seat before rounding it to my own. Uncorking the bottle of dark red wine, I poured a measure into the carved crystal glasses on the table, allowing the swish of the liquid in the glass to soothe my racing heart. I handed one to her before downing my entire glass. The spicy plum flavor coated my tongue, the warmth soothing my belly and steadying my nerves as I studied the female sitting across the table.

I would kill to know what she was thinking. It was as if every time I coaxed her in my direction, she came to her senses and retreated just out of reach.

What would it take for her to fall into me, to say yes to me, to love me as mates should? She had all the power, but I could not let her know that. There was no way I could lose the upper hand, because at the moment she would leave me without a second thought.

No one else was going to leave me – unless I allowed it.

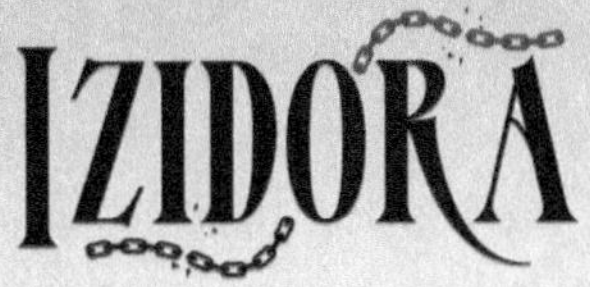

11

Ruslan's demeanor changed completely in the ten minutes between storming into the bathroom and returning to the bedroom. My shoulders were in a constant state of tension around him, his moods and actions unpredictable from one moment to the next. I walked a tightrope with him, waiting to see which way I would tumble. It didn't help that no matter how hard I tried to stay away, something pulled me back to him.

Not something – a thread that I chose to blatantly ignore as much as possible.

The kiss we had shared while we gazed across the Iron Realm was raw, possessive, and ruining. A knot formed in my stomach and my low belly heated as the moment returned to me, clear as day. Only a few weeks had passed since I had been snatched from the feast, and I was already kissing another male.

What was wrong with me?

I continued to berate myself for allowing Ruslan to worm his way under my skin while Kazimir was most likely losing his shit trying to get to me. What I had with Kazimir was uncomplicated, passionate, and most of all, safe. Ruslan was dangerous, possessive, and irrational, and yet our banter made me feel fucking alive.

Was it the years of abuse that caused his stormy nature to call to me more than a male who made me feel safe?

My earlier plan to gain strength and skill, to allow Ruslan to forge me into a weapon and then to turn that weapon on him, felt shakier with each passing hour. But no male would control me again, and if that was Ruslan's goal, he'd meet my wrath. So, I would gain his trust and learn more about the Félvér, all while plotting my revenge against the Iron Realm. Unfortunately, that meant showing him affection and spending time with him – both of which had led to me opening my heart as we shared story after story of those small moments that had birthed the demons that still haunted us both.

I was loath to lock away those parts of me that had burst from the thick stone wall I erected to hide from my abuse. I loved who I was becoming, and I was tired of doing what I had to do to survive. This dance with Ruslan was as familiar to me as breathing, for I had lived my whole life playing this game. I knew I would endure my time here, simply because I was willing to do anything to survive.

But would my spirit survive with me?

Playing the game wasn't the part that worried me – losing myself to it was.

"Where did you go?" he asked, his eyes curious, albeit tense at the corners.

He broke my internal battle like it was glass, and my attention snapped back to the food and male in front of me. "I was thinking about how I've never been given flowers before." Not totally true, there were flowers waiting everywhere I went in the Night Realm, and I used them often in my hair before we reached Vaenor. "I've never really been wined and dined like this, either. It's nice." I lifted my glass to my lips, ready to taste what I was sure was an expensive wine.

His smoky eyes glittered with amusement. "We will have to make up for lost time. I will plan a date for us every evening, so we have time to get to know each other before our wedding."

I spluttered the purple liquid over the white plates in front of me as I choked on his words. "Wedding?" I managed to sound out through my coughs.

"Of course, now that you are here, why wait? It will be the grandest royal wedding in centuries. I have it planned for the final eve of the year, during Béke. All the realms will be gathered in Radence anyway, so there would be no need for them to make another trip." He sipped from his wine like I hadn't just painted the table with it.

Fucking Fates, I'd forgotten all about Béke, and that the Iron Realm would be hosting.

An opportunity to slip away.

A fervent hope that Kazimir and my friends were headed to the Iron Realm with a plan settled into my heart, but I couldn't allow Ruslan to see that hope filling me with light, so I scowled at him. "And I get no say in this? You know I am a princess, right? And now that King Zalan is dead, probably a queen."

He relaxed in his seat, legs spreading wide even beneath the tablecloth. "Of course, you can plan the decor, your dress, the menu, or whatever other things females like to plan about weddings. But the date, venue, and guest list are already set."

I huffed, crossing my arms over my chest, wine glass still in hand while I mulled over my response. I had to play along to earn his trust. "Fine, but I need to see the venue to plan the rest. And I'll need the best cloth weavers you have to design the dress. It's a shame the females who designed the gown you destroyed can't create my wedding dress as well. They would have made me look divine." I sighed wistfully, truly wishing they could design another beautiful gown for me.

"I can make it happen," he said a little too casually, and I narrowed my eyes at him.

"How?"

"I'll offer them a lot of money, and if they refuse, I'll just bring them here anyway." He shrugged like he hadn't just suggested taking them against their will.

"Kidnapping? What is wrong with you?" I seethed, my teeth clenched and lips pulled back as I wished he would spontaneously burst into flames.

He bared his teeth, his eyes flashing black as the beast within surfaced. "I – *always* – get what I want," he growled. "And if my mate, my future wife, wants the females who make the best dresses in the land, then she will have that."

I tore my gaze away and toward my food, picking up a knife and fork to cut into the roasted chicken, which smelled heavenly – even though I was certain I was in hell. Without deigning to respond or give Ruslan any attention, I ate quickly, uncertain whether we would finish the meal with the overpowering tension between us.

Ruslan's hand covered mine just as I was about to cut into a large carrot. Stilling, I peeked under my lashes to find his face relaxed and easy, his earlier rage vanishing like smoke in the wind. "I want to make you happy, Izidora."

"Kidnapping innocents would not make me happy. Don't you see that? I would be perpetuating what happened to me. When I was a baby," I added quickly as his eyes flashed again.

He nodded, as if he understood my perspective. "I'm sorry, I didn't think of it that way. Of course you wouldn't wish for anyone else to go through what you went through in your childhood. I feel the same."

"Will you tell me about your childhood?" I asked, trying to change the subject.

His eyes lost their shine, and his shoulders sagged as if his memories were a heavy burden. "It is not a pleasant story, and certainly not a topic for a date."

I gave him a soft smile. "I'm here to listen whenever you are ready."

He nodded, then dug into his own food, head still drooped slightly. "You know, no other female has ever set foot in here. I saved it for you. I wanted it to be special, for us."

In that moment, he sounded so much like a lost, sad child that my heart broke for him. His previous comments about wanting to be loved mirrored the ones I had made to Kazimir time and time again. As much as I wanted to hate him, to steel my heart against him, to play this game without feeling, I couldn't. Not when I understood his trauma, so similar to my own.

We did have more in common than I thought.

The paths we had walked might have been different, but in the end we were both bruised, bloody, and broken in a way others would never understand, with a void that beckoned our battered souls, always waiting to pounce in moments of weakness.

On tiptoes, I reached for him across the table, stroking his downcast face, and he leaned into my hand, soft stubble tickling my palm. A soft moan drifted across the table as my hand remained against his cheek, not willing to retreat when he clearly needed validation and reassurance. His eyes lifted to meet mine, and the hint of loneliness that usually marked his smoky grays was on full display.

Had he received any affection as a child? Did these small gestures melt his heart like they did mine?

When my stomach grumbled again, I retreated to my side of

the table and reclaimed my dropped silverware. We finished the remainder of the main course in silence, though the earlier tension had dissipated, replaced with an uneasy angst. Glancing around the table once my plate was cleared, I searched for the promised chocolate cake.

Ruslan tracked me with veiled amusement. "What are you searching for?"

"Dessert. I love chocolate cake," I replied, a bit deflated since it was nowhere to be found.

"Cedomir will be back with that. I like it hot from the oven, topped with frozen cream."

"That sounds incredible," I breathed, my body buzzing with anticipation of the decadent dessert.

He flashed a roguish grin. "I know. I have a horrible sweet tooth. I have to train twice a day to work off the calories."

"Guess I should join you if I don't want to be the size of a house," I said.

"I can think of other ways to burn off the calories with you." The low, seductive voice curled my toes, and an image of him moving on top of me flashed through my mind. I broke his gaze, hiding just how much he affected me with his provocative statement.

A knock sounded a moment later – thank the Goddess – and Ruslan waved a hand, the doors opening of their own accord. Cedomir carried a tray laden with massive slices of chocolate cake and two bowls of frozen cream. He placed one in front of each of us, then deposited a small cup of melted chocolate in the middle. He was gone as quickly as he came, and Ruslan turned his predatory gaze on me while the doors swung shut with an ominous finality.

Spooning the frozen cream onto his cake, he licked the spoon slowly, flattening his tongue over it as he pulled it from his sinister mouth. Next, he dipped his spoon into the cup of melted chocolate, drizzling the brown liquid like light rain across his plate.

Forcing a swallow through my thick throat, I turned my attention to my own dessert, mimicking his motions and drizzling chocolate over my slice. With a spoon, I stabbed at the frozen cream before scooping hot cake and lifting the combination to my mouth. It was rich and spongy, the perfect mix of sweetness with a hint of salt, while the heat of the melted chocolate contrasted with the cool cream. Each bite was like an orgasm in my mouth. I moaned with the same level of passion.

Ruslan's eyes were black as he watched me like he would devour me, and I knew once this cake was gone, I was on the menu. He sat preternaturally still, his gaze never leaving my lips, and I was way too warm under his scrutiny, despite the flimsy dress I wore. I dragged out my last few bites, the fluttering in my stomach threatening to return them to my plate, and Ruslan flexed his hands repeatedly, one knee bouncing beneath the table and lightly shaking the floor. On my last bite, he lifted the cup of melted chocolate off the table, stirring it with his spoon to keep it from hardening. The second I swallowed my last bite, his chair legs scraped against the floor with a force that sent the hairs on my arms rising.

In two powerful strides, he caged me in his arms, and I barely had time for a breath before his lips crashed against mine. His kiss was furious, and he insistently swiped his tongue across my lips, begging me to open them. I acquiesced, moaning as our chocolate-coated tongues intertwined.

This was wrong, so wrong; and yet, my body felt electrified under his touch.

His strong hands grasped either side of my hips and forced me to wrap my legs around his waist. Without breaking apart, he walked us to a nearby couch, flattening me against it and peeling my legs from his torso. "Wait here," he instructed, making quick work of collecting the melted chocolate from the table.

My curiosity pushed me to my elbows, and my eyes roamed him as he knelt beside me. The silk slip was barely long enough to cover the tops of my thighs, and I wore nothing underneath. My position lifted the already dangerously high hem, and I tugged at the bottom in an attempt to cover what little dignity remained in my thrumming body. He growled and swatted my hand away, and I stilled, watching him warily as his hand found the strap on my shoulder, pushing it away so that it fell down my arm.

My breath snagged in my chest, my mind screaming no but my body screaming yes. I remained frozen, at war with myself, while Ruslan slipped the other strap off my shoulder. "Wait," I said breathlessly, as the silky fabric came to rest near the crook of my elbow.

His vanilla scent overwhelmed me as he brought his face close to mine. "I told you that I want you to come to me willingly. I won't take what isn't rightfully mine, not from you."

"I know," I panted, shaking my head, guilt and lust shoving at each other to gain the upper hand in my emotional battle.

"Then what is the issue? Don't deny that you feel this pull between us," he growled, and I turned my head, the lie I almost released into the air hanging on my tongue.

Because that was the problem – an all too familiar thread pulled me to Ruslan, just like it had to Kazimir. But that couldn't be right, unless this feeling was only the product of desire.

"Look at me, sprite," he snapped, and I released a shaky breath, meeting his steely gaze with determination not to falter. "Let me show you how much you mean to me." Those words held none of his earlier fire, the usual cockiness absent in his tone, and I wished he'd force me into this, so I could blame him instead of myself. My anger was much easier to wield than what-ever... this was.

"You'll stop when I say stop?" I wanted confirmation, though with his reaction to what I'd told him of my abuse, I knew deep down that he'd never force anything on me that I did not want. The dichotomy of his persona had become more apparent over our time together; with me, he was different than when others were around.

"Yes," he swore, sincerity dancing in his eyes.

Closing my eyes and inhaling sharply, I surrendered. A drop of something fell across my chest, and I remained absolutely still as Ruslan drizzled the melted chocolate across my collarbone and the dip between my breasts. The liquid was still warm, but not enough to burn, and the anticipation of each delectable drip had me clenching my thighs together. He dropped the spoon back in the cup with a clang and set it to the side. Hot breath fanned across my shoulder, and his lips found the pool of choco-late at my collarbone. Planting a featherlight kiss on the bone, he lapped at the delicious darkness adorning it, then drank from the puddle, smearing its remnants on my chest as he trailed his tongue across it. I bit back a groan, attempting to cover my reac-tion to his sensual touch.

I wanted that tongue somewhere else, and I hated him for it; but I hated myself even more.

He sucked and licked his way down my opposite shoulder, stopping to nip at the top of my arm before returning to my heaving chest. My breath was strained as I tried to hide the depths of my arousal, but when he sucked at the dip between my breasts, an involuntary gasp left my lips. I felt him grin against me before he moved on to the melted chocolate that threatened to stain the silky fabric as it mixed with a light sheen of sweat. His tongue mapped the peaks and valleys of my exposed breasts until none of the delicious treat remained.

The fabric barely covered the tops of my breasts, and there was no hiding my desire as my nipples peaked beneath it. His fingers trailed across the silk, the pads barely brushing those aching points. Wetness coated my inner thighs as my traitorous body responded to the touch of the wicked male in front of me. I clenched them together, deluding myself into thinking he couldn't scent me if they were closed.

I reminded myself over and over of Kazimir, hoping that the thought of him would banish my arousal for the male slowly torturing me by licking chocolate from my neck and chest. Even if Kazimir had lied to me and manipulated me...

Ruslan tore me from my internal battle once again with a wave of wispy touches down my torso and straight to my core before leaning away, taking his heat with him, and retrieving the cup of chocolate. He smeared spoonfuls up my bare thighs until the last drop hung just below the hem of fabric, and I shivered as he closed in on that spot that would be a dead giveaway. Climbing onto the couch in front of me, he framed my legs and lowered his lips to my thigh. The first drop disappeared with a flick of his tongue, and his gray eyes turned obsidian as he trailed his sinful mouth up, up, up until he licked the hint of sweetness just below the hem that seemed to drift higher of its own accord. His nostrils flared, and I whimpered as his digits drifted up either side of my outer thighs.

He knew.

With a wicked gleam, he lowered his lips to the seam of my thighs and sank his teeth into them. A cry tore from my lips, body arching off the couch and legs flaring open, baring my glistening folds to him.

"Fuck me," he groaned, staring at my core like he'd found a precious gemstone. "You are so fucking beautiful."

My fists clenched, and I gritted my jaw at his trick. He made to move for my core, and with one swift motion, I planted a foot on his shoulder and shoved. Surprise danced across his face as he jerked back, and then he smirked. "There's my sprite."

He knocked my foot above his shoulder, then pinned me beneath him, my legs split far apart as he lowered his lips to my ear. "I told you I love when they fight back," he purred. "You really are trying to entice me, aren't you, mate?"

Without hesitation, I called magic to my hand and slapped him with all my strength. But he caught my wrist just before I made contact and yanked it above my head, white light vanishing. The heat that flooded the space between our hips was shameful, and he laughed low, the sound traveling from deep within his chest and rumbling against mine as he pressed me harder into the couch.

His nostrils flared and he ground into me with a groan. "Don't be ashamed of your desires, sprite. That's the beauty of embracing your darkness – you get to conquer it, to control it."

He bent his head and captured my mouth in his, the punishing kiss stealing my breath as I tried to wiggle from underneath him. That only seemed to spur him on, and his tongue forced its way into my throat. My moan was heady, wanton, as my tongue intertwined with his, the friction between them mixed with the delectable chocolate alighting my body and sending it arching into him. He sucked my bottom lip into his mouth, nipping it lightly as he released it along with my wrist, his hand retreating to bunch the fabric of my dress higher above my core.

"Stop," I panted, chest heaving and core throbbing.

I couldn't let this go any further – no matter how much arousal soaked my thighs.

With a pained growl, he stilled and sat back on his heels. The fire behind us painted his tattooed chest in light and dark that shifted with each crackle and pop of the burning logs. His eyes were nearly black, and his face was strained as he tried to regain control, his teeth gritted so hard the muscles of his jaw were frenzied. His fist flew faster than I could react, and it landed with a thud on the back of the couch. My reaction was instinctual, borne from survival, and immediately I pushed against him, trying to get out from under him before he could strike me too.

He must have realized the source of my frantic energy, because he snapped back to reality with a hitched breath. "Izidora, I am so sorry, I would never lay a hand on you," he pleaded, his eyes searching my face for any sign of fear or forgiveness.

I let him see just how fearful I was, betting that this side of him would be wracked with guilt. My hunch was correct, and he buried his face in his hands, shaking his head, his black hair tumbling forward and over his fingertips. Scrambling backward, I re-covered myself with the slip, then crouched at the opposite end of the sofa, ready to bolt, if necessary.

But Ruslan remained kneeling, face in hands, in front of me. "I've waited so long for you, my mate, my one true love, the person who would save me and love me no matter what. I wish you wanted me as much as I want you."

My body went cold despite the bronze hearth at my back. Craving unconditional love was something I was intimately familiar with, and similar words had slipped from my lips in my first few weeks out of the cave. Ruslan cracked before me, and my heart dropped at the depths of his sorrow. I didn't know much about love, but I knew how much unconditional devotion from Kazimir had healed me. As much doubt as I held about his actions, that part of us was real.

I hoped.

Ruslan too had built walls around himself as protection from whatever had happened in his childhood. Love and unconditional acceptance had changed the female who'd exited the cave, and perhaps if I could provide that to Ruslan, he would change for the better, too. Regardless of whether we were mates or not, he would understand that he could be loved.

And maybe I still needed to feel loved too, for I was far from healed from my own trauma, the nightmares still sinking their claws into me and flashbacks overtaking all reason as they transported me back to the cave.

I gingerly made my way to him, wrapping my arms around his large frame, fingertips barely touching as I embraced him. He released his hands from his face, encircling them around my waist while he buried his head in my chest. A hand smoothed back his black hair, the soothing touch seeming to relax him with each stroke. "Love and sex are not the same thing. Love is you teaching me to read your favorite book because you want to share something that is important to you. Love is flowers just because you thought of me. Love is riding in the wagon with me because I was cold. Love is revealing the parts of yourself that you would rather not have anyone else see, like when I told you about my nightmares. Love is all around you, and I will shine a light on each part that I can, for you."

He released my waist, then lifted his head from my chest. His sharp features were softened by sadness, his red-rimmed eyes turned a pale gray as he searched my face for a single shred of love. Reaching a hand up, he tucked a lock of hair behind my ear, sighing as I didn't flinch or pull away. "Will you sleep beside me tonight? Close to me?"

His raspy timbre held a shred of hope that I didn't dare destroy. "I will, but I would like something more comfortable to sleep in. Can you show me the options in the closet?"

Without warning, he scooped me into his arms, stealing my breath before carrying me all the way to the massive closet filled with more clothes than I'd ever seen before – even in my room in Este Castle. Placing me on a settee, he ambled to a chest of drawers, pulling at a few bronze handles, peeking inside before he found what he wanted.

"Will this work?" he asked, proffering a long-sleeved tunic that looked like it would be a full-length dress on me.

"Is this yours?" The fabric was soft, and I rubbed it between my fingers, eliciting a hint of cedarwood.

"Yes, but I want you to wear it so it's almost like I'm touching you," he murmured, dropping his head to look at his bare feet.

Rising, I accepted his offering, allowing the soft fabric to slide over my head and cascade down my body. It fell to my knees – much preferable to the slinky silk that hid nothing. I slipped the straps off my shoulders, pulling my arms through beneath Ruslan's shirt, then let the dress puddle on the floor. "Perfect."

Hand in hand, he steered me to the massive bed, an epic story painted across the wall behind it. It was breathtaking, with deep, dark colors highlighting moments of ecstasy and so many tiny details that I could stare for hours and not absorb the full impact of the fresco. The bed was piled with furs, and despite the roaring hearth across the room, a chill wracked my frame. Ruslan tugged back the thick pile of furs, then slid to the middle, gesturing for me to join him after I was hit with another shiver.

Gathering pillows, I crawled toward him, creating a little nest for myself to sleep in – just the way I liked it. Once I had everything arranged just so, I explained, "I'm going to sleep right here, and you can sleep right there, on the other side of the pillow. I'll be within reach, but I will be more comfortable this way."

He accepted the arrangement, though he looked crestfallen, throwing a muscled bicep over his eyes while I snuggled under the covers. I faced him, then tapped on his arm. He lifted it ever so slightly away from his face, exposing the hint of pain and loneliness I'd come to expect from him, then rolled to his side.

With a wave of his hand, he stole the light from the dim lamps that lined the walls until only the crackling fireplace offered a reprieve from the dark, casting just enough light that I could make out Ruslan's features.

"Will you tell me the story of the painting on this wall?" Ruslan's irascible side I could handle, though it left my heart racing and shoulders tense. The angsty side of him on display now was something unfamiliar that left my own emotions a mess, and I wanted to spark some life back into him.

"Of course," he replied, then launched into a tale of two lovers, one Angel and one Demon, destined to be together but forever kept apart. I closed my eyes while he weaved the tale, the wine relaxing me enough to soften the edge of the adrenaline that had run amok for the past few hours. Eventually, I stopped hearing Ruslan's words, his voice trailing off as he slipped into sleep. I allowed myself to fall as well, hoping Ruslan wouldn't catch me in the end.

12

KAZIMIR

We arrived at House Rass's estate just in time to witness a new foal burst into the world. As we crowded around the stall watching the little colt stand on shaky legs, memories of Izidora's first days with us flooded my mind, drowning me in a sea of her. The wariness that took weeks to disappear from her eyes, the first smile she gave me, and her fierce determination to conquer anything we threw her way...

I ran a hand over my face, taking a calming breath and squashing that incessant urge to jump back on Fek and race to the Iron Realm, seeking the female that had captivated me since before I ever saw her face. Izidora needed me, and losing my shit wouldn't help her or anyone. The fervent desire to throttle the next person who challenged me increased exponentially with each passing day, and that lid I locked over the chest that contained my grief threatened to burst free with it.

Liliana and Endre pressed their faces to the silver bars separating us from the stall where mare and foal became acquainted. Endre's hand subtly circled behind Liliana, resting on the warm wood panel and brushing her lower back. Envy clawed my throat, so violent that I had to swallow it down and walk away to maintain my cool. The mere idea that Endre had his person with him and I did not nearly broke me, over and over, throughout the day.

So I imagined her face, her lips, her body pressed against me, falling into familiar daydreams that entertained me in the nearly two decades I'd spent looking for Izidora. My life had been dedicated to saving her, but that was not what I wanted for our future. The life I'd built for us in my head was going to come to pass – that I could guarantee.

The chilled night air was like a slap to the face as I exited the warm stables. I inhaled deeply, the air burning my lungs in a way that was both refreshing and punishing. I welcomed the pain, the sharp sting numbing my inner turmoil in favor of an external sensation. Kaztar had left our party in the stables while he arranged rooms for us with his head of house. Finding him was my best option to stay sane, and sleeping would eat away at the time until I held Izidora in my arms again.

The estate was sprawling, without a fence or wall around it. Thick copses of trees scattered as far as the eye could see, flanked by riding rings filled with all types of equipment. In the distance, two low buildings squatted side by side, one for soldiers, the other for servants. The house itself was not really a house but a castle in its own right, with black spires jutting into the sky and a central tower overlooking the grounds and surrounding area. Around the back, a glassy lake reflected the stars, almost looking like a portal to another world.

As I pushed through the entrance, voices floated from a first-floor parlor, golden light spilling across polished oak floors in the darkness, and there I found Kaztar speaking with a male in uniform who bowed to me as I entered.

"My lord, I have arranged rooms for all of you on the second story. Your bags have been taken up already. Can I get you something to eat or drink?" Kaztar's head of house said.

"Something strong," I replied.

"We'll have two whiskeys and some snacks," Kaztar told him. He bowed, then left us.

"How's the foal?" Kaztar ran a hair through his black hair, straightening the pieces that had fallen loose during our ride here. His jade eyes carried a hint of concern as he examined me. Though he was only a few years older than me, he had been Head of House Rass since the tragic death of his father nearly a decade ago.

"He stood a moment before I left." I shrugged and dropped into a seat.

"Good, Domi's stress will not be so bad now that the mare has foaled. She was our highest-risk pregnancy this year."

"Domi cares deeply for her horses."

"That she does, along with many other causes. Izidora made quite the impression on her," Kaztar remarked.

The rumbling of a cart signaled the return of the servant. He entered, wordlessly laying out glasses, plates, snacks, and a decanter of amber liquid on the table in front of Kaztar. Kaztar nodded his thanks, then poured two hefty measures of whisky into glasses for us, handing me one.

"Thanks," I said appreciatively, then downed the whole glass in one gulp. The burn in my throat was welcome, and as I set my empty glass on the table, Kaztar poured more amber liquor into it.

"Kazimir, I know we aren't that great of friends, but I admire and respect you. If Domi had been taken from me, I would be a wreck. We males may pretend to be the strong ones, but without our females, we are nothing. I learned that the day I married Domi. Though it took her some time to warm up to me." He smiled and took a sip of his drink. "I may not have been part of the Nighthounds, and I can't replace the ones you lost, but I am honored to be riding among you now. I guess what I am trying to say is that I have your back through all of what's to come, Kazimir," he finished.

I studied my drink, swirling the ice through the amber, unable to respond to his kind words when the ones screaming through my mind told me that there was nothing admirable about a male who couldn't protect his own.

Domi saved me from responding, bounding into the room and throwing her arms around her husband, releasing a tension-filled sigh. Liliana, Endre, Viktor, and Vadim sauntered in moments later, all looking travel-worn and weary. "Zelle delivered a healthy foal. He is going to be perfect when he's older. His coloring matches your hair." She mussed his long locks as she spoke.

He gazed down at her, his eyes filled with absolute adoration for his wife. My glass was again more interesting than what was in front of me, and I downed the contents to distract myself, hissing as the burn worked its way down my throat. The grip I held on the glass was sure to crack the delicate detailing, but I could not seem to release the tension from my fingers, even as my head began buzzing and my body sank into the plush sofa. Viktor took a seat beside me, liquor falling from the decanter into his glass and then mine, while Liliana filled a plate with cheese, crackers, and dried meat, then settled on my opposite side.

At least I wasn't pinned between her and Endre.

"Izidora would have loved to see that foal," she sighed.

The alcohol was the only thing that kept me calm as Liliana reminded me, yet again, that Izidora was not here when she should be. "Yes, she would have."

Oblivious to my angst, Liliana continued, "Domi said that Izidora can name the foal once she returns. And that this foal being born today was a sign of good things to come. I hope she is right."

"As do I." I wanted to escape this conversation and these people. "I think I'll go to bed now." My head swam as I stood, but I managed to slur out, "Kaztar, which way to the second floor?"

He didn't look away from his wife to respond. "Out these doors, to the right, at the end of the hall there is a staircase. Your rooms are on the left side, facing the courtyard."

After I bid everyone good night, I made the trek, the rooms not so easily found when the Rass estate was nearly as large as Este Castle. Finally, I found the hall, low simmering lamps indicating that servants had been by recently. The first room was mine, and I locked the door behind me, not wanting to be disturbed. My mind was sinking into a chilled abyss, and no one could stop me from drowning other than my mate. It wasn't worth bothering my friends, who would only look at me with pity.

The bathroom held a shower, and I quickly washed myself beneath the falling water, a week's worth of grime disappearing as I wished the water would wash away the thoughts circling the drain in my mind.

My father...

The twins...

Kriztof...

My mate...

Shaking my head to clear the flashing images of the ones I'd lost, I turned the taps and walked naked and wet to my bags, digging through them until I retrieved those strips of lace that held Izidora's fading scent. Without bothering to dress or dry off, I took them and myself to the plush bed that awaited me, but just before I climbed into it, a knock sounded on the door. Endre's voice floated through. "Kazimir? Are you in there?"

Ignoring him, I threw back the blankets and hoped my silence would drive him away.

"I can hear your breathing, you know," he said, a little louder this time. I only looked at the ceiling, counting the seconds until he moved on.

His sigh was pained, and a soft thud told me he'd rested his weight against the door, head bowed into his forearm, a position I'd seen him take so many times. "Kazimir, I know you are suffering. You do not have to suffer alone. I'm next door when you want to talk."

His footsteps retreated and then reappeared in the room adjacent to mine. The soft click of the door signaled that he'd shut himself in for the night, though I listened for any other sounds indicating he was not alone. The bed creaked once, and then there was silence – at least in my surroundings, if not in my head.

This bed smelled nothing like Izidora. I brought the lace to my face, inhaling deeply as I imagined her beside me. An anguished sigh filled the room as I settled for grasping a pillow to me, covering the top in bits of lace so at least while I slept I might believe my mate was with me.

Sleep eluded me for so long that I lay in silent witness to Viktor, Vadim, and Liliana joining us on this lonely floor, whispering goodnight and settling into their respective rooms. Every time I closed my eyes, I was back in the ballroom at Este Castle, covered in blood, holding my father as he rasped his dying breath. Sometimes it was Izidora lying bloody in my arms, others it was Kriztof's execution in slow motion, each painful second spearing my soul as I watched over and over and over again.

These were not dreams, for sleep was a cruel mistress who would not visit me to carry me through time and closer to my mate. I defied her by fisting my cock and burying my face in the pillow, fucking my hand until my release was imminent, tingling down my spine and tightening my balls. Muffling a groan, I came, my hips jerking to a stop and body temporarily flooding with bliss. Mercifully, sleep let me fall into her, delivering much desired rest.

———

THE CRYSTAL REALM was the most ethereal of all the realms, with its vast, silky lakes stretching for miles in every direction and its lush, green grass that covered everything between them. Near the Agrenak Mountains, massive waterfalls cascaded over the remaining rocks, propelled by the melting glaciers. Unfortunately, the location of House Rass's estate led us straight into the heart of Crystal territory, avoiding the mountains completely as we rode toward the capital. I had been to Vlisa many times, but I never tired of the view each time I rounded the edge of the clear lake. Blire Palace floated above water so glassy it was a mirror perpetually reflecting the magnificence. The palace was constructed from massive crystals, and it was breathtaking in the late evening sun, each spire glittering and bending light into a rainbow of colors, the rays scattering across water so blue it looked painted rather than natural.

Blire's strategic advantage was that any attack could be seen for miles, the land surrounding the lakes flat with only a handful of trees clustered together like someone had captured a fistful of seeds and blown them from their palms, not caring which way they landed.

Small villages hugged the curves of the lake, and Crystal Fae, with their light-colored hair and lithe frames, fished and wove baskets with the reeds that clung to the banks. None paid us any attention as we passed, though the occasional small child would shriek and point at our mounts.

But as we closed in on the capital of the Crystal Realm, a retinue of mounted soldiers waited for us, their icy glares piercing even from a distance. The horses were as white as Izidora's wings, their coats glossy and their manes long and flowing, lifted by the light breeze dusting across the lake. The soldiers' armor was polished to perfection, the silver gleaming in the golden light of the setting sun. Their etherealness was nearly intimidating - definitely unnerving - but I was here to force King Airre and Queen Immonen to help me march on the Iron Realm and save my mate, and nothing and no one would stop me from achieving my goal.

When we rode within earshot, I shouted, "High Lords Vaszoly, Rass, Adimk, and Zadik of the Night Realm request an audience with King Airre and Queen Immonen!"

The soldier at the head of the procession scrutinized us, his piercing eyes taking in our travel-worn clothes and dark coloring before nodding his assent. "Follow me," he ordered, turning his mount back toward Vlisa. Spurring Fek on, we followed the decorated soldier, his legion waiting for us to pass before falling in stride behind us. I glanced at Viktor, whose face betrayed nothing of his thoughts, though a slight shake of his head was enough to tell me that he was unsure why we had a chaperone.

Could Ruslan have gotten word here first? Or had one of their seers had a vision of what heralded our arrival?

Kaztar angled his horse next to mine, dropping his voice so only I could hear his words. "I wasn't expecting an escort. What's the plan here?"

Dipping my head in his direction, I murmured, "I think we assess the mood of the monarchs, then go from there."

His jade eyes went to his wife before he replied. "You don't think they plan on harming us, do you?"

I shook my head. "If I had to guess, they already know why

we're here. The question is, how do they know and what have they decided?"

Vlisa bustled with activity as we rode the short distance through the city to the floating palace. Crystal Fae shopped for fresh produce at a market that sprawled across a large square while blonde children laughed as they tore through the streets, chasing one another until they nearly toppled a cart, earning a scolding from a mother and the shopkeep.

Life was normal in the city, while mine was anything but.

The opaline gates of Blire Palace swung open noiselessly, admitting us to the otherworldly splendor where King Airre and Queen Immonen waited with soft smiles on their faces. Our escort directed us straight across the white stone courtyard, stopping in front of his monarchs before dismounting and sweeping into a bow. We followed suit as a dozen pairs of metal boots clanked against the ground behind us. The hairs on the back of my neck rose only momentarily as King Airre glided forward with open arms.

"Kazimir! So great to see you again." King Airre looked just as young as the last time I had seen him, his white hair flowing past his shoulders, the sides braided back to reveal his high cheekbones and striking blue eyes. The Crystal Crown rested atop his brow, the rough-hewn shards seeming to glow from within as the sun hit them. His embrace was friendly and warm without a trace of deceit, and as he stepped back, I clasped my muscled arm around his lithe one in greeting.

"King Airre, it is a pleasure indeed, though I wish it were under better circumstances."

"Indeed, my friend, but we'll speak on that later." His expression fell only slightly before he schooled his features and moved along to Kaztar.

Queen Immonen waited to take his place. She reminded me of a swan, her frame light and airy with a long, elegant neck. Her headpiece was not rough like her husband's, but rather decorated with perfectly cut and polished stones that refracted the slight and scattered it around her like a halo. Her platinum hair was loose and flowing around her, and she smiled sweetly as she grasped my hands, planting a kiss on both cheeks. "Kazimir, I had a vision of your mate. She is most beautiful, and I cannot wait to meet her. Though I do not see her among your group." Her brows pinched as her clear eyes scanned the faces around me.

"That is actually why we are here, Your Majesty. You see, she has –"

The queen cut me off before I could finish. "Let's not ruin our joyous reunion with talk of politics. There is time for that later."

Through gritted teeth, I offered her a smile, then replied, "Of course, I look forward to tasting some of the Crystal Realm's fine wines over dinner."

My nails dug into my palms until they drew a hint of blood as she patted my cheek, and with elegant grace turned her attention to the rest of the Night Realm's representatives.

There was no time for all this bullshit. Every second away from Izidora was a chance for Ruslan to hurt her, and every time I thought of his smug grin as he ordered his soldiers to drug her, a little piece of me died inside.

I had to play their game if I wanted any chance of making it out of the Iron Realm alive, which meant we had to wine and dine them before we would get the answer I would not leave without.

"Come, we will show you to your rooms! Dinner is in an hour, so you will have plenty of time to freshen up." Queen Immonen clapped her hands in delight, then spun on her heel, her blue dress floating along behind her as she and her mate led us through the open crystal doors and into the glamorous palace. King Airre pulled his wife into his side, planting an affectionate kiss on her cheek, and my heart ached as they shared that intimate moment with us.

Endre appeared at my side, his face etched with concern and words on his lips, but I kept my head forward, deciding I would rather feel the sting of jealousy than the pity of my friend. "We will get her back, brother," Endre said, low enough that only I could hear.

"We're losing time," I ground out, flexing my fingers.

"Izidora is strong, a lot stronger than the female we rescued the first time, thanks to you. You taught her well. She will be okay."

Endre was right, but my instincts had driven me into this obsessive madness. "But I am not okay with her so far from me."

"Of course you're not. She is your mate. I do not dare to say that I understand your feelings, yet that does not change that you are my brother and I support you to the end."

His validation lifted some of that tension that had become a permanent attachment to my chest and shoulders, and a breath escaped me easier than it had in over a week. "Thanks, Endre."

Somehow my friend always got me talking, even when I didn't want to, and each time, a weight lifted from my chest after sharing my inner thoughts. I was not alone in my fight, and I needed to remember that when I was drowning in despair.

"Here we are!" Queen Immonen announced as we entered a long hallway with windows overlooking the lake. At the end, a set of double doors inlaid with gold filigree opened to reveal a living space bathed in the light colors of the Crystal Realm.

"Wow!" Liliana's seafoam green eyes were wide as saucers, mouth slightly agape as she trailed her hand along the smooth walls. The nearly invisible window overlooking water caught her attention next. "It's so clear! I can see all the way to the bottom from here."

Domi's eyes roamed the lofted ceiling that was seemingly lit from within, scattering light around the immaculate room. "Queen Immonen, you must take Liliana and I on a tour later. I simply did not see enough on my last visit, and I am still enchanted by your beautiful home," she said, running her hand across the back of a chair that looked more like a cloud.

"Of course! We will leave the males to talk of boring subjects while we enjoy ourselves," she laughed. "A servant will return to fetch you for dinner. Please make yourselves comfortable in the meantime."

With a quick bow to our departing hosts, I sauntered to a sky-blue chair and made myself comfortable, closing my eyes as I released the lingering tension from our armored encounter.

"I thought for sure we were goners," Liliana groaned as she flopped to one of the blush-colored couches.

"If you can't tell, the Crystal Realm has a flair for the dramatic," Viktor noted as he sank down next to her. "The escort likely was meant as a respectful gesture. With how the last few months have gone, I automatically expected the worst."

As did I.

"If you'll excuse us, I'd like to lie down for a bit before we eat," Domi said, leading Kaztar into one of the bedrooms and closing the door behind them.

I tore my eyes from their retreating forms when Endre cleared his throat. "What do you think of Blire Palace so far, Liliana?" He tried so hard to win and maintain her attention, though he tried to hide it from the rest of us. Only Vadim remained oblivious, almost willfully so. A small smile almost tugged at my lips as I remembered Vadim's comment about my father seeming willfully ignorant of my affection for Izidora, only for my lips to dip into a frown at the memory of his last words to me.

"It is the most incredible building I have ever seen. How is it possible to make a building from crystal like this? All of the houses and shops in Vlisa were made from whitewashed stones, so different from the Night Realm. I cannot wait to see more later," Liliana gushed.

A knock sounded on the door, and a Crystal Fae dressed in white waltzed in with a rack full of clothes. "I have brought formal attire for this evening's dinner," he said by way of greeting.

"Oh, clothes!" Liliana exclaimed, racing toward the male, who disappeared just as quickly as he arrived. I crossed the room to join her in selecting attire, fingering the fine fabrics in an attempt to find a color that matched my mood. Black pants and a light blue tunic caught my attention, their cut simple yet refined.

Viktor and Endre grabbed the last of the masculine-colored tunics, much to the dismay of Vadim, who grumbled the whole way from his comfortable couch to the rack in the entryway. Liliana handed him the blush tunic, teasing, "It goes perfectly with your eyes!"

"But it would go better with yours, so why don't you wear it?" he protested, holding it out to her.

"Because, I am wearing this." Liliana held a shimmery gray dress to her body, twirling and fluttering the light fabric. Endre's swallow was audible as his eyes followed her every movement, a wayward lock of hair falling into his face completely ignored. Ignoring the hollow pit in my stomach, I smirked, imagining what the night would bring once everyone realized there were only three rooms in the suite.

"Viktor, trade with me," Vadim demanded.

"I don't think so. The white makes me look powerful and innocent. Great for wheeling and dealing. Pink makes me look easily taken advantage of," he chuckled.

"When you put it that way..." Vadim sported a wolfish grin. "I'd love to be taken advantage of by a Crystal female."

Liliana's eye-roll was severe. "You're such a slut, Vadim. I'm going to change, see you dumbfucks in a few."

She sashayed her hips as she left us, throwing a heated look over her shoulder at Endre, whose grip on his gray tunic was white-knuckled. Elbowing him in the ribs, I broke his trance, and he joined me in stripping in the foyer, no boundaries left after years spent together. Vadim complained the whole time he changed, while Viktor barely stifled his smile as Vadim buttoned the pink shirt over his broad chest and swept his long hair into a messy top knot.

Kaztar and Domi emerged once we were dressed, and Domi selected a lilac dress to match Kaztar's leftover lavender tunic.

"Don't worry, Vadim, pink is a brave color," Kaztar joked when he saw Vadim's obvious disdain for his attire.

As if they knew we had all dressed for dinner – which was likely, given that the Crystal Fae were gifted with sight – the same servant reappeared to escort us to dinner.

It was an intimate affair in a pearlescent room complete with a cheery, bubbly fountain carved from white marble to look like a mermaid. The whitewashed wood table was only large enough to seat our party and the king and queen, and water lilies adorned the length of the table, bunching together in front of Kaztar and myself seated beside the monarchs, and then trickling down until there was nothing but curled petals on the end of the table in front of Liliana and Endre.

Even the wine glasses were carved from gleaming natural stones, and my stomach curdled as I realized how much gold the Crystal Realm must have spent buying such luxuries from the Iron Realm, whose mountains were tall and thick with precious gems.

Would they risk their relationship with their supplier in order to help us?

Shoving aside my intrusive thoughts, I lifted my glass, the white wine inside it betraying a slight tremble in my hand, and toasted King Airre and Queen Immonen. "We thank you once again for your hospitality, Your Majesties, and may the Goddess bless both of you."

"Cheers!" everyone echoed, and I sipped the crisp liquid that reminded me of fresh fall apples and sweet summer melons.

Talk remained on light topics as an appetizer of a yellow squash soup was served and cleared by lithe females that Vadim eyed a bit too eagerly. Their wispy dresses floated around them as they served the main dish, a pink fish coated in a creamy garlic sauce with a side of wild rice and perfectly steamed vegetables. The fish flaked on my fork and melted over my tongue as conversation flowed as easily as the wine up and down the table. The mood turned jovial by the time our filets were nothing more than errant pieces of pink, and I found myself laughing along as the alcohol swept away all my fear and grief.

A fluffy chocolate mousse rounded off our dinner, its sweetness as delectable as what lay between my mate's thighs. My cock twitched at the thought of her, but I clamped down on my daydream before it took root in my brain, refocusing on the task at hand – negotiating for help bringing back what was mine.

Dessert in the Crystal Realm was meant to be enjoyed, and King Airre patted his flat stomach beneath his icy blue tunic when he'd polished off the last of the mousse. "I cannot eat another bite."

His wife's eyes sparkled as she trailed her fingers along his arm. "Nor should you. I have foreseen what will happen if you continue to snack on desserts when you think I am not looking."

He snorted, and I suppressed a smile as she teased her mate.

"Why don't I take the ladies on a tour while you retire to the drawing room for drinks?"

King Airre plucked his wife's hand from his arm and brought it to his lips. "That would be lovely, mate. But I shall miss you."

I swore Domi and Liliana swooned in their seats, soft sighs leaving their lips as King Airre planted his on Queen Immonen's hand. She batted her lashes at him, then pushed away from the table and beckoned for the love-struck females to join her. "Come, I've been dying to show off the latest addition to our wing. I told Airre for years I wanted a larger shower and..." Her lilting voice trailed off as they disappeared through the doors.

"Shall we?" King Airre said, throwing his napkin on the table and rising. Chairs scraped as we followed him into a distinctly masculine room, pelts and trophy kills lining the light oak panels boxing us in.

"What's your poison?" the king of the Crystal Realm asked, rummaging around behind a small stone bar, pulling glasses and bottles of all types from below and placing them on the bartop.

"We'll have what you're having, Your Majesty," Kaztar replied.

"Vodka it is. And please, let's speak informally." He proceeded to pour the chilled clear liquid across six glasses with near perfect precision before dropping a fat frozen plum in each and handing them out. With a tinkle of glass, he cheered, "To our health!"

The bite was nearly nonexistent though the burn down my throat was welcome as I sipped from my drink. I noticed that a sunken space in the floor held a white fur rug – the bear's head still attached – and a ring of leather couches beckoned us to begin our conversation.

"So tell me, Kazimir, what is the reason for your visit? My seers have had many visions of late, some changing by the day. I am concerned for the fate of our lands." King Airre's white brows pinched together as he sipped from his drink.

"I will spare you the details – unless you would like to hear them – but in short, King Zalan is dead, and our new queen, Izidora, was taken by King Azim's son."

His face paled, and the slight shake of his hand as he took another swig betrayed his unease. "It is as I feared. Queen Immonen saw Izidora, who I believe is your mate, yes?"

A single nod was all I could manage around the lump in my throat.

"And you have accepted the bond?"

His words opened the gate that contained every piece of my shattered heart, and my shoulders slumped forward as I put my pain on full display. "No, for I did not know until the passing of my father."

"My seers saw much death at the Night Realm, and I am sorry to hear High Lord Cazius was among those killed. He was a strong male, and he will be missed," King Airre acknowledged.

"We lost several other friends when Ruslan attacked Este Castle," Viktor added.

"Ah yes, this is King Azim's son?" King Airre clarified.

"Yes, bastard son apparently, yet still his heir apparent. He claimed that Izidora was rightfully his due to an agreement between King Zalan and King Azim prior to her birth," Viktor explained, setting his drink aside and leaning forward.

"I was unaware King Azim had an heir, so this agreement is also news to me. And he simply showed up because Princess Izidora was found?"

A glance from Viktor told me I needed to reveal Izidora's story. "We found the princess chained in a cave in Vasvain. We killed a dozen Iron Fae soldiers to rescue her, and on our journey to Vaenor, we were attacked repeatedly. We fled to my family's home to seek refuge until our safe passage to Este Castle was guaranteed. She suffered greatly at the hands of the Iron Fae, and I fear for her life as we speak. Ruslan also mentioned that she was part of a prophecy – one that would ensure kings fell. He bragged of a plan to conquer the continent with her help. While we traveled with Izidora, she displayed magic unlike anything we had ever seen. It is pure white, and she is extremely powerful." I left it at that, holding the secret that she was half Angel close to my chest.

Viktor added, "Ruslan's claim reminded Endre of the Goddess's Prophecy, though when we searched the library for any mention of it, the pages had been burned or ripped from the books that contained them. Are you aware of this prophecy?"

A frown tugged at the king's lips, and he knocked back the rest of his drink before reaching for the bottle of clear liquor and pouring a hefty measure for himself and anyone else who looked short on drink. "It is a prophecy spoken millennia ago, but one that has haunted me since I heard it. I sensed, even as a small child, that it would come to pass during my reign. If Izidora is one of the predicted from the prophecy, then I fear our world will fundamentally change." He lifted the glass to his forehead, closing his eyes for a moment. "Immonen's visions have increased in frequency, sometimes ailing her for hours on end. She is frantic when she emerges from them, exhaustion bruising her eyes and too-kind heart. She cannot remember every detail, she says, because they are constantly swirling and changing."

During the funeral rites, the High Priestess – possibly the Goddess – had said something very similar, and a creeping sensation crawled up my spine. "Shit," I swore, collapsing against the plush back of the couch behind me.

"She sees Izidora in all of them, though."

His words brought silence to the room as if he had leveled an execution blow.

"She has mentioned on several occasions that she believes

the Goddess and the Fates are battling over the direction of our future, which is why she sometimes sees light and other times sees dark – which tracks with the Goddess's Prophecy."

Viktor and Vadim released a string of curses beside me, while Endre turned a shade of pale that rivaled King Airre. Only Kaztar seemed unfazed.

"Seems straightforward to me. We need Izidora to follow the light," Kaztar shrugged.

A growl escaped my throat, guttural and raw as my feelings. "Prophecies are meant to be vague and open to interpretation. You assume you already know what that light is? What if it is her death?"

Viktor placed a hand on my shoulder, pulling me back against the leather couch. Perhaps I should have had less to drink in my volatile state, but it was too late. "I spent the majority of my life searching for the lost princess, only to discover that she is in fact my mate." My chest heaved as I bit out each word, my neck and shoulders growing hot as my fear masked itself as rage. "I will not lose her after everything I have done to get her." What happened to Izidora while we wasted time conversing was outside of my control, but I could unleash my inner turmoil on the male who only looked coolly at me from his seat.

"I'm going to give you a pass right now because I know this is not your true self, Kazimir," Kaztar snapped. He opened his mouth to say something else, but Vadim interrupted him.

"Alright, knock it off." Vadim leveled a pointed look between us. "We have a common enemy here, and he does not sit in this room. Let's focus on that."

The storm still raged within me, but Vadim was right. My palm rubbed my face as I reminded myself that acting from a place of stability was better than acting irrationally. King Airre studied me, and I allowed him to see how much I struggled.

"We will get your mate back, Kazimir. Yet we must think strategically if we want to proceed with the fewest casualties. I am assuming you have formed some plan, at least?" He quirked a brow, waiting for a response.

Viktor laid out our plans. "We have gathered an army and are sending them in the direction of the pass that divides the Iron and Day Realms. They are only a few days behind us. We are seeking your help and that of Queen Victoria and King Geza of the Day Realm to wage war on the Iron Realm. It is clear they plan to conquer our lands, and we need to be prepared. If we can mobilize quickly, they may not have enough time to do the same. While we attend Béke as if nothing is amiss, our armies will gather at the border and attack while we have an advantage."

"Béke is a time to celebrate peace," King Airre argued. "You would dare upset the Goddess by disturbing it?"

"It seems to me like she wishes for a resolution. She appeared to us during the funeral for our fallen, berating us for not following her guidance," Viktor replied.

The king of the Crystal Realm swirled the clear liquor around the fat plum in his glass. "Immonen's visions would indicate the same," he sighed, as if he were resigned to his fate. "Let us convene tomorrow with my council to discuss war plans."

And with that declaration, the corner of my mouth finally rose in a smile. "Thank you, King Airre."

He dipped his head, then knocked back the last of his drink. "Do you need an escort to your room?"

"I think we can manage. I wish you a good night, Your Majesty."

We took his hint, leaving him with the half-empty bottle of vodka, and pushed into the hallway lined with vase after expensive vase. The halls in Blire Palace were wide and uncomplicated with sharp corners, and within ten minutes we found ourselves standing in front of the doors to our suite, feminine laughter floating beneath them. Domi and Liliana held glasses of wine, their legs tucked beneath them as they giggled conspiratorially with our entrance.

"Oh no, what did you two do?" Vadim groaned as Liliana glanced at us with a mischievous glint in her eyes.

"There's only three bedrooms, and Domi and Kaztar already claimed one." Her cheeks were flushed and she pressed her lips together to contain a bout of laughter.

Vadim scratched his head for only a moment before his hand dropped to his side like a stone. Viktor sniggered as he arrived at the conclusion first, while Endre's cheeks flamed as he nonchalantly sidestepped away from Vadim.

"You and I will share," Vadim hissed.

"Ew, no. You can sleep with Kazimir and Viktor."

"Kazimir has a mate, why don't you share a bed with him?" Vadim demanded.

Domi hid her laugh behind the crystal wine glass, while I bit my lip to contain my own.

"Because Izidora is my best friend and that would also be weird," she snorted.

Vadim rubbed his temples as his sister played him like a violin, finally realizing she'd trapped him between choosing Viktor and Endre as her bedmate. Maybe he would finally acknowledge that his sister had liked Endre since she was old enough to show interest in males. We waited with bated breath and stifled laughter for Vadim's response.

"Don't these couches look comfortable?" His voice rose as tried and failed to stretch out on one, the dainty seating no match for his large frame. Kaztar choked on a laugh, and that was all it took to burst the bubble that held the room captive.

"Liliana wants to share a bed with Endre and has for years,

brother. It's time to get your head out of your ass," Viktor teased, clasping Vadim on the shoulder.

Vadim's glare bounced between Liliana and Endre. "If I hear anything, and I mean anything, coming from that room, I am coming in. I will break down the door if I have to. Mother and father will murder me if they find out I let this happen." Then his gaze landed on Endre. "Take care of my sister, or I will chop off your dick and wear it like a trophy."

Domi spluttered her wine, and we all roared with laughter as Endre flushed the shade of Vadim's tunic. Before he could say anything, Liliana hopped from her seat and yanked Endre by the hand into the bedroom, the door closing with a click.

"I'm going to take that as my cue to go to bed. We've got a big day ahead of us now that King Airre has joined our cause," Kaztar grinned at his wife.

"He agreed?" Domi gasped, rising to her feet, looking at each of us for confirmation.

"He did." Kaztar planted a kiss on her forehead, then led her to their room. "See you in the morning."

"I am calling a bed by myself." I leaped over the chair that blocked my path to the last available bedroom, Viktor and Vadim hot on my heels. We wrestled in the doorway until Viktor broke through our tangle and claimed the smallest bed for himself. Vadim and I flopped on the other, and the lightness and laughter with my friends soothed the deep ache in my soul, that empty part of the bond that called out to my mate all hours of the day.

"I'm sleeping naked," Vadim announced before throwing off all his clothes, his pink tunic landing over my eyes before I snatched it away.

"It's not the first or last time I'll see your dick. It's a shame you are a grower and not a shower," I joked. Viktor barked a laugh, and Vadim glowered at me with a look that said 'the-fuck-I-am'.

"Night, dickheads," Viktor teased, then banished the lights.

Stripping out of my clothes in the darkness, I snatched a blanket at the foot of the bed to cover myself, then allowed my drunken thoughts to wander as I relished the small victory of gaining our first ally.

13

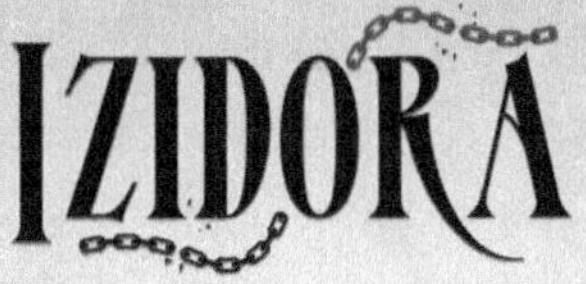

Fire burned all around me, yet I was not afraid. The fire was comforting, familiar almost, caressing my cheek like a lover. The flames were white, yet a hint of black broke through, so subtle that I had to focus on the undulating wisp to see it again. The inky flame held ill intent, and I backed into the safety of the white fire to rid myself of it. Yet it advanced, swallowing the white flames, until all that surrounded me was dark fire. A laugh, menacing and low, echoed around me, first resounding in one ear, then the other, as it trickled through the flames.

"Who's there?" I called, bravery filling my bones.

"Your worst nightmare." The male's voice was sinister, bathing my spine in cold sweat that was immediately banished by the black flames leaping onto my skin and burning me as they forced my mouth open, engulfing my throat as I burned from the inside out. Screams shredded my throat, but my cries were swallowed by more choking flames—

I bolted upright, clutching my throat, sputtering as my breath came and went in short, desperate gasps. Cold air bit into my skin, grounding me to the present moment as I opened my eyes. Black stone walls flecked with bits of gold stared back at me, not a hint of fire in the massive room. The events of the previous night, of Ruslan's tongue lapping chocolate off my skin, flooded my memory and I dropped my gaze to my torso, heaving a sigh of relief when I saw the large tunic I was swimming in. All the warmth had leached from the rooms, and I whipped my head to where Ruslan had lain the night before only to find him gone, an indentation from his body the only sign he had occupied the space. It was cold to the touch.

The windows were covered by black cloth, and I wondered what time it was. The only light in the space was cast by the open bathroom door, and I scurried in that direction, hoping Ruslan did not await me there.

It was mercifully empty, and when I approached the windows, I saw that the mountains cast spiked shadows across the land, the sun not quite high enough to breach their snow-covered peaks.

It was still early.

Turning the knobs for the shower, I stripped out of Ruslan's oversized tunic, wanting to wash the smell of him off of me before I became drunk on the highs and lows of him. This feeling of never knowing what was next was addicting, especially under his smoky scrutiny that sent heat straight to my core. The steam beckoned me forward, and I groaned as the healing spring water coated my skin, chasing away the stone rooms' perpetual chill.

As I lathered lavender-scented soap across my body, my thoughts returned to Ruslan. He was mercurial – sometimes teasing, sometimes furious, and sometimes vulnerable. His triggers were rapid and all consuming, one moment everything fine, the next, everything gone to hell. But he liked the game, he liked the chase, he liked my fire. So I would have to give him what he wanted, not too easily, but just enough to keep him chasing, to keep him engaged enough to open up about his past, the breeding program, and any abilities I suspected he knew I possessed.

He wanted me as a weapon after all.

After shutting off the flow of water and wrapping myself in a towel to lock in the warmth, I perused the walk-in closet, opening drawers, searching shelves, and sliding hangers until I found a suitable pair of pants and cropped tunic to wear. Hunting among the shoes, I spotted a pair of slippers much too large for my small feet and slid into them, wiggling my toes in their fur lining.

Closing my eyes and bracing myself for my first encounter with Ruslan for the day, I slipped through the door to the living space.

But Ruslan was not there, and there was no sign that he had been.

My heart skipped a beat as I realized I was utterly alone.

Was this my chance to escape?

There was no way to take the elevator out of here, but I had wings, and I could fly. Spinning to the spiral stairs Ruslan had pointed out last night, I raced to them, then bounded up two at a time. When I skidded to a stop at the top of the stairs, I called my glittering white wings to my back, hoping that the fabric of my shirt would be magically enhanced. A rush of joy filled my lungs along with a deep breath when my magic flooded my veins, wings popping into existence behind me. I didn't even wince as I flapped them, my back muscles growing stronger with each day.

I regarded my wings for only a moment before my eyes were drawn to a metal hatch notched into the ceiling, and I pulled myself onto the rungs of a ladder built into the wall, my short stature rendering me unable to reach overhead to lift it. It was unlocked, and with all the force I could muster, I pushed the heavy iron door up inch by inch. My wings did not falter at the touch of iron, instead pumping behind me, propelling me upward. Finally, with one last forceful exhale, the door swung over itself, landing with a thud on the roof. I held my breath, certain the door had alerted someone to my presence, but after a moment, all remained still.

Scrambling up the remaining rungs of the ladder, I jettisoned myself onto the smooth rock of the roof, then pushed myself upright, wiping my palms on my pants. A gale blowing down from the mountain tops nearly took me down, and if not for my wings instinctually counterbalancing me, I would have dropped straight back into the hole.

Glorious golden light caressed my face as the morning sun crested the mountain tops, and I inhaled the fresh mountain air, crisp with the coming winter. A gust of wind blew my loose, wet hair in all directions, tangling the long strands in front of my face and blinding me. For a moment, I swore I heard Kazimir's voice whispering by me, but my attention was snagged by a forceful shiver, and I groaned as that rib started to ache.

Shit, I should have grabbed a coat.

There was no way I would make it far in this cold, especially flying among the strong gusts. I'd barely made it off the ground in previous attempts to fly, but this might be my only chance of escape. Torn between fear of death and fear of powerlessness, I hesitated. With a strangled groan torn away by the wind, I closed the door to the suite, then rushed to the railing, peering over the edge of the roof to identify any potential obstacles. The ground looked so far away, and images of plummeting to my death flashed in my mind, my stomach flipping over and forcing me to choose a different path.

I raced to the opposite end of the roof, this side closer to the mountain peaks. But Ruslan had been clever in his design of the palace, and although one would think that entering the mountains from this direction would be easy, the sharp, jagged rocks that waited like the maw of a dragon argued otherwise. If my wings failed me here, I would be impaled without question.

Plagued with indecision, I decided to take my chances over the serrated rocks. Some distance away, there was a flat landing.

If I could only make it there, I could rest and continue on.

Hopping to the top rung of the railing, I used my wings to balance as I steeled myself for the leap I was about to take.

The metal hatch banged against the rock behind me, and I leaped into the air, wings flapping furiously as I spun to see Ruslan's dark, slicked-back hair emerging through it. He hadn't seen me yet, so I flapped away from the edge, trying to appear as if I were casually testing out my wings rather than plotting an escape.

His smoldering eyes crested the hole, followed by his broad shoulders, and his perpetual smirk widened as he took in my wings. His palms splayed across the smooth rock, and corded muscle rippled in his arms as he hoisted himself onto the roof, leaving the door open behind him. "Going somewhere?" he purred.

Swallowing down the fear that clawed its way up my throat, I landed lightly in front of him, plastering a cool mask on my face. "Just stretching my wings. I don't have a death wish." I motioned around me to the obvious death trap that awaited unconfident fliers. "And I haven't used my magic in days. It was starting to itch." I crossed my arms and rolled my eyes as if it should be obvious why I would be up here.

"Well, I'm glad to see your magic well is full enough for what I have planned today," he hinted, and I knew he wanted me to ask what that was, playing on my near-insatiable curiosity.

I caved. "Oh? What is that?"

"We are meeting with Rares. I want him to look you over and test your abilities. Depending on what he finds, you may start training with the Angel in residence to hone your magic," he announced.

My brows shot up, though my surprise competed with rising bile over meeting the man responsible for the misery of my mother and countless other innocents. I let Ruslan see none of that, instead saying, "I look forward to meeting him. I have heard so much about him."

"Good," Ruslan crooned. "Because you and I are his greatest creations. Come, let's eat before we go." He was back to his usual impish, aggressive behavior today, which I much preferred to the despair that had tugged on my heartstrings the night before.

Without taking his gray eyes off of me, he leaped through the trap door, then motioned for me to climb down the ladder. Banishing my wings with a sigh, I climbed down the first few rungs, then was swept off the ladder by large hands gripping my hips. Ruslan placed me gently on the ground, leaving one hand in place while the other pulled and latched the door above us. Then we wound down, down, down, until we landed in the living space where the homelike aroma of cinnamon wafted in my direction, and my mouth watered at the thought of my favorite treat.

My nostrils flared, lashes fluttering as I inhaled the scent like it was my own personal drug, and Ruslan hummed. "I heard that you had an affection for cinnamon rolls. I had Cedomir run out for the ingredients this morning. He's a bit adventurous with his recipes, so you'll have to tell me if you don't like his twist on the classic."

Ruslan guided me to a chair, then proceeded to pile my plate with eggs, bacon, and a miniature cinnamon roll topped with white frosting, lightly torched to harden it. It smelled heavenly, the cinnamon and vanilla joining in a perfect union. Ruslan sat opposite me as I pinched the small pastry in between my fingers, taking half of it in one bite. The light crunch of the hardened frosting offset the warm, fluffy texture of the roll, creating a symphony of flavor and sensation in my mouth. I groaned automatically, unable to help myself, and shoved the rest into my mouth. I didn't care how unqueenly I looked, this was the good shit.

Ruslan's eyes sparkled with amusement as he placed another on my plate. "You need to eat some meat if you want energy to last all day."

"Fine," I sighed, then tucked into the eggs and bacon before finishing off three more heavenly pastries.

Ruslan plucked one of the delectable rolls from the center of the table before piling double my helping of eggs and bacon onto his own plate.

That must have been how he got so big.

He wore a short-sleeved tunic that was tight on his arms, his tattooed biceps flexing and rolling as he lifted his fork to his mouth. The rest of the tunic left nothing to the imagination, and I drank in the muscle on top of muscle that spread across the planes of his chest and shoulders.

He winked when he noticed my scrutiny, and his eyes pooled with a smoldering darkness that sent heat to my core. The way he looked at me made me feel like I was the most alluring female to grace this world, and I was his only reason for living, his next breath determined by me alone. It should have scared me, how intensely he desired me, but instead, my toes curled against the fur of his slippers, and thoughts of his tongue on my folds slipped into my mind.

His nostrils flared, and the corner of his mouth twitched upward. He poured two steaming glasses of tea into mugs, then handed one to me.

"What's this?" I sniffed the slightly green liquid, but there was no scent.

His brows shot up his forehead. "You don't know?"

I placed the mug on the table and pushed it away from me as if it were something poisonous. "Know what?"

"It's a contraceptive tea. To prevent pregnancy. You haven't had it before?"

My fingers curled into my palms in my lap.

Why had Kazimir never given me this, especially after I told him how I felt about children?

I snatched the mug and gulped it down, disregarding the burn on my tongue.

Ruslan's warm hand pulled the mug away from my face, his brows dipping together. "Woah, what's going on here?"

"I've never had it before. Never even heard of it. And more than anything, I do not want children."

Another item on the list of interactions with Kazimir that left a bitter taste in my mouth.

A muscle worked in Ruslan's jaw, and this time I knew it was not because of my actions. "We only have to take them once a month, since Fae cycles are longer than Shifter or Mage cycles. The tea will prevent any unwanted pregnancies. I will make sure you always have it on time, Izidora."

"Thank you." The words came out bitter, but my harshness was not directed at him.

He seemed to understand, because his eyes did not flash at my tone. "For what it's worth, I do not want children either. After everything that happened to me..." He trailed off, and I did not need him to finish his sentence to empathize with him, because it mirrored my own beliefs.

"How will I know... what are the signs..." I began, unsure how to finish my question.

"That you're pregnant?" Ruslan cracked his knuckles, hands shaking with barely contained rage.

I nodded, head falling to my chest, but a finger lifted my chin, and his expression was a stormy mix of anger and pity.

"I hate that I am the one telling you this. Fuck! I hate that *he–*" Ruslan's teeth clenched on that word, "did not take care of you in this way. You are so young and yet your soul is aged beyond its years. You have the most beautiful soul, Izidora, and I hope you know that my desire for you goes far beyond the physical." He released a sigh with his confession. "If you aren't throwing up every morning, you aren't pregnant."

My chest eased with his words, and a hand fluttered over my heart. "Thank you, Ruslan, for not hiding anything from me."

He only nodded and leaned back in his chair, closing his eyes and tipping his head back. He took three deep breaths before reopening his iron eyes.

With an itch to change the subject and discover more about the realm, I asked, "How will we get to wherever it is that Rares does his work?"

"We'll go to Ryza Citadel on horseback. It's beneath it, for protection."

I swallowed my nerves. "And to get down to the stables we have to take the... lift?"

"Is my sprite afraid?" His tone was velvety with a hint of teasing, one that I wouldn't mind hearing again.

I needed to stop thinking like that.

"Yes," I admitted, my fear of using the lift outweighing my fear of appearing weak.

"I can take us down slower, but trust me, you'll like the speed someday soon." His smirk told me he wasn't only referring to the lift.

My cheeks heated, and I cleared my throat. "I need a jacket or cloak and some boots – it is too cold for me to go anywhere wearing only this." I gestured to my thin tunic.

"I'm glad you asked. I have a gift for you." A soft wrapped package appeared from beneath the table, and Ruslan handed it to me with unveiled excitement. "Open it," he encouraged when I eyed it cautiously.

When he released the navy ribbon, the shimmering paper fell away to reveal a soft gray cloak lined with snow-white fur. Pushing away from the table, I shook out the fabric and wrapped it around myself, securing the luxurious gift with a square white diamond at my throat.

"The fur is from hares that live high in the mountains. They are extremely difficult to catch, but it is the warmest fur in all the continents. Since you seem to chill easily, I wanted you to have something warm enough for the Iron Realm. It is especially cold here during the winter."

Who knew such small gestures would be the ones that would ruin me?

His thoughtfulness chipped another crack in my resolve against him, and with my earlier revelation regarding Kazimir and contraception, I worried that the scales were beginning to tip in Ruslan's favor. There was so much thrown into question with my relationship with Kazimir, and I was dying to speak with him, hoping that these issues were oversight and not intentional.

"The cloak is beautiful. Thank you for thinking of me, Ruslan."

"Is that love?"

"Noticing the needs of others, then helping them – that is love."

His smile was devastating, the darkness that swirled around him dissipating enough to reveal a side of the male that was damning. He looked less the broken prince and more a benevolent king, and I caught a glimpse of what could be in his eyes. If it turned out that he was my mate, there was hope he could change for the better.

"One more thing," he said, motioning for me to round the

table to his side. A box sat on the chair next to his, and he lifted it out of my way so I could sit. With the box in his lap, he removed the lid to reveal black leather ankle boots lined with the same snow white fur.

My heart sighed and tears pricked my eyes as his every act of thoughtfulness flashed through my mind. *This palace, the closet filled with clothes, and no other female setting foot here. The cloak and shoes to keep me warm. Sending his chef out to gather ingredients for my favorite treat.*

No matter his father's plans for me, Ruslan only wanted me – us – to be happy, and that was becoming more apparent every moment I spent with him. My heart was at war with itself over the broody, enigmatic male before me, and my mind warred over who lied and who told the truth between Kazimir and Ruslan.

Needing a distraction from the back and forth of my thoughts, I lifted my leg to pull the shoe on. Ruslan tsked, and I stilled, watching him as he grasped my foot with one hand while the other lifted the boot from the box. He planted a light kiss on the top of my foot before sliding the boot on, then repeated the process on my other side, until my toes were warm and cozy in the soft fur lining my new shoes. He still wore that damning smile when he finished lacing both boots for me.

It was nice to be taken care of.

"Ready to go?" he inquired.

I placed both feet on the ground, my weight sinking into the cushioned soles of the shoes. "Slowly," I reminded him of his promise as I followed him to the suite doors.

With a flick of his wrist, the doors swung wide, allowing us to pass through. He closed them in a similar manner, then took to opening the iron doors that hid the lift. The platform awaited our descent, and I sucked down a few calming breaths before stepping onto the stone beside Ruslan. The iron doors swung shut, and the stone beneath my feet jerked. My heart leaped to my throat while my knees buckled, sending me stumbling to the side.

Strong hands grasped my arm before I could tumble to the ground. "I've got you. Always," Ruslan murmured, tucking me under his arm. This time I did not protest, instead clinging to him like my life depended on it. True to his word, Ruslan took his time lowering us to the base of the mountain, and when we finally reached the bottom, I released the breath that I had held the whole way down.

Only once the doors opened did I drop my arms from around Ruslan's waist, but before I bolted, he grasped my hand and strode into the hallway that led outside. Warm sun and frosty air greeted us as we strolled to the stables. The scent of leather and oats filled my nostrils as we approached two black horses, saddled and waiting, with their coats gleaming in the morning light.

"You're trusting me to ride on my own now?" I teased Ruslan.

"Don't make me regret it, sprite."

I approached the smaller of the two, a mare whose gentle eyes reminded me so much of Mistik. She blew into my fingers as I rubbed her nose, her breath foggy in the morning air. Her fuzzy lips nuzzled my palm, looking for a treat. "You're shameless, aren't you?"

Picking my head up, I searched for apples or sugar, and found Ruslan and Drazen, heads bent together and speaking in hushed tones. "I'll be right back," I promised my new mount, then slipped between her and the stallion, headed toward a wooden door that looked like it might be a feed room. Turning the handle, I opened it to find a tack room, but a male stood before a leather saddle, rubbing it down with oil.

"Can I help you?" he asked, giving me a once over that was unnerving, as though he saw straight through me.

"I'm looking for some treats for the horses," I said, puffing out my chest with an air of confidence I currently lacked.

The male fished in his pockets, then revealed three lumps of sugar. "Twilight will eat all three at once if you let her, greedy mare." He stretched his hand in my direction and I scooped them from his palm and retreated to the door, hoping Ruslan hadn't noticed my disappearance.

"Thanks!" I shouted over my shoulder, hurrying back to the horses.

Ruslan still spoke to Drazen, and I heaved a sigh of relief as I approached Twilight again. "Here you go, pretty girl," I cooed, flattening my palm with a single sugar cube offering, and she snatched it, munching away as I tangled my fingers in her mane.

"You like horses?" Ruslan's hot breath fanned across my cheek, and I stiffened, a gasp leaving my lips and nearly sending me into a panic attack as he appeared from nowhere behind me.

Sucking in a shuddering breath and pushing away the urge to fight or flee, I nodded. Ruslan's hand found my back, and I jumped into the mare, still too on edge from my scare.

"What's wrong?" His deep voice held a hint of concern, and he smoothed circles into my back as I struggled to breathe.

"I... You scared me," I managed to say.

Strong arms circled me, squeezing me tight and burying me in his body, which radiated heat. "Take all the time you need to calm down. I'm here."

His tenderness melted me, and I collapsed against him, riding the wave of panic until it subsided and my breath flowed without force from my lungs. His arms did not slacken the entire time, and only when I pushed against them did he allow them to loosen enough to spin me to face him.

Kneeling down so his eyes were level with mine, he said, "I promise not to sneak up on you again. I didn't realize it would cause you to panic, and the last thing I want is to make you feel unsafe, because it is my fault for not protecting you in the first place."

Ruslan had unquestioningly accepted the burden of my abuse, and that alone caused more pin-pricks in my eyes.

"Are you ready to go?" he asked, wiping at an errant teardrop on my face.

"Yes," I breathed, as the male I'd feared from the moment he arrived in my life won another part of my heart.

Backing away, he gave me space to mount Twilight, and I did so with ease. I adjusted my stirrups just a hair shorter, then picked up the reins, waiting for Ruslan. He swung his leg across the stallion's broad back, then clicked his tongue, starting him in a walk, and my mare followed without hesitation. I spurred her forward to ride side by side. "I do like horses, very much, in fact. Learning to ride was one of the best things that's happened to me since I left my cave."

Ruslan's smoky eyes caught the light of the morning sun, the gold highlighting little flecks of blue in them. He slicked his hair back with a free hand, grinning mischievously. "If you like Twilight, she is yours. If you don't – or even if you want – I will buy you another horse. Whatever you want, you will receive."

I couldn't help the grin that stretched across my lips. "I'll hold you to that."

In the distance, small stone houses scattered across fields filled with trees, vines, and stalks. Many Fae bent among them, pruning, collecting, and chopping the last of the harvest. Sheep, goats, and dogs ran among them, chastised when they trailed too close to the overflowing baskets. None paid us any attention as we rode toward the citadel that watched over the fields and city like a sentinel.

"The first snows should arrive any day now," Ruslan mentioned.

I had briefly glimpsed snow on my trips through the

Agrenak Mountains, but I remembered my guards complaining about it interfering with their families' farms.

"I can't wait," I smiled, imagining the land dusted with the white powder. I loved the autumn leaves that had surrounded me on the road to Vaenor, and I was excited to experience a different season. Despite my unwilling departure from the Night Realm, I still held a ferocious curiosity about the world that was hidden from me for so long.

After some time, Ruslan spoke again. "I wish I could have saved you from all of that. I will never forgive myself for allowing King Zalan and King Azim to have total control of your care. If only I had pressed harder for information... I would have protected you."

His confession was merely a whisper and yet it struck me as hard as if he had shouted it in my face. He'd said as much several times now, and I was beginning to think that the male had some semblance of guilt beneath his arrogant exterior.

His pain must run as deep as mine if he had that many layers protecting the most vulnerable parts of himself.

When we reached the outskirts of Radence, the dull thump of hooves on packed earth was replaced by a steady clop against large, square stones dug into the ground, worn smooth by countless feet. As we rode through the streets leading to the citadel, the bright faces of Iron Fae glanced our way, some staring a little longer than appropriate, others sending a friendly wave, while only a few averted their gazes as they hurried on to their destination.

Did the common Fae know of King Azim's experiments?

The longer I studied the Fae, the more I realized that these people did not look at all like what Viktor had described to me when I asked. Skin in every shade, eyes and ears in every shape, and hair in every color dotted the streets of Radence, males, females, and children in all shapes and sizes bustling about the capital city.

We rounded a bend, cutting us off from the colorful residents and beginning a trek uphill to the citadel. Soldiers lined either side of the cobbled road, some headed to and some away from the massive structure that missed nothing with its eagle eyes. Its spires were sharper than an eagle's eyes, too. Black stone formed an impenetrable ring around the edge of the cliff upon which it rested, the stones smooth and without handholds. A surprise attack on Ryza Citadel was impossible, and my stomach dropped at the realization.

Before despair had time to sink her claws in, we trotted through an archway wide enough to ride five abreast, Ruslan angling his horse to the left where young males wrangled other horses deposited by their riders. With the grace of a panther, he slid off his steed, handing the reins to an attendant without a word. It irked me that he didn't even thank the young stablehand, so when I handed my reins over, I offered a polite thanks. He balked at my acknowledgement, his face flushing as he ducked his head and hurried away.

Ruslan watched me with curiosity, a half smile pulling at the corners of his lips. He held a hand out to me, and self-preservation had me accept it. Ruslan might have been an unwanted ally, but he was all I had as we strode toward the citadel where the male who was truly responsible for my abuse awaited. Heavy iron doors marked the entrance, held open by even heavier iron chains to allow the flow of people in and out. A large hall stretched in either direction, and from the shape of the exterior, I assumed it ringed the whole structure. Halfway around the ring, Ruslan stopped at a nondescript wooden door, so unlike many I had seen on the way here. He pressed his hand to the flat surface, and it swung inward to reveal a spiraling staircase leading into the earth.

Sweeping a hand in front of him, he indicated that I should walk ahead. Sucking in a breath, I imagined myself staring out at the vast expanse of land from the roof of Roc as I exhaled, trying to calm my racing heart. He could be leading me into a dungeon for all I knew, and at the bottom of the endless-looking spiral there could be a dozen guards ready to overpower me and lock me in iron. Not that it would do them any good – I could still access my power around it. But they did not need to know that until it was time to reveal my thorns.

Bracing myself for what might be a fight for my life, I stepped past Ruslan onto the landing, then gripped the rail as I began my descent. The spirals were tight and narrow, leaving little room for error in footing. The door swung shut above me, drafting a light breeze on the back of my neck, then Ruslan's heavy steps pounded behind me.

Down and down we went, stopping briefly a few times when the spiral became too dizzying. The walls closed in on me, and my whole body tingled as that helpless feeling of being trapped threatened to rear its ugly head and send me into another bout of panic.

My breathing was labored, both from the effort of climbing down and my fear, and my aching knees wobbled with every step. What seemed like an eternity later, we landed in front of another wooden door and Ruslan pushed past where I had braced my hands on my knees to catch my breath. The panic that tightened my chest in the small enclosed space did not help ease the exertion that still stole my breath.

Despite Ruslan's admission that small spaces bothered him too, he appeared as the ruthless, uncaring prince who had snatched me from Este Castle. With a stone in my stomach, I straightened and followed him into a subterranean chamber devoid of all natural light.

The domed ceiling was filled with floating bubbles of light, similar to those cast by my friends as we'd explored the hidden passages at Este Castle together. Tunnels veered off in every direction, and people milled about in all but the one straight ahead. But there were no guards, no dungeon cells, and no chains awaiting me, and for that I was grateful.

Ruslan carved a path to the empty tunnel, and I hurried along behind him as the others noticed our appearance, many of the males giving me an intense once over despite the cloak clasped around me. We reached a heavy door, and Ruslan knocked once with enough force that the vibration rang in my bones. Footsteps grew louder, and the door was yanked open by a hunched elderly man wearing dark robes that dragged the ground.

"Rares." Ruslan's tone was clipped and strained as he regarded the head of King Azim's breeding program.

"Ruslan," Rares responded, then stepped back to allow us to pass.

I examined Rares more closely, his frail frame not at all what I'd pictured for a male capable of such barbaric deeds. I remembered Ruslan saying Mages were human and did not live very long. And yet...

"You must be Izidora," he turned to me, adjusting his spectacles.

I swallowed, my nervous system on high alert under his scrutinizing gaze. Unconsciously, I scooted closer to Ruslan. "That's me." As much as I tried to keep the waver from my voice, I failed.

"Please remove your cloak and sit here." He patted a table in the middle of the space. I took the opportunity to glance around the room as I reached for the diamond clasp on my cloak. Aside from the central table, there was a desk strewn with paper, no order among the chaos, while books were stacked haphazardly on a shelf and even spilled onto the floor beside it. A wall of instruments that looked like they could easily be for torture hung along the opposite wall, and beneath them were crates filled with something I could not see.

Ruslan lifted the gray fabric from my shoulders, and I stepped to the table, fingering the hard wood. I didn't know what awaited me should I surrender to seating myself, and my every instinct warned me to run instead of obey.

Glancing over my shoulder at Ruslan, he nodded, seating himself in a chair while he waited for Rares to examine me. I chewed my lip, knowing I had no choice and hating the clawing panic that closed my throat because of it. The flat surface was as uncomfortable as I imagined, so I perched on the edge, body tensed and ready to fight.

Rares approached, moving slowly and with a slight limp. I filed the information away for a time when I might need to outmaneuver him. He picked up my hands first, and I flinched, instinctively bringing them closer to my body. He tsked at me, "I am not going to hurt you. I am merely assessing." He yanked my hands to him with more force than I thought him capable. Tuning my hands over, he studied my palms, then slid my tunic sleeves to my elbows, examining each scar and movement in my lower arms.

Next were my legs and feet, and the old Mage muttered to himself the whole way. He alternated between making notes at his messy desk and examining or testing my strength. "Please remove your tunic," he said. Fear flooded my veins, and unfortunately, I only had Ruslan to save me – if he even would. In an instant, he towered over the frail Mage, the sound in his chest more animal than male.

"Turn your back," Ruslan seethed, and Rares did so without a trace of fear in his eyes, despite the violence simmering just beneath the surface of Ruslan's words. The male had no plans to save me from this part of the examination, and I gritted my teeth as he gently slid the back of the tunic over my head so my front remained covered, bearing the scars of my abuse to the Mage who held responsibility for their presence.

Ruslan circled the table, bracing his hands on either side of my legs as Rares began examining my spine. The Mage didn't even comment on the marks on my back, merely continuing his poking and prodding. The intensity of Ruslan's protectiveness was palpable, and his smoky eyes never left Rares's fingers, as though he would not hesitate to throw the male against the wall if he made the wrong move. It made me feel safe in a way that I'd never felt safe before, only serving to confuse me further.

Rares tapped the spot between my shoulder blades where my wings emerged. "You do have wings, yes?" he asked.

I dipped my head once.

"Good. Please bring them out," he instructed.

My lungs inflated with air as I tried to calm my thundering heart. I failed to bring my wings out on my first attempt, my magic uncooperative as it sensed my fear and hesitation to display the beautiful feathers to this disgusting male. My base instincts to fight still overrode my logical brain, but after reminding myself of the benefits of learning all my powers, I managed to get them out. The white feathers arced toward the ceiling, feathers splaying wide and wings flapping a few times in response to my anxiety. Rares touched them, and I growled a warning that surprised even me.

Only one male had ever touched my wings, and that was Kazimir. I wasn't interested in letting another poke and prod them.

The hairs on the back of my neck rose as Rares bent to examine the wings, his hands nowhere to be found. He scurried to his desk, writing furiously for a few minutes. "What is going on, Ruslan? Is there something wrong with them?" I whispered.

"You have pure Angel wings." Rares did not look up from

where he still scribbled notes. "None of the other Angel Félvér received them. It's a shame Ithuriel died after your mother did. He might have been the key."

A choked sob rose in my throat. I had harbored a small hope that the Angel who'd sired me might still live. My eyes burned, and I ducked my head to hide them.

How could one person handle so much loss? Was that all I was meant to receive in this life?

Loss, grief, heartache, abuse, those were the constants of my life. I did not believe the Goddess blessing me with a mate could ever counterbalance the weight of everything I had lost. And even if it was a blessing, I still had no choice in the matter, just like so many other parts of this life I had yet to truly live.

Ruslan wiped a tear that had fallen to my chin, saying nothing.

Rares returned to my back with an order. "Move them about."

I flapped my wings lightly back and forth, then raised and lowered them. My muscles had gotten stronger, but they were still weak from years of disuse. "Ruslan, she needs more muscle work. She is structurally sound, but weak. I see no obvious deformities."

Ruslan heaved a sigh of relief, though my face puzzled at Rares's comment. "What do you mean, deformities? Is that common?"

Rares circled to my front, once more eyeing me closely. His distrust was obvious, but he handed over the information anyway. "Many Félvér are born with deformities. Many times spinal deformities, especially among winged races. That is why we have only selected more powerful lines in recent decades."

"How can you possibly get such strong males and females to agree to this?" I demanded, the knowledge of their trafficking springing to the front of my mind. Ruslan growled low, a warning that this was not a topic for us to discuss. I shot him a glare, indignation overtaking my anxiety.

Rares looked between us, cleared his throat, and changed the subject. "I would like to test your magical abilities now."

Rulsan took one step back, but went no further, watching both Rares and me carefully.

I called magic to my hands, and balls of pure white energy floated above both palms. Rares made notes, then requested I form shapes with it. My magic emboldened me, and that inner fire sprang to life as I tapped into it. I conjured a horse, life size with wispy hairs that moved with an invisible breeze. A hint of my thorns poked through with this creation, if only to deter them from fucking with me while I was in such a vulnerable position. Rares and Ruslan lifted their brows, impressed.

"Have you attempted any other magic other than manipulating energy?" Rares inquired.

I thought about everything my friends had taught me. Endre taught me healing magic, and that was easy. Creative magic and I did not mix. Infusing Kazimir with strength sprung to mind, but revealing that I could influence others' actions would put me at risk. It was one of the only ways I held the upper hand. "I can heal others," I offered.

Rares scowled, clearly displeased with my basic answer. He looked at Ruslan. "I'm going to need to test her abilities further. Please fetch Zuriel."

Ruslan looked down his nose at Rares. "You fetch him. I am staying with my mate."

The old Mage huffed, then shot over his shoulder as he exited the room, "She's not your mate until you both accept the bond."

Fire erupted from Ruslan's body as the comment snapped the last of his self-control. His rage consumed me, eating up my spine until I felt like landing a killing blow to Rares's frail neck.

White magic erupted from my palms, trapping me in a bubble in the center of the space, as Ruslan's fire and fury passed over me like water flowing around a boulder in the center of a stream.

The shield I had instinctively erected blocked more than just physical attacks.

The fire fell away, revealing a panting, crazed Ruslan. The set of his jaw made me glad my shield still stood. Behind it, I breathed a sigh of relief, fear long held in check lifting from my tense and trembling body.

A few minutes passed, then Rares returned with a lanky male, his unbound white hair falling past his shoulders. He was beautiful in a way that was unearthly, a soft glow seeming to fill the air around him when he walked – no, glided – into the room. His eyes were ice blue, so pale and yet so intense in their wisdom, like he had seen more than any of us could ever comprehend.

His face was passive as he took in the scene, though he approached my shield, releasing his clasped hands and touching them to the white energy. His back was to Rares and Ruslan, and he winked at me before popping the shield like it was a bubble made of the thinnest soap. My wings disappeared along with it, and I felt less powerful as my magic slumbered in my chest once more. I pulled my tunic over my head, adjusting it so I was fully covered, then looked to the Angel.

A tendril of something brushed against my mind, nearly startling me with its unfamiliarity. The Angel, Zuriel, held my gaze, his eyes – so similar to mine – pleading with me. He must have been the one asking for entrance, and I opened it to him, curious about this new magic.

"I am Zuriel. Ithuriel, your father, was my uncle. You are an empath, yes?"

"What's an empath? How are we speaking like this? Do they know we can do this? How did you get here?"

"No, they do not know. Let me take your hands so I can examine you. I will answer all your questions in time. For now, follow my lead, cousin."

I allowed Zuriel to take my hands and he ran his fingers across my palms, much like Rares had.

"Being an empath is a very rare gift, even among Angels. Our grandmother was one. You absorb the emotions of others. Have you ever felt emotions that weren't your own?"

"Yes, just now. The shield protected me from Ruslan's rage."

"There is another side to this gift – the ability to manipulate others' emotions. You can push as well as pull."

My brows threatened to lift, but I managed to maintain a neutral expression despite the shock that stole my breath. If Ruslan and Rares knew…

"Yes, they know. They suspected that Ithuriel and Liessa's union would produce an empath. The gift skips generations. But they do not know the full capabilities of such a gift."

"I can manipulate others' actions as well. I imbued strength in my real mate, Kazimir, during a fight once. And another time, I stopped someone from moving altogether. But it was incredibly draining."

"You are gifted indeed. Most empaths can't influence at that level. Do not speak of it to them. But I must tell them you are an empath now."

"She is an empath," Zuriel confirmed, spinning to face Ruslan and Rares, the latter's triumphant grin almost sickening in its glory. "But to hone this gift, she will need special training with me."

"They will try to put a tracking spell on you before you leave, like they have with the rest of us. Do not let them, or you'll never be free. I will help you block it, so keep your mind open to me."

Shit, so that's what kept powerful beings from leaving this Goddess-forsaken place.

"It shall be done." Rares rubbed his withered hands together, a gleam in his eye. His enthusiasm only sent a shudder through my body. I had decided to become their weapon, a true insidious bloom, for one day that power would turn against them and right the wrongs done to me. But this road of surrendering to them in the meantime would not be an easy one.

The Mage crossed to me, and Zuriel stepped aside. Ruslan monitored Rares, who began chanting in a language wholly unfamiliar to me.

"He is going to put the spell on you now. Imagine your magic creating a shell beneath your skin. I will hold it in place, for it is difficult to use such magic without showing it."

Rares weaved his hands in time with his chants. Not a muscle twitched as I tuned in to the fire-wrapped crystal in my chest. Bringing the white energy just beneath my skin was challenging, but I did as Zuriel instructed. My heart galloped as I raced to cover every inch of my skin, straining as I reached my limit at the tops of my thighs. Sweat broke out along my brow as I pushed and pushed, sending it an inch further but dropping the covering on my fingers. It was taking too long, and Rares's words came faster and faster, surely nearing the end of the spell.

"I will hold the magic above the waist, but you need to cover your legs, NOW."

I focused all my attention on my legs, the magic that covered the top half of my body buzzing below my skin. With a final burst of energy I covered my feet, then my fingers and toes, just as Rares placed his hands on me. I yelped in surprise, feeling like a leather whip had lashed my whole body, and doubled over in pain.

"What the fuck was that!" I gasped, leaping from the table, knocking Rares back as I reacted to the pain.

"A tracking spell. Should you ever try to leave the Iron Realm without Ruslan, you will bleed out through your pores." The old Mage had the nerve to laugh.

Sick bastard.

I whirled on Ruslan, stalking over to him and shoving him with all my strength, though it didn't even sway him. Instead his eyes smoldered with a heady mix of lust and power, sending a chill down my spine. The pain was real, still pulsing over my skin, and my stomach dropped as I realized Zuriel and I may not have succeeded.

"You are mine, Izidora, now and forever. You will never leave me," Ruslan purred, his coolness in no way offsetting the rage boiling in my chest.

"This is not love," I hissed, and his eyes flashed with hurt before he bared his teeth at me.

"It is because I need to protect you and keep you safe. That's what a real mate does." His words landed their intended blow.

"How DARE you!" I screeched, launching myself at his face with nails curled into claws. He only caught me and threw me over his shoulder like a petulant toddler.

"You are not bound by the spell, Izidora. Acting like you are was a smart play. I'll be waiting for you to begin training," Zuriel spoke before retreating from my mind.

"Are we done here?" Ruslan asked Rares with casual indifference.

"For now. Have her back later to train her magic," he instructed, waving us off.

Ruslan carried me over his shoulder as we left Rares and Zuriel. I locked eyes with the Angel, who gave me a curt nod, then the door closed behind us. My fists swung wildly against Ruslan's back, but he seemed unfazed by my strikes. I donkey-kicked a leg, trying to break his grip on my knees, but he only tightened his hands so that they were nearly bruising. "Put me down and talk to me! That was not okay." He said nothing, but those remaining in the tunnels quickly scattered at the sight of Ruslan and me.

"I did it because I love you, my sprite," he purred as we entered the stairwell.

"You did it because you are a control freak!" I snapped.

"You don't know the real ways of Fae," he seethed. "Males, especially mated males, go insane over protecting their females. Kazimir clearly wanted your body and title, as he could not overcome the effects of the poison to reach you like a mated male would have."

That made me pause, my fist suspended in midair. It was true that I did not know the ways of Fae, as I had been kept in the dark – literally – my whole life. I recalled Liliana's explanation of mates and her mention of how insanely protective males were.

Could Ruslan possibly be right? Could his insanity stem from a primal urge to protect?

It wasn't until we reached the landing at the top of the spiral staircase that my feet touched the ground again. Not a drop of sweat lined his face, despite the fact that he'd walked up all those stairs carrying me. My knees were grateful that they did not have to make the ascent, but I was beyond pissed at Ruslan for attempting to trap me in this way.

"If you wanted me to accept the mate bond, there's no fucking way I am now," I cursed him as I stalked as far away as I could on the small landing. I wanted to wound him, and it worked. He was on me in a second, pinning me to the hard wall with his harder body. The scrape of rough stone through my tunic was drowned out by the crazed look in his eyes and firm set of his jaw. He dropped his head to my neck, inhaling deeply as he ran his nose up to my ear. Goosebumps spread across my skin, and a shiver wound its way down my spine.

"Once you finally succumb to your desire, you won't be able to refuse me," he growled, his tone as low as it was feral. As if he commanded it, heat pooled between my thighs.

It was so twisted that my body responded to him in this way.

"Watch me," I bit out, the venom in my voice contrasting the softening of my body.

Ruslan chuckled, his hot breath tickling my ear. He nipped the lobe lightly, then trailed his tongue to the crook of my neck, where my pulse fluttered under his lips. He nipped there too, and I clenched my thighs together, both to relieve the tension building in me and to prevent his leg from advancing between mine. I lost on both counts as he hoisted me higher, one hand behind my head to prevent it from scraping against the stone like my back did. My legs fell apart and wrapped around him, and I cursed my body for betraying me.

"I can smell how much you want me, want this." He punctuated each word with a sinful press of his lips against my neck.

I said nothing, unable to deny that my body betrayed my heart and head. He nipped my ear again, and a moan slipped unbidden from my lips. "I get so hard when you're angry." He ground into me to prove his point. The roll of his hips into me was perfectly placed against my clit, and another moan escaped me. I couldn't deny that I wanted him most when we fought. His fire thrown against my own was a force to be reckoned with, and someday soon that reckoning would come for me.

"I want to take you right here, right now, but then I risk someone seeing your flawless body, and I'd have to kill them on the spot," he groaned as he rubbed against my core again. Sparks flashed through my center, and I bit my lip to contain any further sound. His eyes met mine, and he yanked my lip from between my teeth. "Do that again, and I will fuck you right here."

Ruslan stole the whimper from my throat as his mouth

crashed against mine, sucking my lip between his teeth and drawing blood. He lapped at the blood, his tongue dancing with mine and coating my mouth in the metallic taste. I threaded my fingers in his hair, lost to the inferno of passion that consumed us with no care for who might overhear or stumble upon us.

What I was doing was so wrong, yet it felt so right.

Ruslan lifted the hem of my tunic, calloused hand finding my nipple through the lace binding my breasts and twisting hard. I gasped, but he swallowed it, his hand continuing to work over the peaks. Arching my back, I rubbed against him, legs shaking from holding back my desire for so long.

He left me breathless as he pulled away, his hips still pinning me against the wall. He cocked his head, apparently listening to something. I strained my ears, but the only sound was blood rushing through them.

Without a word he released me, retrieving my discarded cloak I hadn't realized he'd been carrying. I wasted no time clasping the diamond around my throat, needing more fabric between me and the male who made my blood sing with delicious darkness. He opened the door to the large entry hall, then guided us back to the courtyard where we'd left the horses.

My mind was spinning, my body was still on the edge, but I could not find words to ask what had us racing from the citadel. Any longer and I would have given myself to him, despite the fact that he had just tried to place a tracking spell on me so I could never pass the Iron Realm's borders without him.

What the fuck was wrong with me?

It wasn't until we breached the city's last houses that I finally asked, "Why did you want to leave so suddenly?"

"My father," was his response, his bitter tone revealing that perhaps father and son were not on the best of terms.

"Would you have been ashamed if he found us in the stairwell?" I prodded.

To say that Ruslan was touchy about the mate situation would have been an understatement. I never knew which side of anger he would land on when the subject surfaced. His head snapped to the side, and his hard expression told me that I treaded dangerous territory.

"I am not ashamed of you, my mate. I simply am not ready to share you with him."

From what I knew of King Azim, I hoped he did not mean literally sharing me, my body merely a toy for his pleasure.

Deciding other subjects would be safer, I asked, "What did Rares mean about needing 'muscle work'?"

"He meant that you need to get stronger. We have an expedited way of doing that if you are interested. But as you said, you do like to exercise."

"So can I exercise when we return to Roc?" I asked.

"That is the plan," he gritted out. Clearly he needed to work something else out, but I kept my mouth shut. We finished the ride in silence, but my head and heart circled incessantly, not leaving a moment's peace on the cold winter day.

14

KAZIMIR

King Airre and Queen Immonen hosted us for breakfast the following morning, a much more casual affair than dinner the previous night had been. A marble table was pushed against a far wall, a spread of cheese, cured meat, eggs, and fruit beckoning me as my head pounded with each step in its direction. I drank far more than I should have the previous night, and I was grateful Kaztar, who walked the length of the table in front of me, seemed to have forgiven my outburst.

Some of the noble houses of the Crystal Realm were also in attendance, and we mingled with them as we ate. Kaztar and I conversed with High Lords Mikko, Aake, and Tukka, males we had met on previous visits to Vlisa. Aake and Mikko had both been married since the last time we visited Vlisa, and I congratulated them on their unions.

"What's this we hear about you having a mate, Kazimir?" High Lord Aake grinned.

"That's actually why we're here. She was taken by the Iron Realm who attacked Este Castle during a celebratory feast," I replied grimly.

High Lord Mikko whistled. "Not okay. Those Iron bastards have been trafficking too long. What would they possibly want with a princess?"

"We'll get into more details during the council meeting later, but she wasn't meant for trafficking. They want to use her as a weapon for war," I seethed.

Mikko's answering grin was filled with mischievous delight. "I look forward to covering my blade in Iron blood."

I glanced at Kaztar, who merely shrugged. If Mikko was restless enough to want a war, I was not going to complain. He and King Airre were close, and having him on our side would definitely sway other council members.

High Lord Tukka interrupted our talk of war as he spotted Liliana laughing with Domi and the two new wives. "Who is that lovely female in your company?"

Kaztar chuckled, shooting a conspiratorial look at us before answering. "That is Lady Liliana Arzeni. Her brother, Vadim, also travels with us. But he isn't the one you need to worry about. She will eat you alive."

Tukka rubbed his hands together. "I do love a challenging female."

I snorted, knowing that Liliana was the ultimate challenge for any male. The only one she did not put up a fight with was Endre – yet. But that day would come. Another Crystal Realm noble stopped to speak with her, and she blew him off as if he were nothing more than a passing servant. It was honestly impressive how handily she turned them down.

Mikko slapped Tukka on the shoulder. "Good luck with that, friend."

We shared a laugh at Tukka's expense, then Kaztar and I excused ourselves, promising to reveal more later. I scanned the room, attention catching on the haphazard mix of Fae, the dark hair and green eyes woven between the light blondes and blue eyes, the strong and muscular males and the lithe females, and the levels of nobility that seemed to matter not in a court that was filled with light and air.

So different from the Night Realm.

And the Iron Realm.

Bloodlust consumed me, as it did every other time I thought of the Iron Fae. It was not really their race I loathed – only their leaders. Vengeance called to me, a sweet song that promised to relieve my pain and return my mate. I imagined the rush I would feel when I sliced Ruslan collar to groin, delivering a painful death blow to the male who dared lay hands upon my mate. I shifted from foot to foot as my blood heated, anxious to begin the council meeting and formally declare war on the Iron Realm.

What seemed like hours later, King Airre called the High Lords to gather. His council was smaller, only six members instead of the Night Realm's seven, and at the snap of his fingers servants carried in more chairs for Kaztar, Endre, Viktor, Vadim, and myself. We almost doubled the presence in the room, and I hoped they would feel the right level of intimidation from our united front.

King Airre called the meeting to order. "It has been brought to my attention that the Iron Realm invaded and attacked the Night Realm, captured their monarch, and plans to wage war across the continent. I believe we should unite with the Night Realm and prepare for battle. It is long past time we did something about this problem. King Azim thinks we must be soft, too comfortable in peacetime to rise against him. But he is wrong, and the Crystal Realm will not bow to the Iron Realm. Do you agree?"

The High Lords of the Crystal Realm banged their chests as they shouted, "Agree!"

"Fantastic. Any questions before we dive into logistics?" King Airre glanced around the room.

"I would like to hear a bit more background on the situation and how it came to pass," a male I did not know said.

"High Lord Vaszoly, the floor is yours." King Airre swept a jeweled hand across the table, inviting me to speak. My chair scraped against the floor as I stood, sucking in a lungful of air before launching into the tale of how we rescued Izidora, were chased to my family's home, arrived at Este Castle only for her to be snatched the following day, and how Ruslan spoke of an agreement between King Azim and King Zalan for Izidora's hand. I finished with his promise of conquering the continent and how many of our close friends and family had perished in the fight against him.

The room was quiet enough to hear a pin drop once my voice died away. Aake shook his head as if he could not believe the madness we had recently endured. Grief surged like an angry wave from the pit of my stomach, and I wished for a stiff drink – at least it would numb me as I drowned in sorrow.

Yet I had no time to process these deep feelings stealing small pieces of my soul when I wasn't looking; I needed to save my mate. I gripped the sides of the table instead, using the pain in my knuckles to ease the pain in my heart. I waited for any glimmer of doubt or second thoughts from the Crystal Realm's High Lords. But none came. Instead, the male who had asked for our story, who introduced himself as Einari, said, "I will offer all my soldiers to the war effort."

Each male seated around the table offered soldiers in turn, until the full strength of the Crystal Realm's soldiers, trained and ready to fight, was offered to our cause. My heart leaped as I calculated our new army's size, surpassing that of the Iron Realm's since the Crystal Realm had allied with us.

The conversation turned to integration and logistics

because, unlike the Night Realm, the Crystal Realm had no standing army, only soldiers who served as personal guards for each noble house's region.

But my mind drifted to Izidora. It had been over two weeks since I'd last seen her, and every action, every breath I had taken since that moment had been for her. Everything I did was for her, and it had been for the past ten or so years. She'd ruined me long before I'd ever laid eyes on her. And when I did? I couldn't help my desire, couldn't hold back despite knowing that she might be ripped away from me. So I pushed her in the direction I wanted her to go, and she gladly accepted my plan because she felt it too. Until Ruslan ripped her away from me.

A sharp elbow in the ribs brought me back to the council room. Endre jerked his head in Viktor's direction.

"Sorry, what was that?"

"I asked if you wanted to explain our army's structure," Viktor repeated himself.

"Go for it, Viktor."

A hint of disapproval etched his mouth, but he continued. "Kazimir is head of the war council, so he acts as general on the battlefield. We also have healers. We could use more, though, if you have any. Our army should move into Crystal territory in a few days' time, with plans to regroup in Zheka. We hope to convince the monarchs of the Day Realm to join our cause before they reach their border."

King Airre rubbed his bare chin, the rings adorning each finger sparkling in the light. "Since we planned on leaving in a few days' time for Béke, most preparations for rule in my absence have already been made. Mikko, Aake, Tukka, you will accompany us as planned, and you will lead in the army when the time comes. We must be strategic in our approach to this. I do not want to plan extensively before we have agreement from Queen Viktoria and King Consort Geza. If they will not ally with us, we will need to change course drastically. We rely on them to solidify the ruse of maintaining peace during Béke."

The males bowed their heads in acknowledgement to their king. He turned to the three other High Lords. "Can you coordinate the troops and send them to Zheka if we ride out at first light? It will likely take days to ready them all, and we must make haste."

"Yes, My King," Einari replied.

"Good. I will ask Queen Immonen to gather healers to join with the soldiers. Now," he rose from his seat, the rest of us rising with him, "I must coordinate our expedited departure. I will see you all at dinner."

We departed the room in waves, the Crystal Realm's High Lords scattering to carry out their tasks, and the Night Realm representatives trekking back to our rooms.

"Well, that was much easier than I thought it would be," Vadim blurted when we were well out of earshot.

"There has not been a war on the continent in almost five hundred years. Fae always get bored eventually," Viktor shrugged.

"Also, King Airre is mated, so he understands Kazimir's plight," Kaztar added.

As we approached the gilded doors that led to our room, Vadim stopped short, grabbing hold of Endre's arm to stop him, wearing a serious expression wholly unlike his usual countenance. "We are going to war soon, so what I am about to say is because of that and not because I'm sentimental, okay? Sorry for being an ass last night, but my protective brotherly instincts got the best of me. Endre, I love my sister. And you are my brother, so I also want you to be happy. If Liliana is that, then you have my blessing."

Endre pulled Vadim into a tight embrace, clapping him on

the back. "Thank you, Vadim. I will protect her with my life, just as you would."

"My earlier threat still stands, though. If you hurt her, I will chop off your dick!"

We shared a laugh, then Viktor said, "You're getting emotional in your old age, Vadim." What was a light laugh turned into a roar, Vadim denying that he was either emotional or old. Kriztof's laugh rang in my mind, and my breath caught as I thought of how he should be enjoying this moment with us, how much he would have enjoyed our banter. As if we all shared the same thought, the merriment died away. "I wish Kriztof and the twins were here with us now," Viktor admitted. "Not that we don't appreciate you, Kaztar."

"No offense taken. I know you all were close, and I do not expect to replace them," he said, continuing forward and pushing open the door to our suite, where his wife waited with Liliana.

"How did it go?" Domi asked, rising from her chair and crossing to greet her husband.

He tucked a strand of hair behind her ear, grasping her hands in his open one. "The Crystal Realm will provide three hundred soldiers to the war effort."

A grin broke out across Domi's face, and Liliana whooped in excitement. "I can't wait to slice up some Iron Fae," Liliana snickered, jabbing her hand at an imaginary opponent.

I couldn't disagree. While we may have already overcome our first hurdle, it was by no means going to be this easy on the rest of our journey. I would rather show up wielding intimidation than be laughed off from appearing too soft. We needed strength – I needed strength, and at that moment, the promise of assistance was not enough to keep me upright. Mind, body, and soul, I was exhausted, my pain pulling at me like I was a horse attached to the cart carrying the load. Rubbing my weary eyes, I decided I needed to sleep, and after a quick glance around the room, I slipped away, leaving my friends watching Liliana and Vadim bicker about where she and Domi would be allowed in the battle formation.

The lock clicked into place when I shut the door. I didn't want to be disturbed, and I fell into the bed, blankets still crumpled in every direction. Kicking off my boots, I flipped onto my back, tucking my hands behind my head as I stared at the crystal ceiling, and lost myself in memories of Izidora, Kriztof, and the twins.

———

KAZIMIR...

I lifted my head, inky swirls painting the world around me.

Kazimir...

The voice sounded like three feminine ones woven together, a slight echo at the end of my name. I whipped my head to the left, but there was nothing save for a handful of trees.

Kazimir...

Spinning to my right, I saw three cloaked figures emerge from the fog, brushing away the somber clouds as they walked. I opened my mouth to speak, only to find that my lips would not move.

Shh...

The word echoed all around me, reverberating off every surface and bouncing around my skull.

Her mates darkness will rise...

The line from the prophecy dripped with a hissing noise akin to an angered snake, and I felt as if one coiled around my chest, its fangs sinking into my magic well, injecting its venom into the moonlight that swirled there. I tried to suck down air, but my nostrils filled with thick, wet vapor, and with the constrictor around my chest I could not breathe.

My heart raced, panic gripping me as I clawed at my torso, trying to free it from an enemy that was not there.

Kazimir...

That haunting voice had my head snapping up, and the three hooded figures towered over me, their faces and hands invisible among the folds of their black cloaks.

Wake.

I jerked upright, my hands scrabbling for purchase around my ribcage, but it was bare. A sharp pain stabbed at the center of my chest, to the left of my magic well, and that red organ that beat for Izidora was bathed in darkness, spilling over from a newfound power taking root among the moonlight swirling there. A small corner of my mind knew something supernatural was at work inside me; but the Goddess worked within the light, and the new gift that threaded itself among the stars of my magic was a black so dark that every speck of light winked out.

Black ropes, unbreakable and corrupted, latched themselves over my heart, over my soul.

Binding magic.

It was a rare gift that rendered every Fae immobile with no hope of escape. A fiendish pleasure rushed through me, and I thanked the Goddess for blessing me in our time of need. Binding magic was dangerous, but I would allow it to consume me if that meant I could save my mate.

But I had to be certain that was what had been gifted to me.

After dressing quickly, I cracked the door to the living space, finding Vadim and Endre snoozing and Liliana reading a book. Slipping through the door, I nodded to Liliana, who briefly glanced up from her book, and exited the suite, spilling into the crystalline hallway and weaving through the glitzy space until I broke into the mid-afternoon sun.

My blood thrummed with a sinister new energy, and as I tapped into my well of magic, it doubled in size to accommodate this gift. There was a wooded area alongside the lake, private enough to practice, yet close enough that I would not need to exhaust Fek before our ride to the Day Realm the following day.

I wove between the tall pines, my fingers brushing their still-green needles, until I found a clearing large enough to wield the power that itched beneath my skin. Focusing on a tall, thin tree about ten paces in front of me, I closed my eyes and tuned in to my magic. When I called it to me, black and silver coated my palms, and sick pleasure ricocheted up my spine. I threw my hand at the tree, calling upon the black binds. A snake of rope burst from me, wrapping itself around the tree once, twice, and a third time before stilling. It felt like an extension of myself, and I squeezed my hand into a fist, the binding cutting into the tree and sending sticky sap bubbling from its core.

With a flick of my wrist, I released my hold and the tree continued to bleed. The part of me that loved nature and felt intimately connected to the forest shouted at me to stop, but this developing menace shushed the pure parts of me, banishing them to a far corner of my mind. I called on my silver magic to create a shield, but the black swirled within, casting me in a smoky shadow instead. I moved through the trees once more, coming upon a deer grazing in the woods. I stepped on a twig, and yet the deer did not move, did not flinch.

Had this rendered me nearly invisible?

My Night Fae magic had allowed me to call shadows to me before. Not enough to cloak me, but enough to distort my image as I moved about. Curious as to this new development, I dropped the shield, and the deer immediately bolted.

Oh yes, this hellish gift was indeed divine.

I called out my wings, wondering if they had changed in any way. While they still sported black feathers, my wings were wider, thicker, heavier, and as I leaped into the air, they carried me higher and faster than before. My agility was not compromised in the least, and I dodged branches and wove between the treetops with ease. I snapped my wings shut, plummeting in an exhilarating freefall to the ground, then caught myself at the last moment, landing lightly on my feet. A manic laugh echoed through the forest, my body tingling as I felt more alive than I ever had before. The rush of this power was incredible, and I wanted more.

Not only could I blast and manipulate energy to subdue my opponents, but I could bind them in place, unable to escape my sword. I would drop from above, piercing them through the middle, then vault into the skies once more, unstoppable in my bloodlust.

In the recesses of my mind, that pure part of me shouted not to fall into the welcoming embrace of reckless power, but the promises it held were too sweet to refuse. I threw bindings around multiple bushes at the same time, pushing the limits of my new abilities. It was too easy, and I wished for something living to test the deadliness of this binding magic.

"Kazimir?"

I was lost to the heady power, and without thinking, I cast a black rope toward the voice that dared interrupt my dance with darkness.

"Kazimir!" The choked sound of a familiar voice ignited fervor in that pure part of me that I kept forcing into silence.

"Kazimir, stop! It's Endre." A strangled noise and gasp for air sounded from the dying male in front of me. He blasted my chest, and I took a stumbling step back, snapping into myself and witnessing the horror I had been inflicting on my closest friend.

Red welts ringed Endre's throat, his skin rubbed raw from the rope I'd thrown around his neck. My sobered body trembled as I placed my hands there, willing him to recover despite my shit skill with healing magic. Between his gifts and my own terror, he breathed normally a few minutes later.

"Endre," I croaked, dropping my face to my hands, too ashamed to look at him. "I would never... I didn't even know... please forgive me."

"What the hell was that, Kazimir?" he demanded. "It was like you were not even there."

"The Goddess was within me earlier, and she gifted me with new magic. Binding magic. I wanted to test it out." I shook my head, still gripped with guilt that I hurt him.

"Binding magic is dangerous – extremely dangerous, Kazimir. And it does not come from the Goddess, but the Fates. There is a reason it is rare – most who carry it do not live long enough to see it passed on."

"I know... I am so desperate to have her back, Endre."

"I know," he said, then pulled me into an embrace.

Endre, my closest friend, the one who always got me to talk. Endre, the kindest of our group, who never left anyone out. Endre, the one with the biggest heart, who cared more than the rest of us combined. And I hurt him because I wandered too deep into a new power that I knew almost nothing about. "I am so sorry," I begged him once again for forgiveness.

"Next time, have someone here to ground you, yeah?" He pulled away, searching for any sign of duplicity.

"I swear it," I promised. "But this could help us win, help us get Izidora back."

"It will. But only if you survive it, too. What good will it do to use it but be unable to return to Izidora when you're finished?"

He was right. "Are you okay now?"

He rubbed his neck, only slightly pink in a few spots. "Good as new."

"Let's find some food. I am starving." Reaching out a hand, I pulled him to his feet, then threw my arm over his shoulders, and we picked through thick roots and dry twigs coating the forest floor, headed to Blire Palace. "What brought you out here anyway?"

"Something has been plaguing you since we left Vaenor. I wanted to make sure you were okay."

I sighed. "You are a better friend than I deserve."

"You've always been the strong and stoic one among us. You are allowed to feel when you need to. That does not make you undeserving of our friendship," he reassured me.

His messy hair fell into his face, and as he tried to swipe it away I ruffled it again, impeding his vision. He swatted away my hands and we laughed together, ease filling the space between us and releasing any lingering tension.

"So, did you and Liliana fuck last night? Vadim snored loudly enough to cover any sounds you two might have made."

"We might have kissed a bit," he grinned, a sheepish expression that told me he was not going to reveal more.

Bringing my thumb and forefinger together, I used my free hand to stick my pointer finger in the middle of the ring, earning another smack from Endre. "One day, but not when Vadim shares a wall with us. You and Izidora were so fucking loud, but she was not the sister of any of our friends."

I grinned. "I can get him shitfaced so he won't even know."

Endre chuckled. "I'll let you know if I need your assistance."

"Can't wait."

A moment of silence passed between us. "I don't want to lose anyone else during this war," Endre whispered, and a pit formed in my stomach at his words. I was so wrapped up in my own shit, I'd forgotten to check in with my sensitive friend. "Liliana makes me so happy, but I feel guilty about feeling happy, you know? Like I don't deserve it until I've mourned them longer. Like if I feel happy, I'll forget all about them."

"You deserve to be happy, and they would not want you to

forgo happiness simply to remember their lives. You can do both."

He sighed, the weight of his breath palpable. "You're right. I don't know why I didn't say that to myself."

"Because friends are for grounding one another when one gets lost along the way." I elbowed him in the ribs, and he shot me a joking glare as I repeated his own words back to him. "I am glad we talked, Endre. Let's not forget to do that again."

"Agreed," he said.

I paused for a moment by the lake, promising Endre I'd return to the suite soon. The sunset over the bright, glassy water was incredible, reflecting the vibrant purples and oranges painting the sky.

"I'm coming, Izidora," I whispered. "And I have new magic that will help me tear the world apart to get to you."

* * * * *

INTERLUDE

The king of the Iron Realm stood with his Mage before the circle of his children in the tunnels beneath his citadel. "The time has come for me to name an heir apparent," he boomed over them. Murmurs drifted through the twelve, before their father silenced them with a harsh look. "You will have to earn the title through a competition among yourselves. The last one standing wins."

And with his minimal instruction, he spun on his heel and exited through the door to the spiral staircase that led to the main level of the citadel.

Immediately, the field of competitors backed ever so slightly apart, eyeing each other warily. Some of them wondered if the Mage would provide more instruction; others were already plotting the downfall of their siblings. But the only words that left the Mage's mouth were, "The competition starts now."

With no warning and no time to prepare, the siblings stood numbly, glancing at each other, waiting for someone else to make the first move. Their father's favorite yawned as if the whole idea of fighting to the death bored him. "If you need me, I'll be in my room."

He turned his back on them all, striding away as if he knew none would try to stab him as he left them. His cockiness angered his siblings, though his nonviolent approach to the competition seemed to ease some of the tension that their father had left in his wake.

The cliques that had already grouped the siblings quickly reformed in rooms hidden from prying eyes and ears as they made alliances and plans to take out the others. Only the favorite remained alone, ambling through the tunnels without a care in the world. Occasionally, he would stop to listen, using his heightened senses to snoop on the others, not even bothering to hide when he got caught. But it was all intentional, for he began whispering in the ears of those he got alone, poisoning their minds and hearts against one another.

That was the benefit of being a loner, he thought. He cared not who lived and who died, who hated him or who loved him. It was, after all, a fight to the death, and he planned on being the one alive and breathing at the end.

It didn't take long for his psychological warfare to take hold, and one by one, siblings turned on each other, slaughtering before they themselves could be slaughtered. When the remaining ones realized who had driven their favorites to be murdered, they turned on their father's favorite child. But they were too late, and he fought them with a deadness in his eyes and an icy cage over his heart.

By the time he landed the killing blow to the last remaining sibling, the favorite was exhausted well beyond the physical realm. As much as he tried to tell himself he did not care, he did. As he lay bruised, bloody, and broken, a lone tear slipped down his cheek, and he found himself profoundly alone.

III

THE REALM

15

RUSLAN

"If anything happens to her, I will flay you alive," I growled at Drazen, the violence in my words by no means an empty threat. My half Dragon cousin snorted and rolled his eyes, accustomed to the vehemence of my words, though he'd seen the consequences of them on more than one occasion.

"There is no safer place in all of Északi than here with us," Drazen pointed out with a sweep of his hand around us. The barracks beneath Roc Palace bustled with the activity of my personal retinue, all in various stages of training and caring for the horses. I had more Félvér within a hundred feet of me than anyone else in the Iron Realm, and with the expanded powers and superior strength our mixed blood offered, no one would go near Izidora and live to tell the tale.

My mate was off to one side, absorbed in petting her new mount and feeding her lumps of sugar. Whether she was oblivious to the heated conversation taking place between Drazen and me was undecided.

"The threat still stands."

Drazen merely shrugged and walked away from me. His

insolence would have normally pissed me off more, but my cock ached and needed release. The scent of my father had broken through my haze of lust when I had her pinned against the wall in the stairwell, but my blood still burned for Izidora.

I couldn't have her – not yet at least. But soon enough, she would surrender to me, and then she would see that we were truly mates.

Without further threat, I called my wings to me, impatient enough that I wanted to go straight to the suite without anyone bothering me. As I snapped them open, Izidora's aquamarine eyes widened, and my dick jumped at the sight of those glassy orbs darkening in my direction.

My wings were unlike those of Night Fae, my Dragon and Demon blood creating black membranous wings that spanned far enough to encompass four of me. With one hard flap, I shot into the air, sending dust scattering across the ground fast disappearing. Izidora and Drazen shrunk to specks beneath me, and soon I could not see them at all. I soared up the rocky mountainside toward the roof and the trap door in it that would allow me to drop straight into the suite.

My boots pounded heavily as I banished my wings and landed, and rather than pausing to admire the view, I yanked open the hatch and dropped onto the landing at the top of the stairs. They vibrated beneath my weight, continuing to do so as I wound down into the opulent suite. I stalked straight to the bathroom, turning knobs and faucets to steam up the shower while I stripped from my clothes, my erection already stiff and wanting.

Bracing one hand on the rough-hewn wall, I stood beneath the flow of water and gripped myself just the way I liked it with my other hand. A groan escaped me as I stroked, some of the ache I'd carried between my legs for days finally melting away. I imagined Izidora on her knees before me, that it was really her hand rubbing my shaft, and that she wanted to do it more than anything. The divine taste of her blood remained on my tongue from when I sank my teeth into her perfect pink lips. The mewl that came between them when I ground my hips into hers filled my ears. Fuck, she was perfect in every way, from her sounds to her looks. I couldn't wait for her to ride my cock, to feel her walls clench me as she screamed my name. The image I conjured of her round breasts bouncing above me as she rode out her release had me growling out my own, and hot liquid spurted into my hand in record time.

My desire was not at all satiated.

I was still hard as the rock I braced my hand on, and my balls were still too full. I needed more – I needed her. The rough wall scraped my back as I leaned against it, but I welcomed the pain as I jerked myself again. With closed eyes, I reached for soap, then rubbed it along my length. The slipperiness reminded me of how soaked her thighs had been as I licked chocolate from them. My next fantasy had me buried to the hilt in her perfect pussy, cock moving in and out of her while I gripped her hips, slapping her ass hard enough to pinken it, her cries of pleasure building with each brutal thrust I delivered. I fisted her hair, tilting her head back and causing her lower back to arch so I could plunge deeper. She moaned my name over and over as I brought her to orgasm again and again. I panted as I lived out my fantasy, every detail so vivid in my mind. My balls tightened, and I was coming again with a frustrated groan when I opened my eyes to find myself alone.

Nothing would satisfy me until I had her.

With the edge of my lust barely dulled, I stepped out of the shower, deciding reading might be a better distraction. Izidora would be exhausted from Drazen's brutal exercise regimen in an hour, so I had time. I dried myself, then slid naked into the bed, her scent still everywhere on the pillows and blankets. My cock jumped to life once again, and I pounded my fists into the bed as that ache settled between my legs.

I had to take my mind off of her.

A drawer beside my bed always held a stack of books, and I snatched a mystery, hoping to lose myself in the story and forget about the world around me for five fucking minutes. I made it all of ten pages before the tent beneath the sheets became unbearable, so I set the book aside, then covered my face with one of Izidora's pillows, burying myself in her rosy scent as I gripped my shaft. Thrusting up into my hand, over and over and over, I dreamed of her throwing her head back in ecstasy from the motion, her breasts bouncing and nipples painfully erect. My fingers stroked her clit, causing her legs to shake as I lifted her from the bed with my powerful onslaught. She mewled my name, telling me how much she loved me, how much she loved my cock, as she came all over our thighs. My balls tightened, and I spilled into my hands like a young male who hadn't found his stamina yet.

Flinging the covers away, I stalked again to the bathroom, using a discarded towel to clean myself off. It dropped to the floor again, and I braced my knuckles on the counter, staring at my haunted reflection. My tattooed muscles bunched and flexed as I shifted my weight, tracing the lines with my eyes and reminding myself of the stories that inspired me to ink them there. Eventually, my racing heart slowed, and I shoved away from myself and returned to the bed.

A frustrated sound between a growl and a moan filling the empty room. I stared at the ceiling, tracing the shape of the Angel wing hanging from the ceiling before tracing the Dragon wing on the opposite side. My eyes grew heavy as I continued to focus on the shape, but my mind wandered, and I tried to think of anything but my mate training with a group of males at the base of the mountain. They wouldn't dare touch her, for they all knew and feared what I would do.

I would do *anything* to keep her with me, including placing a tracking spell on her. In time, she would see that as an act of love. She was simply too upset that her escape plans had been thwarted.

I knew exactly what she had planned when I found her on the roof this morning, but allowing her to think she'd gotten away with it was all part of the plan. She needed to think she had a semblance of control over her life here; I couldn't rip her hope away from her, or she would rebel. But slowly replacing that hope of escape, day after day, with hope for our future would achieve the results I wanted.

Izidora had been shocked at the wedding announcement, but seemed to relax when I told her she could pick everything but the date and venue. She liked to be in control, and if providing her a hint of it got her to lie in this bed, legs spread wide, waiting and wanting when I returned from my official duties, I could release a little of my own control to her.

She could have everything she wanted – so long as I wanted her to have it.

———

AN HOUR LATER, I landed in front of the barracks, where Drazen was speaking with Izidora. She was drenched in sweat despite the chilly day, but her eyes were brighter than they had been when I departed. The flush that spread across her heart-shaped face was nearly as delicious as the smell of her.

Crossing my arms over my chest, I waited for them to finish speaking. She glanced my way, causing Drazen to look over his own shoulder. With one last affirmative statement, he dismissed her. One of the Félvér shouted praise in her direction, and she ducked her head and walked toward me.

"How was it?" I asked her, holding out my hand.

"Helpful, but I am exhausted," she sighed, tucking sweaty strands of her hair behind her ears rather than taking my hand.

I didn't let the rejection pass. Stepping into her, I gripped her by the waist and whispered the spell to move us under my breath. Moments later, we reappeared in the bathroom of our suite. She immediately stepped away from me, her eyes flashing with her inner fire and a hint of lust. The internal battle that played out on her expressive face was intoxicating. She wanted to hate me, but she couldn't. The passion in our earlier kiss was proof of that.

"Take a shower, then we will return to Ryza for your training with Zuriel," I instructed, turning on my heel and leaving her behind in the bathroom. There was no way I could stay in there with her and maintain my fraying self-control.

The sound of water splashing against stone hit my sensitive ears a moment later when I braced my arm on the wall-sized windows in our bedroom and gazed out across the seat of the Iron Realm.

I busied my mind, working over the rest of my plans that had yet to unfold, trying to analyze any potential obstacles and dependencies, rather than focusing on the heated spring water dripping down my mate's body.

I needed Izidora's magic more than her physical strength, but they fed each other, so both were necessary. That was why we would make the trek to Ryza for the second time that day for her to train with Zuriel.

Izidora slipped from the bathroom into our closet with the stealth of a mouse, and I forced myself forward, ignoring her until her reflection appeared in the window beside me. Turning, I raked my gaze across the tight leather pants and flowing shirt she wore, the gray cloak clasped at her throat by a large diamond.

"I'm ready," she stated, squaring her shoulders and lifting her chin.

I lifted a dark brow. "For the lift?"

Her confidence faltered for a moment. "Yes," she lied.

"Come," I held out my hand to her. "I will move us there to save time."

A heartbeat passed, but she accepted it, sucking in a deep breath and nodding. I whispered the words again, and the windows disappeared, only to be replaced by the dark stone walls of Ryza Citadel. With a hand on the small of her back, I guided her through the halls and to the door that led down to the subterranean home of the Félvér.

Izidora paused again at the top of the stairs, but only for a moment, and then she stepped into the spiral staircase with determination written across her face. Only steps apart, We spiraled down and down to the place where I was born and raised. I both loved and hated returning to these tunnels. On one hand, they served as a reminder of how far I had come. On the other, they reminded me how unloved I truly was.

Zuriel was already waiting for us when we entered the large training area, and he dipped his head in greeting to me before acknowledging Izidora. He was quiet and kept to himself, especially after Ithuriel, the other Angel, died, unlike the bawdy Demons who fought and fucked in the open.

"I'll return in an hour," I said, giving my mate one last look before turning to leave. The door closed with an echoing click behind me as I left her in the care of her Angel cousin. Rares was hunched over his desk, papers strewn haphazardly and a bottle of ink nearly tipping over beside him. I cleared my throat, not deigning to speak to the old Mage who brought me so much pain.

He looked up from his work, his gnarled hands pausing over the parchment. "Ruslan," he acknowledged with a grunt. Then he plunked his pen into the bottle with a clink and pushed away from the desk, his bones creaking as he rose. Without bothering to wait for him, I spun on my heel and stalked toward the spiral stairs. We had a meeting with my father to discuss Rares's earlier findings. One by one, I cracked my knuckles, over and over until we finally reached the hall that housed the most important offices in the Iron Realm. The heads of all the noble houses in the Iron Realm had a room along the right side, while on the left, advisors worked away, keeping the realm running smoothly.

Between the doors, finely crafted works of art stood on pedestals, glittering with a thousand gemstones. The artisans of the Iron Realm were the best in all of Északi, which was why the other realms' noble houses sought out our work to adorn their own homes.

My father's office stood at the end of the long hall, and two sentries stood on either side of the door, stone faced and unblinking. "We've come to speak with King Azim. He should be expecting us," I shot at the male on the right, my fists clenching and unclenching behind my back as I struggled to keep my head.

He knocked once, a sharp rap, and my father shouted, "Enter!"

The male opened the door for us, and we strode into the cherry wood-paneled study. The ceiling was a lattice of the same beams, small chandeliers hanging from each hole. A wall of windows faced the snow-capped mountains in the distance, and before them sat the king of the Iron Realm in a plush, high-backed chair, a large desk of the same wood separating him from us and a smattering of other plush furniture. Rares and I bowed, then took up seats in the chairs across from him. Bile rose in my throat at the sight of my father sitting smugly behind his desk, as if he knew I knew what he had done to my mate.

I couldn't wait to kill him.

He rose from his ornate chair, sauntering to a section of shelves that housed various liquors, then grabbed three glasses and a bottle of dark amber whisky before serving each of us.

My father had not let himself go as King Zalan had. While the signs of age showed around his eyes and atop his brow, his gut did not spill over his pants, and he still retained the muscle of youth, even if he moved slower than before. He had the dark hair and eyes of pure-blooded Iron Fae, and his skin was pale but not sallow. There was a little of myself in him, mostly in the set of his jaw, his strong brow, his high cheekbones. But the Dragon blood that flowed through my veins made me measurably bigger, taller, and stronger than him, especially in my prime years.

"My King, you are so generous," Rares thanked him as he accepted a glass.

Ass kisser.

Without acknowledging his gesture, I snatched the glass, knocking back a gulp, needing the burn to steady me. I had words for my father, ones that he was not going to like.

"So," he began, "What news do you have of the princess?"

Straight to the fucking point, per usual.

"She lacks muscle tone, but she has no deformities, My King. Zuriel also confirmed that she is indeed an empath."

Rares could not contain his excitement; she was like a precious gem to him, a shiny object to add to his collection. Only Angels possessed mind magic, but Izidora's empath magic was even rarer, and possibly the crown jewel among his catalog.

A wicked smirk played across my father's face as he held his glass in toast to Rares. "That is excellent news. How soon will she be ready?"

At this question, Rares wrung his hands nervously. "Well… with her weakness, it will take time to make her battle ready. She is not strong enough to fly far. She is with the Angel now, learning how to use her gifts."

My father leaned forward, the temperature of the room rising with his temper. "When?" he asked, the single word filled with a warning that he was not interested in excuses or games.

"Six months or so, give or take," Rares wheezed.

The king sprung to his feet, hands smashing onto the desk in front of him as he towered over our seated forms. His displays did not bother me, but Rares feared him. They would both fear me momentarily, as I waited for my moment to uncover the rage I'd buried after learning of Izidora's abuse.

"I want the continent to fall within the year. How am I supposed to do that if she is unable to join us for half of it? Tell me, after waiting all this time for our final weapon, why is it that I have to wait longer? We already wasted months because those bastards of the Night Realm found her."

I swallowed the rest of the liquid, letting the burn slide down my throat to my gut. Then, so fucking slowly, I placed the empty glass on the desk, the heavy bottom thumping against the wood, then pushed off of it, mimicking my father's threatening stance. His eyes darkened and narrowed as he sneered at me, though he had to tilt his chin up to look me in the eye.

"Because, *father*, you allowed your soldiers to abuse her. To keep her chained to a wall for years. To rape her. To whip her. To beat her. To keep her identity from her. To literally keep her in the dark," I hissed, dragging out each phrase to emphasize my displeasure. "You allowed my mate to suffer, all while telling me she was safe and there was no need to check on her. Did you know what they did to her? Did you know how many males got to taste her before me? Did. You. Know?" The glass splintered beneath my fist with a satisfying crunch as I punctuated my last question with hits to the table, and Rares shirked away as the two alphas of the Iron Realm faced off.

My father's expression was blank, betraying nothing but his distaste for my outburst, though his body vibrated with anger. "She needed to be broken in every way possible so we could make her into whatever we wanted her to be," was his only reply.

"Well, that all went to hell when I wasn't the first one to get to her," I seethed, baring my teeth. I didn't reveal that I didn't think they'd ever been able to break her in the first place. "Now, I have to convince her that everything she was told before is a lie, and I have to wait to have her because she thinks another male is her mate! I have to convince her to accept a mating bond she would have otherwise willingly accepted. But if she had known the truth from the beginning, we wouldn't be in this situation."

"I believe you are capable of swaying her to your cause. After all, that is why you won your place as my heir. Calm yourself, Ruslan, and focus on the plan," he snarled.

"Unfortunately, I do not have anyone to pit against her, like I had to do with my half-siblings," I gritted through my teeth, the memories of their deaths flashing before my eyes, escaping from the part of my mind where I kept them under lock and key.

"You will find your leverage, if you need it," he replied coolly, and I collapsed back into my chair, defeated, if only for a moment. Rares and my father turned to further discussions of the Félvér as I wrestled with the dark memories triggered by his statements.

He had forced us to fight for the right to be proclaimed heir. Only the strongest, fastest, and most ruthless could have won among a field of twelve who all wanted a claim on the land we were born into. I cracked my neck, relieving some tension there, then cracked my knuckles, only hints of scratches remaining from the shards of glass that cut into my skin.

Pain was my anchor to this world. It held me steady in moments when the waves of darkness threatened to veer me off course. Whether I was inflicting it or receiving it mattered not. Pain was a universal experience, the threat of which would bring the weakest to their knees and the strongest to their feet. I became the strongest by welcoming pain into my body, imbuing myself with the ability to rise from the depths as it fought against me, dragging me into the murky abyss.

My sister, Brazren, was on her knees, a bloody dagger held over our brother Orrien's lifeless body, her face horror-stricken as her actions landed squarely upon her shoulders.

Actions I convinced her to take.

I told her that I overheard Orrien speaking with Aztrina about how to kill her.

But I lied.

Orrien was an easy target; his Wolf Shifter nature made him crave the company of others.

"You're a monster," Brazren hissed. "The pain we endured in the tunnels beneath Ryza twisted your mind into something unlovable and irredeemable. You'll never feel remorse for this or anything else."

She was my favorite sibling, but after she turned her back on me, I killed her with the bloody knife.

At least she had her Demon mother around while we were young.

I had no one.

Out of the twelve of us, I was the loner, always reading when I wasn't fighting. My siblings' mothers were around to look after them, to teach them kindness and compassion to balance their warrior training. Yet none of them gave me any thought, for I was the favored one, the one who spent the most time with his father, who received special training from Rares. I often wondered why my father had us fight to the death – whether it was a test for me or simply because he was cruel. King Zalan may have been a jealous narcissist, but King Azim was a sadist – a trait that I sometimes shared, either by his blood running through my veins or by his influence throughout my life. Sometimes, I tried to be better – like how I wanted to be a good male for Izidora – but other times, I needed to satiate my rage, and the only way to calm myself was through pain.

I sought this pain as I stomped from my father's office, headed straight toward the barracks where an unlucky guard of my father's would bear the brunt of my rage.

It was unfortunate Drazen hadn't found Izidora's cave guards, because the release I would get from killing them would be pure ecstasy, and it just might slake this fury burning inside me.

16

IZIDORA

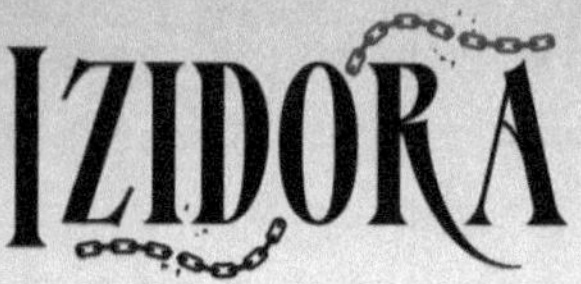

The Angel regarded me with his unreadable gaze as we sat cross-legged in the center of a domed chamber beneath Ryza Citadel. If there weren't a thousand pinpricks of light above us, it could have been mistaken for the cave where I had spent most of my life.

"So, you're my cousin?" I asked, brimming with questions like a too-full glass of wine. I was ready to get drunk on the knowledge about myself and my powers.

"I am," Zuriel began, exhaling a long breath through pursed lips. "We are the last of our family line."

A twinge of sadness stirred within me, despite not knowing a single member of my Angel family – until this moment. It was as if a small part of me held onto a kernel of hope that my people might be out there, waiting for me, ever since I had learned of my true parentage.

"You never fathered any children here?" I had assumed he would have, given where we were.

He shook his head, locks of silky white hair falling over his shoulder. "In my hundred years here, I have not been able to produce offspring."

"You've been in the Iron Realm for one hundred years?" My hand flew to my chest, breath catching in my throat, at his casually-dropped fact.

"Yes. Your father, Ithuriel, and I were captured on the shores of Keleti – the continent of Angels and Demons – as we pursued a legion of Demons who had raided a nearby Angel settlement."

"How?" I breathed. Zuriel looked like a lethal warrior despite his aura of otherworldliness, from the strong set of his jaw to the lithe frame that he carried with a lethal type of grace.

He released a sigh, his icy eyes disappearing momentarily as his white lashes brushed his cheekbones. "Ithuriel and I were locked in battle with the Demons, who outnumbered us two to one, and we didn't notice the wispy smoke curling around our ankles until it was too late. It appeared from nowhere, and the six of us fell to our knees, coughing and choking, as we were smothered in the sickening fog. Everything went dark, and then I awoke here, beneath the citadel, along with Ithuriel and the four Demons. We formed a temporary truce in order to escape, which we did, but when we reached the icy shores of the Iron Realm, an overwhelming pain screamed through us, only relenting when we backed into the mountains, where Rares waited for us along with a retinue of Iron soldiers. It was then we learned a tracking spell had been cast over us, and we were trapped in the Iron Realm until we proved ourselves useful or trustworthy."

Tears pricked at my eyes as Zuriel's lips pinched momentarily, but he was not finished with his tale. "Ithuriel and I tried our best to produce offspring, but to no avail. You see, Angels are a lot like Fae, and conception takes a long time, unless you are very lucky. The Demons remained our allies, and slowly, we grew accustomed to life here. While at first I hated them for capturing me, I learned over the years how lucky I was to speak with so many people from other continents. I had grown rigid in my beliefs, and the others opened my eyes to new ideas that I would have never been exposed to otherwise. And then Queen Liessa came to the Iron Realm, and my world was turned upside down yet again when Ithuriel's mate bond snapped into place."

My breath hitched, and I hung on every word Zuriel uttered.

"That month was one of the most tumultuous times of my life, and I hated that King Zalan forced them to lie together while he watched. It was disgusting, and once again my hatred for the power-hungry ways of the kings flared. When Liessa was carted away after she fell pregnant, I knew it was the last time either of us would see her, and I clung to Ithuriel as much as I could over the next year, for I knew the moment you burst into the world would be his last."

Zuriel paused, steepling his fingers in front of his mouth and staring absently at the padded floor beneath us. "He died in my arms with a request on his lips – that I take care of you, no matter what. I promised him, and I bided my time, waiting for the day you arrived on Ryza's doorstep."

Our eyes locked, though mine were overflowing with tears, and his softened as one spilled down my cheek. With a gentle brush of his hand, he captured it, the corner of his mouth twitching up in a half-smile. "Your grandmother's gift in full effect. You have her eyes, too."

Choking back a sob at that knowledge and the overwhelming emotions that had hooked me as I listened to his tale, I said, "So I am an empath?"

He nodded slowly. "And a powerful one if I am correct in my assessment. You have the unique ability to absorb others' emotions, like you are unconsciously doing with my sadness at the moment, and you can push emotions onto others as well. You said you had influenced a soldier's actions before?"

"Yes, with my mate, Kazimir, and some of the others who rescued me from the cave."

A flash of something I couldn't name crossed Zuriel's face, but he interrupted my thoughts before I could follow them. "What exactly did you do?"

"Well, the first time I did it instinctively, and I filled Kazimir with strength, helping him beat back his opponent and regain his footing. After that, I tried to stop Viktor from moving forward, and his feet stuck to the ground despite his struggle." I shrugged, hoping Zuriel could shed light on my powers.

"Did it drain you?" He cocked his head to the side, studying me.

"Yeah, quite a lot actually. I nearly fainted with the effort. It also took a lot of concentration."

"Mind magic usually does, because the slightest slip of attention breaks the connection. In time, you will deepen the well of magic you can pull from, but wielding it will always take effort. I have some lessons to help you develop that unbreakable focus, but they are for another day." He leaned forward, resting his elbows on his knees, and dropped his voice. "For now, I want to discuss what you should and should not say around Rares."

I nodded, dipping my head closer.

"Rares collects us like prized possessions, and you and Ruslan are his crown jewels. But you must keep the full breadth of your abilities from him for as long as possible, because if he knows that you can freeze people in place, there is no telling what he and King Azim would do with that level of power in their arsenal."

"I don't even want to use that type of magic. I spent too long powerless and chained against my will to do that to others. I refused to practice it with my friends, and I will continue to refuse to use it in the future," I hissed.

"Then we won't. It will be easier to hide it that way." He paused, a question poised on his lips. "Will you tell me what happened to you?"

Drawing a shaky breath, I nodded, then launched into my tale, not sparing my cousin any details of the abuse I suffered. The Angel's unearthly facade gave way to anger, his icy eyes darkening and wisps of magic escaping his fingers as he listened, until finally, I arrived at the point in my story that led to Ruslan snatching me from Este Castle.

Zuriel blew out a breath. "Izidora, there are no words to express the injustice of your abuse. From what I know of Ruslan, he would never have allowed it to take place, and he would have burnt down the whole Iron Realm to get to you had he learned of it sooner. I've known him his whole life, and ever since the day you were conceived, he's been nothing short of obsessed with the idea of you."

"But why? He didn't know anything about me." This question had plagued me over and over, and I had learned nothing that satisfied my curiosity.

"Ruslan was born in these tunnels, to one of the Demons captured with your father and me. She died giving birth to him, which meant he was parentless, the only affection available to him from Rares and King Azim – neither of whom are the nurturing type. Rares took it upon himself to twist Ruslan into a weapon for his own ambition, while his siblings had their mothers to look after them."

"Siblings?" I interrupted, furrowing my brow.

"He had eleven."

Had. The words landed like a boulder rolling off the sheer face of a cliff.

"Where are they now?" My voice was barely a whisper in the cavernous space, yet my words seemed to echo beyond the walls.

"About twenty-three years ago, King Azim announced a competition for the title of heir apparent – a fight to the death. Ruslan won."

Despite freely supplying information previously, Zuriel offered nothing more, which only served to horrify me, my mind painting in the details with nightmarish strokes.

How could King Azim stomach killing all of his offspring?

Not a drop of blood had been spilled by his hand; he'd merely given the order to make it happen.

Was his thirst for power so vast that he truly wanted only the strongest to survive? And if he was so relentless in his pursuit of domination, how did I fit into his plans?

Interrupting my thoughts, Zuriel asked, "Shall we practice flying now?"

I sucked in a serrated breath and nodded, rising to my feet and squaring my shoulders. "I learned how to call upon my wings while still in the Night Realm."

My cousin rose to his feet, towering over me as he studied me. "Show me."

Calling on that well of magic in my chest, I allowed my wings to spring forth from my back, their white, fluffy feathers arcing toward the ceiling above us and catching the light of a thousand lanterns. Flapping furiously, I lifted myself into the air and hovered, waiting for my next set of instructions. Zuriel circled me, then pulled his wings into existence, joining me in floating above the ground. His wings matched mine, though his were larger in proportion to his frame.

"Let's play a game. Follow my lead," he instructed, pulling something from his pocket and racing toward the ceiling. I gave chase, glancing occasionally at the padded ground beneath us.

"Don't focus on the ground, but what is in front of you," he called, and I jerked my gaze toward him, wondering how he knew my eyes were wandering.

Sharpening my attention, I wielded it like a knife as we dipped and dove between the lanterns, occasionally bumping into one before righting myself and giving chase to my cousin. He forced me to forget the world beyond these walls with his complicated flying maneuvers, and for that momentary reprieve, I was grateful.

Because I had a sickening feeling settling in my belly that this choice of light and dark would not be an easy one.

17

RUSLAN

With bruised and bloody knuckles, but by no means any less rage, I swiped sweat from my brow, welcoming the salty sting across the cuts on my hand. I ached for Izidora, my thirst to be near her insatiable, and I pulled on that thread that tied our fates together, needing her light to banish the black blood in my heart.

Darkness called to her just as it did to me, a haunting song that promised relief from the demons that lurked in our minds. We were more alike than she realized, and once I painted the full picture for her, she would understand why we were mated.

My thoughts consumed me as I returned to the tunnels, and I automatically veered left toward the underground training ring where Izidora would be with Zuriel. Lounging against the rough-hewn wall, I watched the tail end of their session, rubbing my knuckles as I went round and round in my head, calculating my next moves.

Izidora's lilting laugh broke through the haze of my thoughts, and I lifted my head to find her soaring to the tall ceiling and retrieving a stone perched on one of the firelights that dripped from above. Zuriel snatched the stone as she landed, then traced a new path and placed it on another lamp. Izidora copied his movements to fetch the stone, almost as if flying an obstacle course, and she mastered the game in minutes, executing a backward roll in the air on her last retrieval.

Zuriel's seraphic and deep voice filled the space. "I think that's enough for today. We'll pick up there tomorrow. Good work, Izidora."

She beamed at him, thanking him profusely, then bounced in my direction, happier than I had ever seen her. My chest tightened as her excitement slipped away with each step closer to me; I sucked the life out of her, like a vampire from the lands of monsters and fantasy. I was torn between self-loathing and apathy, knowing I should not care what her emotions were so long as she served my needs, while at the same time wanting to be better than the monster I was so she might share her light with me.

I held my hands out to her in greeting, trying and failing to bring a smile to my lips, the bitter taste from my meeting with my father still lingering in my mouth. "What did my sprite learn in class today?" The tease was absent in my tone, but my heart leaped as she slipped both her hands willingly into mine. That slight acceptance loosened my tense jaw, and the tightness in my chest that stole my breath vanished as her smile returned.

"Well, you saw me flying just now, but we spent most of the time talking about Angels in general. Since I knew nothing about them before now, I had a lot of questions." She ducked her head sheepishly as if she were embarrassed to be curious.

"What if I told you there is a section in our library filled with books on Angels?" I dropped one of her hands, using the end of my free finger to tilt her chin up. I drank in those jewel-like blue eyes and the flash of excitement in them.

Her pink lips parted over her white teeth as her eyes sparkled. "Will you teach me to read it?"

"Absolutely, sprite. You're learning so quickly, I'm sure you'll be able to read on your own in no time." Her cheeks flushed under my praise, and if my nostrils were correct, I'd bet those words would send her spiraling into an orgasm while I moved inside her. "Let's go home."

"A long soak in the tub does sound incredible right about now."

"What about a bottle of wine?"

"That is also necessary," she laughed. The sound was sweeter than any wine I could bring her, and I wanted to make her laugh again and again. Her spirit cut through the last of my somber thoughts, and I found myself smirking as I scooped her into my arms, intent on carrying her to the horses. I nodded to Zuriel, who watched us with his typical unreadable expression, then I walked with Izidora to the staircase that would lead us home.

"I'm too tired to use magic to heal my soreness," she sighed into my chest, the sound tinged with fatigue.

"I'll run you a bath with extra salts, then give you a massage when you're finished," I promised, my body heating at the idea of running my palms all over her oiled skin.

"Hmm, I'll think about it," she teased, and I decided not to push further, knowing that she was as likely to dig her heels in than surrender to me, and training with Zuriel had lifted her earlier dark mood.

It was only when we returned to the stables that I finally released her to the ground. She yawned, stretching her arms overhead, then took the reins from the stablehand. Watching her mount a horse should not have been as erotic as it was, but my blood thrummed as she nimbly reached the stirrup and pulled herself up and over the saddle before settling in. She rubbed Twilight's neck, cooing softly to the mare. To me, a horse was a horse, but Izidora held an obvious affection toward the animals.

On our ride home, I waged an internal war, my father's request to manipulate her and my desire to make her happy fighting for the top position on my priority list, and Roc towered over us before I knew it. As promised, I ran a bath for her, filling the tub that overlooked the late afternoon sun sinking over the mountains beyond. Healing salts, scented oils, and bubbles mixed with the hot spring water, and I sprinkled rose petals from the bouquet I had given her last night, the final romantic touch that my mate deserved. Once I was certain the bath was perfect, I returned to the bedroom, finding Izidora's face hidden behind a book on the history of Angels.

I increased the weight of my steps so as not to startle her, then threw her over my shoulder and carried both her and the book into the waiting steam. "You better not drop that book into the water. It's an original."

She giggled as she pounded my back, reminiscent of our earlier fight but without the animosity. "I think I read my first full sentence!"

"Oh? What did it say?" Her tiny feet hit the cold tile, and I lifted the book from her hands, turning it so I could check her work.

"Angels have white hair and blue eyes."

"Good work. You are so fucking smart, sprite."

She had to crane her neck to look at me when I stood this close to her, her petite frame dwarfed by my own. Her aquamarine eyes glittered, accentuated by the blush across her cheeks. "Thanks for this – the bath and teaching me to read."

"I'll be waiting for you in the bedroom, ready with scented oils to soothe your muscles whenever you are finished in here." I tucked a lock of her chestnut hair behind her pointed ear.

"Okay," she said, and my breath caught as she took another

step in my direction, without me forcing her closer. Her hand rested on my chest, right over my thundering heart. I dared not move, for she was like a wild animal and one wrong move might spook her. Balancing on the tip of her toes, she ran delicate fingers across the stubble lining my jaw. "You take such good care of me."

Her voice was sweet with a hint of huskiness, nearly sending me to my knees. But before I could do or say anything, she spun on her heel and pranced toward the waiting bath.

That was my cue to exit. The door shut softly behind me, but I did not retreat until water splashed and blissful sighs floated through the door. The tub was one of my favorite parts of the palace, and I hoped one day we would enjoy it together. For the moment, I would prepare to indulge my mate.

After changing into loose pants, I arranged the scented oil I'd selected for her massage – lavender with a hint of rose, reminding me so much of her floral scent. Then, I picked up a book of my own and settled on the bed, facing the mountains gilded by the late afternoon sun. My hearing was trained intently on the sounds coming from the bathroom as I waited. This was my opportunity to bring her closer; I merely had to keep my temper in check while I got her hooked on the passion we shared.

18

IZIDORA

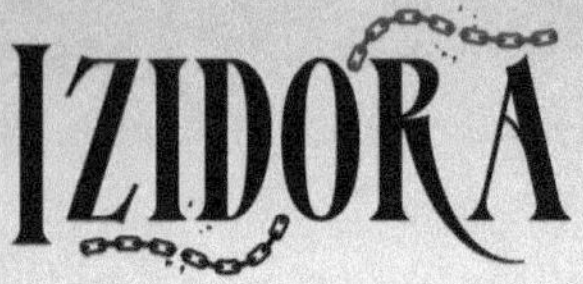

The bath was incredible, and I sank into the steaming water with gusto as the heat sank into my muscles. Aches abated, and the soft cloth rolled over the edge of the tub provided a welcome respite to my tense neck. I was perfectly positioned to watch the creamy golden rays disappear over the snow-capped peaks in the distance. Vanilla and burnt sugar enveloped me as I dispersed some of the bubbles, pulling the floating tray closer, and as I sipped from the wine glass, the taste of plums and chocolate washed over my tongue.

I could get used to this.

Not only the luxurious lifestyle, but being taken care of, like I hadn't been – Ruslan hadn't been – before. Thoughts of King Azim's cruelty caused me to tense once again, and I took a few slow breaths to calm the adrenaline and my racing heart. Another sip of wine helped as I focused on the taste and glide of the liquid across my tongue, then listened to the slight fizz of soap against the warm water, and finally counted the sharp peaks in the distance. Once I felt centered, I surrendered to the moment of peace, appreciating the quiet space to relax – as much as I could with Ruslan waiting to massage my soreness.

Would I allow him to touch me so intimately?

We had a furious passion between us, as evidenced by the damning kiss at the top of the stairs this morning, and my core heated at the memory of him pressing me into the wall, his lips angry and desperate against my own. I would not have stopped him at that moment, of that I was certain. Weeks of banter, seductive words, and possessiveness from Ruslan had my thighs aching and breasts heavy at the slightest provocation. My body responded to his as intensely, if not more intensely, than it had to Kazimir's, and the more I learned about the world, the more I wondered if Kazimir and my friends had kept more from me than I realized. There was simply no way the rest of the realms were totally ignorant of the inner workings in the Iron Realm, of the fact that dozens of different peoples roamed the streets of Radence.

Every day, the seed of doubt grew. If only I could speak with Kazimir, he could explain all of this, and I could forgive him if he'd kept this from me only to protect me.

But I also understood Ruslan's tortured psyche more than before, thanks to the information Zuriel had imparted earlier. It mirrored so much of my own: the scarcity of love and nurture through childhood, the trauma of kill or be killed, the do-whatever-to-survive mentality. Yet I rose above what happened to me, though I struggled with my emotions, and I probably always would. But I tried every day to manage better, to stay open to the wonders of the world around me, and to be kinder to myself and others.

Ruslan walked the opposite path, his experiences creating a wicked male who terrorized others to get what he wanted. Perhaps it was my gifts that guided me down my path, but if I could carve it for myself, Ruslan could follow. Against everything my head screamed at me, my heart softened day by day toward the dark male, and I wanted to see him step into the light.

As the water chilled around me, I made my choice. Downing the last of my wine for courage, I wrapped myself in a fluffy robe hanging near the edge of the tub, then checked my hair in the mirror, pulling a few pieces loose to frame my face. A pink flush dusted my cheeks, but my bright blue eyes held a serenity I hadn't seen before.

It was time to see what happened when I surrendered.

I found Ruslan lounging on the bed, his nose buried in a book, and I paused for a moment to admire his form at ease, a slight crease in his brow as he concentrated on the lines in front of him. He was devastatingly handsome, and as he finished the page, shutting the leather cover with a light snap, I swallowed down a ball of nerves. His muscles flexed and rolled as he pushed himself to kneeling, and my breath fled. Ruslan, shirtless, was what every female dreamed of, and his wicked grin told me he knew it too. But it was the dark fire in his eyes as they locked on my shoulders, where the robe had dropped slightly, baring them and my collarbone, that scared me the most.

"I'll take this as a yes?"

"Yes," I breathed, then with trembling hands I unfastened the belt holding the robe together, slowly pulling the knot apart like I was unwrapping a present. My hips swayed as I walked toward him, eyes roaming over his broad chest and shoulders, following the lines of his tattoos down to the V that dipped below his waistband, where the outline of his hardness grew with each step I took. The robe fell over my shoulders as I crawled onto the bed, and he choked as I shucked it off and lay face down on the soft blankets.

"Tell me how you like it," he croaked, and I celebrated a small victory by having shocked him with my actions.

"Start softly."

He swept a few stray tendrils of hair off my back, then poured warm oil across my bare skin. It smelled of lavender, and the calming scent helped steady my racing heart. With bated breath, I waited for the first touch of his hands.

Rough fingers spread the oil along my spine, fire racing across my skin with each touch. His movements were gentle and slow, with a slight tremble in his hands as if he held back because he knew I would bolt if he moved too quickly.

The bed dipped under his weight as he crawled to my head, and I got a full view of his abs flexing as he stroked up and down my spine, thumbs circling at the base before returning to my neck. My lower belly heated as he worked, both the view and his oiled hands arousing me.

He sat on his heels, using his strong fingers to work knots out of my tense upper back. I groaned as he dug into my right shoulder, and he stayed there a moment longer, delivering extra attention. He only gave at this moment; any hint of concern for his own needs vanished.

Circular strokes worked strain from my arms, his hands gentle yet firm as he loosened my clenched hands. My feet were next, and the pressure he worked into each sole was euphoric. I moaned again, my body relaxing more than I imagined possible. Once he finished kneading my feet, he began working his way up my legs. My breath grew ragged, and as he passed my knees, wetness pooled between my thighs, my arousal unmistakable to his Dragon senses, and I did not try to hide it as I did before.

The first brush of his finger on the sensitive insides of my thighs was like a bolt of lightning to my core. I was wound so tight, despite his handiwork, from denying my lust for him for so long. My body was flushed and hot and wanting, and I ached to be filled already, and for once, my head did not protest. His breath hitched as he slowly stroked higher and higher, and loose pants hid nothing of his own arousal.

Ruslan's eyes were molten, locked on his hands and how close they were to my dripping center. I spread my legs slightly, allowing him access to the highest parts of my thighs. A stifled groan sounded behind me, and I knew this was torture for him. He liked to dominate, but he held back, understanding that in this moment we were balanced on the edge of a cliff, and one wrong move would send us careening down to our deaths. So I spread my legs wider, showing without saying what I wanted from him – because I couldn't say it, couldn't let him win. But I wanted him to fuck me with every ember that burned between us, turning our passion into an inferno that consumed everything in its wake.

When his fingers were a breath from my core, I was no longer sure if oil or arousal slicked my thighs.

The soft fabric beneath my breasts did not provide any friction to my aching nipples or swollen clit, and I longed to rub against something rough. I placed my hands beneath my shoulders and pushed back onto all fours, my center bared to the male behind me.

"Fuck," he breathed, and a small part of me that wanted to please him purred at the strain in his voice. I flipped so I lay on my back, breasts on full display. His nostrils flared, and he closed his eyes, brows pinching as if in pain. A few uneven breaths later, he regained enough control to continue rubbing his hands over my legs, though my own breaths were shallow as he worked up my thighs, the full view of his chiseled body the icing on the dessert that was his hands all over me.

He did not touch my core as he slid his hands over my hip bones, and I groaned as he passed it by. I needed something – anything – to touch the swollen parts of me. His grin was wicked, and I realized the tables were about to be turned. He straddled my body as he worked up my abs, then to my chest, bypassing my nipples, which were hard enough to cut glass. His fingers found the sensitive part of my ribs, eliciting a shiver as he traced a map to my hips. I closed my legs, rubbing them together to get some of the friction I was desperate for; I wanted to be filled, stretched, and rubbed all at the same time.

Ruslan tsked, then reached behind him to separate my legs. "The only one who will give you pleasure tonight is me," he purred. Bracing his hands on either side of my head, he bent his face to mine, waiting, his smoky grays flicking between my lips and eyes.

My whole body was on fire, trembling as the thread pulling us together went taut, vibrating with anticipation. I was so hot, my skin so tight, and Ruslan remained absolutely still, torturing me with that damning smirk of his that melted the moment he crashed his lips against mine.

Where I expected a battle, I received sensuality, our kiss filled with passion of a different kind. His tongue parted my lips, stroking mine and tasting the last drops of wine that lingered on it, before the need to breathe had me turning my head to the side, and I sucked in a lungful of air. His lips found my exposed ear, then my neck as he trailed to my pulse and sucked on the fluttering beat. My hands were pinned beneath his chest, and he lifted his weight off me momentarily, before grabbing my hand and yanking it to his hardness with a growl.

"Do you feel how fucking hard I am for you, sprite? The diamonds we pull from our mines are no match for this, and I plan on making you shatter over it." He stilled, mouth still on my neck, waiting to see what would happen next.

This was the tipping point.

If I touched him here, I would be giving him a part of myself. I would be opening myself to the possibility of us – the possibility that we were mates. The thread I'd been denying for so long vibrated with anticipation, and with a serrated breath, I clasped my hand around him. I ran my thumb over the tip that jutted prominently between us, and a choked groan escaped his lips and ghosted over my neck. Wrapping my hand around the length of fabric, I stroked once, twice, as Ruslan sucked my pulse point. His control slipped with every passing moment, his hips rocking into my hand with each movement up and down.

With his calloused palms, he gripped my breast, pinching the hard nipple that brushed against the hard planes of his chest. Those hands were large enough to envelop it completely, and he splayed them over the mound, providing his mouth access to the pink peak, trailing his tongue around it before pulling it into his mouth with a pop. A cry escaped my lips as his teeth grazed the sensitive bud, and he flicked his tongue over it to soothe the ache before repeating his actions on the other side.

The pleasure and the pain together were a heady combination, and I wanted more. My body arched into his, and I moved my hand from outside to inside the fabric of his pants and grasped the velvety skin. His cock jerked beneath my touch, and the sound that escaped his lips was primal, igniting my core like it was a candle and he was the match. His hands dropped to either side of the bed while he gritted his teeth, breathing hard through his nose as he fought for control.

"Izidora." My name was both a plea and a prayer on his lips, and he stared at me in a state of pure rapture. He drank in the sight of my naked body below him, my hand disappearing between us. He looked at me like I was his salvation, like I was the oxygen he needed to breathe. Our gaze did not break as he rocked back, my hand releasing him. His arrogant face sank to my core, his hands parting my thighs so he could get a good look at me.

"You are so wet, my sprite," he groaned, and my core fluttered as his hot breath swept across my skin. His tongue found my inner thighs, and my hands found his hair as I pulled him where I wanted. A rumbling laugh vibrated my thighs, and he flicked his tongue lightly against that sensitive bundle of nerves.

"Oh!" My whole body jerked as I released a cry of pleasure. It wasn't nearly enough, and I told him so with my hands in his hair. With that encouragement, he latched on to my core, his eyes closing as he groaned into my pussy. He licked from bottom to top of my slit, stopping to swirl his tongue around my swollen nerves before repeating the motion.

"You taste so fucking good," he said as he lapped at my wetness.

I whimpered under his touch, beads of sweat forming on my brow as he dove his tongue into me. But I wanted – needed more. As if he could sense that, he pulled away, hands finding his pants and pulling them off with one fluid motion, and he stood before me, cock swollen and ready, looking like a god as the last rays of the dying sun highlighted his powerful body. The bed dipped as he returned his weight to it, and his carved thighs spread my legs further until his thick length tapped my entrance.

"I want to hear you say it," he purred, a hand on my hip and the other gripping his hardness.

I bit my lip, and shook my head. Saying the words out loud meant that I was choosing this, choosing him over Kazimir, and I wasn't ready to make that choice, not yet.

The grip on my hip turned bruising. "Say it." His eyes flashed with black flame, and the sight excited me far more than it should have. His head circled my clit, then he lined himself up with my core, waiting. "I told you that you'd be begging me to fuck you before the week was up, my sprite."

I cursed the male who was about to drive me as mad as him.

"I can't," I managed to pant, my whole body tingling, trembling, as I waited for him to just fuck me already.

His dark brow rose, and that depraved smirk played on his

lips. "Can't or won't? Because if it is 'won't', I'll make that decision for both of us. You are so fucking exquisite, sprite, and I don't think I can hold out much longer." He slid his length through my slick folds, teasing my entrance. "Because every fucking thing I learn about you makes me want you more – your fire, your resilience, your intelligence. And together they're a deadly poison that I'd gladly imbibe just for one chance to put my lips on you."

My whole body flushed under his words, breath hitching, and that was the only answer he needed from me. With one thrust, he seated himself fully, not allowing me time to adjust to his size.

And I was so, deliciously, full.

He backed out slowly, then entered again, teasing me when I was so close to combusting already, his cock hitting that perfect spot deep inside. His arms fell to either side of my face, and our lips locked in a fierce battle filled with moans and hints of blood as he nipped my lip and licked the beads of metallic liquid away. I pushed back into him, grinding my clit shamelessly against his hips, and he dropped a hand to that sensitive bundle of nerves, circling his thumb over it as my walls pulsed, signaling my impending release. A growl rumbled in his chest as I tightened over his length, hips working faster, bringing me to the climax.

"Ruslan!" I gasped as I fell apart, waves of pleasure rocking up my spine as I arched off the bed, walls clenching his cock. They pulsed and fluttered as my head rolled back, and he caught me before I could fall to the bed. His other hand found my hip, and he pinned me in place as his thrusts became furious.

"Fuck, Izidora," he groaned, burying himself completely, then filled me with hot liquid.

But he did not stop.

Exiting my heated center only momentarily, he swung my

right leg over my left so I lay on my side beneath him, then shoved himself back in, his hands grasping my hips as he brutally thrust into me, our skin slapping as the wetness from our combined release coated our skin.

"I don't want to stop," he moaned. "I've waited so long for this, for you."

"Then don't," I breathed, his girth stretching me in a new way, hitting a totally different angle than I'd experienced before. Ruslan was huge, and I felt every inch of him moving inside me, delivering pleasure to new areas I'd yet to explore.

One hand moved to my breast, the other to my clit as he rolled them both between his fingers. A heady moan escaped me as my senses were flooded with erotic touch, and I twisted slightly so I could reach around my back and cup his balls. His guttural moan sent heat straight to my core, adding to the slickness already dripping from my entrance. Swiping my fingers through the liquid, I brought my hand to his lips, and his eyes blazed as he greedily sucked my fingers.

"You are sweeter than any cake," he moaned, and I trailed my wet fingers down his chest and stomach, dipping them between my thighs to rub my clit so he could hold me steady. His thrusts pushed me across the bed, causing me to cry out. Our gazes locked, our breaths uneven yet synced, and sweat dripped from his body to mine. A wave of pleasure rose from my center, sending my lashes fluttering, and Ruslan growled his approval.

"Come for me, my sprite. I want to feel your walls sucking me dry," he commanded. And with that, pleasure crashed through me, and I screamed his name as stars filled my vision.

"Yes," he hissed through clenched teeth, his pace slowing as his release caught up to him. With a roar, he finished inside me, fingers gripping my hips, holding me to him, as his cock twitched and spurted. Breathless, we remained locked in that position, until a tender hand caressed my face then smoothed the stray hairs that clung to my sweat-soaked brow. He planted a featherlight kiss on my lips before removing himself, but he immediately pulled me into his lap, holding me as if I had given him the greatest gift of his life. His arms were strong and sure – almost safe. His desire morphed into something deeper, something stronger, and for the first time, I truly considered that he might be right about us being mates.

19

KAZIMIR

Endre dropped from the sky, landing lightly next to Viktor and me in the open plains of the Day Realm. It was much warmer here than in the Night and Crystal Realm, the sun shining with all its might on this cloudless, breezeless day. Even standing still, sweat dripped down my spine, and it beaded the faces of all my traveling companions. My tunic was untucked from my pants, allowing the barest hint of relief on my heated skin.

"The armies are about two and a half, maybe three days behind us now. Looks like they will cross paths before the sun sets tonight," Endre reported, wiping at his brow. His long, messy locks were also drenched, and if he had been wearing a shirt, it would no doubt have been soaked through.

"And how long until we reach Zheka?" Viktor asked, shaking his waterskin lightly beside his ear to gauge the contents.

"Maybe two days or so. Aress Keep is visible in the distance. If only they built their buildings more than one story. It would be so much easier to spot." Endre strolled toward his horse, where his shirt was draped carefully over the saddle. He picked it up, then thought better of it and smoothed it back down.

Viktor tipped the remaining contents into his mouth, then shook his head. "I think that is the point."

Fek sank his teeth into a shiny red apple I pulled from my saddlebags, munching loudly and nearly drowning out my friends' conversation. His black hide was even darker, coated in sweat and his tail flicked endlessly back and forth to clear the pests from it. He had been through a lot these past few months, and once this was all over he deserved a nice long break. The stallion nuzzled my hand when the apple disappeared, searching for more of his favorite treat. "You ate it all, you greedy bastard," I chided him before pulling my hand away. He snorted, clearly displeased that I did not hold an unlimited supply.

Domi appeared at my side, another plump apple in hand. Fek's eyes brightened, and he surged forward, barely missing my toes, to snatch the apple from her. She smiled, rubbing his face while she cooed to him. "He may not be one of mine, but he certainly is a beautiful horse, Kazimir, and with such a big personality."

She wiped sweat from her brow, having just returned from training with Vadim and Liliana. We'd stopped daily to allow them time to train, both Domi and Liliana fiercely determined to join us on the battlefield. When King Airre saw them train on the first day, he had requested that Queen Immonen join them. Vadim was going to have his hands full of vicious females by the time the first battle came to pass. Unfortunately for him, they were not the type of vicious females he usually wanted.

"Fek has been a good mount for many years now. I think he will enjoy a nice retirement once this is all over," I said, and he bobbed his head as if he agreed.

"I would love to have him as a stud, if you don't mind. He would produce beautiful and strong offspring," she praised as she took a step back and admired him appreciatively. Fek shook his long mane and stamped his foot, showing off his prowess, earning a laugh from Domi.

"It would be my honor, Domi." That garnered me a wide grin.

Kaztar appeared by her side with a waterskin, which she gulped greedily, releasing a grateful breath when she finished. "We should get going again soon," he said with a sniff. "It has been too long without a proper meal and bath." Kaztar lifted the water from his wife's hands, tipping it to his lips only to find it empty.

"Who knew you were such a princess, Kaztar," I joked, reaching for my own waterskin tucked in my bags and handing it to him.

He accepted the leather with a wry grin and then saluted me with it. "You're used to it, Kazimir, after living on the road for so many years. In fact, I think you probably prefer it to court life," he teased.

"You are spot on with that assessment," I agreed. The longer I spent with Kaztar and Domi, the more I liked them. They were an easy fit into our group, and I welcomed his input on matters of strategy, especially when the topic was court-related. Both Kaztar and Domi were excellent courtiers, which balanced out the brawn and other fighting-related skills the remaining Nighthounds offered. All deferred to me for final decision, as the natural leader of the group. It had been that way long before my father died, as he had said time and time again. I wish I had listened to him more than I did, and that I had not would be my greatest regret in life.

The thought of him ripped open a deep wound inside me, a pain so profound that I wasn't sure how one person could bear it all. Blinking through it, I shoved it away, forcing myself to refocus on the couple in front of me and my mate that needed me.

"We better get going then, so Kaztar can have a bath." Domi smiled at her husband, grabbing him by the hand and leading him to their mounts. He shook his head teasingly, the affection between them apparent. Another stab to the gut forced me to glance away from them, instead, I counted every Fae I saw to ensure every member of our traveling party was present. When I was certain all had returned to the group from their various activities, I called for the ride to continue.

Creaking leather and snorts filled the air as we mounted, and I dug my heels into Fek's sides, leading us down the dirt road that led to Zheka. A loose group formed around me, and jokes flitted through the still air and conversations ebbed and flowed in time with the light breeze that came with the midday. Not a speck of shade dotted the landscape around us, and tall grass rippled like water as far as the eye could see.

What was Izidora doing?

It had been weeks since I'd seen her, and with each passing day my brain found new ways to torture me. Thoughts of her suffering at the hands of Ruslan – or worse, fucking him – nearly drove me mad. Every possible scenario had flashed through my mind, until I was simultaneously convinced she was thriving and dying. But she was my mate, and I would know if she had died, even without our bond solidified – at least that was what I told myself.

That Goddess-damned prophecy. When it wasn't images of Izidora coming undone beneath me floating before my eyes, it was those vague words.

Her mates darkness will rise

My thoughts and desires couldn't possibly get any darker, could they? The number of times I'd imagined draining the life from Ruslan with the assistance of my newfound binding magic filled me with such sick pleasure that I could barely admit it to myself, and the thought of sharing that with Endre was too shameful for me to contemplate.

As if the male knew I had been thinking about him, my messy-haired best friend slowed his mount to ride beside me. "Where's your head at?"

Running a hand across my face, I shook my head. "The prophecy, Izidora, the usual stuff."

"I know you're worried about her," Endre said with a furtive glance toward Liliana. "But she will be okay when we get there."

"What if she's not? What if she's dead, or worse, Ruslan has forced her into something?" *What if he was her mate, and not me?* I had not previously allowed the thought into my head, but it had woven its way in and sunk its claws into my brain.

"Then we snatch her and run, just like we've planned." Endre tried to reassure me, yet his words did not temper the rising anxiety. After all, I had failed to protect her, and what if she thought less of me for not upholding my promise to keep her safe? My hands tightened around Fek's reins, that black beast inside my chest rearing up, ready to fight. I pushed the dark magic down, securing it behind a wall of moonlight, refusing to let it overwhelm me and harm Endre again.

"But that's not what's really bothering you today, is it, Kazimir?"

Fuck Endre and his uncanny knack for making me talk when I did not want to.

"No." I relaxed my grip, and Fek shook his head to slacken the bit digging into his mouth. Then, I dropped my voice to a whisper, not wanting anyone else to hear. "What if Ruslan is her mate?"

Endre opened his mouth, then closed it again. He blew a

lock of hair away from his face on a long exhale, then tried again. "I'm not going to tell you it's impossible, because it's not, and you're not going to be reassured by that statement anyway. But you do feel a pull for her, yeah? That's solid evidence that there's something there between the two of you."

"I don't feel it now."

"If you'd felt it all along, we would have found her sooner. You probably have to be near her to feel it," Endre shrugged, dropping his reins and stretching his arms overhead. We'd been riding relentlessly for what felt like years at this point, and the weariness was not only getting to me. "I'm so fucking ready to be off a horse for a while."

"After the war, I'm sitting my ass on the beach with Izidora for a month," I declared. Then I slipped into a brief daydream of her playing in the surf and crashing into the waves with me on the shores of the Day Realm, which remained warm even during the winter months that blanketed the Iron and Night Realms in snow.

Endre snickered, finally pulling his shirt over his head again. "I don't think you'll get that lucky, not with a coronation to plan and a queendom to run."

My stomach dropped as my worries returned with full force. "What will we do if Izidora doesn't want to come back with us? Who will rule?"

"Probably my father or Viktor's," Endre guessed. "Definitely not Valintin or Luzak, though they won't go down without a fight. Don't worry about it for now, Kazimir. Let's focus on getting the army we need and taking down the Iron Realm once and for all."

He was right. Despite the rising tension in my shoulders, there were more important tasks that required my attention, and focusing on what I could do, rather than the endless possibilities, was what would assuage my fears.

My emotions were frayed after so much time had passed atop our mounts; the days seemed impossibly long, and I had far too much time to think. Between my grief over losing my father, Kriztof, and the twins, and my rage around Izidora's kidnapping, I wasn't sure how much more I could take.

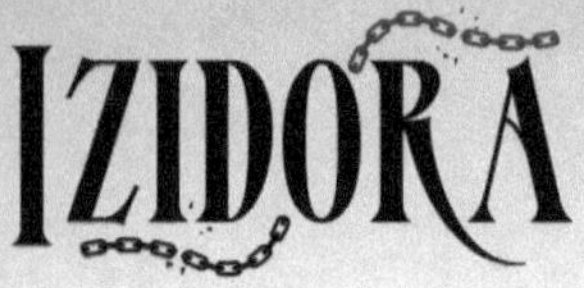 IZIDORA

"**T**ime to wake up, my sprite." Ruslan's rumbling voice against my neck stirred me from a dreamless slumber, and I grumbled at him, yanking the warm blanket tighter and turning over in an attempt to stay in bed. Fingers crept along my back, sneaking beneath the wool and peeling it from my shoulders.

"No," I moaned, but the blanket slipped from between my fingers, and a chill washed over me, quickly replaced by a warm body.

His lips found my neck, and I shivered, but not from the cold. "You've been such a good girl, training so hard these last weeks, that I'll let you sleep for another half hour before we head to the barracks." My eyes popped open as his fingers brushed my hip bones, and he yanked me flush to his body, his erection digging into my back. "Unless you're awake now?"

Goddess damn him, he knew exactly what he was doing to me. "Fine," I yawned, taking a lazy overhead stretch to work some movement into my stiff body. Since I'd arrived in the Iron Realm, I'd spent more hours training than not, first strength and balance with Ruslan in the morning, then sparring with Drazen and the other soldiers midday, and the afternoon hours with Zuriel. When I collapsed onto a soft sofa by the fire at night, Ruslan and I read together, and the previous night, I'd read four pages by myself.

For that I'd earned a rough fucking that I could still feel between my thighs, and the thought of it made my center ache for more. I'd lost count of how many times I had orgasmed, and at some point I must have fallen asleep, utter exhaustion pulling me under when I could no longer keep my head above water.

The bed creaked as Ruslan stepped off of it, throwing on a pair of pants before slipping into the living area of our suite, returning moments later with a tray of food. Stifling another yawn, I reached for a black tunic strewn across the end of the bed and slipped it on, then scooted so my back rested against the wood headboard. Ruslan placed the tray in my lap, planting a kiss on my cheek before crawling onto the bed beside me. He smelled like sex and cedarwood, though my mouth watered from the heavenly scent of cinnamon wafting off the tray. Before I could stop him, he snatched a roll off my plate, smirking at me as he popped it into his mouth.

"Hey! I was going to eat that," I grumbled.

"If you eat all your eggs, I'll have Cedomir make you more for after our strength session."

"I need the sugar to keep up my energy," I said, stuffing a forkful of eggs into my mouth.

Ruslan's brawny shoulder bumped into mine. "That you do. Can't have you falling asleep while I'm in between your thighs again."

I nearly choked on my eggs as my cheeks flamed, along with another part of me. I drained a glass of water to force the food down, and when I placed it back on the tray, Ruslan lifted it, hopped from the bed, and took it to the bathroom, returning with a full glass moments later.

He took such good care of me.

After I'd given myself to him, he'd morphed into something softer, at least when we weren't between the sheets. He oversaw my physical training, tended to my every need, even anticipating them, and ensured I was eating enough. His massages were heavenly, especially as my magic was fully tapped out by the end of the day, not a drop left to ease the ache in my muscles. He showed me a side of him that no one else saw, for beyond these walls, Ruslan was the ruthless prince who demanded perfection from his soldiers.

And yet Kazimir had not left my mind, and guilt gnawed in my belly at every twist and turn down this path I walked with Ruslan.

———

I WAS an insidious bloom in the sparring ring. I was often underestimated due to my size, but just like a rose, I hid my thorns until my beholder had grown cocky and distracted, then struck when they least expected it. Facing one of Ruslan's soldiers, a Bear Shifter Félvér named Savich, I held white flame to my twin blades, the heat cutting through the frosty mid-morning air. Blood rushed in my ears, blocking out all sound as we circled each other.

Savich was burly and moved slowly, often leaving his right side open when he retreated from a series of heavy blows, so I waited patiently, trying to maintain control of my breath, as I blocked and parried.

"Let your emotions go, Izidora!" Drazen called from outside the training arena.

I ignored the half Dragon, instead cutting to my left and dodging a strike from Savich. But the male knew my intention, and a foot slipped out faster than it should have, sending me tumbling to the ground and my blades scattering as I tried to catch myself with my hands. Out of the corner of my eye, I saw Ruslan's white-knuckled grip on the wood panel in front of him, but he would not step in – no, he expected me to perform like the rest of his soldiers.

The ground trembled as Savich's knees hit the ground beside me, his arms latching across my chest and pulling me against him as we tumbled through the dirt. But Savich's arms were like tree trunks, which meant I could use my petite frame to slip out of his grip. I waited until we landed on our sides, then with all my strength, I smashed my head back, connecting with his nose, and walked my feet to the side, bridging off his chest until I had enough space to slide my torso underneath his hands. In a flash, I crouched and backed away, one hand remaining outstretched defensively while the other searched for my fallen blades. My boot hit something hard, and I spared a momentary glance behind me, finding my first sword, just as Savich pushed to his feet and reclaimed his mace.

Blood spurted from his nose, but if it bothered him, he didn't show it. Waiting again for an opening, we danced through the ring, Savich the aggressor and I the supposedly helpless female. But my magic was strong, far stronger than that of the males in Ruslan's personal guard, and all it took was one mistake on their part for me to win.

While he retreated, Savich's legs drew too close together. Using my agility, I sprung on him, building a low block out of white magic behind his feet and causing him to fall flat on his back. The sound was like a falling tree, and his eyes grew wide at my trick. White flames re-appeared on my blades as I wasted no time pinning him beneath my boot, using deadly sharp tips pointed at his throat and groin to subdue him.

"I yield," he said from the ground, and I banished the flames and sheathed my blades across my back.

"You are a tricky little one." Savich's voice was as gravely as the ground around the stables, though the Bear was anything but angry with me.

"Gotta keep you on your toes," I grinned, offering a hand to help him up.

He took it, though I didn't think I was much help in getting the giant male off the ground. "Or off my toes, so to speak."

Before I could respond, Drazen called out for me, and with a sigh I trotted over to the fence where he stood with Ruslan. "You've got to let your emotions flow through you while you fight, especially when you're working with both swords and magic," Drazen chided.

But I couldn't release the death grip I had on my emotions, not when surrendering to the flow meant breaking the last of my resolve to not fall for Ruslan. That part of me that held onto the idea of Kazimir was locked in a wooden box in the back of my mind, though the wood rotted with every small act of kindness from Ruslan, and every reminder that Kazimir might not have had my best interests at heart. If I broke the lock, there would be nothing holding me back from accepting that Ruslan might in fact be my mate.

"They get in the way," I snapped. "Besides, I still won."

"This time," Ruslan growled. "But when there is a battle raging around you? Probably not. You'll never see that arrow flying for your chest until it's too late, or the opponent sneaking up behind you while you fight another, if you're putting so much focus on keeping your emotions locked away."

"Yeah, yeah, I know I'm supposed to be this great weapon for you, you don't have to remind me."

Ruslan's eyes flashed with black fire, and he snatched my arm and yanked me to him, the wood beam separating us digging into my stomach. "You know you are so much more than that to me, sprite. If I thought you'd be harmed on the battlefield, I wouldn't be able to concentrate on what was in front of me. I want you to be strong so you can defend yourself when I'm not there. I'd die without you."

I'd die without you.

The sheer intensity of Ruslan's infatuation knocked me off balance, and I was swept away in his smoky gaze for the hundredth time. To be wanted, to be loved, so deeply was everything I'd ever dreamed of, and there was no doubt in my mind that he meant those words with fervent sincerity.

And that was yet another difference between Ruslan and Kazimir. Ruslan never made me feel like a victim or someone in need of saving. Instead, he showed me how to be my own hero.

"I know," I whispered, reaching a hand to stroke the hair coating his sharp jaw, siphoning away a spoonful of Ruslan's anger with that touch. He leaned into my hand, pressing a kiss to my palm, then released his grip on my other wrist, locking our fingers together.

"Are you tired? Do you need a break?" he asked, the world melting away as his gray eyes searched my blue ones.

I blew out a breath, then chewed on my lip, before deciding to admit the truth. "I am exhausted."

Two strong arms lifted me over the railing, then Ruslan curled me against his chest. "I'll fly us up to the palace, but when we leave later, you have to try flying down."

My palms started sweating at the thought of jumping off the railing on the roof and plummeting toward the far away ground, but I'd never get stronger if I didn't try. "Okay," my voice wavered, and I tucked my head against his chest, letting the steady thrum of his heart soothe my racing one.

Black, leathery wings snapped out behind him, nearly knocking Drazen over, and we shot into the sky.

"Asshole!" Drazen called from below with a hint of a smile tugging at his lips.

Once we'd reached the roof and the wind ceased howling in my ears, Ruslan murmured, "You know I'll be there to catch you if you fall. Always."

———

"I SIPHONED AWAY some of Ruslan's anger earlier," I told Zuriel as we sat cross-legged on the mats in the training area beneath Ryza Citadel.

"And what did you do with it?" Zuriel asked, raising a white brow.

My gaze dropped to my hands, twisting them together. "I forgot to do something with it."

"Let's try a visualization exercise so you can start our training today clear-headed," Zuriel suggested. "Close your eyes."

My lids were already heavy, and it was no trouble to follow his instructions.

"You're standing beside a stream, watching the water flow over the stones, creating a small waterfall. Cup your hands beneath it, feel the wetness in your palms as it fills them. Take a deep breath in." My mind formed the image with perfect clarity as my chest expanded with air. "That little pool in your hands is what you drained from Ruslan. It does not belong to you. Open your palms and release the water back into the stream, breathing out all the air you've been holding."

As my hands emptied in my mind and my lungs emptied in my body, a little of that exhaustion I'd been carrying slipped away along with the emotions that were not my own. We repeated the exercise nearly a dozen times before I felt clear and light, some of my energy returned.

"Thanks, Zuriel, I really needed that," I admitted, rubbing my eyes with the heels of my palms.

"You are an empath, which means you are in tune with the

emotions of every being around you, not only your own. It is important that you clear yourself regularly, especially after you siphon from someone. If you do not, you risk their emotions becoming your own," Zuriel warned.

"Drazen keeps telling me I need to let go of the grip I have over my emotions," I sighed, leaning back on my elbows while the Angel's lips tugged upward.

"Drazen is right. You need to let them flow like water over rock. Holding onto them will only serve to hurt you."

Heaving out a frustrated breath, I asked, "But what if that hold is the only thing stopping me from falling for Ruslan? I love Kazimir – even though I have doubts about his intentions, and I'm afraid if I surrender to them, I'll lose him."

But as the words left my lips, I wondered if I truly meant them anymore.

Another unreadable flash crossed Zuriel's ice-blue eyes, and I instinctively reached out to him with my mind, trying to read his emotions. *Guilt.* I got the sense the Angel knew more than he let on, but he did not seem inclined to share.

"The only way out is through," Zuriel replied. "You must walk the path without obstacles to truly know your heart. You may surprise yourself, cousin."

I gave him a half-smile then pushed myself to standing. "Can we work on shifting emotions today? I think I've got the hang of siphoning and flooding, but some more subtle emotional changes would be helpful."

"Absolutely." Zuriel rose, his frame lithe and graceful as he crossed to the other side of the arena. "I want you to try at a distance, too. You can't always rely on proximity."

Searching inside myself for the moonlight- and flame-wrapped crystal, I filled it with happy memories – riding Mistik and Twilight, reading by myself, besting opponents in the sparring ring – then reached out to Zuriel, searching for his mental barrier across the domed room. It took immense focus, but I finally felt that thin barrier and worked my magic beneath it.

Zuriel was agitated, a mixture of guilt, sadness, and helplessness. With a gentle nudge, my magic spread feelings of calm and peace, and little by little, Zuriel's mood shifted, until he was serene. I retreated from his mind, then opened my eyes to find a wide smile gracing the Angel's face, making him look otherworldly.

"You are brilliant, Izidora. That was the perfect direction to take those emotions, and you did it in a subtle enough way that most would not notice," he praised.

"Do I need to clear after shifting emotions too?" I asked, wiping sweat from my forehead with my sleeve.

"It wouldn't hurt, though you needn't clear right now while we're still practicing. We can finish with another exercise, but remember if you siphon or influence Ruslan's emotions later, clear again," he explained. "Try shifting my emotions again, and this time, I will walk around. You need to maintain a connection with my mind at all times, which can be tricky while I'm moving."

We spent the rest of the afternoon working on siphoning, flooding, and shifting emotions at a distance, until my magic was utterly spent from using my Fae part for fighting and my Angel part for mind-work.

"I'm tapped out," I finally admitted, swaying on my feet. As if Ruslan had been perched outside the training area waiting for me to utter those words, he strode through the door, eyes immediately locking on me.

"I see you've worked her hard today, Zuriel," he said, those gorgeous grays dancing over my sweat-soaked frame.

The Angel crossed to the center of the space to join us. "Izidora is an exceptional student. We're going to conclude our lesson with a visualization exercise. Would you care to join us?"

Ruslan shrugged. "Why not."

The three of us settled in a loose circle, Zuriel inhaling deeply to signal the beginning of the exercise. His lids closed over his icy eyes, and I allowed a sidelong glance at Ruslan before shutting my own. His participation was unexpected, and I missed Zuriel's opening words as I pondered Ruslan's intentions.

Maybe he was changing, and not only because I influenced his emotions.

"...empty your lungs of air and release all tension from your body." The air I expelled from my body was rife with exhaustion, and my shoulders slumped inward with the motion as I unburdened myself of Zuriel's emotions. A brush against my knee had me cracking an eye, and Ruslan's brow was pinched as his fingers settled against my leg before drifting back to his own. That thread that pulled me toward him hummed in a soothing way that settled deep in my bones, chasing away a hint of loneliness I hadn't realized still clung to me. Zuriel's melodic voice faded away as I became acutely aware of Ruslan's presence in my body, in my heart, and in my soul.

21

KAZIMIR

The closer we journeyed to Zheka, the more frequently a handful of trees rose from the plains, until finally the tall grass gave way to farms. The fields were massive, filled with vines, stalks, and dark-skinned Fae using magic to manipulate the earth. The Day Faes' magic was not elemental like that of the Crystal or Iron Realm, but rather steeped in nature, wholly connected to the energy of the flora and fauna around them. Many saw our group and waved, friendly and welcoming. I had always loved the Day Fae, their gentle nature and liveliness brightening the air across the land, but I dared not cross one because they were fierce warriors – relentless, agile, and without mercy.

Eventually, a massive river stood before us, a wide stone bridge spanning across it, and on the other side, Zheka waited. The hustle and bustle of the city that rose from the plains greeted us the moment the river was at our backs. The scent of fresh pepper, rich cumin, and spicy coriander wafted from stalls where meats cooked over open flames, while the laughter of old males drinking wine at open-air taverns floated through the air. Females shouted at children who ran unattended through the streets, dodging in and out of the low stone-and-thatch houses that lined either side of the large thoroughfare that led straight to Aress Keep. The city was alive and authentic in a way that no other in Északi could be.

As we approached the gates to Aress, I examined the sprawl of the keep. It was the tallest building in Zheka, its spread creating an entire network of dwellings and rooms in the heart of the city. In the very center stood a thick, tall tree, its canopy stretching across the surrounding buildings, casting them in much-needed shade. Queen Viktoria and King Consort Geza stepped from the shadows as we approached the open-air entry to the keep. The monarch's clothing floated behind them, rich in color and light in weight, a necessity in the breezeless inner city. A delicate metal crown hammered to appear like tangling vines rested upon the queen of the Day Realm's forehead, emeralds and citrines dotting the gold metal and glinting in the sunlight. Her husband wore his hair in long braids down his back, and the locks glittered with gold cuffs at various intervals.

They stopped before us with hands clasped in front of them, easy postures that spoke of their trust in us.

"King Airre! We were not expecting to see you before the feast," Queen Viktoria greeted us in her fruity voice.

"My apologies, Queen Viktoria, but we have urgent matters to discuss." He dismounted and bowed his head to the queen of the Day Realm. "I am not sure if you have heard the news, but King Zalan is dead."

The smile fell from her face, replaced with a crease between her brows. Her eyes flitted to me, then at the rest of the Night Fae in attendance. "I have not, but this is most worrisome news. Please, let me welcome you inside to freshen up, then we will discuss such matters."

"You are most kind, Queen Viktoria," King Airre replied, handing his reins off before following her inside. Queen

Immonen caught up to him, wrapping her arm around his, and we passed off our mounts before trailing behind the monarchs into a breezeway that formed the inner circle of the keep. A few minutes' walk led us to a set of wood doors that opened to reveal a large central hall with connecting doors leading to other rooms that I knew to be small apartments.

"I'm afraid the guest rooms have not been prepared, but I will have them readied after you have had time to wash up. Meet us in the dining hall in an hour, and we will have a fresh meal prepared," she smiled, yet it did not reach her eyes. She glanced at her husband, King Consort Geza, a subtle but strained look passing between them.

"Thank you for your hospitality, Queen Viktoria," I said, and then bowed. She simply nodded before closing the doors behind us. We split up, enough rooms lining the hall that each could have privacy. After a thorough scrub, I donned a fresh tunic and pants, my hands returning to my bag for a momentary brush of the lacy undergarments and tunic of Izidora's before buckling it shut.

There would be time to hold them later.

I sought out Endre, and found him with Viktor and Vadim, all freshly dressed and deep in conversation.

"You did see how concerned she was, right?" Viktor said as I entered the room.

Vadim nodded, smoothing his beard as he contemplated his response. "Maybe she does not like being in the dark? There is not a great communication network between the capitals, and the Day Realm is as far as you can get from the Night Realm. Speaking of keeping people in the dark, when are we going to come clean about Izidora not actually being King Zalan's daughter?" Vadim looked pointedly at me.

"Not only that, but the breeding program Tamara

mentioned. I think that might be important to our battle plans," Viktor added.

I heaved a sigh, running my palm over my face, tension eating at my shoulders. We were so close to Izidora, and I wanted nothing more than to ride on until I could snatch her in my arms and carry her home with me. I quickly shut down my fantasy, my mind having gotten the better of me the last few days as we rode, distracting me when I needed to focus.

But Viktor and Vadim were right, and both pieces of information were important. Endre quirked a brow over Viktor's shoulder, and I knew he wanted me to share the third piece of information I kept hidden – the binding magic.

"Let's reveal what we know once Queen Viktoria has agreed to join us. Like you said, Viktor, the fact that half Iron - half whatever soldiers might exist in masse will affect our battle plans, though I suspect King Airre knows something, given that he is intimately familiar with the prophecy. But there is another thing I have kept from both of you." I needed to confess before I lost the courage. Both Viktor and Vadim wore serious expressions as they waited for me to continue. "When we were at the Crystal Realm, I received binding magic."

"No fucking way," Vadim blurted at the same time Viktor exclaimed, "Received?"

"Yes fucking way. And he nearly killed me because he lost himself to the madness," Endre snapped.

Viktor glanced between Endre and me. "Is this true?"

I looked at my feet, still ashamed of myself. But I took a deep breath, lifted my head, and took responsibility for my actions. "Yes. I had a dream that felt like it was real, where the Fates allowed a snake to enter my chest, and when I awoke, a dark magic had curled around the moonlight in my magic well. And since the first time I practiced, Endre has helped ground me so I do not lose myself again."

"We should not tell anyone about this. *Anyone.* Binding magic is dark and twisted, not to mention powerful. Most Fae fear it," Viktor emphasized. "But, it will help us win this war. So keep practicing, and let us know what we can do."

Viktor had always been pragmatic.

A knock interrupted our discussion. "Ready to go?" Liliana's energetic voice carried through the barrier between us.

"Fuck off! We're busy," Vadim shouted back.

Liliana's scoff was crystal clear through the door. "When you're finished jerking each other off, the rest of us are waiting." King Airre's booming laugh masked Liliana's retreating footsteps, and I found myself grinning as I readied myself for another game of politics.

"We'll continue this later. We have a queen to see," Viktor said seriously. He led us from the room, all eyes and hidden grins on us as we entered the hall where our companions waited.

"I'll take your lead, King Airre." I motioned for him to lead the way to the dining hall where the monarchs of the Day Realm awaited us. The maze of breezeways passed in a blur until we arrived at a wooden building, glass doors thrown open to allow the warm winter air of the Day Realm to flow through the space. A shallow pool waited just outside them, beckoning the observer to sink into its cool waters on a hot day. But we bypassed it, stepping through the glass and finding Queen Viktoria standing behind a long table laden with food. Her head was close to her husband's as they whispered, breaking apart when they saw us arrive. The queen flashed us a brilliantly white smile that was meant to disarm, her colorful dress floating on the soft breeze that entered behind us.

"Please sit, eat, and drink, my friends," she cooed. She and King Consort Geza took the ceremonial head of the table, and King Airre and I sat beside them, Kaztar and Viktor to my immediate left and Mikko and Tukka across from them. The King and Queen of the Day Realm bit into their food, and then we filled our plates from the smattering of fruit, bread, and meat laid before us. I studied Queen Viktoria, her colorful ensemble enhancing the richness of her dark skin. Yet her dark eyes were pinched with worry, and something was different about her than the last time I had seen her, nearly a year ago at the last Béke.

Her husband cleared his throat, glancing between King Airre and me. "So, King Zalan is dead. His illness finally took him?"

"Unfortunately not. He was killed when King Azim's son attacked Este Castle some weeks ago. He also took Queen Izidora that night." I dropped every major fact in one sentence, its power holding the breath of the monarchs for several moments before Queen Viktoria could respond.

"Princess – Queen Izidora? You found her?"

I nodded. "About three months ago, we found her in an almost impossible-to-spot cave in the Agrenak Mountains. She was chained in absolute darkness, hidden deep in the mountain. We killed many Iron Fae soldiers to get to her."

She hissed, cursing under her breath. "That poor child. Your arrival must have been quite the shock for her."

"It was. It took her time to warm up to us after everything she went through, but she is more resilient than you can imagine. She is incredible, a very fast learner, and so kind."

A knowing half-smile spread across King Consort Geza's lips. "Sounds like you are in love, High Lord Kazimir."

"She is my mate, Your Majesty." I bowed my head and waited for the response this fact would elicit.

Queen Viktoria clapped her hands excitedly, bringing them to her smiling lips. "Mates! Ah, how I enjoy love stories." She glanced at King Airre and Queen Immonen, who gazed into each other's eyes like they were the only two in the world. "And now I see why King Airre has joined you here. You want to rescue your mate and need our help to do so."

"Indeed, that is the purpose of our visit. As we speak, the armies of the Night and Crystal Realms are merging near the Day Realm border, and we would like permission to continue to move through the Day Realm and station them at the border with the Iron Realm as well," I requested.

King Consort Geza glanced at his wife, whose smile fell as she considered our proposal. A heavy sigh escaped her, as if the weight of the world had suddenly fallen on her shoulders, and he placed a steady hand there, giving her a light squeeze as if reminding her that she did not have to carry this burden alone. "If it was any other time, we would have joined in a heartbeat. But right now, we have another priority," he replied.

Red flashed before my eyes, panic gripped my chest, and every muscle in my body tingled as my fear of losing Izidora rushed through me like a tidal wave.

She was mine. Ruslan could not have her. I would force them to join us.

Dark rope surged to my fingertips, begging for release, and I inhaled sharply, ready to bite, when Kaztar kicked me under the table and opened his mouth to speak. "You might not be so quick to decline once you hear more about King Azim's son."

"As far as any of us were aware, only King Zalan had children up until now," King Consort Geza responded, lacing his fingers together and staring at Kaztar over them.

"King Zalan knew about Ruslan, King Azim's bastard. Apparently, the kings made an agreement to unite Ruslan and Izidora in marriage once she turned twenty-one. That is why he showed up, to take her as his. He also said that King Azim plans on using Izidora's power to conquer the continent. You share a border with the Iron Realm, and you are in danger," Kaztar warned.

"And what is this power that Izidora wields? Why would she use it against her own mate?" King Consort Geza challenged.

King Airre interjected, "She is part of the Goddess's Prophecy – the one that predicts a fundamental change to our world. Do you know it?"

"I do, but it has been some time since I last heard it spoken." Queen Viktoria's face was grim, a frown pulling her lips down.

"Queen Izidora has white magic that is stronger than most Night Faes'," I began, drawing a deep breath to steady myself as I realized we had to share the secret in order to gain their alliance. Down the table, Endre dipped his chin, encouraging me to continue. "And we found out shortly before we departed that it is because she is half Angel." I begged forgiveness from King Airre and Queen Immonen with my eyes, while Kaztar sucked in a breath, and Liliana gasped at the end of the table. "The first line of the prophecy states that 'the ones that are part of all will be born under a full moon,' which I believe refers to Ruslan and Izidora. Supposedly, King Azim has a Mage in his employ whose sole focus is to create a superior race. The Iron Realm has been trafficking for years, and now we know why."

The room was utterly silent, so much so that the light breeze through the open doors sounded like a raging battle. So I took another breath, then continued. "King Zalan cared more about power than bloodline, which is why he forced Queen Liessa to breed with an Angel imprisoned in the Iron Realm. The Angel was Queen Liessa's mate, and King Zalan was jealous, so the day she gave birth to Izidora, he had her killed, and Izidora hidden away with a plan for Ruslan to have her once she came of age."

Queen Immonen's jaw hung open in shock, unable to control her features as I revealed the depths of depravity at the highest level of the Iron and Night Realms. Queen Viktoria's hand went to her belly before her head dropped to her chest, shaking from side to side. Both kings looked at their queens, a mixture of disbelief, worry, and anger swirling in their eyes.

"It is all coming together now," King Airre murmured, and I was glad he was not angry with me for withholding this information. But Kaztar radiated tension in my direction, a promise of his sharp tongue once we were alone.

Queen Viktoria lifted her gaze, dabbing at her dark eyes with a cloth. "These are dangerous times indeed, and I sense the only way out of this is through war." She splayed her fingers across her belly and pushed back from the table, chair scraping against the stone floor. She smoothed the flowing dress over her stomach to reveal a growing bump there. Queen Immonen gasped, hands covering her mouth as Queen Viktoria revealed her pregnancy. "This was the reason we declined before... but this is also the reason we cannot decline now. We've waited for over one hundred years for this, and I do not want my child to be born in a world where the Iron Realm rules us all." She turned to look at me. "We will join the fight, but I will delegate to my husband to lead the Day Realm army."

I bowed to them as low as I could while still seated at the table. "I am honored to have your support, Queen Viktoria. Congratulations on your pregnancy and thank you for sharing the incredible news with us. May the Goddess bless both you and your child."

"I am afraid the pregnancy is taking quite the toll on me, so I will leave you all to speak of war while I rest," she said, and we jumped to our feet, Queen Immonen, Domi, and Liliana congratulating her, and waited to retake our seats until Queen Viktoria glided out of the room.

"Shall we move to a more comfortable location to begin planning?" King Consort Geza offered, all plates cleared and glasses empty.

"Lead the way," King Airre motioned.

"We will stay here by the pool," Queen Immonen grinned, rolling up the sleeves on her light dress and stepping into the sunlight, followed by Liliana and Domi. Vadim nearly choked when Liliana hiked her dress up over her thighs, sunning herself and showing off every inch of skin possible. She bit her lip as she looked at Endre, causing him to gulp, and I snickered, bumping his shoulder as I walked past him, following the group into the breezeway.

Kaztar grabbed my arm, forcing me to walk beside him. "Why did you not tell me that Izidora is not King Zalan's daughter before? That seriously changes things about the line of succession, since he did not specifically name her heir apparent. And she killed him," he hissed. "That is regicide. She could be executed for that."

"Why do you think I left that detail out? Don't pretend to be all high and mighty now, Kaztar. We both know she would make a much better queen than he ever was a king. Besides, he went on and on about her being his daughter for years, even more so after she arrived at Este Castle. Whether she was his blood or not is irrelevant when he claimed her as such," I seethed.

Kaztar ground his teeth, a muscle ticking in his jaw. "While you are right in your assessment, I am still pissed. I trusted you, and you lied to me. Who else knew?"

"Viktor, Vadim, Endre, and I were all there when Queen Liessa's former maid found us. I am sorry for breaking your trust, Kaztar, but I will do whatever I have to do to protect my mate. She is my priority in all of this."

"The prophecy says 'the ones who are part of all' and then refers to mates later. Who is to say that it is you? What if it is Ruslan?"

His words echoed the fears hammering in my heart, and brushing against that bruise was all it took for red and black to coat my vision. I slammed Kaztar against the wall, a threatening growl ripping from my throat as I braced my forearm in his neck. Black rope began caging him, and my chest heaved with the force of my fury. Hands pulled on my shoulders, and in the distance someone yelled my name. But I only saw the male who dared insult me, and the male needed to die because he'd suggested another deserved my mate. His lips were moving, but I heard nothing other than the blood rushing in my ears, a song of darkness filling my heart, and vengeance calling my soul.

Hard metal crashed against the side of my head, and I stumbled to the side, dropping the male and my magic. I landed flat on my back, cracking my head on the hard-packed ground, breath leaving my lungs with a whoosh.

"Stop!" I brought my hands over my head to protect it from the next blow as Viktor raised a vase to strike me again. He lowered his hands but did not release his makeshift weapon as he eyed me warily. I touched my temple, hand coming away bloody.

"Shit," I groaned as I realized I had lost control again. "Is Kaztar alright?"

Viktor glanced behind him, and I looked beyond his knee to see Endre healing a deep cut in Kaztar's side. Viktor held out a hand to help me up, and I grasped it, a stone settling in my gut at the fact that I had hurt another friend with this deadly gift that I was starting to think was more of a curse. Kaztar glanced up from where he watched Endre work, and I met his gaze. "I am so sorry, Kaztar. I completely lost control."

He winced as Endre finished the last of his work, then stood eye to eye with me. "First – when the hell did you get binding magic? Is this another secret you've been keeping from me?"

Running a palm across my face, I admitted the truth. "At the Crystal Realm. I discovered it then and almost killed Endre when I lost control. But I only shared it with Viktor and Vadim today."

"Goddess damn it," Kaztar groaned. "Binding magic is incredibly dangerous. You need to get a grip, Kazimir."

"So I've been told," I gritted out.

"But, I did challenge your claim to Izidora. So I will accept partial responsibility for provoking you. I would have been pissed if someone had claimed I did not love Domi, and a mate bond runs much deeper than that," he conceded.

"Can we let this go and promise no more secrets between friends?" I asked, wanting to repair everything that had just broken with the male who was quickly becoming a true friend.

"Let's do it," he said as he clasped my hand, sealing our words.

"No one saw what happened other than us. Vadim rushed the rest of them forward with some excuse," Viktor added as we walked in the direction of baritone voices.

Endre touched my forehead, and I hissed as he began healing the cut there. "Thank you both," I said when blood no longer dripped down my face.

We passed a fountain, and I doubled back to dip my hands in the running water, washing the blood from my face and hands, wanting to be presentable while we talked of war. Endre waited for me while Kaztar and Viktor joined the rest of the group. "I am glad we won them over. I thought you were going to lose your shit in front of everyone in there."

"I almost did. I need to get a handle on this, Endre," I sighed. I hated this side of me that was ready to snap at a moment's notice. Izidora needed me to be calm and level headed, yet the mere thought of her sent me into a desperate rage, unable to think and only wanting to act. My fantasies, my obsession were only fueled by the promise of binding and unleashing fear upon those who stood in my way.

"We will figure it out – together," Endre promised.

I did not deserve a friend like Endre.

The war room held a table with a giant map of Északi, its four corners weighted down by white stones and figurines splayed across it, marking major locations and troop movements. The kings stood over it, adjusting the positions of our armies until all was right and we were ready to begin.

It was time to plan Ruslan's, and the Iron Realm's, downfall.

INTERLUDE

The cozy tavern bustled with Fae from both the Iron and Night Realms. The tiny town on the border between them was not large enough to be marked on any official map, and its inhabitants cared not which Fae sat beside them as they drank from tankards of ale after long days of working in nearby mines or fields. In a corner, four muscled Night Fae nursed their glasses, scanning the crowd as they waited for her to appear.

A bell chimed as a newcomer pushed into the fray. No one paid her any attention as she ambled to the counter and ordered a glass of wine. The barkeep handed it to her, and only then did she push back her hood and scan the crowded room. The four males perked up at the sight of her, one nearly rising to his feet before his companion pushed him back into his seat.

The crowd did not part as she pushed her way through it, angling her approach to the back corner and sliding into a chair beside the male with a thick beard and a pile of hair atop his head. "You didn't hear this from me," she began, her voice low and fast. "My sister has been disappearing deep into the mountains for a week at a time for years. At first, I pressed her for where she went during her extended absence, since I would have to care for her farm while she was gone. The last time she went, I snooped in her late husband's office, only to find a piece of correspondence that indicated her services would no longer be needed in three months' time. It included instructions and mentions of a contract she had signed years ago preventing her from speaking on her activities, lest she wish a slow and painful death."

The female sipped her wine, a shudder wracking her as if the memories were haunting enough. The four males barely breathed as she spoke, hanging onto every word with their hearts pounding. They knew they were close to finding the lost princess.

"Being the nosy sister that I am, I kept searching until I came across a handful of old papers tucked into a book, hidden among old almanacs and farming tables. They detailed specific instructions for caring for a child in Vasvain. But there's no way that's possible, right? The highest mountain in the center of our continent is inaccessible. So I thought nothing of it until my friend overheard you all asking questions about new tunnels in the mountains a few days ago."

Surreptitiously, the scruffy male pulled out a leather sack of coin from beneath the table and slid it to the female. "Your information has been most helpful. We'd appreciate it if you kept this conversation, and the information you found, to yourself."

The female's hands were quick, sweeping the payment into her lap and beneath her cloak and covering her action with a sip of wine. "My lips are sealed." She nodded to them, then tossed her cloak over her dark hair and swept from the tavern without a backward glance.

The nearly identical males slumped back in their seats, releasing whooshes of air. The fourth one with shoulder-length sandy hair spoke first, the awe in his voice audible despite his low tone and the dim roar around them, "We fucking found her."

"We need to send word to the others. Immediately," the shaggy-haired one said, disregarding his half-full drink and the pretty females whose eyes swept over his muscled form as he bolted to the stairs that led to their temporary accommodations. The other three threw back their ales and followed him, hearts pounding with excitement. After all this time, all the years spent riding across the continent, the lost princess had been in the heart of it the entire time.

And they were about to finally save her.

IV

THE RING

22

RUSLAN

I sat in front of the hearth, watching the flames undulate over the burning wood, flakes of ash falling away and collecting beneath it. The smoke filling my nostrils was calming, for my pocket was heavy and my patience nonexistent as I waited for Izidora to finish dressing for the evening.

My thoughts turned to what had transpired since our arrival in the Iron Realm, and I sipped from the glass hanging lazily in my hand, welcoming the burn of the alcohol down my throat.

Unfortunately, my father had been correct in his assessment that I did not need leverage to coerce Izidora into doing what I wanted; she simply needed hope. Her light was both her strength and weakness, one that I was only partially okay with exploiting.

When she bounded to me, filled with brightness after her first lesson with the Angel, the opening I needed exposed itself, and I immediately took advantage. By mimicking her energy, I showed her the potential for me, for us, and what our future could look like, together. Slowly, she fell into the carefully laid trap, and when she let me take her, fuck, it was better than any dream I conjured during the twenty-one years I spent waiting for her.

The only downside to this new plan was that I had been falling deeper into her halo instead of lifting her into my darkness.

Watching as Izidora bloomed into the exquisite female whose fire captivated me at every turn was nothing short of glorious. She had changed me too, as much as I was loath to admit that. In front of her, I was able to keep my temper in check, though I snuck off during her sessions with Zuriel to beat the feelings from my body, either on training bags or the unfortunate soul who sparred with me. The last of my plans had yet to come to pass, and I still struggled to bite my tongue and bide my time. Soon, though, everything would fall into place.

It was not only me who noticed these changes; Drazen pulled me aside while Izidora sparred with some of my soldiers to ask if I was falling ill. I could not admit to him, or to anyone, that my mate's light called to me from the depths of my depravity. I barely admitted to myself that I liked when she eased my pain. I vacillated between denial and acknowledgement, depending on whether I was between my mate's silky legs.

There was no one else for me, and from the moment our bodies joined for the first time, I knew, deep down, that I was forever hers. The thread that tied us together hummed in agreement, and even two rooms away, her floral scent heightened, mixing with the woodsmoke before me.

Downing the last of the whisky, I hissed out the burn, then set the glass aside. Izidora appeared a moment later, the light pad of her feet against the floor discernable to my Dragon senses.

I rose to greet her, grinning wildly. "You look incredible," I told her, gaze raking over the blue dress I had bought her from a shop we passed daily on our ride to Ryza Citadel.

"Thank you," she blushed, and the rosy color only accentuated her radiance.

Securing her hand in the crook of my arm, I steered her toward the stairs that led to the roof, trying to breathe normally.

Our wedding had been a tricky subject the last time I brought it up, which was why I had yet to speak of it again, knowing it would break the tenuous peace that stretched between us. But Béke would start in a few days' time, and I could no longer wait. I wanted to make a grand gesture for Izidora, giving my mate hope and a semblance of choice in the matter. That was all she ever wanted, and had said so many times.

Izidora wanted to be loved, but more than that, she wanted to be shown that she was loved. Words were not enough with her; I had to show her that she was safe with me, that I wanted her more than I wanted to breathe, and that she could be her truest self with me.

We were so alike in our desire to be loved that I knew exactly what I wanted to do for her the moment I decided to make the grand gesture.

Dropping her arm, I climbed the ladder and threw open the door, lifting myself onto the roof. Cedomir had prepared the space for a romantic dinner, setting up a small, intimate table ringed by magic-powered hearths, warming the area so Izidora could wear the beautiful off-the-shoulder dress without the need for a cloak. Rose petals of the purest white and bloodiest red scattered across the table spilled onto the ground, and the sky chose that night to display a rainbow of red, purple, and gold hues, admittedly one of the best sunsets I had ever seen. It was as if the Goddess herself had wished this moment to be perfect.

Izidora gasped at the arrangement when I hauled her through the hatch and onto the roof. My chest was tight, anticipation making it hard to breathe, but I managed to smile down at her as she whipped her head around, aquamarine eyes filled with excitement.

"This is the best date yet," she beamed, and I swooped in, bending her backward as I kissed her deeply.

I rested my forehead on hers. "I'm glad you like it, sprite." Tucking her under my arm, I led her to the table, pulling out her chair and then pushing her close once she had settled in.

I fingered the box in my pocket as I sat, my stomach filled with butterflies. Cedomir had uncorked the wine bottle, and I poured a glass for each of us, the purple liquid sloshing as it collided with its new container.

Lifting my glass, I tipped it in her direction. "To us," I rasped, my voice stronger than the nerves threatening to shake my hand.

She would say yes.

"To us," Izidora echoed, then sipped her wine, a hidden smile brightening her jewel-like eyes as she held my gaze. She was radiant in the low-cut blue dress, a hint of her cleavage on display. Her elegant neck and shoulders were accentuated by the braided crown she'd woven into her chestnut hair. Her cheeks were rosy and flushed from the wine and the slight chill that remained despite the fire around us.

"Are you warm enough?" I asked, just as Cedomir appeared with our dinner.

"Yes," she replied, then thanked our chef as he placed our plates in front of us with a flourish. He winked at me before disappearing through the hatch.

The savory spices from the freshly-cooked chicken wafted off of it with the steam, filling my nostrils and turning my stomach. Soft, fluffy, buttery potatoes nestled against the skin, mixing with the chicken's juices. It looked incredible, but I couldn't imagine eating a bite until I had asked her one of the most important questions of my life. Izidora immediately swiped her fork across both and took a large bite.

She covered her mouth with her hand, moaning around the food. "This is delicious."

"Another one of my favorite meals," I told her, spearing chicken onto my fork and lifting it to my mouth. I could hardly taste it, and I sipped my wine to swallow it down.

Izidora made quick work of her food, and then she drained her entire glass of wine. I wasted no time in refilling it. She grinned, then lifted the glass and leaned back in her chair while I continued to eat. "The sky is incredible tonight," she commented, gazing at the landscapes around her.

The first of the stars had started to appear overhead, though the last rays of the sun still clung to the mountain tops. "When I built this palace for you, I hoped we could share many nights like this, right here," I commented, chewing the potatoes slowly.

"How did you know I would like it?" she quipped, teasing me.

I tried to grin, but my heart was pounding so hard I might have failed. "I figured we'd have similar tastes, since we are mates."

She did not protest or make a face at my statement, and I nearly sagged with relief that she wasn't fighting me on it.

The door creaked open again, Cedomir reappearing with a new dessert for Izidora to try, a creamy custard fired to create a breakable crust on top.

Thank fuck.

Cedomir was aware of my plan for the night, and I knew that he brought dessert early to save me from the utter fear that sank its claws into me. Before disappearing through the hole, he gave me an encouraging nod, though his confidence did not calm the shaking in my hands. Izidora lifted a spoon to the dessert, but I reached across the table, covering her hand with my own.

"Before we eat dessert, I have something I want to ask you," I croaked, losing all confidence and nearly telling her 'never mind.' Rejection was not an emotion I handled well, especially because hearing the word 'no' to a question such as this was about as clear an abandonment as I could imagine. My worst fear, roaring into existence, from my mate no less, did not bode well for me, and I worried about how I would react if a rejection was what I received.

Why couldn't I just take it like a male, unbothered by whether a female wanted me or not?

I hated myself for caring so much.

Izidora placed the spoon on the table, eyes sparkling as a soft smile played across her perfectly sculpted lips. I loosed a breath, a wave of relaxation washing over me, then stood from the table, pulling the box from my pocket. The stone was rough beneath my knee, but I did not care as I knelt before my mate, our gazes colliding with a wave of heat so intense I almost threw the box away in favor of capturing her soft lips between mine. My heart thundered in my chest, and I was hyper aware of every twitch of her gorgeous eyes, my own searching them, pleading with her to accept me, to see me – to love me.

My mouth went dry, and my whole body tingled in a way that was wholly unfamiliar to me.

Was I dying?

Sucking down air, I tried to steady myself as I took her hand in mine. She bit her lip but kept her smile, waiting for me to speak.

"Izidora, I love you," I started. "You are a wildfire that has consumed my every thought since I laid eyes on you. I can't breathe, can't think, when I am around you. You suck all the oxygen from any room we're in, leaving me gasping for breath, and yet I cannot get enough of that asphyxiation. You drive me as wild as you are, making me wait for you, then challenging me at every turn, and I am a better male for it. The light in your soul calls to me, guiding me through this darkness I thought I'd be trapped in forever. You are *everything* to me, sprite."

With shaking hands, I opened the box to reveal the ring I'd picked for her. The color of the square center stone reminded me of her eyes, and two diamonds lay on either side, triangles that reminded me of her angelic wings.

Those eyes widened and she gasped, which I hoped were both good signs. My fear of abandonment reared its head, clawing its way through my chest, and I thought my heart might explode as I opened my mouth to ask the question, nearly closing it again as images of her rejecting me flashed through my mind. But I needed to ask because I needed to show her I listened and I cared. So I took a breath and said in a rush, "Will you spend the rest of your life with me?"

Tears filled her eyes as she searched my face. I waited for what seemed like hours, my heart beating out of control, while she said nothing, and finally, when I felt my chest constricting sharply, neck growing heated as I became certain that she would refuse me, she breathed, "Yes."

I could not contain the roar that left my lips as I yanked her face to mine, kissing her with a passion that spoke of my relief. She opened for me immediately, and I threaded my fingers in her hair, not caring that I was destroying her perfectly crafted plaits. They fell apart and tumbled down her back, and our tongues twined, distracting me from all else.

She said yes.

Izidora broke our kiss with a giddy laugh and reached for the box. I tsked, then removed the ring myself and slipped it on her finger. It was perfect, and the glittering diamonds refracted every beam of light surrounding us. I kissed her hand, each knuckle, and then her lips once more, for once not denying myself the happiness I never thought I deserved.

The euphoria had not lessened when I finally retook my seat, lifting my spoon to the dessert. "Don't worry, it is a cold treat. Dig in," I encouraged Izidora, excited for her to try another of my favorites.

She cracked her spoon against the hardened surface, then lifted a large portion of custard to her lips, and my eye caught on the ring again, perfectly placed on her finger. "Oh my Goddess, this is incredible," she moaned, the sound reminding me of how she writhed beneath me when I filled her completely.

A low laugh rumbled through my chest as I dug into my own dessert. Cedomir was truly a master at his craft. The vanilla was rich, and the texture was dense, and I already wanted another. We finished the last of the vanilla custard together, fighting over the tiny scraps baked into the seams of the cup. The giggle that slipped past her lips and the way she beamed at me made me want to capture her face in that moment so that it would be forever burned into my mind as a memory I could conjure on days we struggled against each other.

"So would you like to start planning our wedding now?" I asked, riding on the high of the moment.

A slight blush colored her cheeks as she finished the last of her wine. "Still for the same date?"

"If you'd marry me tonight, I would gladly take it. But otherwise, the same date." I grinned, reaching across the table and taking her hand.

"Hmm," she thought for a moment, her lips pressed together as she tried to suppress a smile. "I guess I can manage to wait another week or two."

"There is something I can't wait another week for," I replied, voice dropping an octave. Her flush deepened and pupils dilated, and I did not waste my chance to scoop her out of her chair and carry her into our suite.

Cedomir could clean up later. I needed to make love to my betrothed.

Izidora giggled and kicked her feet as we wound down the spiral stairs, her ring flashing in the firelight as we moved from the living space to our bedroom. "It's so beautiful," she sighed, holding her hand out and admiring the stone.

"Not as beautiful as you in this dress," I bantered. "Though, you'd be even more beautiful without it." We had reached the bed, and I tossed her on it, forcing a shocked gasp from her throat. Her blue eyes glittered along with her smile, and as I yanked her to me at the edge of the mattress, she dropped her legs apart. Her chest heaved, breasts straining against the tight band that wrapped around them. Gripping either side of the skirt, I pulled, and ripping filled the air as threads strained and popped.

"Hey! I like this one," she protested, but she made no move to stop me. Instead, she bit her lower lip in a calculated move that drove me wild.

"Then I will buy you another. But right now, I can't wait for you to take it off. I need to be inside you," I growled, shredding the last of the dress. Her arms were still trapped in the sleeves when I sank my lips to her center and tasted her.

"Fuck!" she swore, back bowing as I nipped her clit. My tongue ravished her core, sweeping up and down before diving into the most delicious dessert I would ever taste. Her nipples were hard and wanting, and I pushed one thigh down, opening her for me, while the other trailed up her abdomen to circle the nub. The sound she made when I rolled it between my fingers made my cock ache in the best way. It strained against my tight pants, the fabric digging painfully in.

I pulled away, leaving Izidora breathless and glistening. The ring on her finger shone in the dim light, visible over the sheets gripped in her small fingers. Slowly, I began unbuttoning my shirt, revealing my tattooed torso inch by muscular inch. Izidora's eyes were hungry as they roamed the planes of my chest, and she bit her lower lip again.

"You know what that does to me," I admonished, and she grinned around her teeth.

"I do," she purred, sitting upright and crawling across the bed toward me.

My dick jumped in my pants.

The last of the buttons undone, I let the fabric hang across my body, gazing down at my future wife as she stopped before me. Kneeling, her fingers skimmed my waist, and I had to bite back a growl as she nearly brushed my hardness. Her touch continued up my torso, over every carved muscle, until finally she landed on my shoulders and pushed the fabric off them. It pooled on the floor behind me, and I wasted no time capturing her in my arms and kissing her roughly. Our bare chests rubbed together, and I tightened my grip, desperate to be closer.

Izidora tasted like sweet vanilla, and combined with her floral scent and her acceptance of my proposal, I was about to come undone.

Her nails dug into my shoulders, and I growled before forcing one to my pants and over my erection. She rubbed over it, and we groaned together. The buttons came undone quickly under her deft hands, and she shoved my pants down before gripping me in her soft hand and stroking.

"Fuck, sprite, you are everything to me," I swore, stepping on the ends of the legs and removing my pants while simultaneously leaning her back on our bed.

Her hair fanned out behind and beneath her as I caged her with my arms and settled my hips between hers. Our gazes collided with an explosion of need and love and passion, fucking *everything*.

A moment passed as the world fell away, and it was only us, staring into each other's eyes, a thread of fate tying us together and poised with anticipation for the moment our bodies joined. Slowly, I began to circle my hips, grinding against her. Izidora's mouth popped open slightly as she sucked in a breath. Her eyes rolled back in her head as I brushed against her clit.

Gripping myself, I lined up with her entrance, forcing her eyes open and forward as we joined as one. "Sprite," I croaked as her walls gripped me.

"Ruslan," she whimpered in reply.

I moved slowly, taking my time drawing out to the tip before sliding all the way inside her, forcing her hips to roll backward with the depth of my thrust. Each one drew a breathy gasp from her perfect pink lips, and I throbbed inside her with the force of my desire. This moment was not about claiming and fucking; this was showing Izidora the depth of my devotion, the realest, rawest parts of me that she'd forced into the light.

I loved her so intensely, and it terrified me.

She had all the power, and it terrified me.

Because she held my heart in her hands, and she could rip it out and leave me bloody and broken.

A brush of her fingers against my face brought me back to the moment, and she cupped my cheek, warmth, love, and affection washing over me. I released the tense breath and began moving again, leaning into her touch. Her lashes began fluttering, and sounds of pleasure slipped unbidden through her lips.

"More," she pleaded, her request nearly as raspy as my own voice.

"More what?" I murmured, dropping my mouth to the crook of her shoulder and nipping.

"That," she croaked, and I licked her fluttering pulse before running my teeth over it. "Yes, that, please." Her hands met my chest, nails digging into the tattoos there, and I moved harder, faster inside her, sucking on her neck, shoulder, and chest.

Sweat slipped down my back along with shivers of pleasure as her walls gripped me tighter and tighter.

"Fuck, Izidora, I love you so much," I swore, self-control slipping as I fell hopelessly in love with the female writhing beneath me.

Her hands drifted from my chest to my back, pulling me closer. My mouth left her neck and landed on hers, and I sank my body into hers, so close that we were nearly one. I swiped my tongue at the seam of her lips, asking her to open for me, and she did with a whimper. Our breath combined until I wasn't sure whose air we were breathing, but it still wasn't enough for me; no matter how many times we were connected this way, it would never be enough.

As our kiss deepened, her pussy clamped down on my cock, and I knew she was close. Sucking her bottom lip between my teeth, I ground my hips into hers, and threw her over the edge of oblivion.

"Ruslan!" she cried out, breaking our kiss. Her head tipped back, baring her throat, and I sucked down on her fluttering pulse again, driving my hips in harder to send her soaring higher. Her cries reached a crescendo the moment my balls began to tighten, and with a groan, I came with her, my cock throbbing and her walls fluttering in perfect synchrony.

My chest heaved as I gazed into the aquamarine blue eyes of my future wife, and I wanted to stay locked in that space with her forever. In that moment, she was utterly, wholly mine. She blinked slowly, a soft, serene smile settling across her face. Gingerly, I exited her, then lay down beside her and cradled her to me. Our hearts beat rapidly still, but as she lay her head on my chest, they slowed, entering the same rhythm.

I released a long breath, trying to shove away those intrusive thoughts that told me this peace wouldn't last, that she'd only said yes because she felt obligated, and that she would leave me the moment that Kazimir arrived in the Iron Realm.

Leaving my heart open and vulnerable like this was borderline painful, but I shoved that pain away, focusing instead on the feel of Izidora in my arms.

Because reality would soon set in, and I fucking hoped that I could hold it together long enough to execute my plans, and that Izidora wouldn't abandon me.

23

IZIDORA

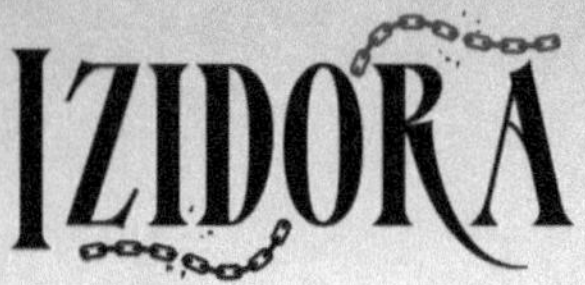

I lifted the hand that bore the heavy ring Ruslan had given me. It was beautiful, thoughtful, and nothing I could have imagined from him when he captured me from the Night Realm. He seemed like a demon sent to make my life hell, cruel and cunning when I screamed at him, raging and vengeful when he felt wronged. He turned hot and cold in the blink of an eye, and I spent a long time tiptoeing around him. Yet, the day I gave myself to him, he morphed into something else. Maybe I had been right before, maybe all he needed was to feel secure in love, and maybe my love was enough for him. He'd told me he loved me at dinner before giving me this ring, but I couldn't say it back to him. Not yet.

A small part of me still clung to the idea of Kazimir, though he seemed more distant as the days passed. My stomach sank every time he crossed my mind, and shame creeped into my cheeks as I wondered what the Nighthounds, what Liliana would think of me.

Would they call me a traitor? Would they stand against me or would they accept the fate the Goddess had granted me?

Kazimir was steadfast, collected, and secure. I remembered

my draw to him, as if an invisible string pulled us together, never letting us drift far. While I had felt safe with Kazimir, I felt betrayed as I uncovered all the falsehoods surrounding my first months outside the cave.

Ruslan was like an all-consuming fire, and when I was with him, I felt *alive*. He pushed me hard, demanding more of me during training every day, and at night, he rode me harder. Yet he could be so tender, and he took care of me in a way that no one else ever had, empowering me so that I could take care of myself when he was not around – though he did everything he could to see that I wanted for nothing.

Did I fall in love with Kazimir simply because he was the first person to show me kindness? Did I overlook everything, accept his explanations, simply because I wanted to be loved? Did he want me as much as I wanted him, or was it all an act?

Which one was my mate?

I searched the prophecy again, hoping to find answers when I had yet to accomplish it before.

> *"The ones that are part of all will be born under a full moon*
> *Her white light will fill the land*
> *But her mates darkness will rise*
> *Kings will fall*
> *Rivers will run with blood*
> *There is a choice*
> *Follow the light*
> *Descend into the dark*
> *The harrowing pass decides it all"*

Was Kazimir losing his mind trying to find me? Had he lost his own light, falling into darkness, to find me? Ruslan had been there long before he found me at Este Castle, his childhood as frightful as mine. My head spun with these unanswered questions, fighting with my heart over the correct choice. Throw my traitorous body into the mix, and it was a real shitshow.

Ruslan stirred beside me, and I decided I wanted to hear the whole truth about his childhood. I knew snippets from Zuriel, and pieces that Ruslan threw out like a trail of breadcrumbs. But if I were going to commit to Ruslan, I wanted to know every horrific detail of what had created this manic Dragon.

"Ruslan, will you tell me what happened to your siblings?" I whispered.

He tensed beside me, and I reached out my mind to grasp his emotions. Anger, guilt, shame, loneliness, and pride wove over each other, crafting a web so thick and complex, I was certain breaking through would be impossible.

"How do you know about them?"

"Zuriel."

He released a serrated breath, struggling for control. As I sent him peace, his shoulders relaxed under my hand, and he turned to his back, pulling me against his chest so my head lay against his slow-beating heart.

"I had eleven siblings, all born within a few years of each other, but my mother was the only one who did not survive the birth. We were all mixed differently, some with stronger Demon blood, others with different Shifter blood, even a few Mages. I was the most mixed, however, and that is likely what killed my mother. Even my grandparents were gone by the time I was born. So I grew up under the care of Rares and others in the tunnel who took pity on me. But Rares's only goal was to create the strongest Félvér for my father. We were the final batch of his years of hard work, and he crafted killers from us as soon as we could wield blades. I guess I shouldn't have been surprised when they announced a competition to the death for the place as heir apparent.

"It was not an all out battle. No, the competition started the second Rares and my father departed. It was as much psychological as physical because some of my siblings were extremely close. They wanted to see who was strong enough to overcome familial bonds and love to take what they wanted. Lucky for me, I didn't care for most of them, having spent twenty years fighting for my place, while they rejected me every time I tried to find comfort with them.

"So, I turned them against each other. I had them start killing each other, cleaning up behind them as they fell one by one. Each of us slept with knives under our pillows, if we slept at all. There were no rules, no breaks, no mercy. It took two weeks for my brother Damir and I to become the finalists. It took another week to trap him in a fight. I left Radence, knowing he would follow, and he caught up to me in the foothills, near one of my favorite spots to sit and read. We fought brutally, first on the ground, then in the sky. We pulled our talons out, slicing as we dove through the air. He caught my thigh as I clipped his wing, and we both tumbled to the ground. My femur snapped in two as I landed, and I laid on my back, waiting for him to end me. I wish he hadn't taken time to gloat, that he would have killed me and ended my suffering. But because he taunted me one last time, I gathered enough magic to move behind him and slice him in two with my talons.

"I had to fly back to Radence, and I fainted twice from pain and blood loss. My father almost lost all his children that day, and if it weren't for Drazen spotting me as he swooped among the mountain tops, I would have died. He brought me to Rares, who healed me, then three days passed before I woke. My father named me heir the next day."

I lay in stunned silence, the weight of his trauma sinking into my bones and settling alongside my own. He ground his teeth, and his darkness fought against the light I pushed into him. He wanted to remain apathetic, detached from what he had done, what he had suffered. Instead I showed him what he had longed for his whole life – acceptance. I wrapped my arms around him, pulling his head to my bare chest, and threw a leg over his back. He wrapped his arms around my small waist, crushing me against him, and I pushed and pulled with his darkness, giving him the space he needed to feel. His breath was uneven and heavy against my chest, and wetness pooled there as I heard a sniff.

My fingers trailed through his hair, scratching his scalp in soothing circles. "I am so sorry no one was there for you Ruslan. I am here now, and I am not going anywhere. I love you."

And with that last confession, he broke down in my arms.

Years of emotional turmoil were released from the cage he'd built around the memories that haunted him, and his breathing remained ragged as sobs choked him. "I can't lose anyone else, especially not you, Izidora. All I've ever wanted was to be loved, and know the person who loved me wasn't going to leave."

Tears burned and overflowed from my eyes at his fervid words, brushing against the raw wound that I shared. I swiped them away before they could fall on Ruslan, but the male must have smelled the salt, because he picked his head up and caressed my cheek with a calloused palm. "I love you, sprite. You are everything to me."

"I love you, Ruslan."

"Say it again."

In the low light, his gray eyes still glistened, so I did. "I love you, Ruslan. You make me feel alive. You understand me."

His brow softened, and I smoothed his hair away from his face as he settled against my chest, still clinging to me like I was the air he needed to breathe.

Questions still burned in the front of my mind, and I needed to ask them so I knew how to proceed. "How did King Azim keep this secret? If the other realms knew this had happened... they would have intervened."

"The High Lords have a vested interest in the program too. My father has shared his power and riches extensively with them. Their offspring are Félvér, so they support the cause of strengthening the magical ability of Iron Fae. Not to mention, it is certainly a more progressive stance than the other realms take on magical purity and maintaining power. Our borders are tightly controlled, and no one enters or leaves without us knowing. When we host Béke, like this year, only the trustworthy ones are allowed to roam Radence."

"So King Azim only wants to create more powerful Iron Fae?"

"He believes that the Goddess turned her back on the Iron Fae, giving them the least power. He wants to grant wings to future generations and strengthen our magical abilities beyond elemental magic. I agree with him to an extent – but I think every race should mix as they wish instead of Rares playing God. I have spent hours pondering the Goddess's logic on separating powers among races to create balance rather than allowing it all to unfold naturally. Perhaps that's what we are meant to bring to this world."

"That makes sense to me, too," I replied. "When we traveled through the Night Realm, we stopped at several large hotels where some of our traveling party could enter these lounges, while others could not. I never wrapped my mind around why only the noble houses were allowed in there, or why they felt the need to be separated from their people in such a way. If the Goddess wanted balance, shouldn't she allow every Fae the same opportunity? I wanted to change that separation the second I could. No one deserves to be treated differently for their power or their name."

Ruslan kissed my forehead, beaming with pride. "My thoughts exactly."

"How many Félvér are there?" My curiosity was piqued, and Ruslan seemed open to talking about it since his emotions were exhausted.

"A few hundred thousand. Those who are of noble Iron Fae blood serve in various positions around Ryza. Those who survived Rares make up an elite fighting unit in the Iron Realm's army, headed by me. Hundreds are in my personal guard, like Drazen."

"Did you take any Félvér with you to the Night Realm, when you came for me?" I chose my words carefully.

"I did, but they all survived. We are much harder to injure, as you have seen."

I considered his words for a moment before asking a question that had nagged me since my first conversation with the Angel. "What did you use to knock me out?"

He stiffened beneath my fingers, and I felt shame rising in him as he recalled the way we'd left the Night Realm. "Rares has spells for such things. He uses them for control. He may not look strong, but he has powerful magic that renders even me immobile if he wishes."

"You told me that Mages are human and have short lifespans... how is Rares still around if this has been going on for over a hundred years?"

"Two ways: my father made him Fae, and he drinks Demon blood. That's why there have been so many of them and so few Angels. He found a way, through his experiments, to prolong life through bloodletting with Demons. It's one of the ways to speed up the training process. If you had wanted to go that route, that is what he would have done."

I shuddered, reading between Ruslan's words to discern that Rares had used such powers to hurt Ruslan in the past.

"How did King Azim make Rares Fae? How is that even possible?"

"The Goddess blesses monarchs with the ability to grant Fae abilities and Fae lifespans to the human Mages and Shifters. It is one of those secrets that are only passed from kings to heirs, for wielding the power takes a significant amount of magic, and if it were widely known, don't you think we'd have a line from Radence to the sea of people wanting to live longer?"

He had a point, and I did not question further, knowing he was nearly spent. So I planted a kiss on his forehead and stroked his back until his breaths evened out, sleep reclaiming him at last.

Bodies were scattered in the grass around me. I bolted upright, and the clang of metal and roars of agony filled my ears. Blood covered every inch of my gleaming armor, and not a single body around me wore metal – only leather. A dozen pairs of lifeless eyes stared into the midday sun. Their eyes were not brown; they were brilliant shades of green. I held a longsword in my hand, it too coated in blood, and I gasped, horrified, when I realized what I had done. I sank to my knees when I recognized a familiar face – Kriztof. He lay on his back, an expression of defiance etched into his face, so like the one he wore the night I was taken. I threw myself over him, listening for the slightest hint of life in his cold body. When I heard none, I broke apart, sobbing as the weight of my actions sank in. I did this, I killed him. I killed my friend. How could I betray him like this? What happened to me?

I woke with Ruslan pressed at my back, his lips skimming my shoulder. "Shh, it was only a dream. You're awake now," he soothed. Wetness coated my cheeks, and I inhaled slowly, settling into his warmth and comfort as the nightmare faded away. Exhaustion still pulled at me, begging for another hour of respite despite the threat of nightmares. My ring glinted in the firelight as I pulled Ruslan's face harder against my neck, and he obliged me with nips and kisses, stoking a fire in my belly that had me arching into him.

What better way to forget a nightmare than to forget my own name?

"As much as I would love to bury myself in you right now, I want to show you something," he purred. A shiver wracked my body as he rolled away from me, taking his heat with him. I groaned, too cold to leave the bed, but he returned a moment later with clothes and a thick fur jacket for me.

"What about breakfast?" I asked.

"This won't take long, and we'll eat after." His eyes glinted with mischief, sending a chill skittering down my spine.

"Fine," I sighed, dressing quickly.

Following him to the lift, I swallowed down my nerves, and he lowered us slowly as he had done every time since I'd asked. Laugher floated down the stone hall that led to the stables and guard house, and I quickened my pace, curious as to why the usually stoic males were laughing. Ruslan pulled back the hidden exterior door, and I stopped short, my breath fleeing as we entered a world blanketed in white. Soft flakes dusted my hair, and I swung my gaze to Ruslan, whose black hair was peppered with white.

"Snow!" I exclaimed, bounding into the knee-deep drifts.

Drazen and a few of the others were locked in a battle, scooping balls of the powder into their hands then chucking them at one another, where they exploded like clouds on impact. I was so enthralled with their game that I failed to see one coming my way, and it landed with a thud against my thigh. I searched for the culprit among the fray, finding Ruslan half-hidden by a rock, grinning wickedly with two more snowballs ready for release.

"Hey!" I shouted, then ran for cover as another launched my way. I crouched to avoid the projectile, then scooped the snow into my hands, the cold biting into my fingers. After making a neat pile, I peeked my head over the small rock, ducking as another sailed my way, bursting against a rock behind me. Gathering a few in my arms, I selected the largest for my first throw, then popped up from behind the rock, heaving the snowball with all my might, only to have it land a few feet in front of Ruslan. He threw his head back, laughing with so much ease it constricted my heart. I tried again, managing to land one on his side while he was distracted in his amusement.

Drazen joined me behind the boulder, and it transformed into an all out war, strategy and all, as Team Izidora battled Team Ruslan for the red flag that looked almost like a smear of blood in the snow.

"Alright, here's what we're going to do," Drazen began, listing off instructions to our group. We worked as we listened, packing projectiles into tight balls and stacking them around us. Savich and I duck-walked to the farthest boulder, per our instructions, where we gathered an armful of snowballs and cocked our hands, ready to strike.

"On three," Drazen shout-whispered, and I had to bite my lip to keep from laughing.

"One…"

Beside me, Savich sniggered, and I sucked in a breath, desperate not to make a sound.

"Two…"

I elbowed the half Bear in the ribs to quiet him.

"Three!"

We popped up in unison, and with his massive frame, Savich shielded me from the brunt of the snow that sailed our way. In rapid succession, I launched my snowballs across the boundary and toward our opponents. Two landed on the guards closest to us, while another, throwing with all my might, sailed toward Ruslan, barely missing his shoulder as he dodged it.

"Down!" Savich shouted, and we both hit the ground just in time, the packed snow sailing overhead and landing behind us.

"Again!" I giggled, grabbing an armful and preparing to pop up.

Laughter roared across both lines, especially as the teams sprinted from hiding spot to hiding spot, closing the distance to the flag bearer. One of the guards on our team snatched it away from another on Ruslan's team, resulting in a wrestle in the snow until I sprinted forward and snatched it from both of them.

Shouts followed me, and I skidded to a stop behind the closest boulder, barely missing a flying snowball. It broke apart on the edge of the rock, spraying me regardless. I was breathless, and my stomach ached from laughing so hard.

These were the moments worth living for.

I was preoccupied with my thoughts and peering around my hiding spot to check for safe passage that I didn't hear the person behind me approach. Two strong arms grasped me from behind, and I screamed, only to realize it was Ruslan a moment later. I kicked and wiggled in his grasp, protesting when he lifted me from the ground and carried me forward.

"I win on both accounts," he pronounced. "I've got the flag and the female."

It was then that the males noticed the ring on my finger, and whoops and cheers resounded around the group. Ruslan tossed and caught me, ripping another scream from my throat before he silenced me with a kiss. I smiled around it, laughing because I was so fucking *happy.*

My hands were utterly frozen, but I grasped his face and kissed him back anyway.

Once Ruslan finally released me, Drazen clapped him on the

shoulder, congratulating him, then he winked at me. "I don't know what you did to this bastard, but keep up the good work."

My cheeks heated, and my stomach dropped, my inner turmoil from the previous night bubbling to the surface. Whether I had made the right decision remained to be seen, but with the change I saw in Ruslan in the past weeks, I had hope.

I was numb from head to toe, and when I shivered for the tenth time, Ruslan took notice. "Let's go warm up." He flashed his teeth in a way that suggested warming up meant a lot of skin to skin contact.

We barely made it inside the suite before Ruslan stripped me of my fur-lined clothes, his mouth attacking mine as he consumed every part of me. A whimper escaped my lips as he bent me back in front of the fire, my hands grasping for purchase as he held me to his hardened body. His cock dug into my stomach as he laid us on a rug in front of the fireplace, our bodies steaming as freezing water evaporated. He paused to admire my naked form, then growled when I spread my legs, showing him how slick my thighs were.

"You are incredible," he purred, sinking between my legs. A hand braced each one, pushing them wider as he trailed kisses straight to the apex of my thighs. He sucked my sensitive nerves into his mouth, then released, fisting his cock. "Fighting with you makes me harder than anything else."

Those lustful lips found my slit, parting my folds with his tongue and thrusting it into my center while he stroked himself. His mouth was like heaven and hell wrapped into one, bringing me so close to the edge with his skillful movements, but it wasn't enough to tear me apart. As if he knew I needed more, he released his hardness, spread my folds with his fingers, and thrust two in. The sucking and curling had me twining my fingers in his hair, directing him closer, needing to feel more, to feel fuller. He spread his fingers inside me, and I gasped as he stretched me around them. I ground into his fingers and face, moaning as my legs trembled from the building tension.

"Someone is in a hurry," he laughed against my center before slipping a third finger into my wetness.

I threw my head back in ecstasy. "Fuck, yes..."

He nipped my clit, and I mewled as it sent me over the edge, pleasure breaking in waves across my heated skin. Fingers and tongue continued to work until my body ceased spasming beneath him. He huffed a laugh, then removed his pants, his thick cock springing free. Liquid beaded the tip, and I turned to my knees, ready to take him into my mouth. He groaned as I grasped his shaft, pumping from base to tip, then flicked my tongue over the drop that gathered there. I worked my tongue in circles around the head while stroking up and down, and he gathered my long hair in his fist, guiding me down his salty shaft until he hit the back of my throat. I gagged, eliciting a growl of pleasure that sent tingles straight to my core.

"Such a good fucking girl, taking my cock like that. Do it again," Ruslan ordered, and I took a few breaths through my nose, then relaxed my throat, trying to take all of his girth. Tears sprang to my eyes as he continued pushing, my mouth so full that it was both pleasurable and painful. He found a steady rhythm, and I dropped my free hand to my clit, rubbing circles over it before slipping a finger inside myself, moaning around him.

I looked up through my lashes, finding Ruslan torn between pleasure and possession, his cock sunk so deep in my mouth while his molten eyes latched onto how I touched myself.

"Keep going," he ground out, and I obliged, sinking another finger into my center. I timed my own thrusts to his, and with a choked cry, I came again. He pulled his cock free, yanked my hand away, then flipped me so I was on all fours.

"Ruslan," I croaked, still riding the edge of my orgasm.

He caged me beneath him as his fingers swept through the wetness between my thighs, coating them in my arousal. He brought his soaked fingers to my puckered hole, and I whimpered at the new sensation. "Does my sprite want to be filled everywhere?" he purred in my ear.

How was I supposed to fit him there?

The tingles that spread over my body as he continued to play with that hole were a heady mixture of panic and pleasure, and when my body pushed back into his hand, he growled possessively. "I told you that those who experienced darkness like us get off at the roughness. I am about to show you just how hard you'll come for me when we let our inner demons out to play."

Oh my Goddess, that statement alone had my nerves on fire, ready to combust once again. He pushed my upper body down until only my ass remained in the air. His rough fingers dug into the muscles there, kneading and relaxing me before running his fingers over my hole again. Cold air pressed against my skin as he removed his hand, only to feel the sting of his strike against my pussy. A sound somewhere between a moan and a whimper caught in my throat, the sensation new and erotic and one I wanted more of.

"Again," I begged. Ruslan spanked my center repeatedly, sometimes hitting my clit, sometimes the backs of my thighs. The pain only served to bring me more pleasure, and I was so turned on that I didn't want it to stop. My breasts were heavy and brushed against the floor, my hands splayed in front of me, unable to move to release any of this maddening tension. Wetness dripped down my thighs, and he growled his approval before smearing it all along my puckered hole.

"Did he take you here?" Ruslan's voice was low, animalistic, and dark enough to send shivers from my spine to where his finger hovered.

"No," I breathed, tense and waiting for his reaction.

My only response was his finger pressing into the tight space, and I gasped as my hole was stretched and filled for the first time. "Fuck, you're so tight. I bet no one has filled you here yet," he growled.

"Only you," I moaned as he pumped slowly in and out, the feeling wholly different from my pussy yet just as sensual. His other hand found my clit, and he circled it slowly in time with his finger. Tension coiled at the base of my spine, and he slipped another finger inside me, causing me to cry out at the fullness, and I tried and failed to steady my breath as he slipped his tongue into my folds. He fucked me like that, tongue in my pussy and fingers in my ass until I was drowning in pleasure, lost to him and his touch.

And I loved every second of it.

He stretched my hole between his fingers, pulled his mouth away from my core, and said, "You're going to take all of me in that tight ass of yours, my mate. You are mine, and I will claim every part of you."

"Fuck, Ruslan," I whimpered. Suddenly, I was facing him again, and he guided his cock into my mouth, so thick I was sure he would combust any moment.

"Be a good girl and get it nice and wet for me," he purred. My tongue glided over his velvety tip before I formed an O with my mouth and sucked him into it. I bobbed my head over him until he was sufficiently soaked in my saliva, and he yanked my head back, forcing me to look up at him with his fingers twined in my hair. "Hands and knees, sprite."

My walls clenched at his words, and I let my hands fall to the floor, then spun so my ass faced him. "Breathe, Izidora," he commanded, spreading my cheeks as he lined himself up with me. He pushed in slowly, eliciting a shocked gasp, his cock so much bigger than his fingers. But I did as he instructed, breathing and relaxing around him until the fullness inside me was bearable.

"Fuck, you feel so good," he groaned, reaching around my hip to stroke my wetness. With the addition of his hand, I fell into a stream of heady moans and whimpers, never having felt so much intensity between my thighs as I did in that moment. Saliva dripped down, joining with my other juices, and Ruslan worked himself a little deeper, his cock stretching me to my limits. His fingers parted my folds, and when they slipped inside me, I thought I might die from pleasure.

"Oh my Goddess," I mewled, my whole body trembling as he fucked me with cock and hand, rubbing against each other inside me. Ruslan pumped slowly in and out, hissing through his teeth as my ass gripped him. My nipples ached, my skin was tight, and sweat slicked every inch of my body as my mind went blank.

I was floating, dizzy and untethered as the most intense orgasm of my life ripped through me. I arched into him, riding the waves higher, higher, higher, until my scream died in my throat and bliss overtook all else. With one last thrust, he emptied his hot liquid into me with a roar that shook the room.

"You are mine," he growled, still inside me, cupping my breasts and yanking me to his chest. "Tell me," Ruslan ordered.

"I am yours," I panted, half-limp from my release. He sank his teeth into the crook of my shoulder, right above my pulse, eliciting another cry of pleasure from me. I shuddered as he released his hold on me, then pulled himself out, and I collapsed forward, utterly spent. Without a moment's rest, he scooped me into his arms, and carried me to the shower, holding me against him while the water rolled over us.

I relaxed into his hold, and he hummed against my back, "How was that?"

"Incredible," I breathed, unable to say more as my brain was not yet functional. A gentle rumble against my back spoke of his amusement. Bubbles coated my body as Ruslan lathered me, gentle despite his earlier roughness. He was my duality, and I wouldn't have it any other way.

He spread my thighs with his hand, soaping my center thoroughly as I wobbled and braced myself on his shoulders. "I think I need to eat after all of that," I admitted, feeling lightheaded.

"I'll call for food the moment we step out," he promised. With one last rinse, Ruslan turned off the water, then wrapped me in a fluffy robe and left to call for Cedomir.

I walked to the mirror, examining myself in a way that I hadn't in a long time. My cheeks were red both from our coupling and the shower, but my eyes sparkled. I looked healthy, strong, and happy. Guests would arrive soon for Béke, and I was unsure who would show from the Night Realm, but there was no doubt Kazimir and my friends would be among them.

What would they think of me when they saw me with Ruslan?

I didn't have long to ponder this question before Ruslan returned with news of food. We ate mostly in silence, both of us taken to reading during breakfast, and I only had to stop every few pages to ask him to help me. But that morning, I struggled to focus as the reality that I might see my friends in a day's time sunk in. I studied my ring once more, then sighed. I wanted to plan the wedding, I wanted to marry Ruslan, but I wasn't ready to commit to a mating bond. There was still something missing.

24

RUSLAN

Béke began the following day, and the halls of Ryza Citadel showed all the signs of it. Extra polish was applied to the already immaculate surfaces, and the dark metal was oiled and rubbed with tender care. Gemstones were cleaned as well, and fresh silks were draped from the ceiling, some with deep, intricate coloring, others with the various sigils of the Iron Realm's noble houses.

Izidora's eyes were bright with curiosity as we passed servants carrying out their tasks, and my chest warmed as I watched her. She stopped at the sigil of my father, shards of iron ore surrounded by diamonds set onto a blood-red silk.

"Whose is this?" she asked.

"King Azim's," I grunted, trying to tug her along.

She followed after a moment, then laughed and shook her head. "I just realized I don't know your family name."

"It's Drakkar, but it comes from my mother. King Azim did not offer the Racz name to any of his offspring," I gritted out, my mood souring as we approached the door that led to the tunnels, where I would have to leave Izidora while I attended to whatever my father required of me that day.

"Oh," she said softly, stopping and immediately slipping her arms around my waist and hugging me.

I didn't know whether to laugh or cry at her open affection, especially with my rising inner turmoil. Wrapping her in my arms, I held her close, then smoothed her soft hair down her back and stepped away. "I'll be waiting for you when you finish with Zuriel," I promised her.

She nodded, holding my hand until she slipped through the doorway and we could no longer be connected.

Once she disappeared, I cracked my knuckles in succession, then my neck, trying to banish the tension that lingered like a permanent fixture around my neck. Rolling my shoulders, I braced myself for the meeting with the king of the Iron Realm.

The door to his office was half-open when I arrived, and his personal guards waved me through. "He's been expecting you."

"Of course he has," I muttered under my breath.

Rares was already there, and I plopped down in my usual seat, taking a cursory glance around the office. The crossed beams of the ceiling gleamed too, as if the servants had spent all night polishing every inch of the room the king rarely left. The bottles of liquor along the wall were brimming, and thick crystal glasses were lined in perfect rows. King Azim's desk was cleared of all papers, too, his more sensitive ones no doubt stored away for the duration of the feast, lest someone try to pry into the secrets of the Iron Realm.

Neither the current king of the Iron Realm nor his loyal servant deigned to acknowledge me. My hands tightened over the arms of the chair. If I had to spend one more minute in my father's office, I was going to explode. My patience with him was fraying faster every day, and just looking at him made me want to bleed him dry. I was more powerful than he had ever been, and his orders were growing old. It wouldn't take much for me to kill him, and as he and Rares traded words, I imagined the moment when I would finally rule the Iron Realm.

"Ruslan," my father snapped, and I finally banished my violent thoughts and gave him the attention he requested.

"Father," I replied lazily, not bothering to pick my head up off my hand.

"How is Izidora's training progressing?" he asked, and my fist tightened over the words as if I could shove them away.

"It's under control," I drawled, acting as if I was bored of this question – which I was. It was the only question King Azim asked me these days, and my answer was always the same.

He scoffed, apparently still unconvinced. "We'll see about that." He turned his attention to Rares. "She is training with the Angel now, yes?"

Rares straightened in his seat – as much as the wizened Mage could straighten. "Yes, My King. She trains with Zuriel at the same time every day."

The king of the Iron Realm flattened his hands on his mahogany desk, spread wide in an attempt at a commanding posture. But his power moves no longer held any sway over me. "We shall attend today's session then, and after, we will take her to Rares's office for more assessment."

I shot to my feet, reacting on instinct. "Absolutely not. She doesn't need you distracting her. She is behind as it is."

My father's face remained neutral, but the wicked gleam in his eye told me I might have shown my hand. "You are the only one who has seen her training and development since her arrival. How would you know if she is behind? Perhaps she has outclassed you in her training and is ready to be deployed."

Gritting my teeth, I sank back into my seat, attempting to slake the fury that burned inside me at the thought of my father looking at or touching my mate. The bite of pain from the tip of a claw digging into my palm wasn't enough to calm me. "There is no one more powerful than me. Even you, *father.*"

His eyes flashed at my insolence, but I didn't give a fuck. I was stronger and faster than him, and it was time he admitted that.

Rares interjected, trying to diffuse the growing tension in the wood-paneled room. "What if we merely observe what Zuriel is teaching her today?"

Both King Azim and myself cut the old Mage a look. Personally, I wished my eyes were daggers so I could stab him until he bled out all over the massive white fur rug at our feet.

"No." My refusal was harder than the diamonds adorning the Iron Crown resting on King Azim's head, and sharper than its spikes.

He leveled his attention on me, and I puffed out my chest, showing him that I wasn't afraid of his threats, or anything he could force Rares to do to me. He appeared almost amused by my defiance, and that made me want to unsheathe the full lengths of my claws and rip him to shreds that very moment.

"Ruslan, you have to agree to something. You cannot hide her from us any longer. Either you can allow us to observe her training today, or you can bring her to Rares's office afterward for assessment." My father's hands lifted from his desk, and the ground beneath our feet shuddered as he called on his magic.

Vines snaked up the chair from nowhere, wrapping around my legs and pinning them to the ground. I burned them away without a second thought, accidentally singeing the fur at my feet. The vines returned, faster this time, and when they crawled over the back of the chair and sucked me back into it, I growled a warning. But my father did not heed it.

Black fire burst from my body and crisped every last living thing touching me.

"Rares," King Azim snapped, and the old Mage began chanting an all too familiar spell.

"Fine," I snapped, shoving to my feet and knocking the chair backward with enough force to crack the wood. "Let's go observe the training."

Without waiting for them to follow, I stalked from the room, slamming the door to the hall with a satisfying crunch and startling the sentries posted outside.

"My Prince," they muttered hurriedly, but I disregarded them entirely. My mood was so foul that if they hadn't addressed me, I wouldn't have cared enough to do anything about it.

The darkness emanating from my being was enough to part the flow of people bustling through the halls of Ryza Citadel, preparing for the upcoming Béke. They shrank to the walls as if by simply being in my path they would end up burnt to ash. Which, at this rate, they might.

Down and down and down I spiraled, both mentally and physically, until I reached the landing for the tunnels that had been my home until I became heir apparent. Sucking in a ragged breath, I waited for Rares and my father, knowing that I had to get my shit together if I wanted to outmaneuver them both and take what should have been mine a long time ago.

25

IZIDORA

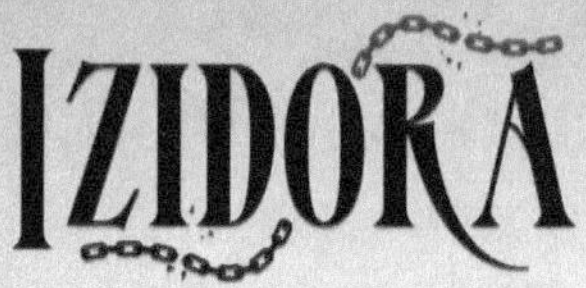

Zuriel waited for me in the training room like any other day, turning to face me as I walked in alone. Seeming to sense my inner turmoil, the Angel lifted my hand to comfort me and saw the ring Ruslan had given me the night before.

"What is this?" he asked, his brow dipping in a frown.

I searched his clear blue eyes, wanting approval and not knowing if I would receive any. "Ruslan asked if I would spend the rest of my life with him, and I accepted."

"Do you think he is your mate now?" Zuriel inquired.

"I don't know." I whispered the thought I was afraid to share with the world. "What is it supposed to feel like? Does my Angel blood make it different?"

"Sit with me, and I will tell you everything you need to know."

We sat cross-legged in front of each other in the center of the training ring. I chewed my lip, waiting for Zuriel to begin. He pulled a chain from an inner pocket of his jacket, a small amethyst pendant dangling from the necklace. "Your mother knew she would die after you were born after what she witnessed with Ithuriel. She came to me the night before she departed, asking me if there was a way to leave a message for you. With the help of one of the Mages, we cast her memories and thoughts into this stone. I have been waiting to give this to you until the moment you began leaning firmly one way or the other with your decision."

I sucked in a sharp breath, freezing as butterflies filled my chest at the promise of hearing from my mother, even if it was only her memory.

What would she have to say?

My mind began spinning over all the endless possibilities, lifted on the wings of excitement and curiosity. Without thought, I reached for the stone, but Zuriel's hand wavered, and I paused.

"There is something else I must tell you." My cousin glanced away from me, shaking his head slightly, then returned his attention to me. Zuriel had always had this air of knowing about him, as if he'd seen more than anyone else could possibly imagine and he knew more than he was willing to reveal, and this moment felt like it was poised on the precipice of life and death itself, though I couldn't discern why.

"I was there when the Goddess's Prophecy was spoken."

My jaw went slack at his revelation.

"You know from our lessons and your books that our continents used to be one, millennia ago. The Angels have always held the closest ties to the Goddess, the Crystal Fae second. That time in our history, the Age of Prophecy, was violent, turbulent, and chaotic as the continents drifted apart, and language has changed since then. In the original prophecy, the language spoke of not one, but two mates."

I could not breathe.

"The Fates are fickle, and the future is always uncertain, but we are at a pivotal moment in the history of our world – one you will play a major part in. Your *choice* in mate will determine the outcome."

"But how do I know who to choose?" My eyes and chest burned as air became trapped in my lungs. Suddenly the space was far too small, my body far too numb, my breath far too fast. My head spun in the opposite direction of the room, and I flattened myself on the floor, hoping for a reprieve from the spinning.

"Breathe with me." Zuriel's blurred form appeared above me, grasping my hand and squeezing to ground me. His nostrils flared, and I mimicked his motion, bringing air into my lungs, then releasing it through my mouth at the same time he did.

"There you go, follow me." We inhaled longer, then hummed together as we exhaled, and the room spun less. We repeated the breath five more times before all was still. With my free hand, I wiped the wetness from my face and Zuriel hauled me upright, sitting in front of me with his hands on my knees. "Are you alright now?"

He enveloped me in a hug after I nodded, and I buried my face in his heavenly scent. Zuriel was my teacher, my cousin, and my friend, and I'd grown to trust the male over our weeks spent together. "Zuriel, I'm scared. It's all too much…"

"I know you are. But you are strong, stronger than you know – stronger than me. You are brave to fight for yourself each and every day, even when it is hard. You are bold, and you want to make the world a better place, despite the world's cruelty to you. Take your fear and harness it into doing what you think is right. You know your heart, and you stick to your values – almost to a fault. Whatever choice you make will be the right one."

I climbed from his embrace to cross my legs in front of him once more. "Does Ruslan know?"

The Angel shook his head, his white hair falling in front of his face. "I have held this secret since I was brought to this continent and realized what their intentions were." He held the necklace out to me, a little piece of the mother I never knew, and my heart panged as I accepted it, brushing a thumb over the purple stone. "Once you put this on, you will fall into her memories. If you want to do it now, I will watch over you."

I wanted it more than anything. With a shaky breath, I grasped either side of the chain, pulling it over my head, and the amethyst settled against my breastbone. Zuriel faded from view, and suddenly, I was standing in the courtyard of Ryza Citadel.

"Queen Liessa!" A white-haired male shouted for me over the buzz of activity in the courtyard, a horse nearly crushing him as he glided to my side. I looked around for my husband, but he was thankfully absent. He would not take kindly to another male speaking to me unchaperoned.

"Yes?" I responded when the male stood in front of me, breathless and wide-eyed. His long white hair was pulled firmly atop his head, the tautness revealing sharp cheekbones and a strong jaw. He was built like a warrior, strong and lean, so unlike my overindulgent husband.

"It's you..." he murmured, taking a tentative step toward me. His hand stretched over the space between us, seemingly of its own accord. The smooth palm found my face, but I did not flinch as I stared into his gemstone-like eyes, sparkling and captivating in their ethereal beauty.

An invisible thread pulled us together, and I found myself dismounting and staring up at the male, as if the hands of the Goddess pushed us toward each other and the whims of the Fates determined this moment. "Who are you?"

"*I am Ithuriel.*" *His voice was like honey drizzled over a warm spring day.*

We were a breath from each other. A small part of the back of my mind reminded me of the consequences of being seen, but my entire focus was on Ithuriel. He consumed me, body, mind, and soul in that moment.

"*What is this?*" *I whispered, unable to break his gaze.*

"*You are my mate, Liessa.*"

His words should have frightened me, and yet, I knew it in my bones to be true.

My mother's memories with Ithuriel flashed through my mind like one lightning strike after another.

"*Liessa!*" *My husband shouted for me through the door to my temporary room. My shoulders automatically rose at his tone. Bracing myself for the onslaught, I cracked open the door to find Zalan, King Azim, and a withered old man standing in the foyer. Tamara slipped into her hiding place as I shut the door a little louder than necessary to cover the sounds of her footfalls.*

"*Yes, My King?*" *I swept my hair behind my back, adding an extra layer of protection to the mark that lay there.*

"*Have a seat.*" *He motioned to the chair before the three standing males. My heart pounded as I did as I was told. I never balked, despite my fears; it only made him angry.*

"*Lean forward.*" *His voice was low, deadly, and instantly my stomach turned over. I had no choice but to obey.*

As I leaned forward, my long hair fell to the side, revealing the low back of my dress. I was grateful my locks hid my face, hoping to spare it from his brutal hand, lest the other monarchs see what really happened in the Night Realm. He circled behind me, roughly swiping the last remaining strands from my back and ripping my dress lower until he found what lay beneath — black marks that indicated I was mated.

His laugh was maniacal, sinister, and raised the hair on the back of my neck.

"So it is true." King Azim's voice was like rocks tumbling down the side of the mountain. "Rares, what do you think?"

The wizened man shuffled forward, lifting my chin with a gnarled finger. He studied me for a moment, then took my hands, turning them this way and that. He touched the center of my palm, and my magic flared to life inside me before simmering to a low boil.

"She has strong power — not only from the Night Fae. Tell me, do you have any other ancestry?"

Mixing between Fae races was rare and discouraged. Those of us who had it in their lineage hid it well, but deep down I sensed he already knew the answer. "Yes."

A wicked expression pulled at his wrinkles. "Yes, she is perfect."

I swallowed down the fear that clawed its way up my throat. What was happening?

"Bring Ithuriel," King Azim commanded a waiting guard.

My heart caught in my throat. "Please don't hurt him," I begged my husband, nearly falling to my knees before him.

"Obey my command, and he shall live," Zalan hissed, shoving me back into the chair.

Ithuriel appeared a moment later with his hands bound behind him. "Liessa!"

I sprung forward without thinking, only to have Zalan throw me with force into the chair, making my head smack the side. I hissed as a bruise bloomed in my hair.

Ithuriel strained against his shackles and the males holding him. "Are you alright?"

A dip of my chin was all I allowed as my husband looked between us.

"Since you have not borne an heir to me yet, Liessa, you will breed with the Angel and produce a powerful one. But there are rules. First, you will only be together in front of Rares and me, who will assist in the process. Second, you will tell no one that the child is not mine and face death if you do so. Third, you will never see each other again after you are pregnant." His tone left no room for debate.

Tears sprang to my eyes as Ithuriel held my gaze. "I will do whatever is asked of me so long as I can be with her."

Every ounce of his love and devotion was poured into that statement, though it broke my heart to know that I would have my mate and then lose him.

"Great. Strip her," Zalan ordered a few unburdened guards milling about the room.

"What? No!" Two males snatched my arms, and a third ripped my dress from my body, baring my naked form to a room filled with males. I struggled as they dragged me to a table in the center of the room, putting me on display like a prized hog slaughtered for a feast, then laid me across it. Zalan pinned my hands above my head, and I was totally powerless as King Azim and Rares settled back to watch the show. Ithuriel was dragged to me and stripped in the same degrading way before being positioned so he stood at the end of the table.

A guard on each of my legs pulled them open and pinned them in place, and tears flowed freely as my husband subjected me to this humiliation – another way to torture me.

Yet, the desire pooling in my belly at my mate's nearness was undeniable – as was his.

"Can I at least have my hands?" he choked on the words.

"He can have his hands. It's not like the iron prevents him from using magic anyway," Rares grumbled from the couch adjacent to the torture table.

The chains were removed, and Ithuriel rubbed his wrists as my chest heaved with silent sobs.

"Get to it, then," Zalan snapped from above me. I closed my eyes, unwilling to look upon my husband's face while my true love, my mate, touched my trembling thighs, parting them slightly.

"I am so sorry, my love," he whispered in my mind.

"Stay with me here. Please don't let me suffer this alone," I thought back.

"Always," his honeyed voice replied. He began to sing a tune in Angelic, the sound soothing in its melody, and I relaxed enough to spread my legs wider. He entered me gently, so unlike our first coupling, and his song never wavered as he moved inside me.

I bit back on my pleasure, knowing that Zalan would be furious if he watched me writhe beneath another male. Ithuriel, to his credit, hurried through his task, quickly filling me with his seed.

The moment he was done, he exited me and the song ended.

The guards tossed him some clothes, and he dressed quickly, though he was left unbound. He shot me a sorrowful look, and through our bond I felt his desire to burn every male in this room to dust to save me from the humiliation I endured.

"She needs to remain like this for twenty minutes before she can move. We'll do it again tomorrow," Rares instructed. And with that, all departed, leaving me alone with my husband.

His grip on my wrists was bruising, and I'd have to wear thick bracelets to cover the rings his fingers left there. He released one, only to thread it in my hair and rip my head back so I was forced to look him in his disgusting green eyes. "You heard him. Don't move, Liessa. The sooner you get pregnant, the better."

He threw my head to the side and stalked from the room, following his new master like a starving pup begging for a scrap of power. Only once the door slammed behind him did I allow the grief and shame of my new position to spill from my lips, and I curled in on myself atop that table and cried until no more tears flowed.

. . .

"SHH, *we must be quiet, my love." Ithuriel dragged me along a dark corridor in a far corner of Ryza. He opened the door to an unused room, sheets covering all furniture. But in the middle, rows of candles lined the floor, forming the shape of a heart around a soft pile of fur. A stifled gasp caught in my throat as Ithuriel led me to it. My blood heated with every step closer to the promise of aloneness with my mate.*

I buried myself in the soft fur, Ithuriel joining me on it, stroking my back and eliciting goosebumps across my skin. "Let me heal you," he begged. The low lighting could not hide the new bruises scattered across my ribs.

"It will only be worse for us if he sees me without them," I whispered, and my mate's stunning blue eyes glistened. His hands shook as he brought them to my face, brushing my hair from it and capturing my lips in his.

"It kills me to watch him hurt you, Liessa," he murmured. "Every time I see him, every time I feel your pain down our bond, I want to kill him."

"But if you kill him, you will die for it, and I'd rather know you still breathe than live in a world without you in it."

"I will find a way out of this, my love, and we will be together and free."

MY MOTHER BEGAN NARRATING as her memories continued to play before me, like my own personal performance.

WE MADE *love over and over and over again that night. It was one of the few stolen nights of aloneness, where Zalan did not discover us. Our love was intense, passionate, and over much too soon. From the moment I met him, I could not deny our connection, no matter how much the threat of Zalan discovering us and killing him hung over my head. Zalan was controlling, aggressive, and violent toward me – all things a male should never do. All he cared about was serving himself and his needs, no matter the harm that came to others.*

My daughter, I love you so much, even as you are just a tiny seed in my belly as I create this for you. You were born from love, no matter the circumstances. One day, you will find love too. Make sure he puts your needs above his own, protects you with the fierceness you deserve, and does not dampen your free spirit. For if you are anything like me, and I hope you are, your spirit will be as untamable as a wild stallion. Do not lose yourself along the way, as I allowed myself to be destroyed. Be free, my sweet angel.

My palms hit the ground in front of me, and my breath heaved in my chest as I wrestled down the anguish in my heart. A waterfall flowed from my eyes as I crashed back into reality.

I felt everything. The intensity of her connection to Ithuriel. Her unconditional love for me. Her fear of King Zalan. Her disgust of King Azim and Rares. It was all too much.

With shaking hands, I lifted the chain over my head and palmed the deep purple stone, holding it to my heart as I broke apart from the inside. "She loved him so much..."

"I know," Zuriel murmured as he stroked my back.

"Thank you," I managed to choke out. "That was possibly the greatest gift I could ever receive."

"I am sorry I did not give it to you sooner." He wiped tears from my cheeks, then handed me a bit of cloth from his jacket for me to dry my face.

I hugged the Angel who had given me so much already. "You gave it to me at just the right time." I'd finally calmed enough to speak of other topics, and I was torn between revealing my plan and risking someone overhearing and wanting to protect him from any fallout should I succeed. He protected me against the spell Rares tried to place on me the first day, and I owed him my life. So, I shared.

"I have been influencing Ruslan's emotions every day since we started training. He has changed, little by little, and I have grown to love him for it. I have hope that he will stand against King Azim when the time comes. And when we take him down, I will release you and the rest of the Telivér so you can either return to your lands or make your homes here. No one deserves to be trapped against their will. I will right the wrongs done to you."

"My dear cousin, your heart is too pure for this world." Zuriel gave me a sad half smile and cupped the side of my face. "I will fight alongside you when the time comes. You have my support in whatever way I can provide it. But for now, let's practice influencing multiple people at once. Béke starts in a few days, and I have a feeling you will need it."

Flooding with light emotions was much easier than doing so with dark ones. It took much more concentration, mostly because I had to feel the emotion to deliver it. My power lay in the intensity of my own emotions, and I hated when Zuriel asked me to make him feel physical pain, because it was so raw, so real for both of us that it made me sick. I gritted my teeth as he writhed on the floor, breathing sharply through my nose as I fought off my own sensation. I released him when I could no longer maintain it myself, panting with my hands on my knees as I grounded myself into reality.

"I am safe here. There is no pain. I am not in danger. I can breathe. I can relax," I whispered to myself under my breath.

"That was the best you've ever done, Izidora." I lifted my head, meeting Zuriel's relaxed smile. How the Angel could receive everything I gave him and not break a sweat, I would never understand.

I straightened, wiping my brow and releasing a long breath. "What's next?"

Zuriel glanced over my shoulder, his eyes hardening, and that familiar thread hummed with life. Whipping around, I discovered Ruslan, Rares, and King Azim had entered the cavernous room. I stiffened, my body on high alert as I laid eyes on King Azim for the first time. He looked exactly the same twenty-one years later as he did in my mother's memories. His eyes were razor sharp and cunning, and I knew this was not a male who could be easily fooled. Where Ruslan had the bulk and strength of youth, it was apparent that his father excelled at strategy and foresight by the way he assessed the whole room with a single sweep of his eyes.

Ruslan's smoky eyes were darker than normal, and as our gazes collided, they held a warning I didn't quite understand.

"King Azim." Zuriel bowed in greeting, and I hastily mimicked them, my shock overriding my ability to move.

"Please, continue, we are merely here to observe progress," he boomed, his voice both bored and commanding authority.

Zuriel wore a mask of indifference, much like the first time we met. "We were working up to Izidora's ability to influence the emotions of many instead of one. She could use another volunteer."

The king snapped his fingers. "Rares, retrieve a few more of our guests for our dear princess to practice on."

Guests? Is that really what he called them? Bile threatened to choke my throat, but instead I reached out mentally to Zuriel, needing to know he had a plan.

"Please don't make me torture them," I begged.

"I will only ask you to apply light emotions. Your well is deep, but

they do not need to know that. We must give them enough to show progress without rousing suspicion that you are holding back."

"Got it."

Rares returned with three others, all Shifters if I had to guess by their looks. The two females' skin was deeply tanned, their eyes golden and hair black as midnight. Wolves. The male was tall and broad with dark skin, two horns jutting from his long brown hair. Centaur. They nodded to Zuriel, joining us in the middle of the cavernous space.

"Konsteon," Zuriel gestured to the Centaur. "Please stand here."

"Rixis, Thalia, if you will head over there," he pointed to the opposite side of the mats, and the Wolves took their places.

"Now, Izidora, I want you to infuse the females with happiness first, then see if you can extend it to us," Zuriel instructed.

I made a big show of closing my eyes, tapping into my magic, appearing focused and effortful. A wave of joy emanated from me, and the Wolves' glowing eyes softened and their barked laughter echoed in the dome. Rixis began howling as Thalia said something I could not quite hear, and I wanted to howl with them, their joy doubling, tripling as I reabsorbed the positive energy into myself.

The magic was slipping out of my control, so I drew a long breath and centered myself before extending my reach. My attention landed on Zuriel and the Centaur, and I imagined the wave spreading from the Wolves to them. Konsteon's neigh filled the air almost instantly, and I chewed my lip as I focused on simmering the emotion instead of boiling it. Zuriel gave me an encouraging nod as the intensity covering them lessened. Sweat dripped down my temple as I held the cover of happiness over them, and as my breath fled my lungs, so too did the magic. My ass hit the floor, dramatizing the act of magic-wielding as I covered the fact that I had been holding back.

A slow clap sounded behind me, and I craned my neck to see who it was. King Azim sat with a smug smirk, and I instantly knew that he did not believe my acting. *Shit.*

"Quite impressive, I must say. But definitely not the best. Show me something better. Something darker," he challenged.

I gulped, looking to Zuriel for instruction.

"Rixis, Thalia, would you mind shifting?" the Angel asked.

"Make them howl with sadness."

"Not a problem," they replied, stripping out of their clothes, completely unashamed in front of the crowd. Two brown wolves the size of horses appeared moments later, and I gasped. It was the first time I had seen a full shift, and their Wolf forms were beautiful and deadly. Their long fangs peeked out from beneath their muzzles, and their golden eyes glowed even brighter against the outlines of their fur. They eyed me like I was nothing more than a snack they were patiently waiting to eat, and I pressed my lips together and refocused on the task at hand.

Zuriel swept out his hand, indicating I should proceed. I drew upon the sadness that some days filled me like an endless sea, then drowned the wolves in it. Thalia released a mournful howl, one that sent chills straight to my bones. It spoke of a home lost to her, a family who desperately loved her, and a freedom to run under the moon she had not tasted in too long. Rixis simply collapsed to the ground, curled in a tight ball, and hid her face under her fluffy tail, a sharp whine releasing with a slow breath. My heart sank, constricted, and collapsed under the weight of our combined sadness. A lone tear trickled down my cheek, mixing with salty sweat, and I could hold no longer.

"You will be happy again, Izidora," Zuriel spoke in my mind, and I emptied my lungs of air as exhaustion pulled at my limbs.

The king of the Iron Realm appeared more impressed, but he was not satisfied. Tension radiated off Ruslan, though he and Rares sat quietly, watching the demonstration. "You can do better than that. Ruslan," he snapped, "hold the Centaur down while Izidora tortures him."

No. I closed my eyes, willing this moment to be a nightmare, but when I tried to wake myself up, I only saw Ruslan striding toward me. He grasped my arm, spinning me and forcing me toward Konsteon. His face was hard and grim, and his emotions were violent, stormy like the blizzard that swept through the Iron Realm the previous night. But he held no hatred toward me when I scanned his emotions.

The Centaur lay willingly on the ground, arms spread wide as Ruslan pinned them. My breaths were cold and rapid as my heart raced out of control, and my whole body tingled, muscles tensing as if I was preparing to fight for my life.

"Do as he says. Konsteon is strong."

"Please, I can't..."

"You must."

"Zuriel, I can't, please, not after what happened to me."

"We will all die if you do not."

Ruslan stared up at me, waiting for me to begin. His smoke-gray eyes swirled with pain as he watched me breaking before him. *Was he really not going to stop this?*

Konsteon must have heard my panicked breaths because he opened his eyes, locking them with mine and giving me a barely perceptible nod.

"I'm so sorry," I mouthed to him, tears falling freely from my eyes. King Azim wanted an empath, and I would show him exactly what that meant. My emotions soared from the peaks of the Agrenak Mountains and dove to the ocean floor, and I refused to hide my tears from another male who forced me to blacken my heart with his own twisted desires.

With a shuddering breath, I implanted sensations of whips lashing Konsteon in his mind, a type of torture I had endured time and time again, permanently marking my skin. Though these lashes would not mar him the way I had been marred, I still gasped as the first one landed, my traumatic memories surfacing with each subsequent strike. Tears streamed down either side of my face as the brave Centaur jerked and grunted beneath Ruslan. After my own back arched in pain, causing me to cry out, Ruslan jumped to his feet and growled, "That's enough." A second before I collapsed against the floor, Ruslan swept me into his arms, a hand cradling my head against his chest, as if he was prepared to flee with me and expected a fight to get us free.

"Did I say we were finished?" King Azim chastised.

"No, I did. If you'd like to continue, you can fight me for the right."

Father and son stared each other down, unblinking, waiting for the other to cave to the rising tension. King Azim was the first to look away, and Ruslan's chest loosened, though his heart still thundered against my ear.

"She looks tired anyway, and we do not want to burn her out before our guests arrive for the feast." The king of the Iron Realm glanced around the room, first at the Angel, then the Shifters. "You are dismissed. I do not need to remind you of the rules for the next two weeks or the consequences for breaking them, do I?"

"No, Your Highness," they all said in unison, then filed from the room, tension lining each set of shoulders.

"I am trusted to be discreet, so I will be in attendance, but in the background. Please do not reveal my identity to anyone."

And then they were gone. Ruslan's glare was sharp enough to kill, and he watched Rares and the king converse, their heads bent together, whispering something too faint for me to hear. But as Ruslan's arms tightened protectively around me, I knew he heard.

"Let's see her physical development," Rares ordered.

"No," Ruslan growled, his voice low and threatening. For once, I stoked his rising rage, his desire to protect exactly what I wanted. "She is developing just fine, as I have seen with my own eyes."

"Your word means nothing when we have plans to carry out," King Azim seethed. "I am growing impatient, and you have blown me off for over a month. I want to see her progress with my own eyes."

Ruslan's fury combined with my own, and I shoved at the his, causing him to open his arms and allow me to land nimbly on the ground. I'd had enough of males thinking they owned me and my body. My voice was laced with venom, and I spat rage at the arrogant king. "I will not be some pawn in whatever game it is you want to play. I am not a tool for you to use at your disposal. I am a fucking Fae and Angel, and I will be treated like one – with the appropriate dose of fear and respect."

King Azim laughed, throwing back his head as I stood there, raging and confused at his sudden change. "Ruslan, you said you had her under your control. That is not what this looks like to me." His dark eyes sparkled with malice as he nudged Rares with the tip of his elbow, then swept a bejeweled hand across the scene before him. "You see, this is why I must keep my eye on everything. No one ever speaks the truth."

Ruslan stepped beside me, half shielding me with his body. "I said that I have it under control, not that she is under my control."

"It appears to me that neither of those statements are true. Instead of breaking her mind like I instructed, you have simply allowed her to strengthen it."

Ruslan grasped my hand, bringing my ring to the light. "Do you not see this?"

"What I see is the son who beat out all others to become heir apparent losing himself to a female. You are pathetic, Ruslan, and I wish Damir had killed you. He would have been obedient without question."

With a roar that shook the very earth upon which we stood, Ruslan launched himself at his father. He had King Azim pinned beneath him for only a moment before the king flipped their positions. Ruslan threw him off, and the king slammed into the rock wall, landing on the ground with a heavy thud. Ruslan was on him again in a second, raining down punches before his father kicked him in the side with a crack that sounded like a broken rib. Ruslan grunted, and the distraction was long enough for King Azim to shove his son away from him. He pushed to his feet, face bleeding profusely, eyes glinting with a hint of madness, as he squared up with Ruslan. "You think you can challenge me, son? You are nothing but what I give to you."

I thought Ruslan was going to rise to the taunt, but he waited, a cold fury settling across him. He took a few steps back, and I realized this was the end of the king. King Azim launched himself toward Ruslan, who unleashed his Dragon, wings snapping from his back, black horns curling from his head, claws replacing his hands, and black fire shooting from his mouth in place of a scream. Rares must have realized what was about to happen at the same moment I did, because he threw a shield in front of the king moments before he would have entered the space bathed in black fire.

My jaw hung wide as Ruslan emptied himself of fire, then sliced through the remains of his burnt shirt, revealing every inch of his tattooed torso, a dusting of black scales peeking through the swirling ink. He was breathtaking in his shifted form, a true predator whose might was unmatched by a simple Fae. He turned upon Rares, who trembled in fear beneath the black fire raging in his eyes. "You will not touch or look upon my mate without my permission. Is that understood?"

The promise of violence in his words, and his lethal body

coiled and ready to strike, had my blood singing, my core tightening, and my heart racing. His nostrils flared, and he shot me a devilish grin as he scented my arousal. He turned his back on his father and Rares, clearly unconcerned with receiving a response from them. In two strides, he held me in his arms, bending me backwards as he captured my mouth. I was so possessed by the heat from the male in front of me, I only realized we were no longer in the tunnels when he lifted me and threw me onto our bed.

"How did you do that?" I exclaimed, blinking as my mind caught up to my body.

"I can bend space, remember?" he smirked, his hands returned save for a single claw. He knelt above me, tearing through every scrap of fabric that separated my skin from his. A whimper sounded in my chest as he flung the ripped garments from my body. His nostrils flared again, a wicked grin settling on his lips. "Admit that my possession of you makes you wetter than any amount of freedom I give you," he growled.

"It doesn't," I breathed. It did, and the slickness of my thighs betrayed my words.

He banished the claw, then tore off his pants and boots, standing completely naked and shifted before me. I raked my gaze across his damning body, every muscle chiseled to perfection, and the scales that graced his skin glinted as he stalked toward me. The bed dipped beneath his bulk, and my breath hitched as he spread my legs with his knee, widening them as far as they would go. "I beg to differ," he purred as he drank in the sight of my bare, soaked core. He caged me in with his arms, bringing his lips a breath from my ear and grinding his hips into mine. "Admit that you have been manipulating me."

My breath hitched. *How could he have known that?*

I tried to close my legs and back away, but he gripped my thigh and pinned it to the bed as his other hand found the back of my head, yanking my hair back so my neck was bared to him. His hips rolled against mine, and my fear only increased the ache between my legs. "Say it, Izidora."

My mother's words returned to me. *Make sure he puts your needs above his own, protects you with the fierceness you deserve, and does not dampen your free spirit.*

Ruslan was possessive in a way that was protective, not controlling. He defied his father's order to break me mentally, instead empowering me with everything I needed to take care of myself. He never hurt me out of viciousness, but only when we were in bed and I wanted it.

Ruslan was darkness incarnate, and I was the fire that lit him up.

"Say. It." he commanded in my ear, adjusting his hips so the tip of his cock lined up with my entrance. I shook my head, unable to speak. He yanked my head back harder, then sucked my pulse between his sharpened teeth, drawing a hint of blood. The metallic scent filled the air between us, and I gasped as he lapped at my neck, then sank his tongue between my lips, sharing the taste. His kiss left me breathless, and when he broke it, his smoldering eyes bored into me.

"This is your last opportunity to speak," he threatened. "I only want the truth from you." He trailed his hand up my thigh to the apex of it, his fingers brushing over my clit. I writhed beneath him, needing more friction, and he responded with a hard slap to my sensitive nerves. I arched off the bed into him with a gasping moan, my pussy sucking in his cock with a wet gulp.

He was right, so utterly right. I wanted him to protect me like he had before, but let me spit fire in my own defense. I wanted him to drag me into the depths with him and light the way out for us. But I could not say it.

Ruslan groaned as he filled me, but his determination to get an answer from me won out. He pinned me beneath him so I was unable to move, but did not remove his cock, its length stretching me but not giving me the sensation I needed to come. "Tell me, my sprite, that you manipulated my emotions, trying to win me to your side. Tell me how good it felt to see me changing. Tell me how you saw hope for us like I did."

I panted as he held me still, panicking because he knew my every thought and because my body screamed for release and I was wholly trapped with no way out. I turned my head to the side, closing my eyes, but Ruslan grabbed my face.

"You will look at me." I did not think I could get any wetter, but another gush seeped from my center, and Ruslan growled as it coated his shaft.

That sinful smirk reappeared, and he dragged his cock all the way to my entrance before seating himself fully again. "Did I not tell you that you'd like it rough? That it would make you feel so alive?" He repeated the motion, and I was trembling all over by the time his balls were flush against me once more.

I moaned, trying to grind my hips against him.

He tsked, then yanked my hair back roughly. "If you won't admit to manipulating me, admit that you like it when I hurt you."

"Yes," I breathed, my body too tight and too hot to deny it.

"Yes, what?"

"I like when you hurt me, and I like when you hurt others for me," I added, hoping that would incentivize him to ease the ache building in my core.

He growled, embers in his eyes as he pumped in and out of me, slowly, dragging out the tension. I needed more, and faster. His hands fell away, but his predatory gaze pinned me as I pushed into him as hard as he pushed into me. "Did you manipulate me?"

"Only because I saw the good in you and wanted you to see that we could be happy without anything else."

In one swift movement, he pushed off the bed and pulled out of me, tearing a cry from my lips as his warmth left me. In another, his hands were on me, flipping me with such force I was on all fours in front of him before I realized what he had done. With one brutal thrust he was back inside me, and he dug his fingers into my hips so hard they bruised. His cock was vicious as it tore through me, so hard and so rough that I cried beneath his onslaught. He bent over my back, wrapped my hair around his fist, then whispered in my ear, "I will not stop until I get what I want. Nothing you can do will ever change that. I want my father dead. I want you as my mate. I want you as my wife. In. That. Order." He punctuated his last words with piercing thrusts.

Fuck, his words were exhilarating, and sparks burst in my chest.

Rearing back, he forced my spine to arch with his fist in my hair, and the chandelier above our bed blurred as tears sprang to my eyes, Ruslan brutally pounding me, over and over and over. My legs trembled as the tension in my core reached a breaking point, the pain in my scalp sending my pleasure higher than ever before. With his free hand, he found my clit, rubbing it in slow circles that were antithetical to his rough pace. "I feel your pussy pulsing around me, sprite. Are you going to come for me?"

"Yes," I whimpered as I ground into his hand, shamelessly needing more friction.

He left me empty, taking all pleasure with him, and my frustrated moan was pure lust, my body still tight and my core still ready to explode at any moment. Ruslan whipped me around, throwing me down beneath him, then knelt over me, looking like a vengeful god as his wings spread wide above us, his horns and eyes glinting. "Tell me that you love me."

"I love you. I really do, Ruslan." The truth fell from my lips with such ease.

"Then scream my name as you come," he commanded, shoving his cock into my core and slapping my clit.

"Ruslan!" I gasped as my orgasm ripped through me, my back arching from the bed, limbs trembling, core clenching, eyes rolling into the back of my head as he continued to pound me, driving me higher, higher, until I was so broken from my release that I could only pant beneath him as he chased his own.

"Fuck, Izidora," he groaned as his cock throbbed inside me, hot liquid squirting from it and coating my inner walls.

When reality returned to the front of my mind, I tensed, wondering what Ruslan would do now that I'd admitted to manipulating his emotions. As if he sensed the direction of my thoughts, he pushed himself up so that I was still pinned but he could look into my eyes.

"How did you know?" I asked.

"Sprite, you are my favorite book. I can read you over and over again and continue to learn something new. As much as you try to hide your thoughts and plans, you can't – not from me. We are too alike, you and I, and when we become mated there will be no more secrets between us." He brushed his lips lightly over mine, a tender kiss that promised so much more.

"What have you been telling your father? How do you have this under control?" I motioned between us.

His face darkened at the mention of King Azim. "Only that you were falling in love with me and would do what I asked when I asked it of you."

I narrowed my gaze at him, irritated that he assumed I was such a willing toy. "I am not interested in being a weapon in someone else's war."

"I knew you would never agree to it. You're not the type of female who does anything she does not want to do. You would only spite the male who tried to force your hand. But my father could not know that, otherwise he would have broken your spirit. And I would never let that happen to you."

Tears welled in my eyes at his confession. He'd protected me from his father, and I understood what that almost cost him, the fight he would have won if it weren't for Rares's intervention. "I'm so sorry I came between the two of you."

Ruslan threw back his head and laughed. "Oh, my sprite, you really do not know, do you? I hate the man who sired me, who forced me to kill my siblings, who never truly loved me and only craved power. The whole time my father has been plotting to use you and I to conquer Északi, I have been plotting to kill him and take the throne with your help."

Stunned to silence, I could only stare at the mercurial male who lay above me. *He wanted me to help him kill his father? He played me this whole time as I tried to play him?*

"So, Izidora, will you help me kill the male who tortured me?"

Abso-fucking-lutely.

While the king of the Iron Realm may not have landed a blow to my body, he was directly responsible for the torture, rape, and abuse I suffered all those years in the cave. I nearly laughed as I remembered the countless times over the past months that I'd imagined killing him myself.

And then there was Ruslan, my broken male, who had suffered at the hands of Rares and King Azim. He was forced to grow up alone, like me. He was forced to fight for his life to earn a place here. He was my Demon-Dragon, his wings flared protectively over me as my thoughts swirled through my mind. He may have started as a villain in my eyes, but the more time I spent around him, the more I realized there was something else behind the mask he wore – a male who craved the love and acceptance he never received as a child, just like me.

"What's the plan?"

Relief and fiendish excitement crossed his face at my question, and he pushed himself upright. He banished his wings and horns, returning to his Fae form, then held out his hand to me. We knelt before each other, a nervous tension filling the air as Ruslan spoke. "You will help me kill King Azim – today – before the feast begins. I will handle my father, but I need you to subdue Rares. His oath compels him to protect my father at all costs. That is, until I am king. Then he will be bound to me."

I nodded. "I have one condition."

He raised a dark brow but said nothing.

"I want all the Telivér trapped against their will to be free to choose if they want to stay or return home. No more experiments."

"All the Telivér may go. But none of the Félvér," he countered.

"Why not? What if they wish to return with their parents, to meet their families?" I challenged.

"They make up a large part of our army, and I will not leave the Iron Realm vulnerable to attack. I must protect you and will do so by any means necessary." His iron-gray eyes darkened with the vehemence in his words, and I believed he would protect me until the very end.

I huffed, displeased with his answer but understanding his logic. "Fine."

"Can I tell you a secret?" He tucked a lock of chestnut hair behind my ear, then rested his large palm on my bare shoulder.

I nodded, placing a hand atop his and stroking the back of it with my thumb.

Ruslan exhaled, long and slow, as if speaking his next words would relieve a heavy burden. "I've always wanted to let the other Félvér roam free across the continent. But with how the other realms are about blood purity, I knew they would never be accepted – that I would never be accepted. I want to change that."

Sincerity was written in the line between his eyebrows as he waited for my response. "Then let's change it together," I grinned at him.

His answering grin was filled with wicked delight. "Good. Get dressed. We have a king to kill."

26

RUSLAN

Vengeance sang in my veins as Izidora and I returned to Ryza Citadel. I replayed my conversation with her over and over. She'd admitted to manipulating me – which explained why I was so drawn to her light. But I no longer cared that she had the upper hand, because it got me to my goal. I was moments away from sinking my claws into my father's stomach and watching him bleed out all over his expensive white fur rug. Oh, how I had imagined this moment, dreamed endlessly of the last words I would speak to him. All the times I bit my tongue, checked my temper, or bent my will to his were in service of this very moment, the moment I had killed for – was about to kill for once again.

In the Iron Realm, there was no council to oppose me, only greedy High Lords who were easily appeased. I had garnered much wealth in my adult years, my inner Dragon hoarding jewels, my inner Demon driving my black market businesses. That night, I would be king. And when the rest of the monarchs arrived on my doorstep the next day, they would see their reckoning standing before them.

Bloodlust filled my veins as I led Izidora to my father's office, knowing he would be there, sitting behind his desk with a drink in hand. His personal guards straightened as I approached, sensing that I was in no mood for bullshit. One knocked on the door. "Ruslan to see you, My King."

"Enter," he called lazily through the door.

Izidora wore a fierce and fiery expression, aquamarine eyes alight, enhanced by the tight braids woven into her hair and the black leathers on her skin. The set of her jaw told me she was more than ready for the fight we were about to have, and as I opened the door, she stalked into my father's office like she was the predator and he was the prey.

My fucking sprite.

The king of the Iron Realm barely glanced up from his papers as we entered. "Have you finally calmed down, Ruslan? Did you fuck her out of your system so we can examine her?"

I gritted my teeth for the last time because I needed Rares in the room before the fight could begin. "Yes, father, you may examine her now. Shall I send for Rares?"

He nodded, and I instructed one of the guards to fetch him. I shifted from foot to foot while we waited for the old Mage to arrive, cracking my knuckles and popping my neck to release some tension. Rares limped into the room, his brows raising when he noticed Izidora was with me, then cracked his creepy, toothy smile at her before greeting my father.

Once the door shut behind him with an ominous click, I jerked my head to Izidora, who waved a hand to lock the door with her Night Fae magic. No one was entering or leaving this room without her consent.

"Honestly, Ruslan, no one would dare walk in without my permission. Strip," he ordered Izidora whose eyes blazed with hate for the male who treated her like an object, who was responsible for her abuse.

A manic laugh burst from my lips, and I threw my head back

with it. "Oh, father, she did not lock the door for her modesty. She locked the door so no one could enter once they heard your screams."

On the last word, I unleashed my inner Dragon, the wind from my wings knocking books from shelves and sending glass objects crashing to the ground. The room erupted in a cacophony of sound as my heavy boot pounded into his desk, launching myself into the air and landing behind my father. He whirled to face me, parrying a strike moments before it would have knocked him over, chair and all.

Izidora cast a net of white energy over Rares, her brow furrowing in concentration as she trapped him, then battled with his emotions.

My father threw up a shield of fire, like I knew he would, and I stepped back, waiting for him to try to spear me with the ground below. The floor hinted at a rumble, and I shot into the air, a spike narrowly missing my feet. King Azim's shield broke momentarily, and I unhinged my jaw, a jet of black flame spewing toward him. He ducked and rolled, his jacket singed but otherwise unharmed. Rares blasted me from the air, and I crashed into the wall of windows behind me with a crunch.

"Izidora!" I barked, a little pissed and a lot afraid that she had been harmed.

"I'm working on it!" she snapped.

A crazed smile filled my face as my father regained his footing. He snaked vines around my ankles and wrists, and with each step toward him, I burned them away, leaving only ashes in my wake. I opened the well of dark flame in my chest, readying my mouth for another inferno, when he dove for my waist, forcing me to backstep as he failed to take me to the floor. His arms clung to my waist for a moment too long, and I latched onto him, snaking my arms around his head and throwing him to the ground. I chased him there, leaning all my weight on his stomach as I pummeled his face with my elbows and fists. Blood coated my hands, the metallic scent exhilarating and fueling my fury.

I was so fucking close.

But another blast from Rares knocked me aside, though it was much weaker than his first attempt, and my head shot up in search of Izidora. My mate was locked in battle with Rares, both hurling blasts of energy at each other while Rares flickered in and out of a rapturous state.

"You have to choose something more intense," I shouted, momentarily breaking Izidora's concentration, and we both paid for our inattention. Rares blasted through her shield, and my father kicked the backside of my knees, bringing me down with a grunt. He followed it with a kick to the stomach, doubling me over, and it was only years of training that helped me avoid the near-lethal knee to the face that waited on my descent.

Gripping the ankle bearing all his weight, I yanked it out from under him, and he fell to his back, landing with a satisfying crack. The air whooshed from his lungs, and I wasted no time calling one claw to my hand and stabbing him through the middle. It was not fatal, but I wanted him to suffer before he died.

"Not so fast, Ruslan," Rares shouted, and I tore my attention from my near-victory to see him holding Izidora by the hair, a knife held to her throat.

"Heal him, or she dies," Rares threatened.

There was not a hint of fear in my mate's stunning blue eyes.

She must hold a secret if she was unafraid with a knife to her neck.

Izidora released a long breath, an almost imperceptible dip of her chin signaling me to finish the job. My father coughed blood on my arms and chest, his teeth bared in defiance, but the gash in his abdomen rendered him immobile.

"You thought you broke me a long time ago, father. You thought that I was completely subservient to you and your whims, ready to bend over backwards to make your dreams happen. But the truth is, that day that I killed Damir, I also vowed to kill you. I have waited for so long for this day–"

"I said heal him!" Rares demanded, his eyes widening as his own knife turned on him, pressing just above his heart, while his other hand dropped Izidora's hair and joined the other as he prepared to kill himself with every ounce of strength in his body. "What are you doing, witch? Release me this instant!"

Izidora's smirk mirrored my own, and I laughed maniacally, realizing my mate had kept this from me, from all of us. She was not only an empath who could influence emotions, she was also able to manipulate the actions of others. Her hate-filled eyes never left the aged Mage, though sweat poured into them as she fought for control.

Using her magic for that was draining her too quickly.

"Ruslan, you are pathetic, always have been, and always will be. You crave love, and that makes you weak. You are no son of mine." My father spat blood toward me, coating my armor in a ruby sheen.

With a roar, I sliced his throat, watching with rapt satisfaction as he clutched at his gurgling neck, the life draining slowly from his eyes. "And you are no father to me." My words rang with finality as he drowned in his own blood, his last wet breath the sweetest sound I had ever heard.

A snap popped across my skin – Rares's oath transferring to me. I straightened, towering over the lifeless body of the male who had given me life, and turned my attention to the Mage who was compelled to serve me. Rares's knife remained poised and trembling above his heart, ready to bury the metal at the will of my mate. "You may release him, Izidora. He is no longer a threat."

She collapsed in time with the knife, and I rushed to her side, catching her just before she hit the ground. Her head lolled, eyes closed, and my chest tightened as panic gripped me.

I couldn't lose her to burnout, not when I was so close to having everything I ever wanted.

With the back of my hand, I touched her forehead, looking for any sign that she might be close, but found none. Hefting her into my arms, I kicked the knife clear across the room, and Rares looked at me with a new loathing that ran deeper than our prior dislike for one another.

"I may be bound to you now, Ruslan, but I will fight every instinct I have to save your miserable life," he spat.

I merely shrugged. "I should have let her kill you, but I think I might find use for you yet. Oh, I just thought of a chore actually. Clean this up."

Rares's glare was hard enough to break glass as I approached the outer door. "Izidora, can you please unlock it?" I whispered. She was barely conscious, and I needed to get her food and a bath, fast. Her hand trembled as she lifted it, so small and so weak, and my heart beat a staccato rhythm as I waited for the telltale click of the lock. I wasted no time bursting through, only to find a regiment of my father's personal guard with swords drawn at the door.

"I am the king now, and as your commander I order you to clean up this mess and ensure Rares returns to his quarters, under constant watch until I say otherwise. Clear?"

"Yes, Your Highness," the soldier in front replied, his eyes wide and bouncing around me, taking in the blood that coated my armor and the trail of footprints I had left behind.

"Good, now out of my way."

They parted for me, and I rushed Izidora to the apartments left unused in the citadel. Along the way, I yelled at a maid to prepare a bath and another to bring us food. My vicious reputation commanded immediate compliance, and by the time I barged through the door, a host of servants followed me, readying the large apartment for occupancy. I laid Izidora on a chair, grabbing a glass of water and tilting her head back, trying to get her to drink the liquid. She sipped from the glass with assistance, then collapsed back once more.

"Stay with me, sprite," I begged.

Though she did not feel like she was burning out, I feared that her Angel blood might make the symptoms appear in a way that was harder to detect.

"Someone fetch Zuriel!" I demanded. While I waited for the Angel, I lifted more water to her quickly cracking lips. She refused, turning her head every time I offered it. The maid running the bath shouted it was ready at the same time Zuriel arrived. His already pale face blanched at the scene before him.

"What did you do, Ruslan?" he shouted, kneeling before Izidora, feeling her head and checking her pulse.

"She might be burning out, I don't know!" My voice cracked, sounding as desperate as I felt, and Zuriel must have taken pity on me because he scooped her up, barking orders at the servants who scurried about. He carried her straight to the waiting tub and dropped a hand to feel the temperature.

"It needs to be hotter. Angels need heat to prevent burnout," he explained.

That I could do. Black fire engulfed the tub, burning hotter than anything an Iron Fae could conjure. Once it was near boiling, Zuriel shouted, "Stop!"

He dropped Izidora into the tub, still fully clothed, and her body was wracked with shivers. My hand shot out to comfort her, only to be jerked back as the temperature burned me.

"How is this not going to kill her?" I snapped.

"Trust me, Ruslan, she will be fine in a moment." Zuriel's tone was sharper than my talons, and I said nothing else.

She sank beneath the water, her shivers subsiding once she was fully immersed. I held my breath, praying to the Goddess that I had not killed my father only to lose my mate in the process. Bubbles burst from her mouth, and she surfaced, fully awake and spluttering. She clung to the side of the tub, and I snatched a towel from a nearby servant. Izidora was delirious and tried to climb out, but Zuriel grabbed her shoulders and held her in place until she regained full consciousness.

"Izidora, can you hear me?" he asked, crouching down to eye level.

"Yes," she whispered, voice hoarse and grating.

"Follow my finger with your eyes," he requested. Those gem-like eyes followed his finger obediently, back and forth, up and down, then in a circle.

"Good. What is the last thing you ate?"

"Cinnamon roll," she stated confidently. Zuriel checked with me to confirm she was correct, and I nodded.

"Let's get you dry and into bed, Izidora. You need to rest now," he said. Together, the Angel and I lifted her from the water and onto solid ground. He held her upright as I dried her, then I carried her to our bed, freshly made with piles of soft blankets waiting for us. A robe hung at the foot of the bed, and Zuriel turned his back while I undressed my mate then wrapped her in it. She blinked slowly as I tucked her into bed, lids growing heavier and lashes fluttering as she struggled to keep her eyes open.

"Don't leave," she whispered as my weight left the bed.

I planted a light kiss on her forehead. "We'll be right here."

She turned so she lay half on her side, half on her stomach, and not a moment later, she was asleep. I waited until her breaths were slow and even before leaving her side and joining Zuriel in the adjacent sitting room.

"She does not need to eat?" I asked.

"She will be hungry when she wakes, but no, not right now," he confirmed.

I dropped my head to my hands, shaken to my core. She was the only person to ever love me. Death would not take her from me. I would fight until my very last breath to keep her alive, and if I failed, I would join her there. We would be together always from this moment forth, and I promised myself that I would not push her so hard again.

"Ruslan, we've known each other a long time. I watched you grow up in the tunnels, and I watched you fight for your place as heir apparent. You are ruthless, cruel, and generally awful to be around. But in the weeks since you returned with Izidora, you have changed for the better. I hope you keep it up. Izidora is special, and if you willfully hurt her, I will ensure the Goddess smites you," Zuriel threatened.

"I had no idea she was capable of manipulating more than emotion," I spoke through my hands.

"What happened?" Zuriel inquired.

"I killed my father. I am now king of the Iron Realm. But Rares, as you know, is bound to the Iron Crown, and I needed Izidora to distract him while I took care of my father. He caught her and held a knife to her throat – until she forced him to turn it on himself."

Zuriel swore in the language of the Angels and shook his head. "Her life was on the line. Angels can do incredible feats under duress."

"Save it, Zuriel. I know it is an empath power, though an extremely rare one." I lifted my head from my palms, glaring at him.

"Fine. But I will have you know, Izidora would only have used it if her life was on the line. I have tried time and time again to get her to practice it, and she refuses. She does not want to take away the choices of others. It is quite noble, although foolish, given that it just saved her life." The Angel huffed a laugh, shaking his head.

I rolled my eyes with a half-smile on my lips. Izidora's heart was much too good for this world. I remembered her one request and decided it was time to offer it to Zuriel. "Izidora asked that in return for helping me kill King Azim, I allow all Telivér to choose whether they wanted to remain here or return to their homelands."

"Did she now?" Zuriel responded, his expression blank.

"I hope you will choose to stay, at least for now, to help her," I sighed, unable to believe I was really about to close down the program that had created me. It was the right decision, though one I knew would have consequences. I only hoped that those who returned home did not rally an army to our shores for vengeance.

"For now, I will stay," he said after a moment.

"Tomorrow, I will have Rares lift the spells tying you to the Iron Realm," I promised.

"Thank you, Ruslan." The Angel stood to leave. "I meant what I said earlier. This change is good on you. Fetch me if you need anything else." And with that, he departed, leaving me sitting with the heaviness of my actions.

I crossed to the windows in the sitting area, looking down upon the city of Radence. Fae and Félvér bustled about, totally unaware that their king had died not even an hour before. The revelation settled in my stomach like a punch to the gut.

I was their king.

I had been so focused on my desire to kill my father that I'd forgotten about the other part of the job – ruling. I popped my neck, shaking out my shoulders as my body tightened, muscles tingling and a bear sitting on my chest.

But the sensation was fleeting as I reminded myself how I'd gained so much power and influence in the first place, enough power and influence that when I killed my father, no one batted an eye. I'd stalked these halls for years, garnering respect, but mostly fear. No one fucked with me, and no one would again now that I sat upon the throne of the Iron Realm.

A wicked thrill settled over me, and I allowed myself to daydream about the day I would be officially crowned king. First, I would marry Izidora. Then, the High Priestess would place the Iron Crown upon my brow, solidifying my right to rule. I'd send Drazen to fetch the Night Crown so Izidora could be crowned after me. And then, we would officially unite the two realms, standing on the balcony that over-looked Radence, hands held high together in triumph. A wave of kneeling subjects would bow before us, the two most powerful Fae in Északi. Izidora would look at me with unfil-tered adoration, and everyone would know she was mine. The scene was so vivid in my mind, it was almost like a memory.

Fear screamed from the back of my mind as I thought about the possibility of Kazimir showing his face at Béke.

Would Izidora run to him? Would she forget about what we had, her guilt getting the better of her? Would she reject our bond to be with him?

I slammed my fist against the window, cracking the glass as the thought of her choosing Kazimir over me unleashed a torrent of rage so intense I thought I might combust with Dragon fire.

She would not leave me. She was already spell-bound to the Iron Realm, but I wanted her heart to stay with me too. I rushed to the hall door, running smack into Drazen as he opened it to enter. I stepped back to allow him inside, then sent the first servant I saw to fetch Rares.

"I heard you killed your father," Drazen stated, arms crossed over his chest as he stared me down.

"I did." I did not elaborate, wanting my cousin to get to the point.

"I thought we had a plan." His normally impassive face was firmly set, and his deep blue eyes were hard as sapphires.

"Plans change." I shrugged dismissively, but Drazen was relentless.

"So you do not wish for me to carry out the second part?" He raised an eyebrow in challenge.

"No need. I have a much better plan now. I need you to fetch the Night Crown and High Priestess from Este Castle. We will ascend on the same day as the wedding, but I need both crowns and priestesses to make it happen," I stated, my words carrying the weight of a king's order.

Drazen pinched the bridge of his nose, sighing heavily. "Ruslan, when are you ever going to make a plan and stick with it? You are too impulsive, and it's going to get us all killed. From what I heard on my way up here, you are lucky that you didn't kill Izidora. Let's just stop and think for a moment, okay?"

"I don't need a lecture from you, Drazen. I am your king now," I hissed, turning away from him and narrowing my gaze on the city outside.

"And I am the only person who actually tolerates your presence and calls you on your bullshit. Don't be the type of king who can't take advice because his ego is the size of Vasvain. You should know from your history books how that turns out for them," he chastised, joining me at the cracked window.

I growled my frustration, but he was right, and we both knew it. "Fine, what do you think our next move should be?"

"See who shows up tomorrow for the feast. We really pissed off the Night Realm, and I have heard whispers that they left with an army. If we can confirm that they are here for a fight, Vaenor will be vulnerable to attack, and then, and only then, will I retrieve the Night Crown. But I think it would be better to crush them while we have a strategic advantage, then wait until they have yielded to retrieve it. If they do not show up with an army, then we have a different problem. We will have to assess if they have chosen Izidora to replace King Zalan, or if they have named another successor. The rules are different in their realm since they have a council. Who knows, maybe the named successor will show up wearing the Night Crown. Wait, just one more day, and we will have a better understanding of our options." The plea in Drazen's voice was hidden, but there.

I cracked my knuckles as I thought through his strategy. Risking Félvér lives unnecessarily wasn't my style, especially because we would need every last one of us for the war that would surely arrive on the Iron Realm's borders. "I can wait, but only one more day. I can't take any chances." My attention drifted to the bedroom door, and the lack of sounds coming from within.

Drazen followed my gaze. "You are worried she will see the other male and go running back to him." It was not a question.

"Yes," I spat through gritted teeth, jaw clenched so tight I thought I might crack a tooth.

Better physical pain than emotional pain.

"Don't let the old Ruslan return, otherwise she will. She likes this new side of you, at least enough to agree to marry your crazy ass," he smirked, elbowing me in the side. I shoved him back with my shoulder, the corner of my lip twitching up.

A throat cleared behind us, forcing us to whip around and face the intruder. Rares appeared at the open door, his wrinkled face filled with hate. "What?"

"You will address your king with respect, Rares," I purred, loving my new power over him. Unfortunately for Drazen, the old Ruslan really, really wanted to play with the Mage now that I was king of the Iron Realm and, therefore, his master.

"What can I do for you, Your Highness?" Rares's words snapped out like he had taken a drink of a bitter potion.

"You will find a way to prevent Izidora from falling back in love with the male she thought was her mate. He is likely to arrive tomorrow, and I cannot have him interfering with my plans." Drazen shot me a dark look, but I ignored him, waiting for the old Mage's response.

"It will take time to develop something, if it can be done. Manipulating another's mind is rarely permanent, as you are aware from Izidora's own abilities," Rares protested, wringing his gnarled hands.

"Then I suggest you start working now, Rares," I replied coolly.

He spun on his heel, stomping away with as much force as his hunched form allowed. I grinned manically, my chest easing with the certainty that Izidora would not reject me.

Drazen punched my shoulder, hard, and hissed, "That is exactly what I was saying not to do."

"I'm not leaving anything up to chance," I countered, heat rising across my neck and shoulders. Drazen didn't understand what this fear was like, how all-consuming it could be.

"No, you are a control freak," he bit out. "You are incapable of trusting anyone or anything."

"My father never did either," I pointed out, keeping my voice cold to mask the heat rising within.

"Exactly. I hope you did not kill him simply to become him," Drazen seethed. "Congrats again, Ruslan. I'll see you tomorrow morning." The sarcasm in his tone forced me to snatch his arm to stop him as he made to leave.

"I am nothing like him," I growled. "I do trust you, which is why I take your council. And why I am asking you to move my personal regiment to the citadel for our protection."

Drazen shrugged me off, but nodded. "Anything else you

need before I go?" The tension between us remained, but it was clear he wanted to leave.

"No. I'll return to Roc later to retrieve clothes and books for Izidora and myself. I need her to wake up first." He turned to leave once again, and when he was almost out the door I called, "Thanks, Drazen."

He grunted and swung the door closed behind him, the force rattling the spiderweb crack in the window behind me, deepening its veins. Blowing out a breath, I surveyed my kingdom, the sun beginning its final descent over the mountains in the distance, signaling the end of a pivotal day in my life.

I was now king of the Iron Realm. A goal I had worked toward for over two decades, ever since my father had announced the competition for heir apparent, was finally achieved.

Except, I felt empty.

Despite the deep well of black fire resting there, my chest felt hollow and cold. I finally had everything I wanted – I was king, I had my mate, and I was the most powerful Fae in the Iron Realm. But why did I still feel like I was not good enough? Why did I still feel so unworthy of it all? Why did I still feel like Izidora did not really love me? Why did killing my father not feel as thrilling as I imagined it would be?

My head throbbed as each question stabbed my brain like an icepick, and I wanted to bury those thoughts in the deep recesses of my mind. Crossing the room, I leaned into the hall, catching the attention of a nearby sentry and ordering him to bring me a bottle of liquor.

I needed something strong to drown my thoughts. The night was not one for wine, not with what felt like my impending execution looming over my head. As much as I knew that Izidora loved me and would likely choose me over Kazimir, my deepest fear was a demon who knew exactly what words to whisper in my ear to make me cow to it.

Minutes later, the sentry returned with a bottle, and I didn't bother to fetch a glass from the nearby table as I settled in front of the hearth. I pulled straight from the lip, loving the burn that seared my throat, numbing my gut and my feelings. The crackling fire held my attention, its wild dance beckoning me to surrender, and so I did, losing myself in the bottle and the flames, the world beyond me nothing more than a distant memory until I succumbed to the darkness.

27

IZIDORA

I woke with a start to the sound of Drazen and Ruslan arguing. Their tension was palpable even through the door that muffled their voices. Curiosity won out, and I crept from the bed to the door to listen. My body was aching and weary, yet my heart and mind raced as I listened to their conversation.

"You are worried she will see the other male and go running back to him." That was Drazen.

"Yes." Ruslan was worried that I would leave him, a constant tension in our relationship.

"Don't let the old Ruslan return, otherwise she will. She likes this new side of you, at least enough to agree to marry your crazy ass."

"What?" A new voice appeared, more distant than Ruslan and Drazen.

"You will address your king with respect, Rares."

"What can I do for you, Your Highness?"

"You will find a way to prevent Izidora from falling back in love with the male she thought was her mate. He is likely to arrive tomorrow, and I cannot have him interfering with my plans."

I swallowed a gasp, shocked that he would really go to such lengths to keep me. Tears welled in my eyes as my heart shattered into a million tiny, jagged pieces, and I had to bite my knuckle to keep from crying out.

I thought we'd made progress together. I thought he was changing for the better, that he would allow me a choice in my life – but that was only a glimpse of what was possible, and not what was probable. Ruslan had spent too long buried in his darkness for me to pull him out of it. My love for him ran so fucking deep, and that was what hurt the most. He'd clawed his way into my soul, and that thread between us hummed with disapproval as I tiptoed back to the bed, wanting to hear no more, and buried myself under the warm blankets, silent tears streaming down my face.

Kazimir lied to me.

Ruslan lied to me.

Kazimir manipulated me.

Ruslan manipulated me.

And the whole time, I thought I was winning them over.

But Kazimir was passionate, calm, and deceptive.

And Ruslan was intense, volatile, and empowering.

Who was the right fucking choice?

My hands covered my mouth and nose as sobs wracked my body. I felt like my heart was being ripped from my chest, stomped on, and then burned all at once. There was only one person in the Iron Realm I could trust, and I reached out to him, mind to mind.

"Zuriel?"

"I'm here, Izidora. Are you alright? You almost burned out."

"I know, my body is weak. But my heart is breaking."

"What happened?"

"Ruslan asked Rares to find a way to prevent me from wanting to be with Kazimir again."

Zuriel swore in the language of the Angels.

"Speak with him in the morning, Izidora. You are brave, and you can talk sense into him. He is afraid of losing you, as you very well know. But you need rest. You are already vulnerable and these intense emotions will burn you out if you are not careful. I will sing to you until you fall asleep again."

"How long until I will be fully recovered?"

"Perhaps tomorrow or the next day. I promise to check on you at first light."

"I promised I would get you home, and Ruslan will release you soon. I will miss you when you go."

"I'm not going anywhere, sweet cousin. Now, rest and listen to my voice."

Zuriel began a hauntingly beautiful tune in a language I could not understand, but the melody ensnared my frayed emotions and carried them along the journey. The sorrow in the song transformed into light, and I lost myself in the notes of his deep, melodic voice. Muscle by muscle, my body relaxed into the bed until I was floating in the words alone. The tears that streamed down my cheeks had long since dried, and as the song began again, my mind finally let go, and sleep carried me away from the world I had longed to see while I was chained in the cave.

V

THE REUNION

INTERLUDE

The tunnels were filled with the screaming of twelve small children training to be warriors. Eleven mothers watched over them, hawk-like eyes on their own. Only one boy with hair as dark as night had no one watching him, and his aggression toward his half-brother had the boy's mother gripping the edge of her seat. Even at the age of twelve, the dark haired one's strength was unmatched by that of his siblings, and with no mother to watch over him, he had raised himself to be cold and calculating.

The Mage that supervised their instruction took to him in a sinister way, often pulling him aside after training for additional one-on-one time, where he pushed him harder and forced him to increase his well of inner strength until it was nearly endless. He subjected the child to all types of pain – physical, mental, but never emotional, for the boy needed no further torture than that of being utterly alone and abandoned by those around him.

The Mage knew that the boy's deep need for affection and attention would keep him in line in the future, and as he watched the day's practice unfold, he rubbed his gnarled hands together with a wicked gleam in his eye. His experiments were paying dividends, and after decades of work, the results spoke for themselves. Out of the twelve children his master had sired, four were his greatest achievements, the crown jewels of his collection.

The dark haired child's eyes drifted to the Mage again and again, especially after he landed a blow that knocked his brother on his back. But the Mage was displeased with his distraction and stomped toward him, shoving him between his shoulder blades until he sprawled on the ground beside his brother. "Once you get your opponent to the ground, do not stop until you finish them, Ruslan," the Mage instructed. "Get back to work."

The children dusted themselves off and squared up again, and that time, when the dark haired one threw his brother to the ground, he followed him there, pounding his face until the boy's mother jumped to her feet and pulled them apart, shooting the Mage a hateful look and cradling her son to her chest. "That is enough! They are just children," she snapped.

"If you cannot handle watching them train, then I shall have to ban you from entering during these hours," the Mage replied coolly, surveying her and the other females in attendance. "In fact, these younglings are old enough now that they do not need your constant surveillance. Get out."

A few mothers opened their mouths to protest, but their teeth snapped shut when the Mage began chanting. They knew what he would do to them if they disobeyed. With lingering looks on all the children, save for one, they exited the training arena.

Most children watched their mothers go with a hint of nervousness, but the motherless one only glared at his half-siblings with sickly green envy emanating from his pores. He cracked his neck when they refocused their attention on the

Mage, icing over the hurt in his heart and channeling his rage into the fight before him. *He needed no one,* he told himself, but deep down, he knew just how false that statement was. All he wanted was to be loved like the others, and even at his young age, he knew that would never happen for him.

28

KAZIMIR

"Fucking Fates, it's cold," Vadim swore next to me. "I don't understand how it's possible to be sweating my balls off one moment, then freezing my balls off the second we pass into the Iron Realm."

"Don't be such a pussy, Vadim," Liliana teased. "It's not that cold."

"Says you, who gets to ride in the carriage with the queens!"

"I'm out here now, aren't I?" She quirked a brow at her brother, daring him to argue again.

"She has a point," I snickered, and Vadim cursed us under his breath, followed by curses to the weather. We stood on the precipice of two realms, staring at the wide path that led straight into the Agrenak Mountains, disappearing around a bend in the distance. The Iron Realm had maintained its secrecy and security for millenia because of the harsh landscape that surrounded it. Only two passable routes existed, the Zherza Pass between the Night and Iron Realms, where one wrong step would send you plummeting to your death unless you could fly, and the Ferzho

Pass between the Day and Iron Realms, which lie before us. At least the Ferzho Pass was even, albeit steep. The road was carved between two mountains, and it was as likely to be a trap as an entrance. We needed to keep our eyes trained above at all times, searching for hidden archers with iron-tipped arrows prepared to knock us from our mounts.

The low-hanging clouds, obscuring the peaks from view, were not a good omen. "I think it's snowing." I squinted my eyes, trying to see if the white flakes dancing in the distance were real or my imagination.

"It's definitely snowing," Viktor confirmed.

"Son of a bitch," Vadim swore again.

"This snow better let up before Béke, otherwise the army will never get through," Viktor grumbled. We briefly reunited with the Night and Crystal Realm's armies in Zheka, relaying our plans. They were worn out from the long days on the road, so we gave them time to rest, and Queen Viktoria ensured they had extra food and places to sleep before we departed. We also grabbed our larger bags from the wagon we'd left them in, and I immediately searched mine for my father's journal, tucking it into my saddlebags.

"We need to get going. The snow will slow us down," Kaztar said.

"Lil, why don't you ride Mistik for a bit and let me sit in the carriage?" Vadim begged, nearly linking his palms and dropping to his knees.

"Not a chance, brother," she laughed, tossing her chocolate hair over her shoulder and returning to the carriage where Queen Viktoria, Queen Immonen, and Domi waited.

"I am glad Queen Viktoria decided to join us for the feast. It would have been awkward to show up without her," Endre commented as we returned to our waiting horses.

"Agreed. It would have been suspicious, and we are going to

be subtle, remember?" Viktor looked straight at me with an expression that said I was not allowed to rip Ruslan's head from his shoulders the second I laid eyes on him.

"I remember," I growled.

"Everything will be okay, Kazimir," Endre reassured me as we guided our mounts toward Radence.

I blew out a breath, fogging up the air in front of me as hot met cold. "I know. Just keep grounding me, yeah? We are so close, and I can't lose her or myself."

"I won't let that happen."

We lapsed into silence, each of us bracing against the bitter wind that tore through the carved path, blowing flakes straight into our faces the higher we climbed. I scanned the mountainside, but it was pointless searching for a surprise attack when the weather was awful. If the Iron Realm wanted easy prey, we were certainly that as we trudged up the hard-packed path that was rapidly icing over. I glanced at the carriage behind us, hoping the procession had broken up enough ice that the wheels would not slip. The six horses that pulled it strained against their harnesses, their hides dark with sweat as they fought the incline. We'd been riding like this for at least an hour, and I prayed that we would reach the point where the pass evened out before the horses slipped.

Endre must have followed my train of thought because he shouted over the wind, "We should get Liliana and Domi out of the carriage to lighten the load. I don't know when the path will level off. I can barely see Geza and Airre."

"If we stop the horses they might not be able to start again with how slick the path is," I yelled back. His brows furrowed, and I understood his worry for Liliana. Ever since Vadim gave them his blessing, Endre and Liliana had been inseparable. "Everything will be okay," I echoed his own words back. He nodded, but we both continued to glance behind us every few paces, keeping watchful eyes on the carriage.

A shout traveled up the line of horses and Fae, and I tensed until Kaztar turned to relay the message to us. "The flat part is just ahead, and we will stop briefly when we get there." His teeth chattered and frost coated his brows. I passed along the message to Vadim, whose beard looked like icicles rather than the lush hair he meticulously groomed.

Silence fell over us the moment we crested the hill, the wind nothing more than a trickle through the mountain. The air temperature rose, though snow continued to coat my furs and Fek's mane. Endre breathed an audible sigh of relief as the carriage rolled to a stop beside us. "We need to warm up," I shouted to Kaztar, who nodded, unable to argue that we needed to continue.

A low overhang that almost formed a cave behind us provided temporary shelter from the cold. Vadim lit a fire using wood stacked as far away from the mouth as possible, and we huddled around it, shoulder to shoulder as snow and ice melted from our bodies. King Geza and King Airre joined their wives in the carriage, Liliana and Domi rushing to the fire beside us to give them privacy. Two of the Day Realm's High Lords joined our journey, and as they shivered beside us, I joked, "Soma, Domon, I've never seen such mighty warriors cower in the face of the weather."

High Lord Soma threw his braided hair back and laughed, loud and deep. "If you grew up on the beaches of the Day Realm as I did, you would cower too."

"I don't know that I would call Soma a mighty warrior to begin with, though. He is soft from his years by the ocean," High Lord Domon bantered.

"The ocean gives you great perspective, Domon," he tsked.

"That's how I knew this war was important. The calmest waters appear after the strongest storms."

"You should write that in your next book," Domon grinned in response.

"Will you actually read this one?" Soma teased.

"Philosophy is boring, my friend. Maybe if you write an adventure."

"I think you will have plenty of material for one after this, Soma," I chuckled.

He waved me off. "Don't assume we know the ending before we know the beginning."

Conversation picked up around me as we thawed, and Soma shared a wineskin with the group, the alcohol chasing away the last of the chill. I was ready to ride by the time the kings exited the carriage, my furs thoroughly dried and feeling returned to my toes.

"How much longer do we have to ride?" Liliana asked Endre as Vadim put out the fire.

"A few more hours through the mountains, and then perhaps a few hours to reach Radence after that."

"Ugh. I am going to take a nap." Her braid whipped behind her as she scurried to the warm carriage.

Fek stomped as I approached him with Endre by my side. "Is she tired because she hasn't slept much lately?"

A lopsided grin covered Endre's face. "Maybe."

"Please, say no more, Endre," Vadim begged, covering his ears from atop Mistik's back.

Snow continued to fall softly, silently, as we traversed the path to Radence. There was no sign of any Iron Fae, and I was grateful for the reprieve. They must have retreated from their sentry posts to avoid the weather; deadly avalanches were common on the higher slopes, especially with fresh snow.

As we rounded the last bend in the road, the sun broke free

of the clouds, the fluffy white powder coating every structure glittering in the light. Radence was bathed in a false gleam, for I knew the evils that lurked beneath the ground there.

"Halt!" King Airre called from the front of our procession. I craned my neck to see what stopped us. A dozen Iron Fae soldiers on horseback blocked the path to the capital of the Iron Realm, and their commander rode forward to greet King Airre, who exchanged a few words I did not catch. When the Iron Fae turned his horse and separated his unit, I breathed a sigh of relief. We proceeded through them, and I studied each male in turn, committing their faces to memory. If any of them had been at Este Castle when Ruslan kidnapped Izidora, I would personally slit their throats. Black ropes hissed like snakes beneath my skin at the thought of each male drowning in his own blood, but I clamped down on the desire before my imagination ran away with my mind.

We left the riders behind as we wound down the mountainside, Ryza Citadel growing larger and larger as we closed in on Radence.

"I'm almost there, Izidora," I whispered on the wind. I was so close I could almost feel her presence. My every nerve was alight, ready to fight, ready to grab her, ready to kiss her, ready to hold her once again. I shifted in my saddle, and Fek snorted at me as if to say, 'calm down.' I patted his black hide, then glanced at Mistik and Vadim beside me. A wave of sadness washed over me as I realized we would have to tell Izidora about Kriztof, Zekari, and Kirigin – and my father.

I've almost got her back, father.

I touched the bag that held his journal, wondering if he could hear me in death. Would he be disappointed in my actions since receiving binding magic? Or would he encourage me to lean into my Fates-given gift if that meant saving my mate?

He always knew the right path, and I wished to hear his

voice guiding me one last time. The ache of his absence had abated during the hectic and hurried race to gather allies, but on that lonely stretch of road, his loss chilled my body beyond the snow.

We entered the city of Radence. The main thoroughfare was nearly empty of life, the thick snow barring many from venturing into the streets. Brief flashes of grim faces appeared from curtain-covered windows that lined the way to Ryza Citadel, each glance at our traveling party carrying a wariness and hint of tension that grew with each step toward the black fortress that watched over all below it.

Something was off, and it was not only the snow that kept everyone indoors this day. Vadim caught my attention, murmuring under his breath, "Do you feel it?"

I dipped my chin. In front of us, Endre and Viktor scanned left and right, up and down, and I tried to look behind us, but my view was blocked by the rolling carriage. Liliana's flushed face appeared in the small window, and she caught my eye, clearly feeling the tension too.

"Do we need to be ready?" she mouthed, her voice blocked by the wall and distance between us. I tapped the boot where I kept a knife hidden, a last resort in case of attack. She understood my meaning, then disappeared from view.

The citadel perched atop a cliff that looked like it had speared the ground and broken through to the skies above, and as we reached its base, we turned onto the stone road that wound around to a sloped incline leading to the citadel's front gates. Soldiers decked in intricate metal armor lined the path that led straight uphill with no way out. Filling my lungs with air, I readied myself for a fight. While King Airre and King Geza might lead the procession, King Azim was surely not stupid enough to think the Night Realm would not attend. But the Iron Fae simply stared straight ahead, unmoving as we passed them.

The kings crested the hill and moved to one side, making room for the six High Lords from their own realms and my friends from the Night Realm.

Dread settled in my gut as Fek clopped closer to the top of the hill. My heart dropped with each pair of riders that disappeared over the horizon.

Eight pairs left.

My palms were slick in my gloves, the fur dampening.

Six pairs left.

My spine tingled, my nerves on fire and sweat dripped down my back despite the chill. Four pairs left.

Fek tossed his head, picking up on the anxiety that wracked my body.

Two pairs left.

Would I crest the hill and find Izidora hanging at the gate?

One pair left.

Goddess, please let her be alive.

And as I finally reached the courtyard of Ryza Citadel, I laid eyes upon the male who had kidnapped my mate and killed my father. We locked eyes, and shock replaced fear when I observed the Iron Crown resting upon his head. He wore a sardonic smirk, and the beast inside me roared, hungry for his blood.

But then I saw her.

29

IZIDORA

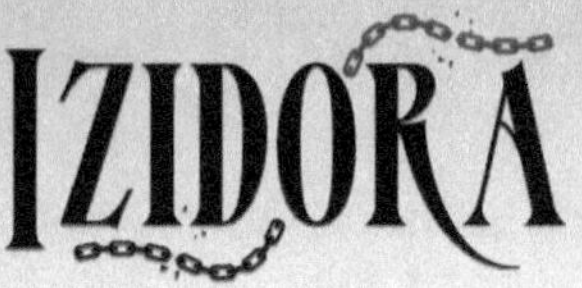

BÉKE DAY ONE

Whatever Zuriel sang to me must have been infused with magic, because I did not wake until the next morning when his voice filled the room beyond. I cracked a swollen eye, finding the bed beside me perfectly intact. Ruslan must not have come to bed the previous night. His raspy voice mixed with Zuriel's, and I waited in bed to see who would come for me. At last, Zuriel slipped through the door, closing it behind him with a soft click, and crossed the large room to the bed where I remained curled into a tight ball.

"How did you sleep?" he murmured when he discovered I was awake.

"Fine, thanks to your song." My voice was thick and hoarse from crying.

"Here, drink this." He produced a steaming mug of chocolate from behind his back. "It is the cure for heartbreak."

I pushed myself upright, closing the robe tightly over my

chest, then accepted the warm drink. "Does Ruslan... Has Rares..." I started, unsure how to finish my question.

"No. He was passed out drunk in front of the fire when I walked in. Seems like he celebrated a little too hard last night." Zuriel scoffed in disgust. "Although now that he is awake, you should probably speak with him."

I took a sip of the melted chocolate, the sweet warmth passing over my tongue and burning down my throat, heating me from the inside as it settled in my belly. It definitely was not a heartbreak cure, but I would take it. "Do you think Rares is capable of that type of magic?"

He pursed his lips and shook his head. "I went out in the middle of the night to check on him, but he was not in his study or the library. I have no idea where he went, but he was not around before I left this morning. Mage magic relies on spells and objects, it is not Goddess-given like our magic. If he could find the right spell or object, it is possible. But could he find it in one night? That I do not know."

I chewed on my lip, Zuriel's uncertainty intensifying my own fears. I wanted a choice with everything in my life, and I had said so to Ruslan countless times. My shoulders tightened at his desire to exert his control over me instead of trusting that I would choose him. Had he learned nothing in our time together? Or were his fears so great that when faced with the reality of Kazimir and I reuniting, his mind simply broke?

As I sipped the chocolate, I discovered my ring was missing. I furrowed my brow, certain I had not taken it off since Ruslan had given it to me. "Zuriel, was I wearing my ring when you brought me in here?"

"I don't remember. Why?"

"I could have sworn I was. It was such a pretty piece, I would hate to have lost it." I paused for a moment, then continued. "Zuriel, I'm not sure what to say to him."

His hand rubbed circles over my back, calming my frayed nerves. "I know, Izidora. But you will find the right words. He loves you, of that I am certain. You did not see his panic over you yesterday. It was very unlike him."

My stomach growled loudly, and we shared a laugh that eased some of the anxiety threatening to immobilize me. "Please tell me you also brought food."

"I did, a full breakfast is waiting for you out there," he jerked his head in the direction of the sitting room. "You need to eat more today to replenish your magic. Especially sugar. Though I don't think you'll have an issue with that." His eyes sparkled as a half-smile teased across his lips.

"Not at all," I replied, hopping from the bed. My feet hit the cold stone floor, sending a shiver from the tips of my toes to the tip of my nose, and I scurried to the wardrobe across the room, clutching the robe to my chest as I opened drawers and shuffled clothes about. There were only male's clothes inside, but I managed to find a loose pair of pants and pulled them on beneath the robe. I had to roll the waist several times to prevent them falling, and they still dragged on the floor with every step I took. The smoky smell of bacon wafted through the sitting room door, and I paused with my hand an inch from the handle, body tingling as fear of opening it to discover Ruslan and Rares waiting to pounce rose within me.

"I'll go first," Zuriel offered, understanding my hesitation. I stepped aside to let him pass, holding my breath until he said, "It's clear."

The sitting room was empty of the male who I both loved and hated at that moment, and I released a tense breath as I walked to the table laden with breakfast for us. Zuriel piled his plate with food, and I pulled the chair beside him back, settled cross-legged onto it and waited until Zuriel finished before making my own plate. Eggs, bacon, toast, and berries squished together on my plate, and after my first few bites, I grew absolutely ravenous, my stomach finally catching up with the rest of my body. I tore through my first plate, then another as Zuriel kept piling food onto it. When I licked icing from my fingers after my fourth cinnamon bun, my stomach finally relented. "You were not kidding about needing food."

"Magic takes energy, and food is energy for our bodies. It is the cycle of life that must be maintained and balanced. Too many sweets," he elbowed me in the ribs, "and not enough use of our bodies throws that balance out of whack. Too much use of our bodies and not enough food also throws off the balance, too."

I remembered King Zalan's rotund belly, his oily energy filling me with disgust and gagging me. Then I remembered my own emaciated body the first time I'd gazed at my reflection in a mirror. I was so much stronger, both mentally and physically, despite the path I had traveled not being an easy one. Despite all odds, I was still fighting for myself, and that would never change.

Whatever lay ahead, I could handle it. I was no longer the victim of abuse, chained in darkness for countless years. I was a powerful Fae and Angel with a deep well of magic who was fiery and fierce and had friends in my corner to fight alongside me. I would not let any male control me, abuse me, or manipulate me again.

A knock sounded on the outer door, and my stomach immediately dropped. Zuriel jumped from his chair and jogged across the room, calling magic to his hand. He hid it behind his back as he cracked the door. "Drazen, good to see you," he said, stepping away but keeping his hands from view. The half-Dragon entered the room carrying an armful of bags, opening his arms and letting them thud against the floor.

"Ruslan never returned last night, and I know you'll be

needing clothes for today, Izidora." He looked at my robe and the oversized pants, the corners of his mouth twitching upward. "Clearly, my timing was spectacular."

"Thanks, Drazen." I gestured to my attire with a lopsided grin. "This is not the proper attire to greet other royals with."

"If you want anything else, just step outside and one of the guards will fetch me. Ruslan's regiment is guarding you now, so you might see some familiar faces." Despite everything, I liked Drazen and some of the others who made up Ruslan's personal guard. I trained with them most days, and although most kept their distance for good reason, I still enjoyed their company. "Have you seen him today? I need to speak with him."

Zuriel responded for me. "He left after I arrived to check on Izidora's near-burnout. Haven't seen him since."

"Thanks, Zuriel. If you see him, send him my way," Drazen requested, then dipped his head to me and departed.

"Let's see what he brought," I said to Zuriel, who banished his magic and helped me carry the bags into the bedroom. We spilled their contents across the bed, dresses and leggings and tunics and lace undergarments flying everywhere. A few books tumbled out at the end, and I silently thanked Drazen for bringing me something to read. I picked out what I wanted to wear, then folded and hung the rest in an empty wardrobe while Zuriel stood by the windows like a sentinel, looking over the capital of the Iron Realm.

The city was still blanketed in white, smoke rising from each building as the inhabitants warmed themselves against the cold, snowy day. A quiet had settled over the city, and barely any foot-prints broke the pristine powder that coated the streets. Unease settled into my belly as I took in more details of the scene before me. "Do you feel that too?" I whispered, afraid to raise my voice and draw the attention of whatever had goosebumps rippling across my skin.

Zuriel nodded, his eyes glazed and far away, but then he blinked and returned to himself, meeting my gaze. "I need to go, but I will see you later. Send for me if you need anything before then."

He quickly made for the door, and I shouted, "Wait! Please don't leave."

"Never forget that you are strong and powerful, Izidora. Don't let your inner fire go out." And with that cryptic statement, he left, leaving me standing in the center of our new room, too confused to move. The unease that wormed it way into me only increased.

What happened and why did he have to leave so suddenly?

A bath was the perfect way to forget the strangeness in the air. A good first impression would be important when our guests arrived later, and I was certain my eyes still held the puffiness that came after a night of crying.

"I am strong. I am powerful. I got this," I whispered to myself as I filled the tub with steaming water. Light floral scents filled the room as I poured salts and soaps into the bath. In the bedroom, I perused the stack of books beside the bed, selecting a romance. Book in hand, I returned to my waiting bath, slipping out of my robe and pants and into the waiting water.

I cracked the book after I got comfortable, wanting to get lost in a world that was not my own. What better way to get over my own heartbreak than to read about another female being swept off her feet by a sexy male?

Since Ruslan was not there, I skipped the words I did not know, but still managed to read over half of every page. When the water's decreasing temperature caught my attention, I decided to bathe. Setting the book aside, I dunked my head and washed my hair, working my fingers through my long chestnut tresses until they were clean, then turned my attention to my body, freeing it of every hint of grime from the previous day's battle. The water had gone cold by the time I finished, and the fluffy white towel warmed me as I wrapped it around my body and stepped from the tub.

Ruslan had yet to return, so I busied myself drying and curling my hair with magic, creating soft waves that cascaded down my back. My magic had refilled, but the well was nowhere near full. I stoked my inner flame, caressing it with love I had not given it in some time. It flared brighter under my attention, and more energy returned to my still weary limbs the longer I focused on it.

The heady thrum of power grew in my chest, intoxicating and alluring and calling me to use it, but I needed to save every drop I could for later, when tensions would run high and the risk of everything falling to ruin would be great. So I returned my attention to the mirror in front of me, staring at the aquamarine eyes filled with fiery determination. After a few more touches to my hair, I was satisfied with my appearance and decided to read by the fire until Ruslan returned.

It was past mid-day, and it was unlike him to let me out of his sight, let alone for hours on end without anyone else present. The uneasy sensation from earlier settled once more in my stomach, and I sensed the wrongness in the air, even though I could not place who or where it came from. It was like all of Radence held its breath as it watched us stand at the edge of a cliff, waiting to see if we would plummet or soar.

And more than anything, I needed to speak with him. My anger had abated with the passing hours, and I understood he had acted from a place of fear. So long as he did not follow through on his actions, I could forgive him.

But he owed me.

I buried myself in the story, sighing when the female main character swooned over the passionate words of her lover, biting my lip in anticipation as the male fought to save his true love, and smiling when at last the couple overcame all obstacles to be together. As I closed the book after reading the last page, I noticed Ruslan sitting in the chair across from me. I screamed, jumping to my feet on pure instinct as he smirked at me. A low laugh rumbled from his chest as I clutched my own, tears pricking my eyes as I tried to breathe through the panic.

"How long have you been there?" I cried, still gasping for breath as my body wound up to fight.

"Long enough. I did not want to disturb you during the climax," he winked. My shock gave way to anger as my heart slowed and adrenaline dropped away.

"Don't ever scare me like that again! At least announce yourself when you walk into the room," I snapped.

"But I like watching you too much for that," he purred.

I scoffed and rolled my eyes, crossing my arms over my chest. "We need to talk."

His playful mood turned somber in an instant.

"I heard you last night, talking to Drazen and Rares."

White knuckles gripped the edge of his chair. "I can't lose you, Izidora." His voice cracked, filled with strain and anguish.

I knelt in front of him, my hands covering his as I siphoned his pain until his breath flowed evenly. I held back my surprise as he allowed it. "I know you are scared, Ruslan, but taking my choice away isn't the answer. Talking to me is."

His black hair tumbled into his face as he dropped his head. "I love you, Izidora. You make me feel... loved. I don't want to lose this feeling I've wanted for so long. You almost died yesterday. I almost lost you. And then the thought of you returning to him... I can't bear it." He pulled me into his lap, burying his head in the crook of my neck.

I wrapped my arms around him, rocking him against me. "I know you're scared, Ruslan. I know you love me, and you know I love you. But more than that, I understand you, and you understand me, and being understood, especially after suffering in the ways we have, is an irreplaceable feeling, more precious than any gemstone, and I will not give that up."

My mate's strong chest heaved as I laid my feelings bare for him.

"I don't deserve you."

"Yes, you do. It will always be us against the world." And I meant those words. We'd both been on the outside looking in for so long that when we were together, I didn't feel so lonely, and I knew with Ruslan I never would be again.

"My sprite," he croaked. "I am so sorry. Can you ever forgive me?" He lifted his head from my chest, staring deep into my eyes with a plea etched on his face.

"Only if you are honest with me. Do you have something?" I asked pointedly.

He nodded, pulling my ring from his pocket. "Rares enchanted this with magic." Then he tossed it into the fire without a second thought. The gems screamed and hissed as if a demon were trapped inside them and the heat burned them out. "I will get you a new one, free of any magic. We can pick it out together."

I kissed him lightly on the lips. "Thank you for being honest with me. Now, what else do you need to feel okay?"

"Accept the mate bond."

My long lashes fluttered against my cheeks. *I shouldn't have asked.*

I had to reveal what I knew. "Ruslan... I have to tell you something."

His breath shuddered, and his whole body tensed as if he awaited a killing blow.

"Zuriel was there the day the Goddess's Prophecy was spoken."

His brow furrowed. "I know that."

I dragged in a serrated breath before imparting the nuance of the Goddess's Prophecy. "But did you know that in the original language, the prophecy called for two mates?"

His brows rose, and he slumped back against the chair, hand covering his mouth. "There is a choice..."

"Exactly. And this choice will determine the fate of the world."

Ruslan gripped my hips and turned me so I straddled him. "I choose to follow the light. Your light." He kissed my neck tenderly, reverently. "Darkness still reigns inside me, but you – you are my very reason for breathing. You are the star that guides my way in the blackest nights. You are filled with fire and spirit and that is why you are my sprite. We bring out the light and the dark in each other. We balance each other. We are better together."

My vision blurred under his worshiping words.

"The weight of the world... it's so much responsibility. What if I make the wrong choice and doom us all?" It was a thought that had haunted me since Zuriel disclosed the true meaning of the prophecy, and now that the reality of seeing Kazimir again was setting in, my anxiety around the choice had increased tenfold.

He crushed me into his chest, his voice thick and cracked. "I know you want a choice, and I will fight my every fear of you leaving me to give you that. But please, please, do not break me."

A lone tear trailed down my cheek. "You have no idea how much that means to me."

We sat in silence for a moment, the gentle sway of our embrace soothing us both. Then, I decided that I needed to bare all truths to him, as he had done for me. "There is something else." I'd already forced Ruslan to endure wave after wave of painful emotions, so I did not pause before confessing another secret I had kept from him. "The tracking spell Rares put on me didn't work. I used my magic to block it." I omitted the part about Zuriel helping me do it, wanting to save my cousin from any reproach.

A puff of breath fanned across my neck as he chuckled. "I should have guessed. You are a better actress than I thought, sprite."

"You aren't upset?" I clarified, almost not believing it.

His arms flexed around me as he held me so close it was like he tried to combine our bodies into one. "I never should have allowed Rares to try anyway," he admitted. "Breaking you, controlling you, neither of those are the way to your heart. Letting you be free is."

Pinpricks filled my eyes, and my heart swelled at his words. I squeezed him tighter, if it was at all possible with my tiny arms. "Thank you," I croaked.

"Make love to me one last time before we go?" the broken male pleaded, his voice as hoarse and raspy as my own.

My body heated, and I couldn't deny that I wanted it just as badly as he did. "Take me to bed, Ruslan."

I wrapped my legs around him, and he carried me to the bedroom. There was no physical pain mixed with our pleasure this time as we hurriedly undressed and fell into each other.

"Ruslan," I moaned as he slipped inside me, my center already dripping for him. His cock stretched me out in the most delicious way, and the thread that tied us together vibrated, pulling us even closer.

He took his time kissing me, stroking me with languid, unhurried thrusts, as if we had all the time in the world. "Faster, harder," I pleaded, needing more of him.

"Fuck, sprite, I love you," he moaned, then quickened his pace, his hands tightening across my back and arching my spine so he could take me deeper.

"I'm so close," I whimpered, digging my nails into his back

and gripping him tightly. My walls fluttered around his thickening cock, seconds from falling over the edge. With one last deep stroke, my orgasm tore through me, and Ruslan followed with his own, whispering my name over and over as he kissed my lips and my neck and clutched me to him like I was the most precious gemstone ever mined in the Iron Realm.

When we finally came down, Ruslan tugged us higher onto the bed and cradled me against him. He continued to kiss me everywhere, showering me with affection until the noises rising from the city below caught my attention and I decided it was time to pretty myself for what was to come. "I need to get ready," I whispered, stroking Ruslan's jaw and running my fingers through the soft hairs there. He sighed, but opened his arms and allowed me to roll out of the bed, mimicking me a moment later.

That hint of strangeness still filled the air, but in my gut I knew that when Ruslan and Kazimir were side by side, it would be apparent which male was the right choice. With that in mind, I hurriedly fixed my mussed hair in the bathroom, applying a few dabs of mascara to my long lashes and charcoal around my eyes to accentuate their brightness.

When I emerged, Ruslan held a shimmering black gown with a sly smile on his face. "I picked this out for you to wear today."

My face was alight as I slipped into the fine fabric. He shimmied the dress over my head, the silk molding perfectly to my every curve. The high neck and long sleeves offset the deep cut into the back, fabric only meeting again just above the lowest part of it, then trailing off into the distance, creating a pool of darkness that spread all around me.

"Won't everyone see my scars?" My brows furrowed as air ghosted across my bare back.

"Do you not want them to?" Ruslan cocked his head, subtle curiosity pulling up an eyebrow.

The scars that marred my back made my trauma visible, and anyone who had seen them thus far had sucked in a sharp breath of shock. I chewed my lip, debating the idea of baring them to our noble guests.

Ruslan's rough fingers grasped my chin, pulling my lip from my teeth. "Your scars are a signal that you are a fucking survivor, sprite. That you remain unbroken despite them, and that you can hold your own against the most seasoned of warriors. One day, you will tell me the story of each one, and when you're through, we will end the life of every male who inflicted them upon you. You will get the vengeance you deserve, and in the meantime, you will flaunt those scars like the badges of honor they are."

The ferocity of his words robbed me of breath, and my eyes burned as I looked up at the male whose love for me was like a violent storm, tearing apart everything in its path to get to me.

"Thank you," I whispered, blinking through blurred vision.

He planted a featherlight kiss on my forehead before releasing my chin. "I have one more surprise for you." He produced a circlet inlaid with rubies, and I bowed my head, allowing him to place it upon my brow with a flourish. "Now, you are perfect."

My cheeks flushed, and I perched on the edge of the bed while he changed into his attire.

Definitely the best view in the citadel.

A dark gray suit molded to his every muscle, perfectly cut to his powerful form. Atop his brow rested a crown of iron, pointed and severe in its profile. He looked every bit the king I wanted to rule my world. His hand stretched toward me, and without thought, I grasped it. "Time to go."

My stomach was in knots as we walked the unfamiliar halls of Ryza. Every Iron Fae stopped to stare at their new king.

Word certainly traveled fast.

We arrived at the familiar courtyard where a path had been carved through the snow, allowing us a dry spot upon which to stand to greet our royal guests. Ruslan settled himself front and center, hands clasped behind his back, eyes trained downhill where Iron Realm soldiers lined the path to Radence. I took my place at his right hand; Drazen, who appeared from nowhere, at his left. I smiled warmly at him, glad he was by our side. He winked in response, nostrils flaring and letting me know he smelled exactly what Ruslan and I had been up to before our arrival.

Rares joined us along with a few other males I did not recognize. The Mage's withered grin made my skin crawl, especially knowing the power he'd tried to wield over me.

I swung my gaze to Ruslan. His countenance was cool, calm and deferential, contrasting the nervous vibration that echoed in my bones. A rough hand found mine, and we stood in front of the doors to Ryza Citadel, the world dropping away as he offered me a devastating smile. We'd come so far since the day he snatched me from the Night Realm.

"How soon will our guests arrive?" I craned my neck, attempting to glimpse a head or two that might indicate the proximity of our guests.

"You should be able to see King Airre's crown in a moment, my sprite." Ruslan cupped my cheek, his smoky eyes filled with adoration, then tore his gaze away to our arriving guests.

My spine tingled in anticipation, and my body thrummed as King Airre rode into view, another king parallel to him. They were followed by pair after pair of riders, most unfamiliar to me. But then, two familiar faces crested the hill. Viktor and Endre. My heart pounded and adrenaline flooded my veins as both their eyes widened at the scene before them. I glanced up to Ruslan, but he only stared straight at them, a wicked smirk lifting the corners of his mouth, spreading into a vicious smile as the last of the riders joined their party in the courtyard.

My stomach turned over as a familiar tug nearly sent me stumbling forward, and I returned my gaze to the last of the riders.

And then I saw him.

30

RUSLAN

Béke Day One

Pounding dragged me from sleep. *Fuck, where was I?* Groaning, I sat up, my head fuzzy and throbbing, but that was not what roused me. The sound echoed through my skull again, and I pushed off the couch, knocking into furniture as I stumbled toward the door. Throwing it wide, I discovered Zuriel carrying a tray laden with food. The smell immediately turned my stomach.

He raked a critical gaze over me with narrowed eyes. "Are you drunk?" His normally melodic voice was flat and harsh.

"I was." I rubbed my temples and eyes, the light spilling from the hall spearing into my skull. Backing away from the door, Zuriel strode past, placing the food carefully on a small dining table in my apartment at Ryza. *Ryza.* I was still at the citadel, which was why everything felt so off. Memories from the previous day burst in my mind, causing another painful throb. Where was Rares when I actually needed him?

And why did I drink so much last night?

Zuriel spoke but my mind did not register it until he glared at me again. "What did you say?"

"I asked how Izidora was," he repeated, a hint of annoyance breaking through his guarded exterior.

Guilt slammed into me as I realized I hadn't checked on her the previous night before drifting off.

I was such a piece of shit.

"See for yourself." I waved him off, not wanting to speak or listen. Any effort was grueling, and I was so close to losing what little control I had over my deepest fear.

"Pull it together, Ruslan," Zuriel hissed. "You have a kingdom to rule now. Act like it."

"Fuck you, Zuriel. If my mate didn't need your help right now, I'd make sure you were gone tomorrow." I didn't have the energy to temper my words, and the glare I gave him was like the icepicks smashing into my brain.

"I'll gladly leave once you fulfill your promise to Izidora and have Rares lift the spell keeping me here," he retorted.

"Yeah, yeah, I am going to see him now. I'll have him lift it later." My fingers tightened over the back of the chair poised between the Angel and me.

"I will hold you to that, Ruslan. I am going to check on Izidora, so I will see you later. Hopefully when you are in better shape." Zuriel looked me up and down once more, disdain dripping off him like water, then disappeared into the bedroom.

Blowing out a tense breath, I shoved away from the chair and headed out of the apartment. I should have checked on my mate, but my head pounded like a hammer on an anvil. Each step I took was excruciating, and what felt like hours later, I finally found Rares in my father's study. Not a hint of blood or battle remained in the pristine space where King Azim had died not even a full day before.

"Rares, you clean up nicely," I commented as I sank into my usual chair, not caring enough to round the table and face him.

"You look like shit," he snapped back.

"I feel like shit, too. Cure this hangover."

He snorted, then chanted a few words and the pulse that resounded in my skull disappeared. "Better now?"

"Much better." I sighed as sweet relief washed through me. Without the headache taking my attention, more of the previous night returned, and I recalled my request of Rares. "Did you find a way?"

Rares held up the aquamarine ring I used when I proposed to Izidora in his withered hands. "This is the solution to your problem. It will only work if she wears it, however. I could not find a spell that would permanently change her, but I found a spell I could bind to an object. So long as she keeps this on her finger, her emotions will be numbed to anything but her love for you – which also means her powers will be dulled and she will be unable to use them. It is not a perfect solution, but it is all I could do in one night."

Accepting the outstretched ring, I pinched it between my fingers, examining it, before turning it over in my palms. It looked exactly the same as before, no hint of the magic that lay within. Izidora's empath magic would be useful during the feast, especially if I needed to sway some visiting noble's opinion or force someone to comply with my demands. But once she was bound to me in marriage and mating bond at the end of Béke, there would be no use for the ring. I would simply have another made and switch them out once everything was settled. "This will work for now," I finally replied, pocketing the jewelry.

"As you wish, My King." Rares wobbled to his feet, but I caught his wrist and he sank back into his seat.

"I have not dismissed you, Rares. I still have need of you. I want you to lift the spell tying every Telivér to the Iron Realm."

Rares looked as if I had just asked him to murder his entire family. Which, in a way, I had. In his twisted little mind, he did care about them and about us Félvér – if only because he wanted to create a power unlike anything before. And I had just commanded him to give it all up.

"Why?" he managed to bite out as his shock gave way to a face flushed with anger.

"That was my promise to my future wife in exchange for her help yesterday," I shrugged.

Rares's face grew redder, his lips a razor-thin line, and his hands shook against the edge of the chair. "Let me get this straight. You asked Izidora to help you kill your father, promising to free all the Telivér in exchange. And yet, you wanted me to find a way to keep her heart prisoner to your whims? And now I deliver this to you, and you still wish to free them? She would have no way of knowing! She would not care if she did, with the magic held in this ring! You wish to destroy all my life's work when I have given you everything you've ever asked for!" Rares was on his feet, chest heaving as he shouted the last of his words.

The corners of my lips started to pull into a smile, so I covered the lower half of my face with my fingers as Rares unraveled before my eyes. "And you will continue to give me everything I ask for until you die," I purred. "After all, you took an oath to this crown. You can do no harm to me, and your only release is death."

"In exchange for freedom to pursue creating the most powerful race!" Rares fumed, but he was powerless in our new dynamic.

"That was a goal you and my father shared, not one that was baked into your oath, if I remember correctly," I drawled, still hiding the pleasure that filled my veins from riling him. He opened his mouth to speak, but I cut him off. "I have a different goal. Well, not so different in the end result, but much different in the execution. Rather than using Telivér and Félvér to help us conquer the continent, I will use my mate's magic to unite it. She and I share similar goals on equality and acceptance. As much as I love slicing and killing, it will not win anyone to our side, and too much powerful blood will be shed. She will sway all who oppose us to our side, and then there will be no carnage Once we have united the realms, and depending on how valuable I still find you, I might consider allowing your experiments to resume."

The sliver of hope shining through my strategy calmed him enough that he returned to the chair with a heavy breath. Hope was a compelling tool when applied correctly. Hope drove us insane with the desire to wait for a change that may never come to pass. Hope was for those who would not take immediate action to get what they wanted. Hope was for the weak, and it was a weakness that I easily exploited over and over again.

Rares narrowed his eyes at me, studying my face closely, and I let my hand drop to reveal the smug expression that told him I knew I'd won. "Fine. I will lift the spell so they may be free to go," he conceded.

"Let's go. I want this settled before the other monarchs arrive this afternoon. They will be welcome to stay if they wish, otherwise they can travel to Stravek and find a ship home." I pushed up from the chair, towering over Rares. "Then afterward, you will gather all the staff in the main ballroom while I explain how I expect this citadel to function going forward."

We left my father's office – my office – and circled our way through the halls of Ryza, seeking the spiral stairs that led to the tunnels underground. Last minute preparations were underway as we wound through the halls, servants decorating every inch of available surface in fine fabrics, floating lights, and glittering gems, displaying the wealth of the Iron Realm at every twist and turn. I made note of a few changes to announce later, then we descended into the earth one step at a time.

When we exited the staircase, the two Wolves, Rixis and Thalia, were chatting in the antechamber. "Gather all the Telivér. Now," I snapped when Thalia raised an eyebrow at me. She muttered something under her breath before stalking off into the tunnels that housed most of the residents. I popped my knuckles one by one as the Telivér gathered on the opposite side of the room. Rares hunched beside me, whether from anger or age, I did not care. I was eager to rid myself of the bullshit tasks on my plate so I could focus on other activities – namely, flexing my right to rule over the other monarchs.

I imagined what their reactions would be when they heard the news that King Azim was dead – and that he had a son. He never announced me as his heir to more than a few trusted advisors and the heads of the noble houses in the Iron Realm, wanting to protect the secret of this place and these people from the other judgmental rulers on Északi. Their shock was delicious in my mind – the pale, bloodless faces with slack jaws formed the creamy base, my radiant mate willingly standing beside me the icing on top. My cock twitched with the exhilarating images springing to life behind my eyes, and I casually adjusted myself before pushing off the wall and surveying those gathered before me.

In all, only twenty-four Telivér remained in Ryza Citadel, most having married Iron Fae, some even finding mates among them, but as I counted them, only twenty-three were present. All twelve Shifters, six Mages, and five Demons stood stoically before me. Zuriel was missing, and I ground my teeth at the thought of the Angel still alone in my apartment with my mate, hours having passed since I left him there. I clenched my fists, about to shout at someone to fetch him, when the Angel himself breezed past me, having just descended the stairs to the tunnels. He checked himself and glanced around before his eyes landed on me, a question dancing in them. Releasing a long breath, I jerked my head for him to join the others. Understanding passed over his features, and he jogged forward, joining the Demons along the back wall.

"For those of you who do not already know, I am now king of the Iron Realm." Murmurs passed between a few of the Telivér, but more passed between the Félvér who pressed against the walls of the tunnels, blatantly eavesdropping. "And one of my first acts as king will be to release the Telivér from the magical chains tethering them to the Iron Realm. Once Rares reverses his magic, you will be free to return home or make one here in the Iron Realm. The choice is yours." The murmurs rose to gasps from those gathered in front of me to grumbles from the onlookers in the tunnels. Once the voices died down, I continued. "But you must make your choice now. If you want to leave, you must do so today. If you want to stay, your room here is available until you can find other lodging."

Rares's fists and shoulders were tight, but he kept his expression neutral. In a low voice, I said, "If any of them die during this process, you will too." I was not one to leave options on the table, especially for those who I already knew resented me. He shot me a sideways glare, then uncurled his fingers and started to chant.

Guess he did not want to give a goodbye speech, not that any of the Telivér would want one.

A faint buzz bounced around the rock walls, mixing with the rhythmic thrum of Rares's voice. Rixis yelped as a popping sound started on the right side of the group where she stood among the Shifters. I scented salty tears of relief as one by one, each Shifter inhaled a free breath, some for the first time in decades. Their happiness was almost touching, and I felt good about carrying out my promise to Izidora when I could have easily kept these people locked in the Iron Realm.

The six Mages stood stoically as their freedom was restored; the only sign of their release was the rubbing of wrists where invisible chains once rested.

Finally, Rares landed on the Angel and Demons, the most powerful of all the Telivér. The moment each Demon felt the rush of freedom, they threw their heads back and released a roar. Zuriel remained ethereal and motionless, watching every move Rares made with carefully honed apprehension. The old Mage completed his work, sweat pouring from his brow, and stumbled to a chair, first bracing himself against the back and then collapsing into it. I did not deign to check on him.

"Those who wish to stay, step forward," I commanded. Zuriel and the Demons all took that step, sending my eyebrows shooting up my forehead. Their desire to remain in the Iron Realm was unexpected, and I studied their faces closely, especially those of the Demons, hunting for any sign of deception. Zuriel remained for Izidora, that much was obvious.

But why would the Demons remain?

The Mages also stepped forward, followed by Konsteon and another Centaur. I waited a moment before asking, "Anyone else?" Silence greeted me. "Very well. Those who want to leave, you have one hour to pack your belongings and head to Stravek. Soldiers will be waiting to escort you in the courtyard. The rest of you are dismissed."

Two of the Mages rushed to Rares's side, checking his forehead and hands for any sign of burnout.

"He needs rest. His magic is nearly tapped," the man said to the woman. She nodded, and they hooked Rares's arms over their shoulders and carried him down the tunnel that led to his workshop and bedroom. At least the Mages who stayed were on our side, clearly taken by Rares's power and thirst for more. I popped my neck and rolled my shoulders, pissed that Rares had expended too much energy, leaving me to gather my own staff.

I needed another assistant.

With a curt nod to Zuriel, I departed, taking the stairs two at a time until I burst into the bustling hall. "You," I snapped, calling out a young but stern looking female. She stopped in her tracks, glaring at me briefly, then continued on her way. My steps pounded toward her, and I grabbed her by the arm, spinning her and forcing her to look at me.

"What do you want, Ruslan? Come to seduce me again and leave my bed cold before dawn breaks?"

Fucking Fates, she was not the right servant to stop. I vaguely remembered her as I checked out her body, but the memory of burying my cock deep inside my mate had erased all others from my mind. "You will not speak to your king that way," I hissed at her.

She scoffed. "I doubt that will ever happen. King Azim would likely have you killed before then."

"King Azim is dead, and I killed him. Which makes me your king," I growled, my voice laced with violence. Her eyes widened, but she said nothing. "Now, I need you to gather everyone in the main ballroom so I can make a formal announcement of the succession. Can you manage that or should I find someone more competent?"

She swallowed, yanking her arm free and rushing off, disappearing behind a door that I thought might lead to the kitchens. The kitchens – Cedomir. I recalled asking Drazen to bring him and my regiment here last night. Had they made the trek already? The pain in my head had required too much of my attention when I stumbled from my apartment this morning to notice who stood outside it. But it was not the time for those questions, not when I still had a list of tasks that needed to be completed before the royal guests arrived.

Taking note of the placement of the decor, I stalked the halls, aiming for the main ballroom where the majority of the citadel's inhabitants would likely be. When I arrived, High Lords Slavian and Anton stood in the open doorway, chatting and oblivious to their obvious blockage of the passage where servants hustled in and out, carrying everything needed for tonight's opening ball.

"Slavian, Anton," I greeted the males, a hint of frustration seeping into my tone.

Both swept into a bow as I stopped before them. "My King," they said in unison.

"So you have heard then?" I clarified, wondering who had spread the news far enough to reach their ears.

"Indeed we have. A welcome change, in my opinion," High Lord Slavian snickered. Slavian was only a year younger than me, and beside Drazen, he was my closest friend. His mother was a half Demon and half Centaur, hand selected for her power by his deceased father. He and Anton were the only two Félvér children to claim their father's noble titles so far.

"I hear you've been busy with other activities as well, Ruslan," Anton prodded suggestively.

"When do we get to meet your lovely mate? The whispers around Radence say she is very appealing." Slavian flashed his teeth in a salacious smile.

Their lustful reactions were the reason I had kept her away from them. I bared my own teeth and clenched my fists, ready to swing at whichever male made the next comment about Izidora. "She is not for you to look at or fantasize about, Slavian. The reason I have kept her hidden is so I do not kill the first male to stare a little too long at my mate. I suggest you keep your eyes elsewhere if you do not want me to peel the skin from your body inch by inch."

Anton's laugh was too light for the darkness of my promise. "Slavian can't help that he is part incubus, Ruslan. I know your pissy Dragon is the one driving you mad right now, and I can't hold it against you. I'd probably do the same for my mate." He plucked a bottle of liquor off a passing servant's tray. "Let's find a dark corner and drink this until the other monarchs arrive. I need to be intoxicated to get through all the formal royal bullshit."

"As much as I want to join you, I can't. I have to talk to all these people, since only a handful know of King Azim's death." Though, that may no longer be the case, since the two young High Lords already knew of his passing.

"Why don't you get Rares to do it?" Anton whined, his Wolf side forcing his pitch higher.

"Because the asshole nearly burned himself out. What I need is a dedicated fucking assistant," I complained.

"I know where you can find a few of those," Slavian snickered, elbowing Anton in the ribs.

I leveled a flat look at both of them. "I don't have time for this. Find me an assistant – for managing my schedule and my people, not my dick – and meet me in the courtyard later when the other monarchs arrive."

Without a second glance, I stomped off, heading deeper into the ballroom where a crowd of Iron Fae gathered, grumbles and murmurs filling the air while fear and curiosity floated into my nostrils. When they noticed my approach, silence reigned, the click of my boots across the lacquered floor the only sound in the vast space. I surveyed the group, deciding enough were present to pass on the information I wanted to share.

"King Azim is dead. There will be no funeral for him, because as you know, Béke begins today. Anything with his personal crest that has been laid out, put away. The Demon Dragon sigil is the only one that any of our guests will see. Understood?" A few nods were visible in the stone-faced crowd. "As your new king, I expect your best performance for the next two weeks. I want to start my reign off on a high note. Anything out of place, any mishaps, you will report to Rares immediately." I turned to leave before I reminded myself to be pleasant. "Oh, and have a nice feast. Enjoy some time with your families, too."

Glancing at the large clock taking up most of one of the walls in the ballroom, I whipped past the crowd, running over in my mind everything else I had to do. First, I needed to return to Izidora with the dress I'd selected for her for this evening, which was likely still at Roc Palace. I didn't have an hour to make the trek, so I let the words for the fast moving spell spill from my lips until I reached our mountain home.

The barracks at the base of the mountain were empty save for a handful of guards who remained to keep watch over Roc. I rode the lift to my suite, jogging straight to our bedroom. Drawers in our closet were left half-open, and lines of empty hangers swayed gently as I breezed past them. Sniffing, I tried to discern who had entered the closet to take the clothes that were once there. Cedomir's scent was the strongest, but it carried a hint of Drazen with it.

Drazen – I needed to find him and speak with him about securing Ryza. I pressed my hands to my temples as once again the pressure of all that I had to do built up in my head, hinting at my earlier headache returning.

I quickly packed Izidora's dress, my suit, and grabbed a circlet for her to wear from my personal treasury. Laden with clothes, I moved from the bedroom at Roc to the courtyard of Ryza, hoping to find Drazen there. As I settled into the new space, I noticed the last of the Telivér mounting horses and preparing to leave the Iron Realm for good. Something like sadness panged in my gut; after all, they had been in the tunnels with me as I grew into the king I was. Despite our kinship, they were wary of me and kept their distance all those years, and that chasm had only widened since I came of age.

I nodded to each of them as they passed, escorted by my father's former guard, until the last of the Wolves stopped before me. Thalia regarded me for a beat before saying, "Take care, Ruslan. You did not deserve the pain you have been through, so don't inflict it on others to make yourself feel better about yours. You are better than that." Without waiting for a response from me, she spurred her horse on, and I watched the sway of its back as it disappeared down the sloped hill. The old me would have brushed off her words, but as I paused for a moment, they cracked a sliver of ice from the case around my heart, a part of me that softened more with each passing day.

Maybe I was making a mistake.

I shook the thought away and returned to my duties, striding for the open doors of the citadel. Drazen rounded the corner just as I exited the bright daylight and entered the dim halls. "There you are, I've been looking all over for you," he panted, his face flushed from exertion.

"Do not tell me there is a problem," I snapped, my patience worn thin.

"No problems, only wanted to check how you wanted to play with the royals when they arrive," he stated, all of the tension from the night before gone.

At least someone was competent.

"I want soldiers lining the path up the hill. Strength, wealth, and power, that is our theme. I want everyone in their best armor, intimidating but put together. Make sense?" My request was rapid fire, but it was not one that needed much consideration. Appearances were important, especially with regard to the monarch of the other realms. If my plans were to succeed, visitors needed to be inundated with the Iron Realm's prowess from the moment they entered Radence.

"Got it," Drazen responded. I made to leave, but one of

Drazen's second in command called for us, his armor clanking as he sprinted toward us.

"They are almost here. Savich just stopped them between Ferzo pass and Radence," he burst out in one breath.

"Did he say who was traveling together?" Drazen pressed.

"Savich said the kings led with about ten riders behind them and a carriage at the back," Artur explained.

"So they are all together, then," I assessed. It appeared the bastards from the Night Realm had been busy. I had no doubt that Kazimir was with them if they arrived together strategically. He would only show up with force, too weak to face me on his own like a true male. But with their traveling party so close, I did not have much time to dress and return Izidora's ring. My stomach sank as I thought about Rares's warning that she would be numb to the world around her. I was protective of her, and fearful that she would lay eyes on Kazimir and abandon me, but more than anything, I wanted to make her happy.

I would not kill her free spirit, even if it meant I lost in the end.

The realization hit me like a punch to the gut, and the need to extricate myself from this conversation and seek out my mate overwhelmed me. "Take care of everything else that needs to happen before they arrive. Drazen, I trust your judgment and discretion."

"Yes, My King," they replied in unison with a dip of their heads.

I was halfway down the hall before I called over my shoulder, "And ensure Rares is there."

My heart raced faster than my feet as I returned to the tower that housed my apartment – and my mate. Two guards from my personal regiment stood on either side of the door, protecting her, and for that I was relieved. They wordlessly opened them for me, revealing a fully stoked hearth and light spilling into the room from the windows beyond. I strode into the living space, arms full of fine clothes, and discovered Izidora curled up on a couch by the fire, romance book in hand. Noiselessly, I laid the clothes over the back of a chair, then sat in another across from her. She had not noticed my arrival, too absorbed in her book, and while I'd taken to announcing myself loudly so as not to send her into a panic, I wanted to watch her moment of stolen peace. With only a few pages left, I sat quietly and allowed her to finish, hoping she'd been able to read most of it on her own.

I loved that she was secretly a hopeless romantic. I loved the way her brow furrowed while she focused, and her lips parted as characters fought for what they believed in. I loved her, and I could not go through with my plan. She deserved better than a male who was too crazed with fear to let her fly free.

Izidora closed the book with a soft sigh that caressed my ears, her happy scent filling my nostrils. A heartbeat later she noticed my arrival and leaped from the couch, her fear intoxicating in its intensity.

"How long have you been there?" she cried, her big aquamarine eyes brimming with tears.

"Long enough. I did not want to disturb you during the climax," I winked.

"Don't ever scare me like that again! At least announce yourself when you walk into the room." Her watery eyes were molten as her cheeks flushed with anger.

"But I like watching you too much for that," I purred.

She scoffed and rolled her eyes, crossing her arms over her chest. "We need to talk."

My stomach dropped like I'd leaped from the roof at Roc Palace without snapping open my wings.

Was this the moment she planned on leaving me? After all we had been through? After how much I had changed?

"I heard you last night, talking to Drazen and Rares."

My knuckles turned white as I gripped the edge of my chair.

She was going to abandon me, just like I had feared, but not because the other male was coming – because I fucked up. "I can't lose you, Izidora." My voice was all anguish as I fought the overwhelming urge to snatch her into my arms and hold her hostage so this crushing pain in my chest would leave instead.

She knelt in front of me, her soft, tiny hands covering mine. A soothing caress licked up my arms and into my chest, and I welcomed the reprieve she offered. "I know you are scared, Ruslan. But taking my choice away isn't the answer. Talking to me is."

She was right. With everything that had happened over the last day, I was not thinking rationally. I should have told her that I was terrified. She made me better, and I fell back into what I knew the moment I felt the crushing anxiety of almost losing her to burnout. "I love you, Izidora. You make me feel... loved. I don't want to lose this feeling I've wanted for so long. You almost died yesterday. I almost lost you then. And then the thought of you returning to him... I can't bear it." I needed her skin touching mine. I pulled her into my lap and buried my head in her neck, and roses calmed me as I inhaled her floral scent.

And she did exactly what I needed in that moment. She wrapped her arms around me, then rocked in a soothing motion, back and forth, back and forth. "I know you're scared, Ruslan. I know you love me. And I know I love you. But more than that, I understand you, and you understand me. And being understood is the most precious feeling in this entire world. I will not give that up."

She understood me better than anyone. She knew what I needed and when. She loved me. She accepted me. She did not want to leave.

"I'm not worthy of you." I said the words, hoping she would refute them.

She did, and every muscle relaxed because of it. "Yes, you are. It will always be us against the world."

"Sprite," I croaked, nuzzling her neck. "I am so sorry. Can you ever forgive me?" My plea was desperate, needy, but I did not care as I begged.

"You have to be honest with me. Do you have something?" she asked, her voice carrying a hint of wariness, and I hated myself for putting it there.

Nodding, I pulled out the ring that had become an unwelcome weight in my pocket. "Rares enchanted your ring with magic." Without hesitation, I chucked it into the fire. I knew it was wrong the second he handed it to me, and I would spend the rest of my life atoning for the fact that I dared think of controlling her like that. "I will get you a new one. We can pick it out together, and I promise to never alter it with magic."

Her featherlight kiss was filled with forgiveness and a chance for redemption. "Thank you for being honest with me. What else do you need to feel okay?"

One action would burn away all fear from where it rooted in my heart. "Accept our mating bond."

"Ruslan... I have to tell you something." Her voice had dropped to a whisper, and alongside it, my heart plummeted to the earth. I held my breath, waiting for the rejection to fall.

"Zuriel was there the day the Goddess's Prophecy was spoken," she said slowly.

My brow furrowed. "I already knew that."

Her chest expanded against mine as she sucked in a deep breath. "But did you know that in the original language, the prophecy called for two mates?"

I did not. The chair caught me as I was too stunned to sit upright. My hand covered my open mouth. All this time... I interpreted it in the modern language.

How could I have been so foolish?

"There is a choice…" I murmured, dumbstruck.

"And this choice will determine the fate of the world."

My hands found her hips, and I spun her to straddle me. I wanted to see her face as I professed every feeling to her. The choice was between following the light and descending into dark. That choice was not only for her, but for all of us. And my actions since we'd arrived in the Iron Realm showed me that I knew what was right.

"I choose to follow the light. Your light." I kissed her neck, just above the point where her pulse fluttered under my touch. "Darkness still reigns inside me, but you – you are my very reason for breathing. You are the star that guides my way in the blackest nights. You are filled with fire and spirit and that is why you are my sprite. We bring out the light and the dark in each other. We balance each other. We are better together."

She blinked rapidly, eyes so blue and filled with love that the final layer of ice around my heart melted away. But the set of her brow told me she was also afraid.

"The weight of the world… it's so heavy. What if I make the wrong choice and doom us all?" she whispered, eyes pinching at the corners.

My redemption started then.

I crushed her to my chest, comforting her as she had comforted me through my arc of anxiety. "I know you want a choice, and I will fight my every fear of you leaving me to give you that. Whatever choice you make will be the right one."

Her tense shoulders slackened, and she leaned deeper into my embrace. "You have no idea how much that means to me."

Silence stretched for a few heartbeats as we rocked together. Izidora tensed and untensed in my arms before blowing out a breath. "There is something else. I used my magic to block the tracking spell Rares put on me."

Surprise flitted through me, but I huffed a laugh, lifting

some of Izidora's chestnut hairs with my breath. "I should have known. You are a better actress than I thought, sprite."

"You aren't angry?" she asked, a hint of disbelief in her tone.

My arms tightened around her, and I clutched her closer, trying to reassure her with my actions that she was safe with me. "I never should have allowed Rares to try anyway. Breaking you, controlling you, neither of those are the way to your heart. Letting you be free is." I was wrong when I told her that she would see it as an act of love eventually. The deep-rooted fears that had haunted me since I was a child were difficult to banish, but during our time together, they had eased – the day's actions excluded.

Our bodies were nearly one with the desperation that held her to me. "Make love to me one last time before we go?"

"Take me to bed, Ruslan." Her words were breathy, wanton, and desperate.

So I did.

Her legs wrapped around my waist as I walked us to our bed, and our tongues twined as I laid her across it, my hips settling between hers. This would not be like our usual fucking; this would be making love, showing Izidora how much I cared about atoning for my mistakes, about protecting her, and about giving her the choice she deserved. We didn't have much time, so I stripped out of my clothes while she tossed hers aside, and the moment we were both bared to one another, I worshiped her, with tongue, touch, and thrust.

"Ruslan," she moaned as I entered her, already slick and wanting. The thread that tied us together tautened, forcing me to wrap my arms around her back and press her even harder against me.

I stole her breath as we kissed, and with long, languid strokes, I brought her quickly toward the edge. "Faster, harder," she pleaded.

"Fuck, sprite, I love you," I replied to her desperate words, and then delivered what she wanted.

"I'm so close," she panted, her nails digging into my back as she pulled me tighter. My abs tightened as I prepared to come, her need feeding my own. She came apart beneath me, her moans driving me wild, sending me over the edge a moment later.

"Izidora, Izidora, Izidora," I whispered, over and over and over with my final thrusts.

When we finally came down, I pulled her into my arms, kissing her head, her hair, her hands until she sighed and blinked lazily up at me. "I need to get ready," she whispered, stroking her small hand across my beard. A pained sigh left my lips as she hurried to the bathroom to fix her appearance.

At least I could surprise her with the elegant dress I fetched from Roc.

Returning to the living area, I grabbed all our garments, laying them out carefully across the rumpled sheets. The light pad of her feet signaled her return, so I grasped the shimmering black dress from the bed, holding it on display as she opened the door. Her eyes were striking with the dark lining painted there, perfectly matching her dress. "I picked this out for you to wear today."

She bounced toward me, running her hand over the silky fabric. She raised her arms overhead, and I shimmied the dress down, carefully lifting her hair out of the way. The fabric hugged her every damning curve, and my cock twitched to life despite our recent lovemaking.

"Won't everyone see my scars?" Her brows furrowed, and a small frown tugged at her pink lips.

"Do you want to hide them?" I cocked my head, curious at her response.

She chewed her lip, an internal battle playing out across her heart-shaped face. I grasped her chin, pulling that perfect lip from between her teeth. "Your scars are a signal that you are a fucking survivor, sprite, that you remain unbroken despite them, and that you can hold your own against the most seasoned of warriors. One day, you will tell me the story of each one, and when you're through, we will end the life of every male who inflicted them upon you. You will get the vengeance you deserve, and in the meantime, you will flaunt those scars like the badges of honor they are."

Those aquamarine eyes that sucked me in from across a ballroom danced with tears, and her voice cracked as she whispered, "Thank you."

I planted a featherlight kiss on her forehead, releasing my grasp on her chin before reaching into my pocket to produce a circlet inlaid with rubies, the perfect match to her dark dress. "I have one more thing for you." She dipped her head, and I placed it upon her brow with a flourish. "Now, you are perfect."

She blushed under my reverent compliment, then perched on the bed as I dressed myself. Her gaze was hungry as she roamed the planes of my tattooed chest, and when the dark gray suit hid my body, she almost pouted. I fitted the Iron Crown to my head, the final piece of my kingly attire.

My hand stretched to grab hers, and she took it, interlacing her fingers in mine. "Time to go." Though my every instinct said to run.

As we wound the halls of Ryza, Iron Fae stopped and bowed to us. We looked every bit the monarchs we would be in a few weeks' time.

A path had been carved through the snow of the outer courtyard, allowing us a dry spot on which to stand to greet our royal guests. I stood front and center, hands clasped behind my back, eyes trained downhill where our soldiers lined the path to Radence, ready to greet our guests with a show of force. Izidora stood on my right, and Drazen on my left. They shared a conspiratorial look, then he elbowed me in the ribs and raised an eyebrow. "I couldn't do it," I whispered to him.

"Good."

Rares joined us along with Anton and Slavian. If the Mage sensed that Izidora did not wear the enchanted ring, he made no indication.

I thrummed with nervous energy, though I schooled my expression to calm and confident. I needed Izidora's comfort again, so I took her hand in mine, and craned my neck to look down at her. She was so small beside me, and I couldn't help the desire to protect her at all costs. Since claiming her from the Night Realm, she had proven time and time again that she was strong and resilient and needed no one to save her, and I was happy to have been a part of empowering her instead of breaking her.

"How soon will the others arrive?" She craned her neck, attempting to glimpse a head or two that might indicate the proximity of our guests.

"You should be able to see King Airre's crown in a moment, my sprite." I cupped her cheek one last time, then tore my gaze from her to face our guests.

As King Airre and King Consort Geza came into view, I loosed a breath and cracked my neck. This was the moment everything I had done over the last few days had been building up to. An impish grin splayed across my lips as two by two, the riders crested the hill and joined us in the courtyard.

Izidora's nervousness filled my nostrils despite the excited smile plastered on her lips. Two males rode into view, their faces vaguely familiar, and I watched a brief flash of shock cross them before they schooled their expressions into cool hatred. Izidora's hand trembled in mine, and I felt her eyes on me, but I only looked dead ahead, knowing that my rival was moments from appearing.

I held my wicked grin as I waited for him to ride into view, the idea of watching his face when he saw that Izidora had chosen me thrilling and intoxicating. And there he was, the very last rider to arrive before a carriage peeled off to the right. Fury, shock, grief, and horror mixed on his face as he took in the scene before him – the Iron Crown resting upon my brow, Izidora staring up at me as if I were the air she breathed. We locked eyes, a silent battle fought between us where I emerged victorious.

But then she saw him.

LINKS

Can't get enough of Izidora, Ruslan, and Kazimir? Pre-order Book 3 of A Choice of Light and Dark here: https://a.co/d/bsIQz1U!

If you enjoyed Light, please consider dropping a star rating or review on Amazon, Goodreads, BookBub or any other platform you prefer to use! Your support means everything, and taking a few moments of your time to let others know how much you liked the book will go a long way for me.

Subscribe to my newsletter and join my Discord Server to stay in the know about upcoming releases, receive teasers and other exclusive content, and connect with other readers.

Where to connect with Lacey:
Instagram - @laceylehotzkyauthor
TikTok - @laceylehotzkyauthor
Discord - Lacey's Insidious Blooms
Goodreads - Lacey Lehotzky

Links

Amazon - Lacey Lehotzky
Pinterest - Lacey Lehotzky

Merch & Signed Copies:
www.laceylehotzky.com

AUTHOR'S NOTE

Trauma shows up in many forms, and the characters in this series all experience a variety of it. Kazimir loses his father and friends, Ruslan was never taught how to love or be loved, Izidora was stripped of her power and identity, yet all of them struggle in different ways with what happened to them. Not only do Izidora, Ruslan, and Kazimir have a choice, but so do we: to follow the light or to descend into dark.

The path to the light is not an easy one, but as someone who has been on both sides of it, every ounce of effort to get there is worth it. I would not be here writing these books if it weren't for that spark of hope that kept me going in the hardest times, and the desire to someday see what lay beyond the endless dark.

There are others out there who understand what you have been through or are still going through. You are not alone in your struggles. Asking for help can be the hardest step, but don't let fear of judgment hold you back. You might be surprised just how supported you are when you open up about your experiences, and your vulnerability allows others to share theirs in turn.

We heal together. We cope together. We love together.

United States

USA Suicide and Crisis Lifeline: dial 988

Crisis Text Line: Text REASON to 741741

United Kingdom

SHOUT: text SHOUT to 85258

Samaritans: call 116 123 (free from any phone), email jo@samaritans.org, or visit some branches in person

National Suicide Prevention Helpline UK: call 0800 689 5652

Australia

Lifeline: call 13 11 14 , text, or chat online 24/7

ACKNOWLEDGMENTS

To my dear readers - Thank you for taking a chance on Chained and then following up with such enthusiasm for Light. To say that I am humbled by the attention is an understatement, and I am incredibly grateful for every single one of you. Thank you for rocketing Chained to the Amazon bestsellers charts and keeping it there!

To my beta readers - You are incredible. Thank you for your feedback, letting me ask you follow up questions, and being such supportive friends. I am lucky to have you in my corner!

To my ARC and Street Team - You are the most supportive group I could have asked for. Thank you for your feral support on social media, and I love connecting with each and every one of you!

To Beholden Book Covers - Thank you for another breathtaking cover and for formatting Light. You truly help bring my vision to life!

Kristina - You're going to ugly cry reading this too. Words can't express how grateful I am to you. Not only are you the best hype girl, you're also so responsive and helpful when I need to talk out different parts of my books. Thank you for being the first to jump on a new chapter, and I'm sorry (kind of) for all the emotional pain I've caused you. On to the next one!

Kaitlin - Not only are you a fantastic editor, but you are also an amazing friend. I'm so glad we've continued to grow our friendship, and I love every post-BJJ writing session we do. We're going to have to start a Gracie-adjacent writing club at this rate!

Angel - There are some people who are meant to come into your life for a particular reason, and I definitely know why you came into mine. Your support so far has been incredible, and you give so much not only to me, but to countless other indie authors. I see how hard you work for us, and I want you to know that you are so appreciated and loved! Can't wait to see what you put on the edges of Light.

Renee - TikTok knows who our besties are! Even half a world away, I feel like I know you like a sister. Every time a man in a mask pops up on my feed I will think of you. Thank you for being my first international signed copy, for sharing your story with me, for hyping up Chained, for being the incredible human that you are. I can't wait to meet in person one day!

To my author friends - Logan, Courtney, RM, Shelby, NR, KL, Julia, Vee, Ree... team work makes the dream work. Our group chats give me life, and together we will all rise.

To my Gracie Raleigh friends - one of the best days of my life was walking into the gym. There I met my husband, and every day I get to hang out and roll with you fills my heart with joy. Your support has been incredible, and from the bottom of my heart, thank you for buying and reading and sharing my book with the world. The BJJ community is one of the best, hands down.

To my friends - Matt, Melissa, Stacie, Sam, Christen, Kristin, Sophia, Dan, Ryan, Ben, Zach, Chris, Gretchen, Haleigh, Angelina, Bekah, (I know I am missing someone), thank you for sharing my excitement and supporting me along the way!

To my family - thank you for reading (and skipping over the sexy parts) and spreading the word about my books! Grandpa, I can't begin to express how happy I am that you found reading because of Chained. Mom would be so excited we're sharing this hobby now.

Andrew - thank you for everything. For supporting me

through the long hours, emotional moments, celebrating the highs and the lows and every little moment along the way. You believed in me when I didn't believe in myself. Sorry that my accounts are always a mess, and I appreciate you figuring out all the accounting stuff so I can focus on writing. I love you! :)

ABOUT THE AUTHOR

Lacey is a writer, photographer, and author of the Amazon bestselling dark fantasy romance series, A Choice of Light and Dark. She is most often found with her nose in a book when she isn't training to be a fighter like her main characters. Lacey has her best ideas while traveling, where she finds inspiration for people and places in her books. She especially loves exploring the dark side, writing characters with deep flaws and even deeper trauma, and strapping her readers in for an emotional roller coaster that will leave them breathless by the end.